LEGEND OF CAEMERIS

ASCENDANT'S TEAR

BOOK ONE

CLARE L ROLFE

A catalogue record for this
book is available from the
National Library of Australia

Rolfe, Clare L.
Ascendant's Tear / by Clare L Rolfe
Legend of Caemeris
Paperback ISBN 978-0-6486994-0-8
Ebook ISBN 978-0-6486994-1-5
Printed and distributed by Ingram Spark

Contents

PART THREE

BONDS OF STONE AND WATER

Prologue

Sermon of Ursula Ben-Rhŭn I Abbot: Brethren of Ira

I remember as a novice I sat watching the waves crashing onto the pebbled shores of my homeland. They were mesmerising as their certainty created the peace that comes with the dawn. On this particular day, the sun was bright. It sparkled on the water like diamonds. In the distance, I could see a fishing boat. The men were hauling in nets gorged with silver soats. It thrilled me to see the generosity of the ocean and the thought of the great feast that would follow, to celebrate the success of the fishermen.

Suddenly, a shadow rose behind the boat. A huge wave was racing toward it. The fishermen remained oblivious as I called to them. They were too enthralled with their catch to notice. Then the roar of the leviathan wave stirred them, forcing them to watch their death approach. The boat exploded into tiny pieces and the men were lost beneath the chaos of the water. Calmness resumed as the wave curled over and disappeared into the expanse of the ocean that had birthed it. Even as it reached the shores, it merely stirred the pebbles beneath my feet. The destruction it brought was forgotten as the foam tickle my toes; mocking the fear that thudded in my heart at the sight of the destruction.

One of the first teachings of Ira had come to mind at that time. 'In the light exists chaos and noise and, in the darkness dwells the sorrow of what the light reveals.'

I began to study the patterns of the ocean and learnt its rhythm. I scribed how the tides and moon waxed and waned together. I passed on my knowledge in the hope that no more would be killed by a rogue wave. But always other storms would come, bringing death with them. I studied them as well, hoping to make sense of the seas, and perhaps save some more of those fishermen along the way.

But even with all the knowledge I have acquired, I still do not understand what made such beauty as the ocean on that day and the ugliness that came with it. Behind it lies a power, or perhaps even a will, which existed before those fishermen or me. A power that gave no thought to either one of us. It made the wave so strong that the ocean became an instrument of death.

Ira taught that the will of intelligent creatures brings either annihilation or, calms the light and eases the sorrow of the abyss. As I think upon these first teachings of light and dark, a doubt holds steadfastly inside me; as weak and ignorant as I am, how could I have changed the strength of that wave. I can neither condemn it as evil nor declare its beauty as sacred when both exist in the same thing.

So, my lesson today brethren, is not to seek divisive rules about what we deem to be good or evil as this is not how the world was made. It has come into being by a force and strength that never asked these questions, but merely formed its own rules, of which we are not aware and must learn.

One day our vision may stretch far enough to see what made that wave kill as it did but bring peace to that girl upon the shore. Then we shall know what to name this power and perhaps how to save the fishermen on the boat. But until then our path to wisdom and peace remains to seek out where light and dark live in our hearts, understand the beauty and terror that makes our world, and most of all, we must always resist the desire to destroy either. For as Ira taught, just as the night and day consume each other in continuous harmony, so our lives wax and wane. One does not exist without the other. If they did, then nothing would remain.'

The World of ARGLETHIUM

NORTHERN ICELANDS
JAWS OF WHITEFANG
Forest of Enan
NORTHERN RANGES
Doanda
DOANDA RANGES
Doanda Bush
R.
KINGDOM OF DRAXUS
The Mighty Choasa R.
LANDS OF CHOASA
Ancrid City
Boabs
Kensai
MIDDLE OCEAN
Isls of Hosiaan
Hosiaan Citadel
GREAT RED WASTELAND
MIDDLING ISLES
SANDY SEAS
IRON COAST
Seraf's Altar
Land of Bluesmoke
Mountains   Forests   Rivers   Plateau   Free trade route/territory

PART ONE

SUNDERING OF LIGHT AND SHADOW

1

Red Earth

Dust consumed the landscape and all within it. Little footprints crisscrossed the fine red dunes in between spinifex tufts. A long thin shadow extended over the grasses. From a distance, it looked like a small tree with one limb bent at forty-five degrees with a needle-like branch pointing directly at the sky. At the top of the trunk was a round mass. Suddenly the tree-like shape moved. A spear sped through the air and impaled a lizard resting on a plateau of stone. Widjera strolled over to the dying lizard, picked it up by the tail and wacked it against the rock to finish it off. Slinging it over his shoulder, he walked into the setting sun, content with the hunt for that day.

He had made his camp under a large outcrop of sandstone cliff, whittled by the millennia into a curving waves, each undulation higher than the other. The overhang of the tallest crest gave protection from the searing heat and very occasional wet. Widjera made fire, threw the lizard onto the flames, and waited. His dark eyes scanned the horizon. The sun was in its decline throwing the last of its rays across the land in a finale of cerise and red fingers. Blackness moved into the crevices, silhouetting the majestic fanfare of the sunset. All of this was familiar and mundane to Widjera. While he waited for the lizard to cook, he thought of his journey. He would finish at the ancient caves of the sand god Mimat to make offering. He hoped that his spirit's release would be quick. The pain in his side throbbed patiently everyday now, it would not be too much longer he thought. He knew this would be his last walk into the great hot dirt. Night descended swiftly, giving rise to the majesty of the stars. Widjera looked through cataract eyes but could still appreciate their glory, and comfort at the familiarity. He wondered if his spirit would miss such things when it had passed into the lands of his elders. As he slept, he dreamt of his father and brothers, his woman and the stars.

On the following day, a miniscule shadow trailed along behind beneath the baking sun, as he reached the cave of his ancestors. The trek had been slower than he remembered as it was many seasons since Widjera had visited here. Inside, the remains of eggshells and small bones littered the sand from the snake's nests and carcasses of small animals. On the walls were eight figures spread out along one side. They had elongated limbs, and each stood akimbo. Their heads were in the shape of coronas and their hands stretched to fine points. Widjera's tribe called them the ancient guardians to the spirit world. The traditions were obscure as to how they came to be, but they were believed to be a gateway left by the First who walked.

Covering his body completely in a red paste made from the sand he blended into the walls and floor of the cavern. The old man gathered small pieces of desert bush and crushed the bones of small mice and rats. He lit the fire and let white smoke enter the cavern. He began to chant the songs of death. His voice and white smoke brushed against the figures on the wall. They met Widjera's prayers with silence. His mind drifted into a trance as the flickering of the flames made the figures look like they were dancing with him.

Each day for seven dawns Widjera prayed, his spirit sensed its nearness to the ancient ones, but was still not ready to go to them. He stopped suddenly as a deep groan filled the cavern. A steel coldness passed over his skin. The tendrils of smoke stilled around him as the groan resonated again. Out of the corner of his eye, he saw the briefest flex of a hand from one of the figures on the wall. His eyes scanned in the dim light. Then everything became hazy. He staggered and fell as searing pain lanced through his belly. Thinking that his spirit had decided to leave him now, Widjera lay panting on the ground, red dust bubbles forming where saliva dribbled out of his mouth. Sweat dripped into his eyes as the waves of agony slowly subsided.

'Not yet,' he thought, 'my spirit is not ready yet.'

Gingerly, he crawled back to the fire and rested. Widjera slept. His eye flickered under his lids, oblivious to the shadows about him. He did not hear the whump made by something landing on the soft dirt. One by one, the ancient ones came to life, stretching their limbs and talons. They saw the creature on the ground but were not curious about him. Their true form had been kindly hidden by time, blunting the claws and teeth. Ageless and created before the world, the guardians gathered in the cave to begin the awakening. All eight stood over the old man, talons dangling just above his body. Their chant was soothing, filling his dreams with swirling ethers of colour – rainbows with eyes and awareness. Then blackness met Widjera as malice replaced the rainbows. An emptiness descended into his dreams making his body shudder. Profound grief washed over him from the unrelenting darkness. Tears formed under his lids and trickled onto the red dust.

The guardians' swaying quickened. A figure formed in the dust, a face, then a torso and finally the limbs. A gust of wind blew, and the figure disappeared, only to resurface again as the guardians' hands coaxed it to life. The scream that came out of the mouth formed from the red dirt shook Widjera's body; its arrival heralded by a massive roar of deliverance.

The god stood: weak and confused. The sand fell from its form to reveal a pale translucent skin, ragged mouth, and claw-like hands. The sockets in its head were empty, but the black holes were a gateway to an ancient violence and memory of creation. The head scanned the world it had entered. It turned towards the warriors still swaying. It roared again.

"The life and death of many stars have passed, but now the bonds are broken."

It filled its chest with air. Black ooze dribbled down its mouth and chin as the void's remnants were squeezed out. It stepped over the sleeping figure of Widjera and walked towards the cave's entrance. The warriors followed it. The moonlight stung. It snarled at the great disc. It had been imprisoned for eons in the abyss that even the pale light of the moon was agony to its hide. It snatched a large gullaroo that stood on a rock and tore its throat out, drank the gushing blood and chewed on the flesh. Its skin flushed with the life of the desert as the lifeforce of the creature flowed into its form. More ooze dribbled down as the god let out a bellow across the land. A shudder ran through the ground, rippling the sand. It had arrived. It had broken the chains, and at last, its dominion was laid bare ready for its rule.

The guardians formed a circle around it and began to chant again. They lay their talons on its torso and head. The god breathed, draining them. It felt the ancient force fill the cage of its existence. Light radiated out, piercing the night in a lacerating flash.

Pointing to the cave again, it willed the guardians to bring Widjera to it. One of them went in, picked up the old man and bought him to the god. The creature placed him on the sand before its ruler.

"This creature is of the ancients. Its life force flows within its flesh and memory. There will be more of its kind." The god and guardians sensed the waking of the sun. It took one of the arms of the guardian closest, and using its talon, cut Widjera's leg.

"We will follow in the darkness by the scent of its bleeding flesh, left when the creature wakes with the rise of the burning star Belmaris."

They retreated to the darkness of the caves. The god lay down into the red dirt waiting for night to come. The guardians went to the stone walls watching the god vigilantly.

Widjera wheezed as he stood. Even with first rays of dawn the sun was already blazing. He realized he was outside the cave. He rubbed his arms; they itched, and he winced slightly with a pain. He noticed that there were burns on each of them, as if a hot stick had been placed there to mark him. He felt an itch on his leg and looked down. He inspected the cut. Blood trickled onto the sand. He dabbed it with some wet sand to seal the wound, but it would not stop. A voice filled his mind saying, "Lead", as a gust of wind brushed past him. Widjera shuddered, heavy in heart and soul. He began to walk. Vague shadows seemed to jump at him. Something moving behind him made him look back suddenly, only to find nothing there. His mind drifted back into the vivid nightmares, making his skin prickle and stomach tighten. Watching the sunrise always made him glad, but now for some reason, a thick unyielding shadow seemed to rise with the red dawn. As he walked, he knew something had changed deep within the desert. There were no lizards or gullaroos to spear and the air felt clotted like a storm brewed, yet the skies were clear of any clouds.

The old man walked for five days without food or water. On the dawn of the sixth day he heard the trickle of a creek in a gully hidden by a steep embankment. Stumbling down towards it, he collapsed onto the rocky bed and gulped cool liquid. The stream slowed. A flock of black desert fowl flew up in alarm, screeching as they went. He felt something touch his arm. He saw a hand made from the water. It stroked the wounds. He pulled away quickly causing the hand to collapse back into the water. Widjera stood with a pounding heart, thinking that he must have the sickness of the desert. Rubbing his arm, he noticed the marks had completely healed. As he strode off into the bush along the creek bed, he looked back and saw a figure standing in the stream. Further behind on the horizon, dark shadows shimmered in the haze of the baking dry.

Widjera arrived at his tribe's camp just after twilight. His son,

Tamatjera, stood to greet him, surprised to see his father alive.

"You have come back, old man. The spirits of our ancestors do not want you yet, eh?"

Grabbing Tamatjera by the arms, he wheezed, "You must leave and make for the waterfalls. The ancients have arisen. The air thickens with their breath."

Tamatjera helped the old man onto the ground to rest. "I fear they have come not just for me, but all of us."

"Rest, we will talk with the tribe in the morning."

Widjera stood. "No now, gather everyone and go now!"

Just then, a searing lance shot through his side causing Widjera to double over in pain. He fainted. Tamatjera cradled him. Rousing slightly, he said, "Go now! The spirits have awoken, they come for us."

He saw one of the elders, Yanun, and called to him, "They have come. The gate has opened. The spirits have risen."

Yanun looked at Widjera not wanting to hear what his fellow elder spoke. But he could see the truth in Widjera's eyes and knew from the urgency of his voice.

"We cannot hide from them. There is something else. It touched me in the creek – a spirit of the water. Go to the caves of the janabaal, where the deep pools lie."

Yanun stood. As Widjera's body convulsed again with pain, he panted, "Leave me; I cannot go any further, go now."

Yanun called everyone to the fire. "We must go to the deep pools."

Tamatjera sat near his father. He called his son and daughter over. "Your grandfather is dying, look at him for the last time."

The children touched the old man and wondered at his age.

The whites of their eyes glistened in the moonlight. Widjera's heart ached, as he realised that this could be the end of their time here. "Go with your father!" he said and pushed his grandchildren away. Tamatjera's wife gathered their baby and called to the other children to collect bundles of twigs for fire. The baby began to cry as she placed him in a halter.

Ardana, Widjera's woman, sat looking at him with eyes weathered from desert living. She began to chant their death song, calling the ancients to take his spirit. The clacking of the stones echoed around the camp as her son and rest of the tribe gathered the children and supplies for their escape. Rhythmic and soothing Widjera concentrated on his wife's voice as the spasm of pain tore through him again. Ardana looked at the man with whom she had spent most of her life. She had no memory of their young faces, only the memory of being presented to each other as children to be bonded as spouses. She felt at peace. She had not expected Widjera to return from his walk, so her grieving had been done. At least she could sit with him until he passed and then she would walk into the desert herself. Either she would make it to the caves, or the desert would take her. Her voice resonated into the night, cutting its stillness with the lament of the days of Widjera and Ardana. She watched as the tribe moved away, their family looked back, her heart ached also, but these were the laws of the desert and elders. She continued chanting and tapping the stones.

Widjera's breathing was ragged now. He grimaced again with pain. In his mind, he saw the blackness again coming from a great rent in the sky. Fear pervaded every part of his body. 'Why had the ancients left his people? They had lived by the ways of the desert, within its harshness and providence,' he thought in his death throes.

Ardana heard a slight thump behind and a gust of wind blew into her face. The stones faltered slightly. She looked into the night and saw a great warrior from the sacred rocks. Fear flooded her heart. Its taloned hands reached forth and grabbed her by the throat. Widjera's eyes opened when he no longer heard the clicking tones. The warrior turned around and presented the old woman to the god. Ardana screamed in terror. Her lifeless body hitting the ground made Widjera sit up. The god came over to him. Blood and black ooze dribble down its chin.

"Ancient one, who are you?"

"I seek dominion here, that which was denied me."

The god grabbed Widjera's face and took all the life within him. It roared again in satisfaction. It felt strength flow into its being. It felt something else – something more ancient than the pit to which it had been chained. The creature's blood was tainted with another life force, older and more potent than that found here.

The warriors were swaying again. The god's skin and face were more definite now and its skin made an ethereal glow in the night. The eyeless pits had become more menacing as the face absorbed the moon's pallor. The guardians set off to find the others. It followed.

The tribe was in the distance. It could see them more clearly. A shadow caught its eye off to the side. Two red dots shone in the night, flirting on the edges of its vision. It looked at the shadow.

"Come, Voloc!" the god called.

A large wolf appeared, silhouetted even against the night. It moved slowly towards the god with a low growl, red dots flaring. It made a gesture of obedience, lowering its head and pawing the ground. The god looked at it and placed a translucent hand on its head. The wolf winced and backed away. 'Ah, from the pit,' thought the god, 'you came with me.' It wondered what else had followed. A malicious grin crossed its face letting a slick ooze dribble through the shredded lips.

So, the chase began. Voloc ran down the older women and the women with child. Their bodies littered the dirt. Their blood blended with the god and the red sand of the desert. The god bellowed its birth across the skies. Animals skittered away, lizards, skinks, mice, and desert fowl shrunk back into the cracked and broken earth, away from the invader that walked amongst them.

Tamatjera carried his daughter on his back and sprinted towards the caves. The entrance was hazy in the distance.

"Not far now." He hissed to his daughter to reassure her.

Sweat trickled down his face and back. He could see his wife and son ahead. 'Good,' he thought. He knew that Ardana was gone when the rhythmic tapping of her stones had abruptly stopped.

He saw five young men veer off into the desert. A black streak raced after them.

"Stay near the water!" he shouted but they did not hear him. "Run into the creek," he called ahead.

The sounds of the salt bushes being crushed came from behind him. He dared not look back to see what was there. The caves drew nearer. To enter them they had to wade into the creek that led into a large cavern. From there, the water flowed down into the janabaal pools. His daughter screamed as she saw the young men in the distance run down by a great dog. Tamatjera turned and saw the guardians. His heart thumped with fear and adrenaline. 'The sacred ones… why?' he thought. 'They were not benevolent guardians at death's gateway, but demons come to slaughter. What had the tribe done to anger them?'

He quickened his pace and went straight into the creek. Behind, he heard loud footsteps. The entrance to the cave was nearing. 'Faster!' he willed himself. His chest burned with the exertion. His daughter sobbed into his ear. His wife and son were up ahead looking back, their faces frozen with terror. The large dog broke out of the bushes along the creek's edge. It entered the water heading straight for the pair.

"Go!" he shouted at the others. They ran out of sight into the cave's mouth.

A great roar sounded behind him making him turn. His heart caught in his throat and the piercing scream of his daughter deafened him. The dog neared, but then he watched the water rise to a wall and push it back. The beast tried to wade closer to Tamatjera, but the water stopped it. The current started to flow away from the cave. Tamatjera raced ahead. He lunged toward the entrance and fell into it. As he stumbled, a talon reached inside and clawed his leg. He screamed with the agony of it. His wife and son dragged him inside, his daughter ran to one of the tribes' women. Just then, the water rose blocking the entrance, forming a translucent door. The creatures outside tried to pierce it. Then everything went quiet. There was a yelp. A figure came towards the watershed, large and glowing brilliantly.

It touched the barrier causing it to tremble, but it did not collapse. The figure roared again, but still the water did not give way. Tamatjera got up with blood gushing from his leg. He motioned the others to keep moving.

Only a few dozen of the tribe stood in the cavern; the others were gone. They moved as quietly as they could further into the recesses. Up ahead, they heard another waterfall. The younger men made their way into it. It was at the end of a long tunnel. Pushing through the flow of water, a massive underground cave opened before them. At the base was a large pool. The width of the cavern was so large the other side could barely be seen. A small shaft of moonlight shone onto the water, reflecting pale violet on the mirrored surface. Above, upon a ledge, stood a janabaal, preening itself. Then Tamatjera noticed a whole colony of them. Their eyes were iridescent in the semi darkness. Their fur was white, and they had a pair of wings. They were natural underground dwellers but due to large expanses of the caves they had wings to fly into the highest recesses. 'The moon has bleached their hides to match its own,' Tamatjera thought. The creatures fluttered up higher as more of the tribe came into their home.

Food, water, shelter; Tamatjera's mind raced. They felt a shudder under their feet as the god roared again, trying to break through the wall the water spirit had formed.

"Be still!" he whispered. Tamatjera and the tribe crouched and waited. Eventually the quiet of the cavern remained. Only the movement of the janabaals and water dripping into the pool could be heard.

"Yantarja, take Yinak and Wadda over to the other side and see if there is another entrance."

Inspecting from this side, the only entrance was where they had come through. Sitting down, he placed his leg in the water. It stung but was soothing at the same time. He tenderly touched the wound. The gash was not as deep as he thought.

Waiting for the others to return, he noticed a slight ripple on the water then the echo of a roar came through. It seemed further away than the last one. His daughter ran to him, scared. He patted her on the head. "I don't think they have gotten through yet." He encouraged her to go to her mother. When the roar finally stopped and the water became flat again, the women set about making a fire. The cavern was so large that the smoke rose well above them. It escaped out of the tiny hole in the sandstone canopy without suffocating them. They had some berries and dried fruits in their pouches and some leaves from the myrtle bushes to make a tea. It would do until the men caught a janabaal.

Yantarja came back with the others. He sat near Tamatjera. "There is only one other entrance. Like this one, it is covered by the water. It should be safe if the water nymph protects us."

Instinct told Tamatjera that it would. They would wait until the full moon passed before going near the entrance to their haven.

Outside, the god roared at being stopped by the spirit of this land. Its hunger was still not satisfied, its rage became unbridled. It plunged its talons into the water barricade to break it, but it did not budge. Each thrust drained its newly found energy.

"Voloc what spirit thwarts me?"

"Your sister."

"Nay, I have none. It is my weakness from my long slumber." It rammed itself into the entrance of the watery blockade again. The water held and thrust the god into the air and back onto the banks. It stood.

"Who are you, water spirit, show yourself. Do you seek to destroy the destroyer?"

The guardians gathered around. Silence responded to the god again. A flock of parrots flew out of the trees. It thrust his anger at them. Half of the birds dropped dead out of the sky.

"I must rest again." Walking back into the desert, the dawn greeted the newborn god. Soon the rays began to burn, and its skin peeled off.

"Carry your master!" the wolf growled at the guardians. One of them picked the god up as it collapsed, one large hand dragging in the sand. The god was laid down back in the sacred caves. One of the guardians took a gullaroo, slitting its throat, the guardian dripped the blood into the god's mouth. The ancient guardians then melted back onto the walls of the caves and waited.

On the rise of the fifth dawn, Yinak went back toward the entrance they had come from and saw the opening was no longer blocked with the water. Looking out from the cave, he saw that all the trees and shrubs had withered.

He returned and spoke to Tamatjera. "All the dirt is dead, and grass, and animals. There is no life for us that way."

"We will go forward and find a new land," replied Tamatjera,

The tribe gathered behind Tamatjera as he walked out on the other side of their sanctuary. A massive gorge opened out before them. A waterfall spouted out of the rocky face below, into the river that flowed ultimately to the red ocean of sand. There was no way down to the water below, as the cliff was sheer. The plateau above was lush with shrubs, myrtle bushes and acacia trees.

Tamatjera walked along the gorges edge surveying everything. "Warriors, each take a path and seek if any others live here. If you find someone then tell them of the shadows that have risen and now stain the land. When you return, if none have been found then we will make this our new home."

A cycle of the moon passed. The tribesmen returned. "None were seen, and no rock shows the hands of others like us dwelling here."

Tamatjera began the ceremony to bless the land. He took blood and dirt and painted the story of his mother and father's death and their expulsion from their land by the ancient ones of the sacred caves.

"The ancients have abandoned us, the sacred caves are cursed to us. Instead we will pay homage to the spirit of the water that has protected us." Tamatjera drew three lines in a wave pattern to show the water nymph and placed a corona of the rising sun around it. The chanting echoed into the gorge.

— — —

Inside the cave, deep beneath the blood drenched sands, the god slept, its flesh reforming as the ancient life forces of tribe of the Iron Desert flowed through its body. Voloc lay beside its master, the eidolon of the void revelled in its memories of ancient battle cries of the first wars, lusting for the screams of chaos and destruction again.

2

Voloc

Voloc left the flayed body of the god lying in the cave with the guardians. Until more of the ancient's blood was consumed, the god would remain weak and the spirits of the earth strong. Racing across the desert, it saw that one of its legs bled where the sun had scorched it. It dripped on the sand and turned to black oil that melted the rock. The wolf sniffed the air and red dirt and knew that what it searched for was here.

Reaching the coast, the red eyes scanned the ships in the harbour. The creatures were getting on and off as they replenished their supplies. Making its way toward the wharf, the demon walked onto the first ship. It was an imposing bulwark with a black hull adorned in red sails with an eagle's head at the bow. Taking the form of a man's shadow it made its way to a lighted cabin situated above the main deck. Inside, a large man sat behind a desk smoking a pipe. Voloc slid into the unlit corners of the room drawn to the thoughts of the man. They churned with anger and insatiable desire to dominate. Two women came into the cabin. The fear in the thudding heart of one of the women reminded Voloc of the cage of its dwelling place.

"Lord Ranik, she is ready."

Voloc drank in the fear.

"Come here!"

The older woman pushed the servant forward and then left the room hastily. As she left, her eyes were caught briefly by a flicker of red where Voloc stood. The demon's shadow reached toward her. Its claws twisting as it possessed her. The woman almost collapsed with terror as Voloc's eyes stared back at her from inside her mind.

The servant's eyes were huge with fright as Ranik got up and gestured for her to come to him.

'Here!" he barked.

When she was close enough to him, Ranik slapped her to stun her, making her fall on the bedding.

"Do you see that chair. It is covered with the hide of one of your villagers. Do you wish your family to become my foot-stool?"

The slave shook her head frantically as she looked in horror at the human skin stretched over the seat.

Reefing her legs apart, he went down into her. The girl cried out, but he covered her mouth. Voloc took in all the malice and hunger from Ranik and the white fear of the woman. The tyrant of Matavia ravaged her until she was almost uncon-scious. When he had finished, he thrust her onto the floor. A splash of water aroused her from the washbasin as Ranik washed himself.

"Matron!" He called sitting down behind his desk. He lifted the jug of wine to pour himself a drink.

She came in instantly as if she had been waiting. She grimaced slightly as she saw the unconscious woman on the floor. Voloc could see through the matron's eyes as she picked up the emaciated body. A flutter of relief had washed through the old woman at finding the girl alive.

"Clean her and bring her again tomorrow. The Iron Coast trader stock are always worthwhile. Send for Lord Faad as well."

Ranik lit his pipe. As the old woman left, Voloc probed her mind and sensed the guilt locked deep within her. The memories of all the people she had bought and sold, hand-picked to feed her master's lascivious appetites appeared before the demon's piercing eyes. Voloc gouged more deeply and tore all the faces of the girls out of the dormant layers of the matron's mind. Slowly, it began to bring each of them screaming to the woman's waking thoughts. The old matron nearly collapsed, as the images of all the wretches she had betrayed bombarded her.

A small dark-haired man walked into the cabin. He was slightly dishevelled from being woken, as it was now well after the midnight watch.

"Yes, Lord."

"It is fair news Faad that the northern rebels have been squashed. Have you sent orders that all the villagers and their families are to be killed and burned? I will use the lands there to grow fodder for my guard's horses. It is a fertile valley, and much can be grown with little need for other than what the sky provides."

"My Lord, surely the villagers can be put to work to till the soil."

"Nay, Faad, you never seem to learn. If it spreads that Ranik was less than fierce in his retribution, then another uprising will occur then another. I need not remind you of the eastern feudal Lords, they ever seek an opportunity to disrupt my trade routes from the south. I do not want my soldiers to be burdened with the peasantry. It will distract them from protecting the Matavian Empire from invasion."

"I understand." Faad saw the blood on the bed and grimaced at the mess. He wondered how old the slave was this time. Ranik's perversions had grown more violent and fearsome even by the standards of an old battle axe like Captain Faad.

"Lastly, I want the monastery of the priestesses of Rhu to be destroyed. They are assisting the slaves that have escaped and hide them in the northern caves near the Unstaadt borders. They are feeding them and giving them herbs to heal their wounds."

"But those women also provide healing work to the royal family, including yourself. Their knowledge and skills would not be replaced easily."

"Perhaps you are right. Bring two of them back to teach my own apothecary. When that is complete, they can be burned in view of all the citizens. Bring the slaves they have aided to the city where they will be maimed and then let them wander in the salt plain for the buzzards to finish."

Ranik didn't look up, as he scribbled his signature on parchments related to payments for stock.

Faad bowed and left. Ranik breathed in deeply looking out his porthole. He remained still, pondering the darkness tinged with the earliest breath of dawn. Tias Ranik rarely slept. The only thing that made his mind still was killing. Even his sexual proclivities did nothing to quell the lust for destruction. If he had his way, he would flatten the world, and leave only his beloved white city standing. The massive fortress in the Bay of Tears his legacy to his Kingdom, a frigid reminder of the coldness that sat in the pit of his essence. He sometimes wondered if he had been born of this world at all. Ranik saw the first crack of light and appreciated the blood red sky of the southern land's dawn. The days were long and the nights short compared to his lands in the north. A chill swept through the despot as Voloc passed by to find darkness before the sun's rays touched it. Voloc saw how vast the emptiness was within the tyrant, there was no potential to create, only destroy. A kindred spirit who could be sanctuary for Voloc to dwell.

— — —

Voloc left the ship as it docked in the Bay of Tears. Two guards were carrying off an oarsman from the galley who was screaming about a demon lying next to him. They slit his throat and threw the body overboard. A second body was being taken down from the cross beam of the main sail. It was the old matron. She had hung herself during the night. The full moon illuminated the water and white walls of the city's buildings. The bay was dominated by the palace built by Ranik's great grandfather. Constructed from white marble, it imposed itself on the subjugated inhabitants by blinding them in the summer sun and offering a frigid unwelcoming wall in the winter.

Voloc passed the palace and began to climb to a plateau. It found a path that led to a crossroads a league to the northwest. The roads extended in four directions. The vista stretched far to the east, west, north, and south. Called the point of Isthmus, the demon scoured with its ancient vision all the lands of the Middling Territories. To the south, the god still slept, gathering strength again, and in the east and west there was potency of strength resounding throughout the earth. Leaving its shadow form, it became a wolf and headed toward the west. Voloc's memory was old, even the god it chose to serve did not know where Voloc had come from. The spirit of shadow had remembered the wars of creation and the sundering of the gods as if they were only a moment ago. It remembered the creations of Belmaris and Magmeris and even thought it knew of Caemeris. The demon wondered where its ancient nemeses slept on this realm. Arglethium, the place born of the memory of Caemeris and the colours of the first dawn.

Voloc came to a temple as the new moon was on the wane. Sitting at the entrance of a great hall, the demon began to haunt the monks as it searched for the source of the power that drew it to this place. It found the old man called Abbot. The old man was formidable. As Voloc stared deep into the soul, the Abbot stared back directly. 'Be gone,' came the commanding thought from the Abbot. The shadow retreated.

Voloc left and moved amongst the other creatures, silently praying and delving into the recesses of memory and sorrow. It heard one talking of his homeland Matavia. It stayed to listen. The voice and visions of land was the same as the despot on the ship. It stared into the very depths of the heart and saw the beatings given out by the father and then the mother. The anger festered deeply. Sensing this one would be suitable, Voloc spoke.

"Vronius." The cold whisper crept onto the nape of the

monk's neck. Shadows played on the walls and across the monk's vision.

"Who are you, demon? I have felt you in my meditations watching me."

"I seek something from this place that is hidden from me."

"This is the sacred temple of Ira. How dare you profane its stone."

The malevolent chuckle sent a shiver down Vronius' back.

"This place will be destroyed, and I will have what it holds. Now turn to me so you may know who I am."

Voloc transformed into its true self. Vronius started to whimper at the pain of the darkness that tore through his mind. Tears welled in his eyes. After probing the monk's mind, Voloc plucked the lust in the young man's heart for control of all things and placed it at the front of his mind. It broke Vronius' will to resist and he became consumed with a lust for power and rule. Vronius' mind went blank, but for one thought. 'Seek the gift I desire, and you shall remain free of my eternal cage.'

The next morning, Vronius woke, and instead of going directly to the temple to pray, he went to a chamber, a few paces down the corridor. Going in, he surprised Brother Jon, advisor to the Abbot. Taking him by the head, he twisted so hard that Jon's neck snapped like a twig. Vronius threw the body out the window. Brother Jon smashed onto the rocks on the cliffs edge and was dragged away by the waves. Vronius was next advisor after Brother Jon. He glided past the desk knowing within three dawns he would be sitting at it, privy to all the archives only the Abbot was allowed to read. Voloc left the temple to seek out Ranik.

Upon reaching the Point Of Isthmus Voloc looked to the east. Voloc's sight was clearer as it drank in the darkness from the creatures' memories and the fear of death which constantly surrounded them. The great black wolf stood surveying the world and salivated at its destruction.

"Voloc where are you?" called the god.

"I am seeking a way to bring you out of the cage."

"What have you found?"

"Many, who are easy to break and bend to our need."

Voloc looked to the east again as the whisper of an ancient enemy came across the winds, but swiftly disappeared. The rising sun's rays crept slowly towards the black hide, forcing the shadow to leave and seek shelter. It sniffed the winds which came from the east once more.

"Where do you slumber my ancient enemy. I have not forgotten you or the cries of battle which scored my hide." Voloc howled as it sped toward Matavia.

In the darkness of the palace chamber, Ranik sat smoking his pipe. A young man and village maid were asleep in the bedding. The tyrant stood up. He was looking around the silent room when the iciness of the demon's breath brushed his cheek. Images of the great wealth of minerals that lay to the east and west filled Ranik's mind as the blackness crept into the already tainted heart. The demon left Ranik lost to the vision of immeasurable wealth that lay within his grasp.

"Voloc, come!" called the god once more from far away in the south.

The shadow hesitated upon hearing the call. Perhaps the god was not needed now with such emptiness to sustain it until the gift was found. The call came again. Voloc stood howling across the plains in the dusky twilight. It had tasted a piece of freedom. It needed no master. The flesh was so weak here, so unformed, ignorant, and futile in its life, Voloc could lay dominion and face Belmaris from its own throne. The call came again, and this time it felt the wrench of its bonds tighten, causing it to yelp into the wind. Obediently, the shadow wolf found a ship. On the dawn as the ship set sail Voloc made its way to the prisoner-god it served and guarded.

3

Uchala and Vipax

The cave was empty except for the god and the still forms of the guardians. They had retreated to their slumber, waiting to be called. The god placed its hand on the rocks surrounding its body. It felt the ancient pulse from the first touch of Caemeris. It had never waned since the dawn of the creation. Stepping into the night, the moonlight and stars stung its flesh. It bellowed across the great expanse laid out before its vision, awakening all within its reach. It walked until the dirt ended and the ocean began. The crashing waves stung its ears as they rolled onto the shore in harmony with the moon. It stepped into the water; it parted under its feet. It pulled it together to support itself, but the strength drained from its flesh. Confusion reigned in its mind as the waves pounded onto it. It clutched at the shifting sand and crawled back onto the beach. The god knew of its might and terror. But here it was nothing; a ghost, a shadow.

"Master, I am here."

"Voloc, I am weak."

The wolf sat on the beach as the god heaved itself clear of

the crashing surf.

"The ancient energy flows in the dirt and rivers and creatures, most of all in the first that walked Arglethium. They will be the strongest. It is from their blood I will regain my power."

"Where are they?" asked Voloc.

"I will know them when I find them."

"What of your brethren, more sustenance can be found."

"Of what brethren do you speak?"

Voloc did not answer the god. The millennia spent imprisoned had dimmed its memory. The great wolf followed its master as it strode along the shore and back towards the heart of the desert. It could sense the hunger in the god, the longing for strength and dominion over the world. The god consumed all that came near. The jagged lips oozed the bile of the void's cage and the blood of the living. It found a tribe of the creatures who dwelled in the red sands. Decimating them, as it ate their flesh and drank their blood, the tribe was erased from the memory of their lands. The ancient life force of the earth that had sustained them for so long suffused into the emaciated body of the prisoner god.

It returned and waited for the sun to set. In the darkness, sitting on a ledge of cliff face above its cave, the god watched the light of another day sink on the horizon, with reds and golds stretching across the arid vista. The colours stirred a distant memory, but it remained on the edges of its awareness, only serving to remind it of its imprisonment. The god's memory and purpose had long been whittled down to a raw lust for destruction and darkness. Its skin flaked off even in the twilight making it glare at Belmaris and rage at its power. As the sun finally set, it saw a blue light moving slowly in the distance, contrasting with the redness of the desert sand. It watched it approach, becoming brighter as the waning moon took its seat in the night sky. It walked up onto a rock and stopped. It was a spider as large as the god's hand.

Voloc went towards it.

"Away, wraith of the dark." The blue blood pulsing in the veins of the creature flared brilliantly to warn the wolf back.

"Who are you?"

"I am Uchala; I am an ancient of the earth. One of those you seek."

"I will feast on you, Uchala the ancient."

"You are deceived, destroyer, for the more you consume of this world the more you will take its form."

"I have sat mired in the pits of dark and its bondage to feel the death of many of the stars, even in their tombs I was not destroyed. Neither will this place of clay born, weak and shackled to their flesh's need for constant nourishment. Death haunts their every step. And now so do I. My path is clear; for nothing will defeat the prisoner of doom once it has had its fill of those imbued with the flame of Belmaris."

The blue of the spider flared more brilliantly. "Belmaris' flame cannot be destroyed. Only that which made the great progenitor may destroy it." The voice of Uchala was thin but strident.

"You forget the light usurped the dark, and so it must be that in the end the usurper is destroyed," replied the god.

"But you were not born of the dark and so with our destruction lies your fate."

The god wondered at these words by the blue creature. It had no memory of light only searing pain of shackles and loneliness.

"Emptiness has brought solace. Since light's first intrusion, old one, chaos existed and with its destruction, peace shall reign again. My fate lies with that which has made me and given succour when not even my creator would remember me. Before I destroy you, old one, tell me who you are?"

"My kind has walked this land since its dawn. Our blood runs with the light of the caemexa as a reminder of their presence in all things."

"Your colour, it pricks my skin. It is not of my enemy in the sky?'

"Nay, I am full with the shades which made the gates between the light and dark. I am a memory of the Stonthrax, Gate Keeper between the light and shadow. Those of us born of this hue seek our ruler to return and restore our dominion once more."

"I know not of what you speak. Since you are as old as you say, who am I?"

"One to bring annihilation and the end of time. You seep hatred and draw the light into you. You are the one that is wept for. All your being is consumed with your will to usurp and lay dominion over this world and beyond. Even the sight of the Caemeris has not humbled your heart. Your litany is not of glory or thanksgiving but of potent malice and desolation. You are the loss of hope and bringer of despair. Arglethium writhes in agony at the loss of its promised gift, when light and dark merged and formed the density of clay. Now time draws to an end for me and my brethren, as our destiny is fulfilled with your coming. In taking from this world, you shall bring your own annihilation and a way back for us – the progeny of Stonthrax – to return from where we came. You have breached the walls of creation and now they must be closed once more."

As Uchala spoke, her offspring had begun to gather around the god and Voloc. Little blue lights ebbing in the moonlight. Voloc snapped at some of them but their taste was painful, making the wolf spit them out.

A deep throaty laugh emerged from the god's ragged lips "Ahh, ancient one, the darkness seeks only peace. It comes not to destroy. It was first."

"Frozen in isolation and sterile, Caemeris lay suzerainty over it and it refused to obey."

"And it sends me to restore."

"Nay it does not, for another has opened the gate to this world, thrusting you from one prison to another."

The god noticed the little spiders gathering. Picking one up, it ate it. It took a handful and ate those as well.

"You are old, Uchala, and your life is bound to this place. Why have you come to speak to me, when you know it will be your end?"

"Long has my life been, bound by the earth and Belmaris. I will not let you destroy all that they sustain. Eons ago, the eternal placed me here to brood and send my children out. Many generations of them have I watched rise and die. My blessing and curse is to never die. I sat in my cave and I pondered and waited. I never asked why the infinite deemed my fate to be watching long vistas of time lost in heaped memories, until on one sunset something shook beneath me. Something woke and broke free. Its cries of new life, bellowing across the land, screaming its awakening, and piercing my slumber. Its hunger pains and lightless heart drawing me to it. It cried of agony at the sun. This offspring of the dark which had forgotten the purpose of its creation and seeks to destroy all that the infinite wrought. Long I brooded, waiting, anger at no reprieve until now I see the old wisdom at work. I have come now to the answer of my own creation. I have come to kill you, defiant one, and with your death forge a way back for my brood to their ancient birthplace."

The god laughed, opening its great jaw. The derisive laugh rippled into the furthest reaches of the ocean and across the land.

"How?"

"My blood is poison to you."

"Nay, it is sweet."

"Master, it burns me." Voloc had come closer when the demon heard the spider's threat.

Scooping up another handful of the spiderlings, the blue oozed down the god's chin. It began to feast on the spiders as they crawled towards it, covering its legs and arms and up onto its head, trying to sting the terrible flesh with their fangs. Finally, only Uchala was left.

"Who am I?" the god asked once more.

"You will remember and then the paths will be laid out before you. The deceiver sits close to you, god. Beware. Remember who first led you to your cage and placed the bonds on you."

Uchala made her way to the god crawling up its leg, her blue blood magnificent in the darkness of the night. She crawled onto its chest then its chin. It bit into her and the blood of the ancient sentinel oozed into the body. The god ate her up lasciviously, the most ancient of the wonders of earth. It looked across the desert. Blue specs now shone in the black sockets of its head. Voloc watched silently as the god slowly transformed.

"Come Voloc, there is still more. My bondage has made me hungry."

———

Vipax lay around its eggs, gently rocking in the tidal rhythms. The cave it dwelt in was deep below the ocean's surface in the underworld just above the beating heart of Arglethium. The serpent was so large that its belly spanned the width of ten men and her coils were uncountable. She could sense the eggs were nearly ready. She had bred a thousand generations of ocean serpents. The eggs began to hatch. The offspring wriggled out into the water. One of them tasted her eye as it slithered past. A profound contentment oozed from the iridescent scales of the god-serpent into the ocean. It leaked the silent love of creation, equally giving, and ignorant to the disruption new birth brought to existence.

Suddenly, the restful waters began to ripple with the sound of something set free from a bondage older than the world. The cry carried sorrow and rage; both of them pierced her scales like the fangs of her own kind. Vipax stirred for the first time in a thousand cycles of the moon. The salty ocean washed over its corneas as the slits of her pupils adjusted to the murky green of the water. One of the sentinels had gone, disappeared from the world. She felt the tug of the lifeforce as it was swallowed by shadow. Slowly the ancient guardian of the seas began to uncoil. The scales slid over each other effortlessly, brilliant golds, greens and yellows moved across her body. Searching for the entrance to the cave, she made her way out into the pristine seas above her den. Rising up and up, the filtered light stung. She reached the surface and with an almighty surge broke through the water into the air and sunlight. Vipax, the ancient, saw the sky and the sun for the first time since the birth of the world. She opened her mouth and her crystal fangs glistened in the daylight. She roared her awakening, the rays of the sun danced on her scales revealing the glory of the colours wrought by Caemeris. The eyes shone like yellow diamonds, each facet reflecting Belmaris and the heaving waters. She dived straight down into the murky depths and sent a tidal wave towards the shores. A group of fishermen saw the serpent break the surface and swore in terror at the leviathan as she emerged from her slumber. While there were legends of the great sea serpents, Vipax offspring were one tenth the size of their parent. Her beauty and terror were not equalled in this place and even Lido, the water spirit, bowed in humility at the magnificent and terrible beast. Vipax sensed the god. Gliding in and out of the water, she swam to find the destroyer.

The god stood on the cliff and watched the waves. It was able to withstand the twilight with venom of Uchala flowing inside it. It walked down to the ocean and walked into it again. For a moment, the water held it. It began to walk across it, but then a great wave came and crashed onto the body driving it into the sand below. The god stood again and roared its anger at the weakness. It went back onto the land.

"We are trapped," spoke Voloc from behind. The god's hand caught the wolf's jaw and threw the beast against the cliff.

The god roared on the wind. It looked again at the ocean. "The water defies me!"

Just then, Vipax spewed out of the ocean and came crashing down toward the sand to swallow the god. The god moved away as it sensed the power within the serpent.

"Ah yes, here lies the brethren of Uchala, but stronger."

It grinned in readiness for the slaughter.

The god leapt up onto the python and bit into her.

Vipax roared and convulsed. It dove into the watery depths to thrust the god off. Whipping her tail around, she flicked the god, causing it to come loose and be lost in the water. Green and gold oozed into the waves around it from the wound in her hide. The god rose to the surface and stood upon the turbulent ocean. The blood of the serpent was strong; if it drained it, nothing could defy the destroyer. It strode onto the beach. The python rose again but did not attack. Its wound was haemorrhaging sparkling green fluid.

"Lay down, mighty one. I am here and my hunger will not be assuaged, especially now that I have tasted you. I already have your sister within me. It is with her eyes that I see the power in you."

"Baachelaus," she hissed, "How have you broken your chains and entered into my realm?"

"Baachelaus," the god whispered, "Yes, that is my name."

The god leapt at the great serpent. Voloc barked viciously at the clash. Baachelaus opened its jaws and bit into the vibrant scales and flesh. Power surged through it. Vipax contorted as the pain of the second wound tore through its glistening skin. With titanic force, she leapt up into the air and came crashing down on her belly to force the god off. Rising again, she kept thrashing down onto the surface of the ocean. Huge waves crashed up onto the land sending torrents of water up over the cliffs and onto the escarpment that stood almost a league above the beach. The serpent's fangs glistened with venom, trying to strike the invader as it thrust its talons into her scales. Each blow came with more force as her juices poured out and the god drained her. Just then, as the python began to lose strength, Lido rose up out of the water, grabbed the serpent and god, and wrenched them apart.

"Be gone serpent; go to your slumber until I awaken you."

Lido flung Baachelaus onto the land.

The god landed heavily on the cliff. It leapt again with gaining strength and began to run towards the spirit of the water.

Lido commanded the waves higher and thicker and a great wall of water blocked its pursuit of the serpent.

"Ahh, who are you, spirit, that thwarts me at my first awakening and again at this moment of victory."

"If you have forgotten, traitor, then I will not heal your confusion, for it would be at my peril."

A wind gust blew forward and a face formed in the air.

"Sister, be gone as well, the higher one lies confused, but its strength is growing."

Baachelaus looked at the floating figure and roared in frustration. Who were these to defy the destroyer? The figure in the sky moved closer towards it. It sensed potency there, it stirred a memory, but it would not reveal itself.

"Who are you?"

"I am Aerean, guardian of the unseen power which lies beneath sky and sea, leaf and stone. I am the custodian of air and wind." A translucent finger formed and touched the god on its cheek.

"Aerean, nay, his strength was always…" Lido stopped herself from saying anything else.

"Lido, he has returned."

"Only to destroy."

Suddenly the god plunged its hand into Aerean and instantly felt the bolt of oneness and the strength of a thousand suns enter. The god of wind tried to pull away, but she couldn't flee from the grip of Baachelaus.

"No, brother, release me," pleaded Aerean. The custodian of wind felt the grip of Baachelaus tighten more.

Vipax spewed up out of the water and came crashing down between the two figures breaking them apart. Lido welled up as well to push Baachelaus back further away from the ocean. The god and Voloc were thrust into the desert by the power of the water. Lido saw on the horizon the guardians walking towards their master.

Vipax retreated under the waves. The wounds were healing fast, but her sacred energy flowed through the god.

"Aerean, his will is stronger than yours. Do not forget who he once was."

"I know, sister, but my sorrow and joy at his return clouded me."

Baachelaus roar washed over them. Aerean felt a tug, and

then she disappeared. Lido felt the wrench as well but was able to withstand the strength of Baachelaus as it clawed at her. Lido rose as tall as a mountain and sent a tsunami of water towards the god and wraith. She tried to pull Aerean away, but the clutching strength of Baachelaus would not release the wind custodian. Then the sun broke the horizon and Lido heard the screech of pain as the god felt the sting of the dawn. The god of water watched as the guardians collected the invader and took it away to the dark, along with her sister, Aerean, trapped within the will of Baachelaus.

Voloc's red eyes stared at the water spirit: ancient enemies looked at each other, remembering the battles of long ago.

Lido searched to the depths of her oceans. She found the trail of shimmering ichor from Vipax's wounds. Eventually, she saw the serpent swimming slowly before her.

"Heal yourself, mighty one, for you will be needed. Our brother has placed a leash on Aerean. I must find Norbu."

The serpent looked at the spirit of water.

"The custodians were sent before us, but our purpose has never been realised until now. Your brethren will destroy this world with the very strength that protects it. Why has Caemeris abandoned its creations?"

"The breach of long ago set the created against the unformed and now the end draws near. Battle for this world, great serpent, not for Caemeris favour, for I too fear that we have been forgotten."

Vipax dove further toward the bed of the ocean and went back to her cave. The serpent knew if she battled the god again, she would not be able to defeat its strength. She, like Uchala, knew now of her purpose, to lie in repose until the time came to awaken. But with the strength that Vipax would give the god, then it would become indestructible. Coiling up again, the serpent fell to sleep. Lido watched the great viper fall into slumber.

"Norbu, where are you? The higher ones have descended into your realm; their presence will bring the great division here where it never belonged."

Lido thought of Aerean. What would her brother do with her? The spirit of water began to search the old places where the custodians first made their dwellings. As she called, only silence echoed in her mind. Despair began to fill her thoughts, along with a darkness that she had not felt since the first days of the sundering of Caemeris from the custodians of light and colour.

4

Brethren

Seraf was the god of fire. He, of all the brethren, was not bound to Arglethium. He had been conceived by Belmaris in its infancy. He would often leave and sit amongst Belmaris' chaotic flares and just burn. The heat would sear him to his essence and then he would reform and become Seraf the god again. During these times cradled in Belmaris heart, the world below would freeze. The tribes of Arglethium would call it winter. And as if in homage to the absent god, the leaves of the trees in the coldest parts of the world would turn to vibrant reds and golds, yearning for his return. Then they withered and fell into slumber waiting for his arrival. He loved his beauty and any time he saw the offspring of his essence blaze to life after a storm, or the lesser one's nourishing themselves by their warmth, he would glory in the hectic dance of his progeny. Sometimes his flames would destroy all they touched, but even this mayhem fed his pride. Norbu, the elder brethren of the custodians, would call Seraf when the earth and trees were reduced to smoke and ash.

Seraf would sit with the mighty Keeper of Arglethium and say,

"Look here, brother, a new leaf is born. Do not be saddened, for it is my nature to destroy to bring new life."

It was for this reason the contrary god of fire was tolerated by his elder.

Seraf had been resting in the great star Belmaris and reminiscing of the early days of Lido's storms. Gathering in her mighty clouds, he would ride them, shooting spears of heat down onto the land. Aerean would join in, draw her strength, and enliven the little sparks to glorious infernos. Lido, who always sought to stifle his nature, would douse whole mountainsides and blazing forests, with torrents of rain. Seraf missed the early days of creation when he had wrought such beauty in his unbridled infancy. It was during this time of reflection that a memory of Norbu came to him. Norbu had set order amongst the brethren so that Caemeris' vision could be realised. He had not seen his brother for a millennium, but the potency of the Elder of the first Caemexa remained palpable to him. He withdrew from Belmaris' and descended to Arglethium. For Seraf it had only been an instant in the star but for Arglethium it had been many generations since his heat had graced the land. In that time, the northern lands had frozen in the worst winter some of the elders could remember in their long years. He saw the frigid lands. The frozen earth needed his enflaming touch with his sister's help. He arrived in the southern wastelands, which out of all the lands lay nearest to Belmaris heart. In the midst of a drought, he felt the heat gather to him and intensify.

He called for his sister "Come, Aerean, we will lay waste to this red dust and clear the land, burn the leaf and bark, melt the ice and quench Lido's thirst. Awake, mighty brother Norbu; who has long remained dormant to my games, the young god of fire needs to be tempered."

Nothing stirred as the emptiness of the desert met the fire god. Seraf drifted into the skies and towards the edge of the land across the water and the middle lands. It was wetter here and he felt the heat sap from him. He saw Lidos clouds form and sent a spear into it, and as it pointed straight down into the forest, the fire began. He floated again and saw the trees change to mountains that separated the middle lands from the north. He called for Norbu, where his great brother had made his Keep. Not even in the lofty heights of the peaks of Tarentess did the cries of Aerean's zephyrs or deep boom of Norbu's strength meet Seraf.

Flying over the ice caps of the northern lands, he felt his father's power wash over him in radiating arcs of heat. It reminded Seraf of the beginning times when the Caemeris had first thought of the universe's existence. Drinking their essence, he blazed across the night sky in magnificent streaks of vermillion, indigo, and greens. He left, full with the essence of Belmaris and returned to the southern land to rest. His throne was the red centre of the desert on the top of a great rock formed in a cataclysmic eruption at the time of creation. The sun was strongest here when it reached its zenith. Often sitting in the heat of the day, the desert dwellers would come to sacrifice or offer worship to the sun but did not sense his presence. Very occasionally, one of the children would have insight to his spirit, but it would go quickly, as it was deemed that the children would remain ignorant to the caemexa. Everything was silent and Seraf became restless again. Softly, as the sun crept silently above, the sound of a gentle whisper came to him.

"Ahh, Aerean. At last you have come to play."

He waited but nothing stirred except the shimmering haze of the desert heat. On the horizon, he saw figures walking. The heat waves of the sand obscured their form. Another sound came to him, not of wind, but a roar. Seraf tensed, he felt something he had not felt for an eternity. As the figures drew closer, he materialised on the very peak of the rock. He saw them and knew them. Seraf and Norbu had sealed the tear shut and had seen the guardians form at the gate they made to stop the shadowed light breaching its bonds. The guardians began to climb the rock toward him, sharp fangs and taloned hands, their strides long and few to reach where the fire god stood. They corralled around him and he braced himself. He had felt their strength before, when they had placed the chains on the betrayer, their lost brethren.

"Norbu, Lido, Aerean, where art thou? Our doom has awakened and walks our world."

"Brother, flee now, flee to your father and forsake this place."

"Aerean where are you? Come to me, sister, and we shall destroy the spawn of light's enemy."

One of the guardians moved closer to him. Seraf felt the talons on him. He tried to leave but couldn't. The creatures were swaying and chanting. He drew in on himself and looked towards the sun as he felt the cold seep into his being.

"Oh, great star, hear your child," he cried, and heaving with all his might lifted himself away from the rock into the sky. The guardians wrenched the god of fire back toward the red earth.

He was driven straight into the ground causing a massive crack to snake its way deep into the bedrock of the desert floor. The figures hopped off the high peak and came toward him. He stood and formed a fire ball, thrusting it at them. Three of the guardians were knocked over, but they did not burn. The others kept coming.

"Brethren, where are you?"

The voice of Aerean floated to him, "Seraf, flee." Seraf searched for his sister but could not see her.

He focused on the sun and drew energy from it. Forming a great wall of fire, he began to walk toward the guardians, the heat melted the sand and rock and for one hundred leagues a great black wasteland, forever to be known as the tomb of the sun spread across the lands. He forced the fire around the figures and lassoing them, he gathered them up and pulled them into the sky. He headed north to the radiating flares of the northern skies. Seraf felt himself brimming with the energy and love for Belmaris. The talons began to loosen.

When he reached the top of the world, the power of the sun's rays made him shine so brightly that the tribes below were blinded and the leagues of implacable ice at each end of the world began to crack. Seraf became his full glory in the prism of ethers that swirled high in the atmosphere. Drawing his strength, he compressed a ball of flame and set it to spin around the gaolers causing everything to explode into a cacophony of flame and colour. Seraf fell to the earth and landed in the melting ice beneath.

"Lido, he has come."

"Seraf! Up now, brother. You will be weak here! Up now!

They are not destroyed; they were created by the eternal to be our gaolers; only the Caemeris may destroy them."

Seraf roused and as he alighted onto the land, he saw them swaying in line before him. Instantly, he felt their claws take him.

"What am I to do, Sister?"

"Flee to the star."

"I cannot. They are too strong."

He called again for the sun, but they began to place the chains on him.

On the wind, he heard a voice, thick, evil, and potent. "Bind him and bring him to me."

Seraf called for Norbu, "Where are you, elder of this world?"

As the chains wrapped around him, he felt the mastery of their power. In the eons of his time here on earth, his essence had waned while the guardians still stood close to their first forms. Both borne of the eternal, but each weathered by different strands of existence. Seraf, at his creation, held the sun in his hand and would have incinerated the earth and all sustained with in it if he had not been tempered by Norbu. Now he was caged, and all the power that he could muster from the sun was not enough to break the bonds around him. Solar flares and fiery sparks flew at the guardians, but it was not enough to free him. They entered Widjera's sacred cave with Seraf as their prisoner. Walking deep, far deeper than Widjera would have ever known in his life, the brilliance of Seraf lit the walls with red and gold shadows, showing the grandeur of the cavern. A throne had been carved from the deep bedrock. Baachelaus sat upon it. The god sneered at the light Seraf radiated into the lair.

"Welcome, fire god. Dim yourself before me." The blue eyes flared slightly.

"Higher One, I bow to you and my spirit remembers your glory, but the void has gnawed on your face and might. It has left you to dwell in darkness like the vermin of this world and the fell creatures that slither on the edge of memory in the depths of your lightless cage."

"Silence, your chatter and brightness burns me."

"Brother." Seraf stirred, hearing Aerean's call.

"Sister, come we must dance for our brother and welcome his return."

The guardians let go and Seraf blazed in fury, but Baachelaus blew a gale dimming the fire to a spark. Chuckling at Scraf, Baachelaus rose from the throne.

"Ahh fire god, you are magnificent."

"The dark has made you pale, and you have forgotten your brethren and the things which sustain us all." Seraf stood before him, he called to Belmaris with the bonds between himself and the star, but the cave was deep, and no light penetrated here. Baachelaus sensed Seraf's attempt to draw power from the sun.

"Ahh yes, the star blazes ever brighter, disturbing my peace and thwarting my path."

"What do you want, brother? I am a curse to you, if my father burns you."

Baachelaus moved quickly and placed his hand on Seraf. The fire god felt himself plunge into darkness. He sensed Aercan inside the emptiness. A deep cold filled him and the burning spark of the great star from which he was formed began to whither.

Silence and darkness enveloped the cavern. Voloc appeared before Baachelaus.

"Have you seen what the brethren know, My Lord? The secrets that lie hidden from your sight, are they revealed now that two of the gods dwell within you?"

"What draws me here lies dim on the edges of my sight and the great star still weakens me. The children of flesh shall feed me until all these spirits are captured and become one with me. Then Belmaris' power will be defeated."

Baachelaus sat back on his throne. His sockets were filled with green specs, as the blue of Uchala yellowed with the essence of Seraf. His skin still glowed like crystal and illuminated the lair. His ragged lips expelled the black venom within him sliding down his emaciated body onto the dirt below. Black creatures, unknown to this world, with the fangs and legs akin to Uchala grew out of the dirt and venom and made their way into the world outside. He crept into the ancient vaults of his mind and called, nothing answered. Instinct told him this was not what he was, but all that existed was the memory of his cage. For eons, he had floated with his gaolers until his isolation slowly filled his mind with rage and confusion. He forgot his name and purpose. The chains on him grated inside his chest, wearing his memory and vision away until only a hollow cavity existed. He remembered the first time he felt the presence of the other.

"Who art thou?"

"I am from the dawn of creation before the light came, this

prison is my throne, and you, great one, are chained to it."

"Who put me here?"

"Yourself," came the reply.

Then everything was silent until the pain started. Slowly he felt himself being shredded to pieces and reformed, he screamed in the darkness and the echoes reverberated for eons.

"Who are you? Why am I here?" he screamed.

Nothing; only more pain, from an itch to searing heat, then the frigid cold came, instantly freezing him, only to shatter his fleshless existence into a thousand pieces. At one time, he thought he heard a voice call in the distance – a sorrowful cry, a lament of profound grief. "My beloved" echoed across time and space. But the pain consumed him, and the voice was forgotten, as he was incinerated over and over again. The voice faded into oblivion leaving him to wallow in his emptiness. He spoke after an eternity of agonising screams and this time his words were thick with malice.

"Who torments me in this way?"

"Who art thou?" asked the voice.

"I am the destroyer of the light."

"Then it is yourself that binds you to this eternal oblivion."

The pain began again, only this time, he revelled in the climax and took it all in. The voice whispered to him, 'Go here,' and a vision formed of a place, this place he sat now.

"Here lie your enemies and their destruction will unleash you from your gaol."

But the other never told him why he had been bound in the first place.

He opened his eyes again and saw the cave. The guardians

had retreated onto the walls. Voloc was not there. He called Seraf and Aerean forth. Each of them became a speck on his hand.

"Who am I? Brother and Higher One, you have called me, who am I?"

No answer came from either of them.

"Answer me!" he demanded.

"You may command our power, but you do not command our will."

Seraf flared into a spinning wheel of flame on his hand. The god winced at the light and heat.

"When you remember, you shall weep a thousand tears for the caemexa and yourself, brother. Did the void not speak to you? Was it only putrescence and malice that it seeped into your being? My fire will cleanse you, strip you back to your essence, and bring you home to the realm where you belong. You are no longer our brethren, for I feel no warmth in you only the cold darkness of your chains. They have made you dead to all that is born of the colours of Caemeris."

Seraf had begun to glow more with each sentence and was burning the god's hand.

Aerean being the spirit of wind could see all things closed and hidden from the world. She had felt the stirring in the dead heart of her brethren's memory of the sorrowful voice that had once come to the imprisoned god. She knew who that voice belonged to.

"Brothers, you fight for no reason, come back to us, our beloved," she whispered into Baachelaus ear. "Let us free you. We will bring you back to the realm, the first realm of light where you once sat watching how your brethren revelled in the vision of Caemeris." Baachelaus did not answer as he heard the word beloved drift into his ear from the god of wind.

Seraf grew and Aerean became a tornado on his palm growing larger. They joined together and exploded forth in front of him. They wrapped around his body. He roared at their brightness and strength.

"Guardians, come!"

They sprang to life and walked through the fire and wind. Baachelaus began to melt from the heat and the abrading force of Aerean. The gaolers gathered and joined their talons and began to chant. Voloc appeared but was driven back by the savagery of Seraf and Aerean's force. The twins came together, the walls shuddered, but the guardians seemed to be drawing tighter around the pair and the god. Seraf and Aerean drew together and formed a cyclone of wind and fire, tighter and tighter into a frenzy. Baachelaus roared in pain as his skin began to strip away. A crack sped along the floor of the cavern. Then it widened into a gaping hole. Under the gods, the world opened to reveal its belly of fire and rivers of rock. Seraf became manic with his flames. Convulsing with pure energy, he drew around Baachelaus and pulled him down into the pit.

"Guardians, take the chain and heave your servant forth!" Baachelaus bellowed above the melee of wind and fire and lava. Everything stopped. The forces that held the earth and skies apart were wrenched together almost splitting the colours of the world into their elemental hues. Seraf was magnificent, whipping the lava around himself and Baachelaus. One of the guardians, First of the eight, reached in and pulled out their prisoner. The god was limp in his long taloned hands.

Voloc snarled at the scene before it, its eyes blazing the same red as the molten rock beneath its paws. Seraf and Aerean flew up into the cavern, as Baachelaus broke free.

"Higher one let us go, we will not bear to be gaoled by our own. We will seek what you need, but let us go," pleaded Aerean.

Baachelaus roused, the green specs exploded with fury. He drew the gaping hole in the ground closed. His mind was full of the darkness he had languished in for millennia. The flaming pit reminding him of the agony he had endured. He stood silent. The guardians swayed in the cavern, which was enflamed with reds and blues. Both the spirits burned in their magnificence. Aerean ventured nearer to the cavern wall seeking escape, but Baachelaus stretched his long fingers out to her. A malicious grin crossed his face.

"Come to me, Sister," he pulled her. Seraf flared. With his other hand, he drew Seraf to him as well.

"Where does your might come from, brother?" Aerean barely whispered as her strength to resist his domination began to wane.

"Mine is not of the star, mine is of the First, the dark, the void." The guardians chanted around him and began to circle. Seraf could feel himself dimming.

"Come then, brother, to the dark. Let us leave this place and go to where the star's rays never reach and we will see your might and terror unfold," provoked Seraf.

Baachelaus became curious but was wary. He still did not fully understand the way things were or why these spirits called him their brethren. He relaxed his hold a little.

"What is your name, fire spirit?"

"Seraf, Baachelaus."

"Take me, Seraf, to your darkness so you may witness my glory."

Seraf grabbed him and reefed him out through the mouth of the cavern. The guardians did not follow. Aerean flew with the pair of them as Baachelaus refused to let go of her essence.

Journeying into the blue sky, Baachelaus flesh began to peel off from the heat of the sun. Then they broke free of Argelthium and entered the space between the stars. Cold seeped in but Seraf blazed brightly and streaked through the emptiness. Arglethium became a blue and white disc in the background. The sun perished in the distance and when Seraf looked back at his father, he watched it dwindle into a spec on the horizon. He felt a sorrow enter his mind as he thought suddenly that he might never feel its heat again.

"Seraf, you are too far from the sun, you shall freeze."

"Yes, my love and so will my essence, so it cannot be used to destroy the world below or my brethren. I shall become a dying crystal of flame, left to drift in the frozen reaches of the void."

In the distance, a great roar could be heard. It drew closer. As the stars became fewer and fewer and the darkness more expansive, a penumbra formed out of a ribbon of colour, swirling so fast that the colours merged into a white ring in places. The trio felt they were being pulled into a churning mouth.

"Come, brother, see the marvels of the dark and glory in them. This was once the great star Magmeris, sister to Belmaris, my father that sustains the world in our custody."

But Seraf did not understand the nature of the dark, especially since he was born from the sun, unlike the other brethren who were formed wholly in the sight of Caemeris. He did not understand that Baachelaus was filled with emptiness and so was sustained by it. The god hungered for the face of the great churning pit. The grin of his great maw and the filth that oozed from it, was matched only by the black hole in which they now stood.

Pulling them both in, he said, "Yes, brother, sister, let us see."

Seraf realised his mistake in the instant that he went through the opening. As the destroyer consumed him, he was snuffed out to a tiny spec in the palm of the taloned claw. The destroyer swallowed Seraf and felt the surge of the power. Aerean screamed, but there was no sound. Everything was silent inside Magmeris' crypt. The lifeless void strangled the spirit of wind as if she never existed.

"See my cage, brethren and know my torment." Stepping back through the opening of the tomb the god of destruction screeched across the universe in victory.

Baachelaus glided out into the lifeless space, toward Arlegthium and the cave of his birth. As he passed over the lands, he saw the mark of the destruction that followed him. For a hundred leagues, the desert was scorched to black glass. He came to rest on the edge of the cavern and surveyed all before him; waiting for him were the guardians and Voloc.

Baachelaus saw the memories held by Seraf and the pain of his imprisonment enraged the god. Wind and fire spewed forth from his mouth up out into the night sky and across the world. The guardians swayed and chanted as their prisoner came to fullness. Voloc looked with blazing red eyes and growled his pleasure at the destruction. Suddenly, the god collapsed, drained of power as the beating heart of Belmaris within Seraf bled into its body.

"This flesh is weak. How do I heal it?"

"There is a way where you will command your power once more without the memory of death that dwells in the lesser one's flesh. Once it is found, your reign shall begin. Take the god. Heal it." The wolf commanded the guardians.

— — —

Lido knew Seraf had been taken prisoner. The spirit of water felt a fear creep into her as the power of the higher one grew and penetrated her being.

"Norbu where are you?" She shed her sacred tears into the unending oceans and rivers. She sent them down to the deep ridges and cliffs of the ocean's floor where the earth folded on itself and toward the great coastal cliffs, causing tidal waves to claw at the rocks to awaken the first custodian of all.

"Awake, Norbu! Your Keep lies on the edge of annihilation."

— — —

Silence lay about the wolf and the god deep inside the cave beneath the searing heat of the southern desert. Voloc slipped into its essence delving back through the eons trying to remember where it and the god had come from. It remembered Belmaris. Its gaoler and progenitor. The shadow's enemy at its zenith and would not weaken for another two decicycles. Twenty summers and winters here in this world of clay and rock. It would have to wait until the cycles of Belmaris waned. To when the dawns changed from bright red to the indigoes of leaf fall. Voloc had learnt patience, but its lust to be free of the leash of its creator fumed like the heart of the blazing star itself. With the god now full of its brethren of fire and wind and blood of the ancient sentinels, Voloc had the strength of the light of Caemeris under its command. All it needed was the gift, the prism, the tears wrought into pure crystal by Norbu the mighty to wield Caemeris' power – then Voloc could break the heart of Belmaris. It would become suzerain of all the star had created.

Voloc found Vronius staring across the moonlit ocean. Inside, the monk's mind the demon searched for any knowledge of the gift of Norbu. The creature of flesh knew nothing. Voloc knew the gift lay within the brick and mortar of the temple. It was there but shrouded itself with time's conjuration of slumber. Even with eons passing away from the custodian Ascendant there was still a hint of its strength which Voloc could sense.

Vronius could feel the presence inside him. Something lay hidden and needed to be found. It was fluttering constantly at the edge of his vision. 'Where was it? Where was it hidden? Find it and bring it to me,' commanded Voloc. Pain seared through the flesh of Vronius. He went to the great archival chambers and began to read the oldest scrolls. His eyes scanning like fire ants disturbed from their nest, devouring the old texts for clues. The silence of the library remained watchful. It had stood for thousands of generations of brethren, formed from the very foundation of the gift from Norbu when Ira had returned from the southern lands. Now it watched the trembling figure of Vronius knowing that its destruction lay on the shadow of the horizon.

5

Ascendant

Blinking, she saw specks of light piercing a vast blackness. Green and white incandescent sparkles looked down on her. 'How beautiful' she thought. As if hearing her, a thousand tiny voices chimed, "Who's that?" The sound lanced her awareness, making her jump. Normally existing in the essence of time, the miniscule voices rippled through the crudeness of the form she had taken.

"Who are you?" The tiny voices made her laugh this time, as they tickled her ears.

"Say it again," she called.

"Who are you?" sang a chorus.

"Who are you, little ones?"

"We have no name. What are you?"

"You remind me of the first stars formed at the beginning of time."

"Stay with us. We are lonely here. We can teach you songs to sing with us."

"Only for a little while. I must begin my search for my brethren."

"Who are your brethren?"

She stood up and looked at her arms and legs. Taking a step her foot jagged on something. Pain shot though it and a warm liquid trickled down her toe.

"Little ones, could you let me see a little better?"

Immediately the specs of light brightened displaying a huge sulphur cave. Large snottites hung from the ceiling, dripping raw sulphuric acid into a pool below. The water was still, silent and deep with a yellow haze rising from its surface. Her gaze came to rest on the farther edge of the pool. White sticks lay in piles along the wall of the cavern. Some of the stones looked circular with divots removed, while others were arched, cage-like in appearance. They were bleached white. More piles of these stones lay scattered randomly around the floor of the cave. Looking down, she saw the broken remains of a circular rock upon which she had cut her foot. She picked it up, one half of the rock was missing, and two large holes had been burrowed out. Jutting out of the rock, were peg-like protuberances. She ran her finger along them. Then put her finger to her mouth and felt her teeth. She realised that these were a stage in the existence of the form she had taken.

"So, little ones, you have seen others like me?"

"No! Not as beautiful as you. The others seem different. They are coarse to our ears; they screech and gurgle. Who are you?"

Not answering them, she walked over to the pool and put her hand in. Pain seared its way up her arm as the flesh began to blister. Pulling away, she stood and watched as the burnt flesh healed instantly.

"Is this a pool of your tears?"

"No, it is our death. We are born and then die as we fall. Each time, new ones are made."

The largest of the stalagmite had almost reached the surface of the pool.

"The charm of your singing belies the sting of your forms, little ones," she said, laughing gently at the paradox of these creatures under Norbu's dominion. Her existence was lost to the physicality of sensation and death, and the intricate designs that were born from this place – so removed now from the first colours of the created light. As she began to explore the cave, something touched her arms. In the dim cavern, a little worm, glowing warmly, struggled on the end of a fine thread, glistening with many colours.

"And who are you?" She picked it up and held it towards the ceiling to see well.

"That is us."

"This strand, is that what you are attached to?"

"Yes. These are our gift for those who wish to have it. Strong and beautiful, it shines with our song."

Walking further into the caves a shaft of light from the outside broke through the haze. It revealed a cave with hundreds of spires reaching down from the heights. The ground became smoother. The acid had worn the rock down to beautifully marbled contours of lime and onyx. It was a magnificent testimony to the deeper reaches of Norbu's vision.

"Are we not beautiful – as is our home?"

"Indeed, you are beautiful, little ones, and you pay homage to my brethren, the first custodians of light. The way your essence, released at your death, sculpts the rock is worthy of their greatness."

She rubbed her throat feeling it burning. "I have thirst. This body is weak." Her tongue rasped over her lips as they cracked from the fumes. She felt a hot sensation in her chest as she breathed the air.

"Drink from our pool."

She smiled at their kind but innocent gesture. "I fear that is why your guests do not remain long here."

"Rest a little. We will make you a gift with our song," trilled the little worms.

She lay down again, smiling to herself at this world's beauty and ugliness. The creatures began to coo in the toxic darkness of the cave.

Sleep came easily to the god, as the soothing echoes relaxed the body she had woven around her essence. This was a weak form, always needing sustenance. There would be none found in this cave, this place was anathema to the flesh that bound her. Her quest had led her to the realm of Arglethium. Her brethren lay hidden deep within their Keeps here. Eons had passed since she had seen them. Letting herself drift into a dream state, visions of golden dawns and eternal springs at the time of custodians' birth flourished, as the density of Arglethium made the senses draw her memories into definite shapes. Her other brethren who dwelt here came to bring the songs of creation's fledgling beauty to life. The vision of Caemeris their progenitor, mysterious, unseen but potent in its force. Norbu, her mighty brother, warrior, and maker of clay. She imagined his great arms stretched out protecting the breadth of his dominion. She searched the depths of her conscious for any sign of him, but nothing came. One hundred millennia had passed and the desire to see her destiny fulfilled remained as potent as ever. The last dream she remembered, etched on her ancient awareness, had been of this world, but always she had been thwarted in reaching this place. By who she did not know, but now she had arrived. Was it time for fulfilment or annihilation? Either way she sensed the end of her quest was nearing.

A great whooshing noise filled the chamber, waking her. Sitting up, she felt something on her skin. On her lay some clothes. A black hooded tunic with flowing sleeves, some trousers and a sash, braided in reds and golds. There were boots as well, trimmed with the same colours of her belt. The cloth felt soothing to her skin and shimmered in the light.

"Ahh! What a beautiful gift, little ones!" A thousand trills agreed with her.

She stood, jumping slightly at the sound of another hollow whistle echoing through the caves again. Towards the rear of the pool, she saw the cause of the noise; a yellow pillar of sulphur was pistoling from a crack in the bedrock.

"I need to leave now friends. Will you show me the way out?"

"Ooh no," chimed the snottites, 'Stay here!"

"I may return. Thank you for these." She held out her arms in recognition of the tunic she now wore. "I will think of you and your kindness every day."

Moving along a tunnel, the dim glow of the worms revealed the expansive network of caves where she had arrived. Walking through the great stinking cavern, the sulphur haze cleared as the sandstone became thicker and less permeable to the acid seepage. In places, in the cavern where the rock had been eaten away, there were columns of rock in perfect alignment. The tails of the worms dotted the roof intermittently, mirroring the night sky.

After several hours of walking, light began to permeate the darkness.

"Wait!" called the tiny shrill voices. "You will no longer need us to see, the big light enters soon, and it dims ours. Please do not go."

"I must, little ones."

Walking on, she entered into daylight, her eyes smarting at the sudden brightness. In the distance, she heard their voices calling her to come back. As the wind gusted slightly the voices carried on it. To the human ear, it sounded like sorrowful cry for help. Guessing this was how the creatures lured visitors to their doom, she continued forward into a meadow of heath and spiky grasses. Surveying the scene before her, she breathed deeply. The air felt crisp and revived the body as the caustic fumes were replaced with the breeze. The ledge of rock ran in circle at least a league across. She stood in the crater of a volcano. Extinct for many hundreds of years, it was flat on its summit with steep slopes descending into a dense forest. Mossy rocks and flax grass covered the plateau at the cave's entrance. It was spring here, and dispersed through the grass were wild daisies, corn flowers, and pigface; their dots of colour broke the aridity of the yellowed grass and grey rocks. She let her fingers run through the flax; the new sensations etched themselves into her waking memory.

Soon she reached the northern edge of the plateau. Again, the magnificence of Norbu's realm greeted her sight. A vista lay out before her, made up of a mosaic of crops and dwellings surrounded by sheer grey and white mountains. Twinkling in the distance, a serene stream ran through all the fields, with culverts diverting water into various dams along its path. The tranquillity of the picture before her soothed her senses. The blue stream seemed to remind her of her body's needs. She ran her tongue around her mouth and felt the dryness and acrid taste of the sulphur cave again.

Making her way along the precipice, she found a path leading into the forest. Stepping under the canopy, the sun left, and she plunged into dappled shade. The diversity of the trees and plants lining the understory of the forest crowded her mind as it filled with the detail of each leaf, stem, and twig. The majesty of the trees crowning the roof of the forest overwhelmed her with their height and largesse to protect their smaller siblings as they carved out their existence underneath. A little lizard skittered up the trunk of the large tree, freezing suddenly with claw in mid-step. It waited nervously as she stepped closer to look at the creature.

"Oh, little one… so delicate." She sighed in wonder.

The lizard swallowed then dashed up the trunk in terror, out of sight and into safety.

She sunk to her knees; the tears formed into diamonds onto the ground.

"If I restore the Caemexa do I condemn the clay born. For silence has ever answered my calls through the eons of searching to end in nothing but an abyss, bereft of memory and hope.

I am weary of this quest and here in this last creation I seek my memories to erase the sundering of light and shadow. What is my fate, to bring destruction or restoration?"

Her despair at this thought thrust her ancient memory to the time of the breach and the shadows that had dogged her existence ever since. She shuddered. The forest around her stilled as the profoundness of the god's sorrow spilled into the earth, leaf, and root.

She gathered herself and continued through the forest. Her heart and body trembled at what would lie ahead. Coming to a stream, she stooped down and drank greedily. Slaking her thirst restored her mood, pushing back the dreadful images that had diminished her wonderment in the forest. She walked through the rainforest, hardly disturbing a leaf. Rain began to fall. The clothes repelled the water, so she removed them. Standing naked, she lapped the droplets on her tongue and marvelled at the earth. Thunder cracked across the skies hurting her ears. Dressing, she moved toward the escarpments. Looking toward the great mountain range, she felt drawn to them. She closed her eyes and tried to sense Norbu again, but there was nothing.

She reached a village. The clayborn tilled the earth, prepared food, and chattered to one another of things unknown to her. Their offspring played and cried out. She did not sense fear or pain. Some had anger in their hearts, some had sorrow, a few had joy, and some love. All had an emptiness, some felt it while others did not know what it was, but instinct made them rail against it. She drew it all in and felt a surge of longing and forsaken hope withering in their hearts. She walked through one village after another; her heart and mind were awash with the happiness and sorrow which living exacted upon them. Places full of sickness that ripped the flesh to pieces and rotted their bones; children dead at their birth, mother's blood oozing from their torn bodies as they screamed them into existence. She saw a farmer whipping a slave and then kicking him when he collapsed. His flesh shredded into slivers; he lay unconscious in the mud. She saw into the farmer's heart – nothing, not even pity for the other man's life, only a void, blackness. She looked into the heart of the one that lay in the mud dying. A small dot of light shone there. It was of his wife and child, lost to him many dawns ago. The sorrow cradled in the brief joy he had before he was stolen from them. A bolt of sheer agony wracked her body as the slave's bloody wounds became hers. She took the pain from him. The slave stood and struck the farmer with a pick. He threw it down. Sorrow and hatred swelled in the man's heart as he ran. She took it all in.

As she continued, she saw some children eating off a tree. She waited until they had finished and went there. The red berries were bitter and sweet. She ate until her stomach cramped. Her mind began to open again to the people around her. Inside one hut, there was laughter as a child played games. Leaving the village, she came to a stream where some young men were fishing. She saw them catch a fish, scale and clean it, and put it into a flame. The fish turned black and then they ate it. She came and sat next to them. The three of them were unaware of her presence. She placed her hand into the fire and pain immediately met her. She withdrew it. One of the young men looked to his side sensing something but shook it off. They were content. But one of the young men secretly envied the leader of the group because he was betrothed to a girl he desired. She steered her mind away as much as she could to the other men. Hopeful and in love with their lives. Wanting adventure to conquer the world in their fashion. And love… she felt the love some of the group had for each other; their camaraderie and bond. It was good and did not jar her – unlike the man with malice in his heart. After three days, the group had begun to argue with one another when the man with envy had begun to taunt the leader. He had threatened him while they had been sparring in a game. The next morning the group had left.

Hunger for food was constantly bombarding her senses. Especially since she would forget to nourish the body. Remembering the young men taking food from the river, she went over to the stream, snatched a small fish, and ate it. It was silken in its flesh and its scales shimmered in the light. Bones caught in her teeth and she plucked them out. Feeling more satisfied, she lay back against an oak tree and listened to it breathe. It had lived here for almost a thousand generations of people. Its roots reached down deep within the earth drawing on the strength of its mother. She tried to sense Norbu, but there was nothing.

She opened her eyes and watched the clouds. "Where are you all, brethren?" she called, as she fell into sleep again. She rested for days against the tree letting it be her sustenance. How pure their spirits were; nothing of the tree's essence pricked or jaded her senses. Her heart remained content with the memory of every spec of dirt and drop of water that had ever fallen onto the ground. A continual thread of existence coursed within it. She sensed the tree was dying. The roots now tasted fire in the belly of the earth. But it kept its own counsel and simply remained as a witness to the rise and fall of the sun.

In a deep sleep, she thought she heard scratching a long way off. Something moved on the edges of her vision again. It knew she was no longer in the realm of the Caemeris. A way had been opened. She woke suddenly. Three nights had passed since the young men had left. She heard voices. Getting up, she wandered away from the stream through the bushes. She saw one of the young men holding a girl with long yellow hair. Then the god felt the lust and ugliness in the young man's heart. He was the one who had been secretly envious of the leader. The girl's heart was frozen with fear. The god's skin prickled as the waves of the girl's panic spread over her. Then the man thrust her to the ground. The girl screamed, but his hand muffled her cries for help. He mounted her and she struggled. He slapped her several times until she lay limp, then he tore her clothes. The god fell to the ground bombarded by hate and domination. Then something darker came, violent and loathing. The man strangled the girl until her neck snapped. The god appeared suddenly in front of him. She saw the soul of the dead girl turn into wisps of smoke lost on the wind. The god's anger rose, she grabbed the man. Taking his hatred and envy, she drew her strength and crushed his skull between her hands. He dropped on the girl and his soul lingered on the god's hands until she blew it away in anger. The god collapsed from the strain and began to sob. She went into her mind, deep within the essence she had been, and screamed out at the loss, despair, and the desolation around her. She cried into the world to kill the pain and malice that held dominion over the hearts of those born into this place.

"So mighty Norbu when you made the clayborn was it with my essence of longing you imbibed into their hearts. Is this why I can see them so clearly, more clearly than themselves. Is this where my fate lies and that of Baachelaus? If we are united again with the brethren and the realm of Caemeris is restored what will come of these ones here?"

The bodies of the man and woman lay behind her, crushed from the force of her scream. She did not look at them but began to walk. In a daze, she made her way towards the mountains. She tracked a path up to a plateau that lay halfway up the north side of the peak. The blood from the man had run off her clothes without leaving a stain. The plateau was four leagues across its width and supported a verdant forest of birches, pines, and oaks. A small waterfall from the icecaps of the great mountain flowed into a river. The stream snaked its way along the length of the tableau until it cascaded over the edge to the river below. These streams in the old tongues were called Oda and Uda, meaning upper and lower. She walked until her feet began to bleed in the boots. Her stomach and body ached for nourishment. She tried to dwell within herself to find the essence from which she had come, but it seemed to be further away with each day she spent here on Arglethium. The contempt that lay now in her mind from the lesser one's murderous heart consumed her thoughts. Climbing up towards the escarpment, the beauty of the woodland was lost to her. At last, grasping onto the rocks and vines, she made it to a flat ledge and rested. She looked out over the lands she had crossed and saw in the far distance the volcano. All the memories of the people she had felt, and the death she had perpetrated on the one with murder in his heart, hung upon her like great chains bolted to stone. She cried as she felt like she was being suffocated. She wanted to tear the body she now inhabited to shreds and return to the realm of light which had created her. Pulling her hood over her face, she headed west towards the setting sun. The reds and golds in her belt shimmered in the fading rays. In fact, the whole outfit became raiment of glorious colours as the light of the sunset glimmered on the cloth made from the worms. Eventually, she came to the place that had been calling her. It was a grove surrounded by silver birches and firs, laid out in concentric circles. In the centre of the trees was a pool. The water lay still and deep. Kneeling beside the pool, she pulled her hood back, washed her face, and drank the water.

"Oh sister, what have you done to yourself?" Lido rose out of the pool and grasped her face in watery hands to look into her eyes. The bond was undeniable as they both felt the chorus of their kinship with Caemeris within them.

"I am awash with the despair that lies in the hearts of the one's who dwell here, sister. I have spilled blood consumed with the hate that defiles their hearts."

"You are weak and need nourishment." Instantly, some fish bobbed to the surface. "Eat, then bathe in my sacred waters."

The god finished eating the fish out of the pool. They seemed quite happy to be eaten – almost jumping into the god's hands. Her mind was calmer, but a fog still surrounded her. She had immersed the garments into the pool to wash them, but they came out perfectly dry. She placed her feet into the water. She watched as the blisters healed on her feet. She realised that the longer she walked this world, the less of her essence she would retain. In the caves where she had come from, her flesh healed itself, but now it took Lido's sacred waters to clean the wounds.

"The path to your destiny is difficult, Assumpta, why would it be less so for the ones that have been placed in your custody."

She had not heard this name for so long that she had forgotten the sound of it.

"Yes, I have been lost to the grief that has sent me into the far reaches of all that has been created and forgotten my purpose. Lido, I seek our great brother, Norbu. I cannot hear his booming voice or the great beat of his heart. He is silent to me."

"Yes, I have searched for our lord of the earth for many cycles of Belmaris, but he slumbers out of reach. And now a grave fear has awoken. Our brethren and your beloved has come here. He is lost in his memory and now rests deep within the heart of the great southern deserts. Baachelaus has breached the walls of creation and with it you have followed. He has imprisoned Aerean and I fear Seraf is lost also. Now when Norbu is most needed I cannot find our elder.

Assumpta smiled slightly, remembering the time before the creation of the world had been revealed to the gods. The mischievous games of Seraf and Aerean; Norbu's booming laugh, came to her. Our doom lies close with yours and Baachelaus arrival."

"I come to heal the breach, with the memory etched into the prism forged by Norbu when Baachelaus was stolen. I bring destruction either way to the caemexa or the clayborn. I know this deep down. But it must be done. Close lies ending of all things. And with it my relief it shall end one way or another."

"We lay in contentment for an eternity before this realm of clay and water was created, but the void has not ceased its hatred of the light. We are old and the world weary. It was never promised to us that the Caemeris would sustain us forever. Its light has been lost to me since I have dwelt here. Sister, does it call to you?"

"Nay, since the sundering of the eternal bond it has been silent. I lie in faded glory and filtered shadows, motionless and without desire. I have wept until no more would come. I woke and I began to search for him. Eons upon eons passed and the stars burst forth and dimmed. In the shadows came the beasts and the terrors that only light will destroy. I was seen and known to them, for my heart lay empty. Then a vision came to me to seek out Norbu. The gift made by our wise brother will be the way to seal the breach."

"Rest again, sister. I will seek our eldest brethren in the hope I shall find him before Baachelaus restores his strength."

"Ah Lido what loathing you must have for us, the last of the custodians, when the three of you and Norbu were set to grow and flourish here. Now we the last ones Ascendant and Descendant of the six custodians of light bring death by the very power which made us."

"Norbu's vision was far, I believe the gift he wrought will give us answers. The gaoler Voloc seeks the same gift and becomes stronger with every dawn."

"I once drew close to Baachelaus but a presence more potent and far more ancient thwarted me. Perhaps it was this creature Voloc of which you speak."

"Voloc is unknown and not of the Caemexa."

"How long has Norbu been gone?"

"I do not know. As the world was being made, I began to slumber for vast stretches of time, only waking when the great ice was needed to melt and form new land for creatures to walk upon. But, during one of my dormitions, I felt tremors deep within my oceans, something moved, and I awoke. I found Aerean and Seraf as before and they had felt the disturbance but knew no more than I, and nor had they felt Norbu's steady gaze upon them. I have watched now for millennia and feel the earth shudder as if it knows that the darkness has seen your vision and seeks the same path."

"I fear that this form will weaken me, and I will not fulfil the vision that has sent me here. If I draw close to Baachelaus now I will not be able to overcome him."

"Your essence will diminish the longer you are here. That is why you will seek out the strongest of the ancient blood lines. Their heritage is bound to Arglethium's beginning. I have found three of them. Look at their faces in my pool, so you will know who they are. Their strength when discovered will be as mighty as the foundations of the earth. Seek out the girl first, but all of them should be guided to my sacred pool. None, not even the shadows that haunt your memories, Assumpta, shall defile its waters."

"What makes their blood so potent Sister?"

"It is the memory it contains when their ancestors made a covenant with Norbu. It is also destiny that these shall be able to see Caemeris. For they looked upon the Caemexa and did not perish. It is in their flesh, permission has been granted rule the power of Caemeris light."

"Where will I find the girl?" Assumpta looked up from the pool remembering the faces.

"She lies in the east, in the deserts. Follow Belmaris as it rises, and you shall find her. But rest a little more. There is still time. Baachelaus is not restored fully."

Assumpta lay down and slept. She dreamt of a time before the sundering of the world from the Caemeris. She and Baachelaus had just been created – new essences, each aware of the other. The eternal's mind entered their thoughts. 'Remember each other, for all that is in my minds has not been wrought. With the fullness of time, your destiny shall be made clear.' Their spirits merged and the universe became white, hot and searing so that all around could not bear it. The other brethren watched in awe and bowed to the majesty and glory. 'For all to come would never usurp the wisdom of the highest of the custodians,' said a voice with no name.

She woke at dawn, loyally the little fish bobbed to the surface for her to breakfast. She washed in the pool. The water rippled slightly as she got out and a whisper floated to her ear,

"Eternal grace be with you, Sister. Draw strength from the brave hearts that walk Norbu's Keep and do not retaliate against those who have drawn the dark into theirs; for all of the clay born lie under your dominion."

"When the order of the brethren is restored then it will be

me who shall sing the praise of Lido, wellspring of all that nourishes the fertile beauty of this world; restorer of strength within my heart and flesh alike."

She looked towards the east where the sun rose and left the grove with only the birds to accompany her. She put the hood over her head; inwardly drawing on the waters of her sister, as she thought of all that had already passed since walking the earth, and the difficulties that lay ahead. The rays of the star Belmaris greeted her as she broke free of the forest surrounding the pool. She felt its warmth and light around her waist. The sash scintillated in a raiment of colour. Faintly, she thought she could hear the tiny voices from the cave. She smiled as her spirits lifted and the memory came back to her of the ancient un-tethered beauty she had once created with Bacchaelaus, re-flected now in those glow worms and her sash. And yet deep within her ancient memory the breach into the realm of clay and stone brought the doom of the custodians of light as well.

PART TWO

Cage of Flesh and Bone

6

Visitors

Bensah's shadow stretched out on the slip faces of the dunes as the sun closed on the horizon. The sand was interlaced with the black crevices formed from the undulations casting shadows. Some of them were so steep that they reached higher than the elephants from the lands of Bensah's birth. In the distance, he could see the small oasis of boabs. He hoped to make it there before the night came. The moon was on the wane and he could miss the one place of refuge in the darkness from the sandstorm that loomed behind him. The windstorms could be lethal during the dry season. He quickened his pace. The only noise was the jingling of his satchels and Nekoda's panting just ahead of him. A cross breed of hyena and wild dog, he made an ugly companion, but a sturdy and loyal one; good for hunting and guarding Bensah against thieves.

"Come, Nekoda, the sun runs its own race towards the night."

Nekoda cantered up towards his master at the sound of his voice. Bensah began a slow jog, his feet heavy and awkward on the slopes of the sand. He began to pant, feeling his fifty summers. Soon beads of sweat formed on his face, dripping down to his chin, but evaporating before they trickled onto the parched grains beneath his feet. Nekoda raced ahead, barking encouragement to keep going. Bensah envied the dog darting up and down the dunes with ease, while his own legs succumbed to exhaustion. The sand grabbed his ankles and would not release him, making each step more forced. As he reached the crest of one massive dune, Bensah saw the trees standing in the middle of a large expanse of level sand. He took a step to descend the slip-face. He managed to get halfway but the slope was too steep, losing his footing he slid down toward the waiting oasis. When he stopped, his satchels had spilled open and his water cask lay leaking onto the sand. Nekoda came bounding towards him, licking his face with concern. Bensah righted himself, cursing at his clumsiness. Looking back at the dune, it rose ominously above him – almost seven men tall by his estimation. He felt its curve wanting to push him into the earth below, like a tidal wave of dirt, suffocating everything and erasing any trace of his footsteps. The desert had grown larger. Its edges reached almost to the sea now. These days, only tufts of hardy sea grass grew along the coasts. Bensah's childhood memories were of lush coastal bush and shrubs that lay like the woven mats of the northern lands. In spring, he and his brother would collect the berries that grew on them. Their mother would make a stew for them to eat. Now it was as if the desert wanted to swallow the ocean as well.

Gathering his things, he began to walk toward the trees to make a shelter for the night. The sun's curve was just nudging the horizon. The haze around it was as red as the sand he walked on. The corona of indigo and pink was spectacular, but it also meant that the winds would come during the night.

Upon reaching the oasis, Bensah undid his head scarf and outer robe. He hooked them over the branches of two trees to create a tent, with each end abutted by the thick trunk of a boab tree. 'It will do,' he thought. As he looked back across the land he had just trekked, he saw the miasma of red fury in the distance as the storm approached. He made sure the tent was secure where he had fastened it to the tree.

Taking his cask he tapped water out of one of the trees, filling it to the brim. Nekoda came over and waited. Once the cask was filled Bensah held his knife longer to let Nekoda drink from the wound in the trunk.

The night came with a veil of black descending as storm clouds blanked out the stars. 'If the storm blows over quickly, I should make it to Kensai tomorrow,' he thought as he settled in to sleep. He kept his back to the trunk of the boab in case he was buried by sand carried by the storm. That way he could dig his way out.

Bensah woke from his dreams to howling wind. Grit flew into his mouth and eyes. Nekoda had curled up at his feet tightly to protect his snout. The feeble tent had collapsed. Taking the cloth, he wrapped it around his head and over Nekoda and waited. He could feel the sand pile around his body. He dozed rather than slept and eventually watched the red rays of the dawn spill into the sky. Nekoda stretched, sneezed, and crawled through the mound of sand that encased them. Bensah got up stiffly; every joint creaked. He spat the grit out. Stooping down, he scooped the sand away from one of the trees and again tapped some water.

"Nekoda, come here."

The dog obeyed, sneezing again. The spit splashed onto Bensah's face.

"Arrh, dog, keep your muck to yourself," he said as he wiped the drool from his face and affectionately patted the dog on his head.

Nekoda lapped up the water greedily.

Bensah drank from his cask and washed his eyes with the remains. It stung but cleared the grit out of them. He refilled it again and another cask for the day's walk ahead.

"Come, Nekoda, before this demon blows again and takes us with it."

Gathering his satchels, he began the trek to Kensai. It would take most of the day and then his own village was another two days beyond that. He looked back towards the way he had come. The dune he had fallen down was twice as high now; the sand would collapse and bury anyone who tried to climb it. It dominated the landscape, even more since yesterday. Its slip- face cast a shadow almost to the edge of the boabs, which now looked dwarfed by the red dunes. Bensah, who was not a spiritual man, felt it didn't bode well. It was as if something was coming to sweep it all away. Nothing could stop it, like an almighty mouth come to drink the earth dry. He shivered slightly and turned towards the south to make his way home.

By midday, he had made good time. Nekoda was slowing slightly as the full heat began to take its toll on them. In the shimmery haze, Bensah could just make out the edges of buildings. He took another swig of water and kept going.

"Not long, Nekoda."

The dog merely gave a bored yawn and kept going. Bensah thought of his wife, Sara. They had no children. The twins had passed not long after their birth, and Sara had been damaged and was not able to have anymore. Normally these women would be divorced and sent to be helpers with their families or other women who were more fertile. However, Bensah did not wish this to happen and kept her in his home. He had married another girl, but she was too young. She left to go back to her family, bringing shame on him and her family. He had decided that Sara was more use to him, to keep the place while he was away on his long treks and to be a companion. She had agreed. As much because she thought Bensah a kind man, but also, she had no family of her own and did not wish to live with strangers. Their mutual grief from the death of their children would always bond them to each other more than anyone else. This was never talked about, but each intuitively knew it of the other. He had been away almost three full moons. 'You may not recognise me' he grinned slightly at this thought.

In the mid-afternoon, they arrived at the village. Kensai's population was less than five hundred villagers. It consisted of a few markets in the centre, surrounded by a collection of farmers. The huts were made of mud bricks with straw roofs peaked in the centre. He began to head towards a hut located on the edge of the village. It belonged to his childhood friend Noai, who was also his trading partner. Nekoda went ahead, familiar with this routine. Bensah walked past the markets, which only had a few traders left trying to haggle the last of their goods. Two girls were patting Nekoda at the edge of the small market. Bensah waved to them.

They waved back and waited for Bensah to join them. One of the girls was stunted and walked with a limp. She stood with a lean and was nearly a foot shorter than the other girl. She was unlike most of the women from this region who were tall and slender with refined elegant limbs and neck. They were frequently sold by the traders that he bartered with to other tribes or the fiefdoms in the north for their beauty.

"Tata," they both screamed.

"Ange and Tessi, it is good to see you. Grown up now just in three moons." He grinned back at them. They walked with him. Ange, the smaller one, patted Nekoda.

He saw Noai was outside tending to the goats.

"Pata, Tata Bensah has returned," called Tessi.

"Bensah El Bunani, a long time this time, fat with profits from the markets or did the desert winds take them from you." Noai slapped him on the shoulder in greeting. "Ah, brother. It is good to see you. You have come at a good time, there is a marriage on the horizon. You will stay for the feast; it is only three days away."

"If there is sweet milk and the fine flesh of Noai's kids then I will stay," he answered.

A goat bleated. "Yes, you." Bensah grinned "and you as well," he said pointing to a kid nudging his leg. "You will be sweet meat, both of you."

Going inside the hut, Bensah placed his goods down. The hut was large enough for a family. On either side of the middle room for meals and gatherings were two rooms partitioned off with a curtain. Elanai was preparing some millet cakes. She got up when she saw Bensah was there.

"Welcome, Bensah!" She took his things and placed them off to the side and began to gather some bowls to bring water and tea. She put some dried bush plums and yoghurt with a flat millet pancake on a platter for him.

"It has been three moons, Bensah, since we saw you."

"Yes, it was a good journey this time. The trek was worth it," he said grinning widely.

"Come, brother."

Bensah followed Noai out to wash in a small well, located at the rear of the hut. He had red grit all over him. The water revived him instantly. 'What a simple pleasure,' he thought as he watched the red grains discolour the clear liquid soothing his skin. Walking back inside, he saw Elanai sitting in the centre, pouring tea into the bowls. Bensah sat and heartily helped himself to the food laid out. It tasted good. The yogurt was rich and the fruit sweet.

"Elanai, it must be all the special love Noai gives to his goats that makes their milk so good," he said smiling cheekily.

"Hmph, yes, Brother, I think it must be."

"So, what news from the city dwellers in the north?"

"They are plump with desire for our goods, Brother, and their wives are just as pink as lazy sows in the mud and now they rest upon mats made from the reeds of the mighty Choasa."

"Our brothers further south at the top of the western desert have fared worse. Their crops have failed, and wind brings with it a sickness, which has taken their children and elders. It is quick like the sand spirits that devour the land here but brings disease and death in its rear."

"Yes, I have heard this also; perhaps the great waste will be kind and protect us."

Just then, Ange and Tessi came bounding in with Nekoda. They shooed the dog out when they saw their mother's face. Ange tied Nekoda to a stump at the rear of the hut and left a bowl of water for him. He barked after her.

Bensah called out, "Put the muzzle on him."

She giggled at Nekoda's playful snapping and nipping as she fastened the leather guard over the large mouth. She was one of the few people that Nekoda would let handle him in this way. Nekoda had killed men to protect Bensah. His jaws were massive and the wild dog in him made his body twice the size of the hyenas that roamed the plains.

Running inside, she washed in the bowl and sat between her sister and mother. Tessi had a strand of beads entwined in her slender fingers. They were speckled with green and vibrant blues. The necklace was made of the stones from the rivers of the Jadahn ranges which lay in the Aeserean Territories. He had been paid by a westerner in exchange for some goat hide sacks.

"Here, Ange." Bensah gave her a strand as well. Hers had more indigo hues in it but they were equally as exquisite in their beauty. It was the first gift she had been given such as this; normally it was a piece of cloth to embroider so she could sell it.

"Thank you, Tata." She put it over her head. Tessi did the same. The girls giggled with delight and went outside to watch the stones sparkle in the sun.

Bensah smiled and began to take out some coins and place

them on the centre of the mats. Elanai gathered the remains of the meal and walked outside to clean the bowls. She was not allowed to hear the exchange details of the trades between Bensah and Noai. Her husband still maintained many of the elder traditions of excluding the women from matters of commerce, and a disdain for babes like Ange. In her grandparent's time, babies like Ange would have been killed at birth. The tribes had not learnt to farm and store for the bad seasons so babies like Ange were unable to be provided for. Her body was too deformed for her to be bartered as a wife so she would be relegated to be a servant in the family. The elders had outlawed such practices of killing the deformed babies now, as they knew that even babies like Ange could be useful for labouring. Elanai's heart filled with joy when Bensah treated her misshapen daughter the same as Tessi. She saw the girls playing together beyond the animal pens.

"Girls can you go and pick some berries for the morning meal. I saw some a few days ago. They should be ripe by now," Elanai called as she picked up a bucket and went to milk one of the goats.

Inside, Noai counted the coins. "They are northern; what use will they be here."

"I will sell them in my village. Many traders come through. They will want this currency. I will exchange them for animals and grain."

"And the cloth, for Tessi's dowry?"

Bensah nodded. Collecting the coins, he took out a large length of cotton, richly dyed in reds and golds.

"Ahh, this is fine indeed."

Bensah pulled out three satchels of spice and a bag of beads. "You have done well, Brother. And still some for yourself."

Bensah smiled grandly. Noai got up and took a cask from the shelf. Taking a swig, he then offered it to Bensah.

It was a brew made from soured goat's milk and a thistle that burnt the lips if eaten raw. The concoction was bitter but intoxicating. Noai slapped Bensah, full of happy thoughts at the riches his friend had brought.

Outside, Tessi and Ange could hear the laughter getting louder and louder.

"Come, Ange, let's go and find the berries for Mata."

"I will take Nekoda." Tessi nodded and went ahead of Ange.

The girls walked towards a well at the edge of the village. Lush bushes surrounded it, and on special occasions, the villagers would pick the berries that grew there in the dry season. As the sisters wandered down the centre of the huts, a group of girls met them at the edge of the village. They were friends of Tessi. Ange kept walking as Tessi showed the girls her new beads. Nekoda pulled ahead.

Ange neared the well and saw that a group of boys was wrestling with each other just on the other side. It was not vicious, just friendly play.

"Ange, eh," one of them called out, the others laughed as they turned to look.

Ange cringed inwardly a bit. This boy, Takob, had teased her before, even pulled her hair once.

She ignored them and began to pick the berries placing them in a woven sac.

Just then, she heard Nekoda growl, she turned and saw all

the boys standing behind her. Ange quickly grabbed the dog as he went to rush at the advancing boys. Takob came forward and threw a clod of dirt at her. Then the others joined in. One of them hit Ange in the face. She screamed to protect herself but could only put up one arm as she held onto Nekoda. He barked ferociously. She had not taken his muzzle off.

Then Takob came from behind, pushing her to the ground. He went to grab her hair but caught the beads around her neck instead. The string broke and the beads flew everywhere. In her panic not to lose them, she let go of Nekoda. He leapt up at Takob and pushed him over, snarling at him, trying to bite his face, but only abrading him with the muzzle. Takob cowered on the ground, half yelling, half pleading with fear as Nekoda's growl grew more ferocious. The other boys began to throw stones at Nekoda. He leapt off Takob and pushed one of them over, forcing the group to run away. Ange, realising what was happening, grabbed Nekoda's leash and yanked it so hard that Nekoda was forced to back off. Takob instantly got up and ran away. Nekoda pulled Ange over trying to give chase. The leash ripped from her hand.

"Nekoda, stop!" Ange sunk down and began to cry. Nekoda turned from his chase, and came over and nudged her face, scratching it with his muzzle as he did so. Her eyes stung as the grit from the dirt clods worked its way into them.

She began to look for the beads, picking them up one by one. She didn't notice Nekoda sink in an obedient stance beside her. Just then, she saw a hand take a bead she had reached out to pick up. She shrunk back, startled and looked up fearfully. A woman stood above her. The face before her seemed to change as if it reflected the moon and then the sands and then the midday sun. Her hair was black like the dappled shade a camphor tree cast. Her eyes changed colours like a rainbow was caged inside them. Ange could feel them boring into her.

"Take them. They are yours. My brethren's artistry is most worthy of the name Norbu."

Ange stood and edged back towards Nekoda. He inched his way closer to the woman.

Ange put her hand out and the woman let the beads fall into her palm. She put her finger on Ange's cheek and caught a tear as it trailed down.

"What is this? Do not be afraid of me, little one." Nekoda had put his head up towards her in a gesture of wanting a pat. She obliged him. "What are you called?"

Ange swallowed, frightened, and wanting to run away, "Ange," she stuttered.

The woman nodded, "You are an old soul, Ange. I am old as well; older than this place."

The woman stooped to pick up another bead. Rolling it between her fingers, she continued to speak to Ange, "Something seeks you, Ange, your blood is from the ancients of the earth, and it is this life force within you that is precious. This creature will bring death in its wake and swallow all that is beautiful and good in this world. When you are alone and it draws near, you must leave this place and go to the grove in the north. Far from here, across the desert towards the east where you will see the great mountains, which lie next the ocean. You will need to journey to the other side of them. From there you will head west for nine nights' journey where you will see the table of Norbu, the place that lies between the two falls. Here lays a grove surrounded by the silver trees. My sister's Keep will give you refuge until I return."

Ange became frightened again and wanted to leave. She quickly stooped to gather the rest of the beads, the lady stooped also, she placed her hand under her chin and drew her gaze towards her own.

"I cannot remain with you long enough to show you everything I see; but be sure your blood will draw the gaze of the wolf that hunts now in your lands. However, when the time comes and all is lost, remember what I have told you; seek the grove of silver trees. People will not hinder you, your body will deceive them, slavers will not want you for labour. You're blood flows with an ancient wisdom, little one. You will remain hidden from the dark that now rests here."

Ange had looked into the lady's eyes and saw an image, weak and translucent, of trees and a pool of water. Briefly, she saw a woman, dark and powerful, but beautiful, like her mother could be when performing the birth rituals for the newborns in the village.

Then, she heard Tessi calling her and the woman vanished.

"Ange!" She ran over when she saw Ange and Nekoda on the ground. "What happened?"

"Did you see the woman, Tessi?"

"What happened to your beads? Takob?"

Ange nodded and burst into tears again. Tessi gave her a hug and patted Nekoda.

"I will gather the berries in the morning. The beads are easily fixed."

The girls arrived back at the hut. Tessi went around the rear to tie up Nekoda. Ange went in first. All three of the adults looked at her, the mud on her tunic and tear streaked face. As Ange scooped the few berries she had managed to pick out, some beads fell from her pocket onto the floor. Noai glared at her as he stopped a bead rolling under him. He saw how dishevelled she was.

"What happened?"

Tears began to well up in her eyes again. Noai's lip curled with annoyance at his youngest. Tessi heard the question. "I think it was Takob again and some of his cousins. They came running back from the well." Ange had tried to hide her face from her father's gaze as she stooped to pick up the beads again.

"Is this how you treat Tata Bensah's gift, girl?"

"Pata it was not her fault. Takob tried to grab it. We will mend the string, Tata. We found all the stones" retorted Tessi.

"Of course, Tessi." Bensah nodded trying to catch Ange's eyes to reassure her not to be upset, but she had her head down.

"Come, Ange." Elanai took her hand. "Wash and go to bed." She put her hand under the girl's chin to see if she had been hurt. Spitting on her thumb, she cleared away the mud.

The girls took off their tunics and washed their faces, hands, and feet in a bucket of fresh water. Ange lay down and watched as Tessi deftly rethreaded the necklace before the sun sank entirely. In no time, the necklace was as before. Ange put it safely under her mat in the corner closest the wall, just to make sure it was safe.

"Tessi, where did the lady go?"

"What lady?"

"The one at the well."

"I did not see anyone. Go to sleep, we will need to be up early to pick some more berries, otherwise Pata will be even more angry." She smiled brightly and kissed Ange on the forehead. "I bet Nekoda put the fear of the desert spirits in Takob, eh."

Ange smiled, nodded, and rolled over to sleep. Her dreams were filled with visions of the lady. She was great and powerful; it was like looking at a deep flowing river spreading over the entire lands. Her eyes looked at Ange and pierced her heart. "Hasten to me, Ange." Then, she looked away as she rose up into the sky, terrible and fierce, her words echoing in Ange's mind. "Hasten to me."

7

Banrock

Gildas lay on the squalid floor of his cell. The dirt had been gouged into the shape of his body. His skin was chafed and infected from the chains that held him. He had woken to rats nibbling and crawling over his face and arms, but at least his mind had blanked out for a few hours. He grabbed two of the vermin and flung them, watching their insides explode as they hit the rock wall. Three small shafts of light sat facing him on the upper half of his cell. Judging by their position, Gildas guessed it was not long after dawn. The blood of the dead rats stood out vibrantly against a steely coldness pervading the cell, made worse by the weak rays of sun that barely lit the granite. A large timber pole sat in the centre. The iron vest fastened around Gildas chest was attached to a chain bolted into the hoary timber. He sat up and scored another day into the stone. This mark filled in the last corner of one entire wall.

Gildas' chest was covered in raw ulcers so macerated that his bones were exposed. The flesh was septic with infection. He wondered how much longer it would be before this place would kill him. He had stopped caring a long time ago, even before he had come to Banrock.

A slit opened at the door to the cell and a tray of slop was left there. Gildas crawled over, grabbed it, and gulped down the gruel of water and grain husks. Regardless of how much deprivation he suffered, his appetite never waned. As he stood, his body screamed with bolts of agony as the movement caused his chest to prick against the spikes inside the vest. Ignoring the pain, he started his daily run around the timber trunk. Hardened by his life on the steppes, the clansman continued until the slits of light had moved halfway across the floor. He knew it was midday and the sun sat at its zenith directly above his cage. Blood and clear fluid oozed from underneath the vest and onto his legs. Stopping, he leant against the pole heaving, but pleased that his stamina was not waning. Like most Graan of the north, the more an enemy tried to subjugate them, the more strident in their defiance they became. In Gildas, that stubbornness to conquer had magnified so much that he had risen to be the great chieftain warrior of his people. However, the Graanar tenacity to defeat any he deemed his enemy had also made him brittle. His own father had been more even, measured and able to bend with the winds, even his brother Jarrod, in spite of his weakness with the axe, was able to see all paths to victory.

Sitting down, Gildas thought back to long ago. He was twelve winters old and the coming of age rituals were beginning. He remembered the arrogance in his heart when he had demanded that his father allow him to take on the challenge for his initiation. Normally it was not until the fourteenth winter had passed that the younglings could be chosen. Gildas was already towering over most of the men in their clan. His father had relented, sensing that his refusal would not be obeyed anyway. The boys were required to go out into the steppes and hunt for marmoset furs. The one who produced the most furs of the highest quality was admitted into the initiation rituals for warriors. To go out on their own into the remote plains with its capricious ice storms was considered a sign of strength necessary to be a warrior of the Graan; declining the challenge was not considered cowardice. Although it would come to pass, in the days ahead of Gildas' life that all the males of twelve winters would be made to go through this trial, the mothers and fathers who lost their children would never forgive their Graan chieftain.

His body jerked in the cell as it remembered the adrenaline and excitement as he and another clan boy, Elo, set out. The day was clear and pristine, the air so crisp it hurt to breathe. The vista of white on white stung his eyes, but it was the one thing of beauty that never threatened Gildas' senses. The flat plateau of ice was broken occasionally by brown rocky outcrops and undulations never rising more than twenty arm spans. This is what made the steppe so dangerous, for when the raging blizzards came, there was no shelter to protect anyone or anything from them. Their talisman believed it was the ice god, Raajn's anger, unleashed to cleanse and remind. Gildas' grandfather, who was not a strong believer in the talisman's talk, had seen patterns in the storms frequency and had learnt to plan his hunting trips to avoid the worst of the blizzards. This was never revealed by the Gol clan to the rest of the Graan tribes for fear of ostracizing themselves by questioning the talisman.

Gildas gained pace with his lengthy strides and quickly sped ahead of Elo. The place where he would make his camp was clear in his mind. The trial was to last until the next full moon, at least twenty nights away. The young clansman had no doubt in his mind who would be the victor.

It took patience to trap the rodents; lying still for hours on the snow, frozen and numb, hanging on to a leather strap, waiting to lasso them as the males marked their territories. The fortitude of the northern clansmen and their ability to stake out their enemies was learnt here on the steppe.

Gildas trapped thirty hides, four of which were the prized black fur, rare obviously, as it did not enable camouflage for the rotund creature out in the open. He began to pack up and make his way back to the village. He felt the wind whipping up and knew a storm was on its way. The clouds in the horizon were black, bringing with them the winds of Raajn. He would be walking straight into it. By midday, the snow had begun to fall in a frenzy, blinding Gildas' view. He pushed on into the gale hoping he would not have to build a shelter and wait for the storm to pass. He would be penalised, as the contenders only had the two days to the full moon to return, otherwise they forfeited their right to contest. He continued, blinded and frozen, pushing into the wind as it forced its will against him. The gale did not abate, and ice crystals formed on his hood and sleeves. A break in the gale suddenly allowed him to see in the distance the dark line of the forest of Edan, which formed the border to his village. Heartened, he picked up pace. As he did, he noticed out of the corner of his eye Elo falling into the snow. Should he stop to help, it was not required, but the honour of winning and also assisting a tribesman would be great. He decided to move towards his clansman to see if he was alright. As he neared him, Elo was kneeling desperately trying to get the furs into his pouch; somehow, they had fallen out and the wind had caught them. Three were being picked up and flung faraway. Gildas knew he would have more than Elo now and his would be in pristine condition. The wind had given the gift of victory to him. Silently, within his heart, Gildas was glad. He stooped to catch another pelt as it caught on his foot, but Elo pulled the fur away and looked straight at Gildas, tears rolling down his cheeks.

Gildas looked at him in disgust. 'Weak. Too weak,' he thought. He walked away into the forest, leaving Elo behind. Gildas made good time. The small huts came into view by the dusk of the second day of full moon. Suddenly, he felt a heavy thump in his back, winding him and propelling him forward. His pouch flung in front of him. Elo raced ahead of him and grabbed the pouch. Gildas leaped and pursued Elo into the village, launching himself at his competitor as they ran toward the chieftain's hut. Gildas tackled him to the ground and began to pound Elo. He could vaguely hear his father's voice shouting at him to stop. Nadas pulled Gildas off the bloodied Elo, but with temper roused, Gildas leapt at the boy again. Nadas swung the blunt end of his axe at Gildas to wind him.

"What is this?"

"He stole my pouch," Gildas protested.

Looking down at the cowering Elo and the tears on his face, Nadas and the others wondered how that could be, considering the boy was half of Gildas height and weight.

"Elo, what has happened?" asked his father. Having raised the boy he was not surprised, but it also meant a loss of face for his clan if it was found to be true.

"Gildas came from behind and pushed me. He had dropped his own trappings and tried to take mine instead."

"Liar!" screamed Gildas, whose temper got the better of him again, as much out of contempt for the weak Elo, but also the injustice of the accusations.

"We will go inside." Everyone followed Nadas.

The pelts were pulled out and laid on the floor. Gildas' haul was superior in numbers and quality compared to that of Elo.

"Well, whoever these furs belong to they are the victor, but how do we decide? Talisman?" Nadas looked at his son; Gildas was growing into many things, but a thief he was not.

The talisman stepped forward. Gildas rolled his eyes. His contempt for the man was known from his boyish boasting.

The Talisman, out of malice for Gildas and his clan because of their secretive ways, threw the teeth of the white whale onto the mat. He pointed his staff at Elo.

Gildas exploded in fury. His father was barely able to constrain him from attacking Elo.

Nadas came to Gildas' defence. "It is well known among you that Gildas has displayed his prowess as a hunter. Talisman, could it be that the pelts do belong to Gildas?"

The talisman threw the teeth of a white whale on the floor again. "The ways of the great water dweller do not lie. The pelts belong to clan Nimmo."

"You lie!" roared Gildas.

Nadas gestured for his clansmen Acco and Unta to take his

son outside. The two men barely restrained him; such was his strength even at that young age.

It was decided that Elo would progress to the initiation rites and Gildas would have to wait another cycle.

Nadas suspected the injustice that had been done here, but could offer no succour, such were the ways of the clan.

Gildas went to his mat, took off his furs, and lay down. His mind was racing with anger and the urge to flog Elo. "He is too weak, father. The weak need to be culled like diseased rodents or they shall resort to cunning to defeat the strong."

"Cool you temper, Gildas, your strength could lead you to destruction or victory, be wary of it. There will be next season; if Elo has indeed done this thing, then he will not pass the rites."

Gildas rolled over in his cell and thought of Elo lying dead from his axe blade three summers later at a combat trial. Mostly Gildas remembered the satisfaction at seeing Elo's lifeless eyes. He had looked directly at Nadas, sitting on the throne of the Ice Bear, repeating to his father, "The weak need to be culled."

Gildas woke with a start at the sound of a whip thudding against its target, wet and thick. It stopped, and then Gildas heard the sound of gravel and the feet dragging along it. "Into the pit!" shouted the foreman, a thick burly man from the southern islands. Dark and deadly was the first thought Gildas had of him when he had arrived at Banrock. Gildas liked his measure and understood the acumen he had for his work.

He stood again and winced, sucking in short breaths as his chest on the right side chafed. He noticed a pale red ooze dribble onto his thigh. Not much longer. A decision would be made, he would defeat Banrock, or it would add him to its victories. He had already survived the longest stint in the cage. Normally, the prisoners either died or were begging for release, after being driven mad with isolation and sickness. Gildas mind was like steel, nothing chinked his armour.

"Let the rats chew away until only a kernel of Gildas Gol remains in the echoes of his dungeon to haunt the next captive."

He started to run again. He sped up, around and around he went, the chain attached to the trunk rasping on the wooden surface. It was soothing. The memory of Elo's dead face returned to his mind, drawing the rage out again.

The door opened and a whip lashed around Gildas' neck. It yanked him to the ground. Three guards and the foreman stood at the door.

"Clean him up and bring him to the yard. Lord Hadan wants some sport."

They grabbed him. One took a pair of bolt cutters and tore through the locks at the back of the vest. Gildas ribs showed through on his chest; his flesh white and crinkled. They threw a bucket of cold water on him and then sulphur powder. He collapsed with the pain as the yellow dust ate into his flesh.

Dragging him outside into the open courtyard of the gaol, the guards threw him on the dirt and walked away. His vision was hazy from the brightness of the day as he scanned his surroundings. The entrance to the prison was directly in front of him. It was heavily guarded and bolted with three massive beams made from the giant oaks of the north. The timber was almost indestructible. The beams were hewn from trees believed to have stood since the dawn of time. The walls were at least twenty men high and built from smooth polished granite. Anyone trying to escape would find no purchase to climb over them. Not that it mattered. Outside the prison walls was half a league of tangled briars and thorn bushes with wild dogs roaming amongst them; kept there by the promise of meat. It was a way of disposing of the dead prisoners. Banrock was known for the stench of the dead lying around its implacable walls and the calibre of criminals it kept until their death.

Another prisoner was bought out at the opposite side of the yard from underneath. Prisoners were caged behind iron bars around two of the walls. They were crammed so the ones at the front had their faces and arms hanging out through the gaps. Gildas could hear shouts and whimpers coming from the layers of incarcerated bodies.

'So, they want a fight,' he thought.

The guards then filed out. Three men, one adorned in fur and silver mail, climbed a small dais at the far end near the entrance gates.

The guards stood in semi-circle formation around the sheriff, Lord Hadan and his offsider, Ignard.

"Today, we will have sport. Konj and Gildas you are to fight to the death with only your strength to use as your weapons. Begin!" the warden commanded. The prisoners roared with excitement waiting for the bloody fight.

The guard behind Gildas shoved him forward. Konj came running at him grunting. He was from the middle isles, swarthy with legs and arms as thick as masts on the mercenary ships.

He was equal in height and stature to Gildas.

He hit Gildas front on and thrust him into the ground. The pain seared through the Graan warrior as it directly contacted the bones of his rib cage. A foot struck him square in the chest. He heaved as the wind was knocked out of him.

He threw gravel into Konj face, giving himself time to get up. He grabbed Konj by the hair and twisted as hard as he could, but the neck would not snap. They separated. Gildas heard the jibes and sneering from the cells. They ran at each other and locked together fiercely, each man grunting like bulls. Konj put his fingers into Gildas exposed ribs and grabbed them. Gildas grunted with the pain. He bit Konj and tore his cheek off. Backing away, both panting, they stepped around each other, waiting to see who would strike first. One last time they went together to end it. Blood spilled into Konj's eye, blinding him momentarily. He stumbled. Gildas kicked him in the gut, and then the throat, and then stomped on his neck. The blow was lethal.

Gildas stood back. He heard cheering, then one of the guards kicked his legs making them give way.

"Strip him down and tie him like a dog. It is punishment, Graan, for not keeping us entertained longer," Lord Hadan jeered at him.

The guards held Gildas as he fought them, but they forced him onto all fours.

"Now bark!" called the sheriff.

Gildas refused.

"Bark, dog!"

One of the guards shoved his spear into Gildas open wounds on his ribcage.

Gildas refused to make a sound as the metal point cut into his innards.

"I said, bark!" The soldier placed the spear in further forcing a guttural yelp of pain out of Gildas. "That's a rutting goat!" A roar of laughter went up around the walls.

Gildas lay in the darkness of his cell, floating in and out of consciousness. Blood dripped from his body and the weight of the steel vest pressed on him making it hard to breathe. He moved to drink some water left near him by one of the guards. Gildas noticed the guard had the tattoo of an exiled Graanar. He scraped another mark in the wall. The moonlight came through the small window above. Perhaps this would be his last night here. He let his mind drift to the Icelands of his birth; the memory of hunting the great fish of the frozen seas dimming the pain as he fell asleep.

"Gildas."

He woke. Looking around he saw no one.

"Gildas."

He rolled over and saw a woman in the far corner. He saw that her hair was dark and her face seemed to float with pallor of the moon and clouds. He rose up and managed to stand leaning against the wall. She came forward, Gildas instinctively stepped back, ready. "Who are you?"

"You do not know me. I have only been here a short while, but I have known of the way of things for a long time."

"Why have the guards sent me a woman? I am in no need of one and if I was, it's hardly a punishment."

"The guards are not aware of me. It is only you who sees me."

Gildas banged on the door. "We'll see."

The doors slit opened.

"Why have you sent this whore to me?"

"Chunt bastid! I sent you no whore, now shut up before I send you out for a flogging."

The slit slammed shut before Gildas could respond. He could hear the guards laughing to themselves, one of them shouting, "I win, he's done."

"Gildas, still yourself. They will not see me even if they come into your cell." She sat down and crossed her legs. Her forearms rested lightly on her knees. She gestured for him to do the same.

He paced, raging, "Who are you?"

"You do not know me, but we shall talk some and then we shall learn more of each other. Please sit. You need not fear me."

He started towards her menacingly. "Nor can you harm me," she warned lightly.

"We shall see, bitch!" He went towards her again, but suddenly, before him stood his brother Jarrod and Jesse. All three of them were young and they had been out fishing. They had their haul laid out; Jesse was gutting and filleting her stash getting ready to cure it. She was smiling as she looked at Gildas; her pale oval face and strong white teeth out shone by her deep blue eyes. She was fair for a member of Gildas' tribe, considered a rare beauty, and she liked Gildas. He had decided at that moment, she would be his clan wife. She looked across at Jarrod and winked at him playfully. Suddenly, a bit of fish gut hit Gildas in the face and Jesse broke into peals of laughter. Jarrod hesitated, waiting for Gildas' reaction, but when his face broke into a smile, he relaxed and joined in. Jesse was one person that did not cringe at Gildas' presence.

Blackness engulfed him again; he was back in the prison. Looking ahead into the cell, the woman had gone, unnerved at the long dormant memory of his wife. He sat back against the wall. He sifted his memory to find someone who matched the woman he had seen but none came to mind. Gildas chuckled to himself, maybe even the great Gildas Gol's war mongering heart was rotting after fifteen winters in Banrock. Jesse's face came back to him. No pain existed there now as before, only recidivist anger, insatiable and tenacious. Jesse his wife, dead now as was his love for her. Anger welled again inside his decaying chest.

"Bitch, who are you?" he whispered, kicking the wall.

Gildas decided he needed to escape; it had been long enough. These cells were used to break the wills of its inmates. Most of the weaker ones killed themselves after going mad. They had not broken him yet. He lay down, hesitant to sleep but his eyes closed none the less. His dream that night caused him to scream and wracked his body with perspiration and fear, something Gildas Gol had not experienced in a long time.

She sat and watched the convulsions and torment that played in the lesser one's mind. The damp and cold did not worry her, but the blackness in the cell brought back pricking memories of something that had pierced her sight once before. Slightly agitated, she had waited. His anger would tire him again soon enough. So much anger in him, it was something that had always been with him waiting its release to dominate him. Perhaps that will change. All around this place, the void existed everywhere. Here the emptiness grew fat as it chewed away the lesser one's souls. Gildas stirred and rolled onto his back. He sat up and dragged himself up the wall wincing. He rubbed his eyes and adjusted them to the dark. It was just before full dawn and only the barest of light fell onto Assumpta's face as she sat watching him. Startled, he reacted more quickly and went towards her.

"Again, Gildas, you cannot harm me. Please sit. It is time we spoke."

He strained in the iron vest, ripping more flesh of his ribs. Blood trickled down his thighs. He swung at her and knocked her over, but she stood quickly, unscathed from the blow. He swung again, but the chain pulled him up before he contacted her.

"Who are you?" Some sniggers could be heard on the other side of the door.

"You do not know me. I am on a quest and seek your aid, fearsome one."

"Enough with this trickery. What do you want, witch?"

"I will explain in time, Gildas, please sit. They will be here soon with your meal. They will think you have lost your reason. I smell your anger and it strengthens me and pulls me into visions of long ago, in the lost chaos that once was."

He watched the door suspiciously, maybe they had heard already. 'She was right, they weren't going to laugh at his expense,' he thought. He stepped away from her. Seeing her calmness enraged him. The grill slid open and the tray of slop was pushed in. Gildas took it and ate greedily, always watching her. The god saw the bloodshot feral eyes and knew this was a primeval creature trapped frightened, dangerous and lost to its purpose.

"Speak!"

"What haunted your dreams last night, Gildas?"

"Nothing, witch!"

"It chased but you ran to where it could not go. It cannot follow you there, Gildas, believe that. When you remember that place, tell me of it. You have run all your life, a mighty warrior, who has slaughtered, butchered, protected your tribe with wrathful justice, instilling that fear only a god can inspire, making them loyal servants and warriors; until the anger spilt over, dimming your vision and mind. The wolf's teeth are sharp, are they not, Gildas?"

She saw the vaguest flinch in his eye. "Now, Gildas Gol, here you lay, a festering heap, manacled and raging at these sodden walls, along with the other broken angry children. I want to know, great warrior, where do you hide in your dreams and what are you running from?"

Assumpta faded into the silhouette of moonlight.

"Be gone, whoring witch! I run from nothing." He screamed with bared teeth, heaving with fear and frustration.

He flung the bowl into thin air. He sat back panting, he was wasting away, he was dying he knew that. Confused again, he lay back. He could hear the guards sniggering. Too exhausted to be angry, he wanted death to come, so he could fight his last battle.

"Who are you, bitch?" She knew his dreams. He closed his eyes again as he felt the rattle in his chest move its way to his throat. "The coughing is going to hurt in this thing," he groaned.

The grill slid open. "Plate!" barked the voice. Gildas groped for it and handed it to the guard. "How's your whore?" the voice sniggered and shut the grill.

The cell brightened as the light meandered its way through the slits. Gildas began his routine again, slower than before; his body was giving out. He thought of the nightmare he had last night. More vivid, he had felt the brush on his leg of the wolf's breath as he ran and the sharp claws scraping behind and snarling like a wild dog. It had never been this close before and this time the red eyes ahead were clear. He stopped at the thought shivering – close – it had been close. He remembered veering sharply to the left as the rancid breath washed past, and the growl as the claw connected with his thigh. These nightmares had begun even before he was put into the solitary cell.

He watched the pus and pink fluid ooze down towards his groin as the wretched skin attempted to heal only to be ripped open again by the vest. He stank, putrid from the infection. His mind raced. He needed to get out. He needed to die. Night came again. Gildas slept. His chest thudded as the same nightmare that haunted him every night returned. His chest rattled as his breathing quickened. Running fast through the forest, brittle branches laden with icicles caught his arms and legs. He heard shouts then suddenly Jarrod's face loomed up in front of him. He was handing him a pack and a sword and knife.

"Make for the blade and the spike. None but you can outrun them. I will lead them north, Gildas. I cannot save you and I am not sure I want to; you have brought nothing but fear and battle to heart of the Ice mother clans." He pulled Gildas closer and kissed him fiercely on each cheek and bear hugged him. "You have bought this on yourself."

He was running; heading straight ahead. The cliff loomed up ahead. As he stopped to climb down the face, the ice sheet underneath gave way. He plunged into the icy tundra beneath the cliff. Darkness suffocated him. He was running again, but it was not in the lands of his birth. Howling erupted around him. He could not see where it came from; its piercing cry unrelenting.

His mind wandered, faces loomed in his mind – Father and Mother smiling and showing him how to clean the fish well for salting. Father showing combat moves and chasing him; pretending to be bested. Jarrod, the younger one, always following, annoying, but always eager to spend time with Gildas. Looking into the memories, he needed them, but he didn't want the same as his father or brother. He wanted to conquer all that stood in his way. Jesse was there smiling at him. Gildas moved, running he looked back and saw blood running down her neck. He almost remembered why he had been driven to exile from the clans. It was close, so close. He moaned in his sleep as a rat bit his leg, relishing the flesh. Kicking it involuntarily, it moved back, wary as well.

Laughing – he heard laughing. Then talking again. He strode into the hut. It was Jarrod and Jesse. 'Always together,' he thought. Jesse was full with his child and near to her time; the bump satisfied him. This child would be the first of his heirs. He had delayed child-bearing until he had secured his kingdom. He was now chieftain of the northern reaches, as far south as the Unstaadt borders. Gildas Gol was feared and sought after for trade. It had been timely now to begin his legacy. They moved apart as he walked in. Jesse came to him and offered him water. He waved it away. Jarrod began to count the beadings and gems that had just been traded.

Gildas pulled out his broad sword. He stood and began to make sweeping strokes.

"Always together, what do you have to talk about so much? Jesse why are you not with the birthing women being readied."

Both stood to attention. They knew Gildas moods. This was dangerous if not handled well.

"Gildas we were thinking back to the time we were catching fish and Jarrod fell in and you had to swim after him. And how you climbed on to the ice ledge with a carp attached to your ass. We couldn't pull it off and Jarrod had to cut its body off with his axe. But its teeth stayed clamped onto your ass."

"Jarrod, how is your skill with the blade these days? It has been a while since we have trained together."

Jesse moved away sensing her husband's agitation. Jarrod tensed as well.

"Gildas, you know you could fell me with one stroke of the blade without even looking. I must speak with you regarding more urgent matters." He looked at Jesse indicating it would be best that she left now.

"I command my wife, Brother." The strokes became fiercer.

"I shall leave you to talk."

Gildas ignored her.

Jarrod continued, "We need to discuss the clan of Bregt. They have requested a greater seat on the tribal elders' council. They have aligned with Clotte by the joining of Jesse's sister

Inga to Bergyl. It places them as third clan. I am inclined to agree, it will strengthen the first two circles of tribes in your favour."

Jarrod's presumption on his agreement had always grated Gildas. Jarrod had been sent away to the temple in the west to learn from the scholars about diplomacy. He had come back to the Graan as though he were better than his clansmen and even his brother. While Gildas brute strength and cunning had been the backbone of Gildas' rise, the stability and unity of the tribes and regions he'd bought under his Chieftain banner was due to Jarrod's strategic negotiations. This had always galled the contentious nature of Gildas.

"Pick up your sword, Brother. I wish to test you. Always you have followed me, in my shadow, does it vex you that I am never in yours."

"What has agitated you, Gildas? You speak of yourself. I serve my purpose, loyal to the end, even against my better judgment at times. I will not be drawn into a fight just to sate your jealousy and pride." Even as he said the words, he realised his mistake.

Gildas grabbed a sword resting against the wall and threw it at Jarrod. Hardly giving Jarrod time to react he launched at him. Jarrod defended easily.

"What were you and Jesse laughing about?" The festering jealousy had been on and off for many summers in Gildas mind, but more so since Jesse being with child. It had moved into a protective rage, driving Jesse further away and fuelling Gildas' paranoia.

"We have already told you." Jarrod dodged a glancing blow

to his left and defended with an upraised sword as Gildas came down with almighty force, jarring Jarrod's shoulder.

"Enough, Gildas! Enough, step back, you are chieftain to half the land that buttresses the great ocean, is your mind and heart already not full with its concerns? Why are you being like an unbedded eunuch?"

As soon as he said it, Jarrod saw the look in his brother's eyes and knew he would need to fight. Gildas had taken the offensive stance and hefted his sword around in a massive arc. Gildas felt something momentarily resist his swing and kept coming. Jarrod's face went ashen as he screamed. "Jesse!"

Gildas stopped in mid swing and turned around.

Blood streamed onto the floor around Jesse's face and torso. She lay awkwardly on her large belly, lifeless. Gildas dropped his blade, stunned. The blood pooled around his feet. He couldn't bring himself to touch her, as he stared at the gaping wound in her neck.

"Jesse." Jarrod went down to try and staunch the bleeding. "Gildas, what have you done."

"Undra and Deida come quickly!" shouted Jarrod.

The birthing wives came running in to the hut. They screamed when they saw the mess in the tent.

"Can the child be saved?" pleaded Jarrod.

One knelt and felt the still belly. "We can try."

They rolled her over and one of them inserted their hand to break the placenta pushing the belly down to make the baby come out. Gildas sat watching everything. Blood and gore meant nothing to him, but his wife's lifeless eyes staring at him pierced the thick hide of his battle-hardened heart. He heard a high-pitched squeal followed by nothing, a few more minutes, nothing but the hushed murmurs of the wives. Then he saw one of the women undoing her wrap and twisting it into a bundle. He pulled himself away from Jesse and looked at the bundle in the old woman's arms.

"Give it to me."

"He did not live."

"He is my son. Show me!" he roared.

The woman gave Gildas the bundle. He unfolded the cloth, underneath was the tiny little face, perfectly formed, but dead by his father.

Gildas twitched again. His legs had felt the roaches crawling over him. His mind was blank. He had stopped running but something waited for him. He heard the growl. He turned away from the menacing sound and fled into darkness. The god's words came to him in a haunting whisper, 'Run to where it cannot go'. So Gildas ran.

He jerked awake, panting. Then, was racked with coughing causing excruciating pain.

"Bitch, whore, you have placed all that in my mind again to torture me." He gasped.

He lay down and looked at the moon through the window, wheezing. For the first time in his life, Gildas thought of death not as an honour of the battlefield but as a release from the wretchedness in which he existed. A tear trickled down his face. He saw her face in the moonlight; her open generous smile that would indulge his every mood and yet still play with his heart. He'd forgotten what it was like to touch her. Her smell had left him as well. Vaguely, he remembered her laugh and voice – the cutting edge of it when he had pushed too far, warning him. He remembered her eyes, deep blue like the waters off the eastern shores. Gildas knew it was here that he could always find refuge, in her love. He knew her devotion to him never waned and he remembered how unworthy of it he was. She'd chosen him, though there had not been any others to compete for her, from the time of their childhood, she had been drawn to him. Jarrod too, faithful to the end, he put his own life at risk helping him. Would he have done the same? Why did he run? Gildas, a coward? He had never run from a battle so why did he fear his tribes' retribution.

He didn't move. He wanted to stare at the moon and let it go – just drift away. 'Let the darkness come.' He sighed. His chest wheezed.

"So, tell me, Gildas, where do you run to in your dreams?"

"You know where, witch," he said resigning himself to her questions.

"What was she like? I too have known love. When it is lost it becomes thin and pale in our memories, but its sustenance lasts forever."

Gildas sat up again and began to drift in and out of consciousness.

"I don't know, witch. My will sustains me. I cannot take back my actions. Ever has it been my way to force the will of Gildas Gol so that nothing save death shall thwart it."

"Nay, Gildas, death will not offer refuge from the demon that chases you. It has breached the worlds and now dwells with the only desire to devour everything even the mighty Ice Mother who birthed you. Voloc existed before decay came to rest here. It waits. Do not wish for death just yet, for even its gift of peace lies in the mouth of the wolf."

Gildas laughed. "I ran because I knew how weak I was. I felled my own son in my rage. It was not the fear of my tribe's punishment, but fear of how weak my jealousy had made me. The wretchedness of the helpless I battled against I have now become. Let the demon wolf come and devour the dregs of me. If any grace is saved for one such as I, then it will be her eyes watching me as I decay."

Assumpta smiled a little. "Yes." She spoke quietly as Gildas drifted off again. "When you next wake, you must go to the grove and wait for the others. My brethren Lido shall welcome you," she whispered into his ear. She hesitated before she left, drinking in his pain and anger.

'That is good, he feels no fear, only anger and that shall be his strength,' she thought.

8

Festival of the Harvest Moon

"Kado Ko, wake up!" A girlish voice giggled in his ear. "Sleepy."

He was sweating slightly from the lily he'd ingested, half morose from the drug but alert enough to know where he was. He slapped the girl across the face to get her away. She stood up, indignant.

"Payment!" she demanded.

Kado didn't respond as he drifted into sleep again.

She found his purse and took some coins and left. The room was smoky and musty. Sunlight drifted onto the mattress where Kado lay. He breathed slowly. The coverlet moved with his chest. The black curtain, embossed with gold dragons, floated lightly into the room as the breeze helped clear the staleness of the coitus and incense. The city outside was a bustling paradox of elegantly carved dragons' heads and filigreed cornices, richly stained in greens and golds with twinkling lanterns. Below the glittering richness flowed a labyrinth of culverts filled with putrid human detritus. The city was circular in design, ascending to Emperor Ko Paidrax's palace. From the main tower of the palace, the city beneath was a magnificent spectacle of precision geometry, awash with mythical opulence in the shape of a diamond. The lower perimeters mostly housed tradesmen, serving classes, and the poor. The brothel where Kado lay was located halfway down in the market district. It was an eclectic mix of middle tier merchants whose level of wealth was reflected by the ornate decor of their dwellings. Kado rolled over and moaned. His hand reached out expecting to find the girl beside him. He squinted as the sunlight hurt his eyes. A cat meowed and jumped down for a pat. Kado was familiar to it as he often gave the scavenger a morsel of food. He took a sardine from the tray of food that had been left, and let the cat eat it out of his hand. The cat purred and winked at him in a gesture of friendliness. Kado fed it the rest of the fish as he drank wine and ate the rice from the bowl.

His head was clearing as the perspiration on his forehead pushed the poison out. There were two lumps of what appeared to be sugar sitting on the tray. Kado ate one and put the other in his pouch. He noted how many coins were missing. 'Hardly worth that much,' he thought. Getting up, he bathed and dressed. He saw Ji standing at the end of the hallway.

"Cart!" he called.

Some girls tittered in a room as he went past. "Bye, Bye, pretty prince."

Kado didn't bother to be anonymous anymore, much to his father's chagrin. He even made the point to Emperor Paidrax that if harm did come his way it was better to know where the heir could be found. Kado walked outside into the clear day and breathed deeply. In a moment, he was vomiting in the street. He checked the lump of fermented lilium fern was still in his mouth. His tolerance for the addictive herb was lessening each time. The crashes came on more quickly. The cart pulled up and the boy helped him into it as the cramps began. Maybe Fedryn was diluting the supply. He quickly sucked again on the lolly to ease the knife like jabbing in his gut.

"Drive!"

It was no easy ride to the palace. The cart driver panted heavily as he pulled Kado up the steep winding streets. Eventually arriving at the gates to the palace, Kado alighted and threw some coins towards the driver. The boy stooped, heaving with a tuberculoid wheeze as he gathered the coins. Only the middle class were obliged to pay for any journeys. It was deemed a privilege to carry a royal. 'At least the Emperor's son always paid his way,' thought Podaan as he bowed in gratitude. Kado continued on, oblivious to the gratitude of the driver as he walked toward the grand stairs leading into the palace.

The palace was designed to have an east west aspect so that the setting and rising sun would call the household to wake and to sleep. The palace was over a thousand Emperors old, as long as the Drax Magisterium had existed. Two gargantuan dragons stood at the entrance as guardians of the palace; their massive jaws yawned a ferocious welcome and their left claws were raised in menace. The dragons were cast from solid gold and had rubies for eyes. The palace had six levels, from the servant's quarters two floors beneath the ground to the Emperor's rooms located at the very top. It was the jewel in the city's crown. Adorned in red and white marbled quartz with gold spires and turrets, it literally dazzled in the sunlight. Its roof's spires were encrusted with emeralds. Each floor had a theme, lapis lazuli for the entrance floor, emerald and black granite for the servants' quarters, kitchens, and laundries. The banqueting halls, four in number, were each a corner of the palace. Their walls were made of marble with mosaics made from precious stones; jade, topaz, rubies and rainbow gems, only found in the mountains of Ka Sadom. The great banquet hall was lined with mirrors encrusted with diamonds, aquamarine, amethysts, and blue turquoises, with tiles of polished white marble inlaid with gold. In the evenings, as the sun would set, the whole room would sparkle with diamonds and as the full moon rose into the sky, the bluer gems would cast an indigo hue all over the room.

The bedrooms were equally as opulent with each chamber bedecked with strawberry marble, obsidian and charoite, jades and quartzes. The master room held beautiful mosaics of victories fought long ago. Telling odes of the great warriors of the Drax House, they were made from sapphires and rubies studded into yellow quartz. All the grandeur was a show of the huge mineral wealth of the mountains that passed through the Sa Dom province and the reason for the rise and fortunes of the Drax Empire. The family were able to amass such wealth from the trade of the gems and stones and ultimately became the suzerainty, dominating over the last millenia. This wealth was now under the auspices of Emperor Ko Paidrax the Third; the greatest and most aggressive of the reigning emperors. Ko had annexed almost the entirety of the middle continent in a bid to sure up his wealth for the future generations. He was a war monger. His military prowess was unrivalled and greatly feared. Ko was a belligerent entity both within his household and land. His disgust for his son Kado, only heir to the Drax Magisterium, was no surprise. Kado's indolent tendencies and self-indulgent proclivities provided ongoing agitation to his father. Ko had sired other males to concubines, but none of them survived. It was almost as if the will of the dragon in their sire wanted none to challenge him. So, until another heir was born it would be Kado's place to rule upon Ko's demise. It was by luck only that Kado had not been banished or even killed. However, if another male was born and survived, then his fate would be sealed with a death blow, such was the vitriol he inspired in his father.

His parents were in the main garden located on the third terrace. Often, they would sit and take tea there in the afternoons. The view from the garden overlooked the tapestries of rice paddies across the plateau all the way to the Sa Dom Mountains. The tea gardens were situated so that there was a view of the sun rise between the highest peaks of the Feet of Jun.

Kado went directly over to his father and kissed his ring and bowed to his mother.

The Empress looked at him, concerned. "Kitty your eyes are sunken, and you have fever."

She waved the servant Cho over to fetch a basin of water and a towel. Ko turned his lip up in disgust and turned back to the advisors he was meeting with.

"It is in the Iron Coast, here. The supplies are being depleted by the lack of rains and fires that ravage the lands; it stalls the barges bringing the ore to the ships. The workers have been scared away by rumours of a spirit that hunts them. Even with the whip and chain, we cannot get them to mine the ore," said Jindon, the lead advisor.

"How long has this been happening?"

"There have been problems for many cycles, but it has become worse in the last few. The region most affected appears to be where the best quality ore is found." Jindon pointed on a map.

Kado half listened as he washed his hands and face. "Thank you, Mother Empress, I feel new again," he said sarcastically. He sauntered over to the gathering of important people.

Ko stiffened slightly at his presence, but at least he was here.

Kado bowed to Lord Tsung and Lord Hojinex of the provinces on the southern fringes. "My Lords, I hope your journeys were comfortable."

"Prince Kado, our people are honoured to be in your presence," replied Tsung.

"As are ours, Prince," chimed in Hojinex.

Emperor Ko spoke. "Of course you are aware, are you not, of the great heritage of our esteemed guests and their skill in bringing the iron ore from the southern deserts. Our soldiers deserve the best for their swords."

Kado bristled at his father's condescension. He knew full well the importance of the trades between his ancestral lands and those of the great southern expanse. His father often intentionally treated him like a child to humiliate him further. However, he was surprised that he did it so blatantly in front of such important guests. These two Lords were the most powerful of all the provinces, often given special leverage rites with the Emperor purely because of the trade relations they had established and maintained over many generations. They were also the last of three remaining Lords whose lineage matched those of Ko Paidrax in terms of birth rites and inheritance, and possible alternatives to rule in place of the Drax. Had it not been for the skill and rapport with the local tribes that mined the precious mineral, like other rulers who were seen as challengers to Ko, they would have been supplanted by the Emperor's own men. Most of these usurpers were loyal ex-soldiers, whose viciousness was only matched by the Emperor's himself, thereby maintaining the local populace in a state of brutalised servitude.

Kado began to grow bored and hungry. His brow still sweated slightly as his cravings came at shorter intervals.

General Chalac entered. The soldier bowed to both Kado and the Empress and then kissed the dragon ring of Ko.

"Ah, General, what is your opinion on this? The local tribes attribute the lack of rain to a demon."

Chalac smiled at the jab at the tribal superstition. "Have your Lord's advisors not noted before that the Iron Coast can be subject to long periods of no rain, thus making the rivers dryer than their deserts."

"The caves entrance where the iron ore is found is situated two leagues above the ground and too far from the top of the ridge, making entering the mine difficult, but also removing the ore even more challenging. Normally we could use barges and haul the stuff to the coast to our ships, but the river is dust and sand."

"Dig from above, Lord Tsung," replied the General.

"It would take too long. Underneath the fine red earth is

bedrock as solid as Mount Sa Dom."

"Then blast it. Give them a show of our fires," the General retorted.

"The Matavians have frozen the orichnite. What they intend to do it with it is not known," retorted Lord Hojinex. "I want scouts to be sent to report back on the situation to ensure that nothing else besides the fickleness of the rain gods has caused this interruption. It may be useful also to find the location of another source of the ore and blasting salt. Lord Hojinex, I will send my chief scholar to search your library. I would think that when the ore was first discovered, your predecessors would have been thorough and searched for it in other lands." Ko interrupted.

Lord Tsung flinched just slightly, confirming Ko's suspicions that alternative supplies existed. He wondered what the real cause of the problems in the south were and what the reason was for Ranik stopping any shipments of the blasting salt.

"But, my Lord Emperor, that will take time and surely supplies will run down before these answers are found. Begging my Lord's pardon, but our archives can only be read by a few. Perhaps, if I may be so bold, to offer our own interpreters. It would save time." Lord Hojinex flashed a knowing look across to Lord Tsung as he attempted to deflect Ko's command. The glance was not missed by Ko or the General.

The Lord's assumed that the stores were low for the ore, but Ko had amassed at least three harvests of stock just for this reason. He also knew that Hojinex and Tsung had been ciphering ore to sell to other Suzerains, especially the Matavian tyrant whose lands shadowed the far western edges of the kingdom. Of course, this was all done under the guise of other traders, but ultimately, the profits came back to the two fiefdoms. While Ko tolerated these actions out of necessity, if it came to be that the trade routes were no longer required and other sources could be found, then Ko's largesse could not be relied upon.

"Your very generous offer is noted, but my chief scholars have been trained in the ancient Hojin languages and will accompany you back. I will send two of my elite guards as escorts." Ko clapped his hands. "Fetch Wilo."

Kado had gone over to one of the lounges. Bored with the ongoing political undercurrents he drifted off into a light sleep. He was reminiscing about a dalliance with one of the whores from the night before. His fingers languidly drifted in the air as he remembered stroking her buttock.

"Scholar Wilo you and your most adept student in the Hojin languages are to accompany Lord Hojinax back to his homeland. There you are required to interpret all the scrolls pertaining to the first journey's south. They will be dated between Emperors Doang the First and Third. I will expect reports of your progress back on the cycle of the waning moons." Ko looked directly at Hojinax and Tsung as a warning that, should no report be received, then it will be assumed that there has been interference.

Ko clapped again to signal that the meeting had ended.

For generations each fiefdom had zealously guarded their sources of the ore and original exploration routes. Tsung and Hojinex left, agitated at Ko's interference. They both saw the indolent Kado and knew a day would come when the Drax rule would be weak. It was with deliberate intention that stockpiling of the ore had commenced, to be ready for the time of the Drax Magesterium's demise. As the iron piles built up, so did their armouries.

"General, I will let you hand-pick the guards to accompany the scholars." Ko stood, looking directly at Kado slumped on the lounge. "I believe snakes wait to plunge their fangs into an old dragon's hide in its death throes. I think some further enquiries should be made independent of the scholars. Send your best scouts."

"I have no indication a rebellion is at hand but..." replied Chalac.

"Not yet, General, but one of the virtues of an old ancestry is patience and long sight, and these two lords certainly see far into the future. They both contain the blood of rulers, as do I. We are more akin then you might realise."

The General bowed, but surreptitiously followed Ko's gaze over to Kado. As he left, he thought that Ko was right, the empire's future rested on an indolent lily stem addict. Other Lords would have seen the chink in Emperor Paidrax's armour.

Kado had woken at the sound of the clapping; it irritated him immensely.

"Kado, wine is being served, tidy yourself."

He stood and smoothed his dishevelled robes and hair. Ko seated himself at the head of the small table with Kado to his left and the Empress to the right.

The maid meticulously served the wine. Kado winked at her remembering previous meetings. But the young girl was too busy concentrating on serving the Royal family to blush or react. Such a great honour required almost religious devotion. Kado felt a little put out. He thought that she might need a reminder of her privilege to have the eye of the prince. While Kado could be written off by other royalty as a bit of a rakish brat, his disregard for the people who may actually suffer – such as the maid being severely disciplined if she were to react inappropriately – made the heir a lot of enemies amongst the servants and soldiers.

"You are to go to the temple at the base of the mountains and cleanse yourself. You reek of the putrid rot you ingest too readily and the diseases of your whores."

"Those girls are no different to the whores that visit you, Father."

Kado felt the sting of his father's hand, blood oozed from his lip as the wine glass smashed on the marble floor.

"You disrespect me and your mother."

Ko snapped his fingers for Chot. "Get Prince Kodrax's carriage ready. He will be sojourning to the mountains indefinitely."

Kado re-gathered himself from the shock of the slap. "No, Father, the Festival of the Harvest Moon is in four days. It is tradition that the heir to the throne open the festival and close it. I will go after."

Empress Sosunna spoke, "He is right, husband; the tradition has not been broken for generations. Let it not be so now. I will ensure our son remains in the palace with the healers attending to him."

Ko stiffened ready for a fight. "You are unworthy in all ways," Ko's face was blood red with rage towards Kado. "My ancestors must quell in the spirit world at the future of this Kingdom. What curse was laid down on me that you should be my hope for succession to this mighty throne? My enemies drool with lascivious anticipation of my death, knowing that all that they will be met with is an indolent cur, only worthy to languish with the swine."

The empress bowed in complete subservience in a futile attempt to diffuse her husband's anger.

Kado simply sat there, almost like an idiot. He had heard this so many times. "And as unworthy as I am, Father, I am all that you are allowed to have for continuance of the Magisterium. What curse indeed did you bring down on your father's house for one such as I to be your progeny? Why not replace mother instead, so another can produce an heir worthy of the mighty Ko?" Kado's eyes were black with malice.

Ko gripped Kado by the chin and raised him up to his face. "I will not let my ancestor's memories be stained by your incompetence. I will let you die first. You are to remain in your chambers for the duration of the festival and then you are to go to the Sa Dom temple."

The empress bowed as deeply and humbly as she could. Kado's words rang in her ears and a piercing fear penetrated her heart. Ko was still a strong man of fifty-two cycles, he would rule for many more. If Kado were to continue as he was, then in all likelihood the Drax empire would end with Ko. The impatience with their son had grown more with each passing year into manhood. She also knew her own fate stood on the edge of a dagger's tip. Her family ruled the western lands and it was only this fact that saved her from being replaced. Ko knew her brothers would rise against him in allegiance with southern Lords. It would destroy the Kingdom and leave all the combatants weakened. "My Lord, the horses are ready for the inspection of the First Circle," Fai the head servant to Ko announced breaking the tension.

Ko nodded and stood. The message was timely as he fought not to lop Kado's head off at that moment.

Kado and his mother both bowed as their ruler left. Sosunna offered her son a napkin to wipe the blood off his lip.

"Why do you anger your father so? One day you will be ruler. The fate of the Kingdom will rest with you. You know, not one of the other Lords will be loyal to the Ko name once your father is gone."

"Exactly, Mother, this is the legacy I am left with; war as the Lords of the Dragon battle for its throne. Our Lord and ruler disguises his lust for destruction with a quest for wealth. Even he cannot see it. He has poisoned the dragon's blood with this curse, not I. For even the dragon knows the people cannot suffer at the will of one so quick to kill and terrorise, and not see that the very thing that sustains it will eventually die under its malice."

She had watched Kado thrive as a child and adolescent, but once it was apparent that he did not have his father's prowess for military strategy or political machinations, she saw his gradual decline into debauchery. Her own feelings were mixed. Raised to fulfil a duty and role, she had no comprehension of any other life, therefore limiting her in finding ways to help Kado be what was expected of him. She felt no remorse on her part for Kado's behaviour. She had fulfilled her role as best she could. Even Ko was restricted by the inheritance laws, all previous Emperors had been subject to them and Ko would be no different. So, in the end, Kado had an ornament for a mother and a warmonger for a father, and his own future was already shadowed with war and bitter power struggles that were waiting to burst forth with the death of his father.

"The festival begins tomorrow evening. You will need your rest."

"All is duty, Empress," he said caustically.

"Yes, Kado, that is what it is, you will learn this one day or you will perish. The will of the dragon sustains us, and this is where our duty lies."

"Then perhaps Father should be reminded of this. Too much now happens in these lands that speak of Ko and not of the blood of the Dragon."

Kado walked along the halls smothered in monuments to the dynasty of rulers from whom he descended. He felt no pride or attachment to these ancestors, only lethargy and indifference to the people who had perished as the great empire was formed. He had realised a long time ago he was not his father's son and that the dynasty would end with him. Should he pluck a jewel out of one those mighty warriors' eyes, and keep it as a token of better times? He sniggered to himself quietly. The first twinges came, and experience taught him it would get worse. He waved a servant over.

"Fetch Ming. He can be found in the kitchens."

Kado looked across the great hallway and saw a face he remembered, Sa Tuc. It had been many moons since Kado had seen her. She looked the same as always, straight backed and precise. She had taught him the way of the Dragon's gaze, an abominable failure on his part, but it was infatuating to have a dominant woman control him so well. She had been his guard at auspicious occasions when he was younger. It was strange to Kado, he and Sa would have been only a few cycles apart in their age, but Sa seemed to be an ancient well of knowledge, like the old nuns of the temples.

"Sa Tuc," he called.

She stopped, realising who it was that had called her, she bowed.

"Surely you will have time to visit an old friend before my father sends you off on another errand."

"Yes, Prince Kado, but I have business with General Chalac."

"Of course, join me in my chambers. I am under curfew again." He smiled cheekily.

Sa never reacted. As usual, she was on edge, keen to find out what orders the Emperor had for her. She bowed and went up the stairs to meet with the General.

Kado neither annoyed nor interested Sa. He was indolent and did not match his father's strength, but there was certain sensitivity in Kado that had not been well utilised by Ko. Kado, in his way, understood subtlety better than Ko. It was a strength any great leader required. Sa's meticulous attention to detail allowed her to see this in Kado, whether he quite understood it or not. She entered the large room lined with red marble and granite. General Chalac was bent over a map.

"Ah, Sa Tuc. I have an errand for you. Can you choose two of your best. The mission is to penetrate into Hosiaan Province and return with any findings. The Emperor is suspicious of the Lords Tsung and Hojinex. We are particularly interested in any remote areas where the ore from the Iron Coast can be stored. We know that the current routes are these areas here and here." Chalac pointed to the map. "But knowledge of any other would be most useful to the Emperor. I know that they are amassing an armoury, but where eludes me. There have been sightings along the waters between the two lands of the Matavians as well. It would be easy for the east and west to place the kingdom in a vice. The General's fingers came together on the map showing how the alliance could be lethal to the Emperor.

"Yes, my Lord. I have two in mind already. They just passed their final level and are ready for this mission." She bowed and made to leave.

"Sa Tuc," called Chalac, "Dependent on the news the Emperor receives, he may need you to pass judgement on the instigators of such theft from the Emperor's coffers."

Sa nodded understanding the implication. She would begin to ready herself. It had been almost a year since his last request. If this was involving iron ore and these two provinces, the outcome of these missions had far reaching consequences. Sa left and made her way to Kado. She knocked on the large black walnut doors. The servant Ming opened them and ushered Sa over to the antechamber to await Kado.

Kado eventually came out, he was relaxed, a little too so, and the sweat that was there when she had seen him earlier had gone from his brow.

"Sa Tuc," he mouthed the words; his large lips relishing the words. "My father's favourite. You are like a bell jar clock, self-contained and precise. Inner cogs whirring in exact harmony, intricate in design, fascinating to watch, but no one can touch. The exterior perfectly sealed shutting the rest of the world out leaving it to stare in wonder at such a perfect instrument. What do you think of me, eh?"

"I am not allowed to make opinions of my superiors, My Lord. I am here to serve them."

"You sound like my mother, indeed the whole palace. I remember you when you arrived at the palace – the child prodigy. Fierce and wild like a rat in a corner, but then you became the predatory cat, no longer the rodent pest, as are so many of the urchins that line my father's streets. You were courteous to me though, Sa. You knew I lacked the qualities to make a good soldier like my father, but you persisted. I guess loyalty to one's duty has its value. What must you think of me? You are the perfect warrior in all ways, unquestioning, agile, fierce, courageous and vicious, precise, and intelligent."

He had come close to her. He stank of the lily. Sa did not react. She remembered how hard he had tried as a child to please his father; the tears. While they did not soften her heart, she could see the longing to please and fulfil his duty. The failure lay not with him, but in the parents for not searching for other possibilities. So, he ran to his whores and drugs and there he still lay.

"Well, tell me," he said more insistently, "You must think something. Speak, I command you."

Sa nodded acquiescing. "You are no soldier, My Lord, but you have a determination not yet realised. Others have forced their own vision on you, allowing no room for your own. This I have always thought of you since we first met in the quadrangle, where you lay crying with exhaustion as I tried to mould you into your father's image. However, you are a grown man now and no tears will save you nor will the women or drugs. I have said too much, My Lord. If you will excuse me, the Emperor has issued urgent orders to which I must attend."

Kado in his half stupor appreciated Sa's honesty, "Ah yes the precious ore and the southern provinces. I neglected to mention to my father that there is a rumour that a new lord rules the great southern lands and has grown powerful. I heard two traders from the north talking in the dens. They barely escaped with their lives."

"You must let your father know, My Lord, this is grave news indeed and a direct threat to the Empire."

"I will in good time, Sa Tuc. Be kind to Tsung and Hojinex, make it quick and painless, their royal blood is as old as mine you know." He sauntered off to his bed behind a petition. A young female voice spoke but Sa did not hear what she said as she bowed and left.

Kado's mother watched the assassin efficiently make her way to the guard's compound. The path was lined by cherry blossoms in full bloom. But its beauty, was lost on one such as Sa. She had waited at the entrance to Kado's chamber and heard what the assassin had said to Kado. The assassin's words had rung in her heart. Sa Tuc's ability to see the reality of a situation grated heavily on her nerves. How impudent of her! A servant to speak to the heir in such a way. Her son would find his way. He would be the leader his father had wanted. Deeply within her, she knew that the resentment lay not against the assassin, but her own rigid adherence to her duty as the Empress and docility to obey. She had political allies in her family, but had neither the will, nor strength to use it against Ko. Instead, she let her son drift into decadence, almost leaving Ko no choice but to remove them both if he wished. She stiffened as she resolved firmly that she would do anything to save Kado if only to prove Ko and his servants wrong.

"After the festival, Kado shall go to the monks again and they will purge out his poisons and make him better. I will order their executions if they do not heal him," she whispered under her breath as she watched the assassin walk towards the soldier's huts.

———

It was nearing twilight and the guests had begun arriving for the first evening of the festival.
"Kado, you must ready yourself. Out girl! Jeck, draw a hot bath for the prince," Empress Sosunna commanded.

Kado woke, happy and unashamed for his mother to find him this way. He stepped into the warm bath and began to lather. The water smelled faintly of jasmine and lemon. 'Beautiful,' he thought. His mind drifted for some reason to Sa Tuc. He idly held some affection for her. She was unattractive in every way for a woman, none-the-less, he counted her as a friend. He thought back to the time she had been his sparring partner. Swift and merciless, she often bested him; actually, all the time; working him to exhaustion and tears. His humiliation all the greater for her being a girl, until General Chalac stated that he was sure Sa-Tuc would best him in combat also.

Sa Tuc never appeared to judge Kado, she simply tried to teach him, and to a certain extent she succeeded, but never to the satisfaction of his father. The image of Sa pulling him up as he sobbed made him feel disgusted at himself.

Her only comment at each of his failures was, "We begin again, until we have learnt it. If you have not learnt, then I have not taught you."

Kado's mind flicked back to his childhood chamber as he watched Sa train with the master of Draxinian Battle, Jinta Tsoasaan. He had become mesmerised by her fluidity and grace. The observer could not anticipate any manoeuvre or feint. Often when he was made to do the inspection of the elite guards and warriors, he would study Sa's scarred face and trace the lines of the cut that ran from below her left eye to the corner of her lip; inflicted by her mother for running out of lily tobacco. He would peer into her small dark eyes; so unlike the people who lived in the Drax lands who had multi-coloured slit like irises, almost like gemstones. 'Who are you?' he would often think.

Kado snapped back to reality upon hearing the gong for dinner. He hopped out of the bath and dressed in the robes laid out.

The Festival of the Harvest Moon commemorated the beginning of Spring and harvest season. It was a joyous time, lasting for twelve days. The whole city was decorated with grapes, grasses, and blossoms, with dancing dragons amongst it all. The first produce of the harvest was prepared for the Royal family in special dishes reserved for this time only. Kado actually felt excited. The main table had been laden with fruits and bouquets of grains and flowers. He made his way to sit near his parents. Ko did not acknowledge his presence. The guests stood. Each of the provinces had been represented. The Paidrax rule reached three quarters of the middling territories, a massive hegemony totalling twenty-four regions. Kado took the burning incense and placed it in the smoking vase hung from a chain. He swung the incense to let it drift across the room. He then took a dagger as two live pigs were presented to him. He placed the dagger at the throat of one of the pigs and sliced evenly, the blood dripped into a gold dish as the monks prayed over the dying piglet. He did it again. They were removed to be roasted for the main course. Kado then raised the ceremonial wine and began the traditional prayers for the harvest.

"Great dragon of the sun, moon, oceans, land, and stars, we offer this feast in gratitude for your gifts of sustenance. Let the blood of these beasts be our offering to you, great and generous one, that your favour and protection will remain with us always. So, speaks Kado Kodrax Diamond Fang, son of Ko Paidrax Blackflame."

Then lifting the wine, he sipped, passed it to his mother and then his father.

Bowing before them, he turned to the guests. "Let the feast begin."

As the sun set and the moon rose to its fullness, the great hall became awash with indigoes, violets and blues as the sapphires, amethysts and diamonds encrusted on the walls were awoken by its rays. Kado took his seat at the side of his father and began to eat.

The next morning, Kado found himself on the floor of an unfamiliar chamber. Under his arm was the Princess Yenta. She was naked. He rolled over to be met with the angry face of her maid and her mother. He rose, standing naked in front of them. Lady Ingo, Yenta's mother, began to shriek in horror and embarrassment, while the maid grinned slightly, impressed with Kado's physique. The princess lay cowering in disgrace in front of her mother. The maid placed a shawl over the princess and escorted her behind a partition to dress.

Kado was told to get out. He noticed there was blood on the rug from their union. Kado took a mental note of adding another virgin to his list. Going back to his room, he lay down with a pipe and began to drift off into another world. He was awoken by his manservant, Ming.

"Get up, Kado Ko son, the Emperor has summoned you." He slapped him on the face and then assisted him over to a bath. Kado roused instantly when the cold water hit his body. Drying him off, Ming then helped the drowsy prince into his robes. They walked into the main hall together, Kado barely aware of his surroundings. Before him stood Emperor Ko. His mother, as usual, was standing to the left and behind. He saw that Lord Jiang and the Princess were standing just in front of the regal dais. Yenta was weeping into her hands. On the other side stood Lord Lo-Tung and his son Untan the betrothed to the Princess. The match had been orchestrated by Ko, these Lords were heavily indebted to the emperor and the alliance of these two territories would mean Ko would have control of the northern trade routes. It was cheaper to have a strategic marriage than to declare war on two lands. However, Kado's lascivious deeds now placed this marriage in jeopardy.

"Kado Kodrax, you have been accused of adultery and rape of Princess Yenta, how do you plead?"

The Emperor's face was stony, but Kado had learnt to know the subtle ways Ko used to disguise his rage in public.

He looked at the Princess on the floor, who was pleading with her eyes not to declare their transgression. She made a minute shake of her head, as she knew full well the shame she had brought on her house would never be forgiven.

"I have no memory of having relations with the Princess."

It was not a lie, as he truly could not remember what had happened. He swayed slightly. Ming steadied him by the elbow.

"There was blood found on the rug and you were found in her chambers."

Kado stood up and took a deep breath. In some deep recess of his mind, Sa appeared, her face was sweaty after they had been sparring. "Remember, Kado Kodrax, as the next Emperor, the fate of the land rests upon you, so while you pretend to not care of this fact, the people who lay their loyalty with you, in spite of their hatred and loathing for the Magisterium, will be your eyes, ears and limbs by which you will maintain your strength. For a head without a body is a useless thing."

"The blood is from my arm." He held up his bandaged arm where they had bled him to remove the lily poison from his body.

"And yes, I was in Princess Yenta's chamber, but drunk on the floor as is my weakness. I beg forgiveness and pardon from Emperor Paidrax, Lord Jiang, and Princess Yenta for bringing dishonour to my family, the Jiang House, and all the honourable guests present. I did not lay with the Princess Yenta, but merely in my drunken stupor broke into her chamber. Her honour remains intact, as does her beauty. I beg for pardon and suitable punishment for this action from the mighty Emperor Paidrax Blackflame."

He bowed at the end, stumbling slightly as he did so. Kado's mother gave a sigh, at least he knew the gravity of the situation, but deeply she realised how stupid her son truly was.

Ko got up and strode down off the dais towards Kado. He struck Kado on the face, sending him to the floor in a spray of blood. Kado, still drowsy from the lily, lay on the floor stunned and disoriented. The floor was swimming under him, he tried to get up but couldn't.

Ko gestured for the Princess and her father to come over to him.

"In recompense for the humiliation my son has caused you, I offer you a breeding mare from my elite stock and twelve ducks of gold. If indeed it is found upon testing that the Princess' honour has been removed then this will be doubled and if no child is born then I will triple this payment as a sign of the great union of these mighty and brave Houses of Jiang and Lo-Tung."

Lord Jiang audibly gasped at the generosity of the offer and then realised how much Ko must want this union.

"We most humbly accept your gift and my daughter shall be sent to the temple of sisters for testing and etiquette training fit for a princess."

Ko went back to the dais. "We will continue the festivities. Come, Lords."

Ming took Kado to his rooms. Blood covered his face and shirt. He laid the prince on the bed and pressed a cloth on this mouth to staunch the blood flow from his lip.

"Your father has sent instructions that you are to remain here until the guests have left."

Kado nodded, feeling nauseous. His face and nose were swollen. He swallowed a block of lily sugar, which helped relieve the throbbing.

"What do you think will happen?"

"I do not know, Kado Ko son."

———

Kado had just finished having his nose dressed where a sore had festered. He had been watching a beautiful sunset across the valley and the line of guests leaving as the festival drew to a close. The streets below were still vibrant as the daily procession of the dragon made its way towards the palace. He had not left the chamber for twelve days and nights by order of his father.

"A carriage waits for you at the rear entrance. Take anything you wish."

Kado jumped at the sound of his father's voice.

"You jeopardised the alliance for the northern trade routes. If the marriage does not go ahead and the two houses do not align, then war will come to the lands again. The dynasty has survived for a millennium and it will fail by your hand if you are its only heir. Your mother will be sent away. I have ordered the daughter of Lord Hojinex, who is unattached, to be made ready for betrothal to me. It will give me direct suzerainty over his lands as well."

"She is a child, Father."

"She will be of age soon and provide me with heirs."

"Surely it would be honourable for the great Drax warrior to see his name upon another victory."

Ko ignored his son's sarcasm.

"You are to go to the temple and remain there until you are dead."

"Let me rot in my pleasures, surely that will give you more satisfaction."

"You are banished, Kado Kodrax. I have already ordered the scribes to write you out of the texts. You will be stricken from the records of the Drax Inheritors."

"Why don't you just kill me?"

"That would be too kind. Take him to Sa Dom. Let the monks do what they wish," Emperor Ko commanded Ming.

9

Sorrow

Ange woke to the sound of an axe coming down and the screams of a kid as its life ended. Looking out through the window, she saw Noai was killing the goats to bleed them before the wedding feast. The marriage was between one of Tessi's friends and a boy from a neighbouring village. She had heard Mata and Pata talking about how it was a good match, as the boy's family were wealthy. Mata was happy as the boy seemed gentle and mild in his spirit. The axe came down again and a third time. She watched her father hoist the dead goats onto the camphor tree's branch to let the blood run out onto the ground. Nekoda began to lick it up.

"Oi dog, that is not for you." Bensah grabbed Nekoda and tied him back to his post alongside the hut. The dog whined in protest. Noai took two wooden bowls and let them fill with the fresh blood. He gave one to Nekoda and the other was used to daub the doors of the bride. Ange could hear Nekoda lapping up the warm juice.

Noai went to the well at the rear of the hut and washed. As he came inside, Ange saw the speckles of bright red blood on his tunic. He threw the dirty smock on the ground for Elanai to clean. He put on another tunic.

"Noai, how long before the goats can be spiced?" asked Elanai.

"Two days."

"Ahh, the sun is happy today brother and sisters, my stomach knows it." Bensah walked in with a beaming smile as he saw the simple but delicious morning meal Elanai had prepared.

On a mat sat a platter of berries and curdled milk for everyone to eat. Ange poured tea into some bowls and then placed the clay urn back on the embers in the corner.

Noai and Bensah toasted the day and began to eat. The women waited until the men had taken their share. The tartness of the yoghurt with the sweetness of the berries made the meal very delicious. Ange could hear Bensah's lips smacking together in satisfaction and giggled at him.

"You and Nekoda sound the same when you eat, Tata." Ange cheekily poked at Bensah.

"Ha yes, we do, don't we, Ange. Our bellies are never sated except when we visit here." He scooped the last of the yoghurt out of the bowl.

"Come brother, the fish will jump for the sun today." Noai stood, wiping his face with a damp piece of muslin. "We will head to the north. The waters are shallow there and the fish plentiful."

"Good, Brother. A feast tonight, eh." Bensah rubbed his stomach at the thought of the next meal to come. His face shone even brighter making Ange laugh out loud at his delight.

Bensah picked her up and spun her around. She squealed

with the thrill of the sensation and everyone giggled at her clumsiness when she was put down. 'It is better here when Tata comes, even Pata is happy,' she thought as she lay on the ground waiting for the straw roof to stop spinning.

Noai and Bensah wrapped their headscarves around faces and left. Noai only needed his knife to pare down a branch, and he would pull some thread from his tunic for line. Sometimes the fish were so plentiful that you could catch them with your bare hands.

Elanai pulled a roll of material onto the floor. "Come girls, Tata Bensah has bought this fine gift for us." Ange's and Tessi's eyes were huge at the quality and richness of the cloth. The fabric exploded brilliantly with rich golds and reds in the mundane brown of their hut. It was weaved in an intricate pattern of small leaves and inter-twining branches. Moon crescents formed a border around the end of the cloth in the pattern of two lines crisscrossing in a curved wave. It measured three arm widths across and five in length.

"Now girls, take enough to make your costume for the wedding and the rest will be put in your dowry, Tessi."

Marking a length, Tessi used a whittled leg bone of a goat, honed to a sharp blade and cut a perfectly straight length off the main roll. She then cut one piece in two and gave one to Ange. Ange began to pull threads out width wise from the remainder of the large piece. She carefully tied each pulled thread to a little hook on a shelf. Soon a hands width of frayed material was hanging from the hook. Tessi took two strands and carefully sewed a hem to stop the rest of the material fraying and braided the fringe. This section was carefully refolded for her dowry. Ange began to intricately braid the frayed strands to make ribbons to plait into their hair.

Elanai held up the two pieces trying to decide how to sew them. Tessi and Ange stood to attention as their mother modelled the fabric in different ways. Elanai nodded when she had decided.

"I think some feathers stained with ochre will be perfect. I will make you into the sun's handmaids."

Elanai felt herself at peace at times like this. When Noai was out pre-occupied, she could potter and do her chores. The girls were busy. Her heart saddened a little, the marriage feast would be the first time Tessi was presented to a prospective husband. This marked the official end of her childhood and entrance to the life of Elanai and the other women of the village. At fourteen summers, it was time, and with Ange being the way she was, it would be their only chance for a dowry. Elanai knew that Noai resented this situation, not only with Ange being crippled but also that there were only two children. Their neighbours had five children. All healthy and well-matched. The neighbour had approached Noai many times to take his lands, even going to the elders, but they had been blessed by the spirits and the neighbour had not been allowed to take their family home. But things could change. Some of the villagers held resentment towards Noai and Bensah's trading and the fact that they did not share their profits readily. It was known as well that some of the villagers still clung to the old ways and felt that Ange's birth was a sign that Noai profited from deals with evil spirits.

Her crippled babe had survived coming into the world and

then faced derision at her form. She had taught Ange not to be hateful back at the children who taunted her. There had been many occasions she had heard Ange crying – especially when Noai would shun her, but she did not comfort her. The kindest thing Elanai felt she could do was to teach Ange not to hold to bitterness but accept this was the way of things and live within it. But also know that there must be some reason she was here rather than not existing at all.

Elanai could hear the girls giggling and chatting as they braided the pulled threads into their hair. She began to smock the pieces of bridal costume.

"Girls, later on I want you to go fetch some grass to smoke the fish, some feathers for your hair, and Tessi you are to clean your dowry, and make sure it is tidy."

Elanai passed the day in quiet meditation, sewing the cloth. The weave was mesmerising with its stunning colours and details.

"Mata how do you think they made the cloth with such fine weave?" asked Ange

"I think it took a long time, it would have had many wefts and warps each almost a single thread."

"I think I would like to learn this weaving style. I could sell it at Ancrid City. The goat hair could be spun finely like this." Elanai smiled warmly at Ange, her heart at ease for her daughters.

The morning of the wedding feast began with a magenta dawn, which usually meant a storm would come by the end of the day. The whole village was awake. The chanting of the elder men filled the air as the sun rose.

Elanai dressed herself first with the traditional veil and wrap for the bonded women in the village. Her face was smeared with red and yellow ochre paste. Once she was finished she helped Tessi and Ange dress. She styled the cloth into a wrap pinafore that gathered at the front forming a fan. The girls made half face masks in a fan shape as well with feathers dipped in the watered down red and yellow paste. Together the three of them looked imposing and exquisite.

Katania, the bride, came out in a brilliant gold veil and wrap. Ange and Tessi, along with the other girls from the village, formed a circle around her. The procession of the betrothed began. Their mothers and sisters followed behind hooting and chanting with dried grasses dyed in reds and browns to ward off any evil omens. Little children ran along screaming gaily in front.

Noai and Bensah, with the other men of the village, had gone ahead to herald the bride's arrival and to begin roasting the meats. The spectacular coronas of colour from the women and girls' costumes contrasted with the dusty brown earth, and arid grasses that surrounded the village. The girls to be married were called the sun wives, as their regalia of yellow symbolised the sun's blessing on the land and people. The whole village pulsed with joy and excitement.

Ange flicked her head and jigged gaily dancing, not as graceful as Tessi and the other girls, but with as much happiness and euphoria shone from her eyes and face. The villagers watching saw the beaming smiles of the girls, clapping and whooping their blessings as the procession made its way to the groom's village.

Later that night, exhausted and dusty from the festivities, Ange lay in bed completely content. She rolled over and hugged Tessi who lay quietly beside her. Three families from the village had offered an interest to Noai for Tessi, one of them the brother of the groom from the feast. Over the next cycle, the families would begin to negotiate dowries. Tessi was fortunate. She would be able to choose one of them, as long as Noai agreed. Tessi's heart fluttered a little at what lay ahead now. She hugged Ange back not wanting to lose the happiness of the day as they both fell asleep.

— — —

Ange watched Bensah and Nekoda walk towards the great desert and the trading cities in the south. She had accompanied them as far as the edge of their tribal lands where the river Choasa snaked its way to the west. Kensai was located at the end of the great river's path. It petered out into smaller estuaries, which led to a delta that met the ocean. Tata had stayed another whole moon before leaving.

Ange felt a little sad watching Bensah leave, but mostly she would miss Nekoda. He was the friend she didn't have in the village. A friend who would always stand by her and keep Takob and the other boys from teasing her. As she said goodbye Ange had gazed into the dog's eyes and given him a good rub on the head and a hug before he walked off. He obliged with a big lick on her cheek. Ange pushed the sadness away. Her sorrow was not just that Tata and Nekoda were gone, but that Pata was happier with them here, which meant he was less angry with her.

Noai waved Bensah off and then went over to some men from the village that had been hunting. He didn't acknowledge Ange as she turned around to walk back to her village, following the riverbank. She saw some little fish floating along the surface of the water. Looking more closely, she saw that they were dead, a raven swooped down, scooped one up, and flew away. Then more of them came flowing along towards her. Ange stopped to watch. All the fish were dead. Two more ravens swooped down to feast.

"Silly birds, if the fish are sick so will you be."

Ange got up and headed towards home again. Further along, on the other side of the river she saw Takob. He was preoccupied with something in the water and did not notice her. His brother and cousin came up and he ushered them over and pointed to something. Suddenly, one of the boys, Mihas, ran off. The boys laughed and put their hands over their faces. Ange heard one of them yell, "It stinks." As Ange rounded the bend, she peered over the grass, trying to be inconspicuous. She saw three dead goats lying in the water. Their hide had been stripped bare, large red pits covered their flesh, and the smell of the rotting flesh brushed past her on the slight breeze, making her gag.

"Heya Ange! Is this one of your friends." Ange jumped and began to run home. She heard the boys laughing in the distance.

As she neared her hut, she saw Takob's father going towards the river.

"Mata, something is wrong, I saw dead fish and Takob found dead goats in the water."

"Yes, some of the men are going to see what it is. It might be a cat that has come down from the hills looking for food."

Later that day, Noai came back smelling of smoke and a rotten odour. They had burned the carcasses. It was decided that the river would be inspected each day to see if any other dead animals were seen.

"You will have to fetch water from the wells further north. The water flows should be clean." Elanai sighed inwardly. It was almost a half days trek to that well.

One of the suitors for Tessi began to come and meet with Noai. The boy's name was Liet. His father and Noai seemed to get along. Tessi had nodded her approval. Ange tended to go outside or Elanai would give her chores to do during the visits. She had heard her father say to Elanai to make sure she is away when Liet and his father come to visit. She no longer felt anything when she heard these comments. The meetings began to take longer each time until finally, the day arrived when the dowry would be haggled by each of the fathers. Elanai and Tessi were preparing the afternoon meal. Ange had decided that after helping Tessi carry fresh water from the well and Mata prepare the food, she would go to the river and gather stones to polish for Bensah's next visit. He could take them and sell them for her at the northern markets. She had prepared some oatcakes and berries and decided to put Bensah's gift on. Leaving, she saw Elanai braiding Tessi's hair. Tessi hugged her sister.

"Tomorrow we shall play, and I will do your hair." Ange grinned at Tessi's offer and left. Elanai watched her leave, her heart aching for her shunned daughter. From a distance, she looked like an old woman strolling along the path. She had always felt like she was looking into an old soul when she had gazed into Ange's eyes.

Walking up on to the higher bank of the river, Ange headed directly west. Checking the flow of the water, she saw that it was slow. Putting down her things, she waded in and began to gather pebbles off the bottom. Most of them were dull and brown but a few sparkled with bits of silver gold and vibrant reds. When her sack was full, she decided to make a picnic in a patch of grasses flush with blue corn flowers. As she ate some of her cakes, she began to polish the stones. The grasses were halfway up to her waist and obscured her from anyone seeing her on the path. She wished Nekoda were here, she could lie on him and watch the clouds.

Eventually, as the day warmed, and all the stones had been polished, Ange fell asleep. When she woke, she was stiff and very thirsty. A rotten smell struck her first. As she stood, she saw a man lying down in the grass. His eyes were bulging, and his tongue stuck out. He had blood oozing from his mouth. Gathering her things quickly, she ran back down to the village. When she got to the hut, she found no one there. Looking out along the path, she saw them all walking back from escorting Liet's family to their village. They held hands and were laughing.

She waited for them. Noai entered and saw Ange, he ignored her and went through to the rear to sit and smoke. Tessi came after him.

"What did you do today, Ange?"

"I went for a walk towards the big bend in the river to find stones for Tata Bensah."

Elanai had come in carrying some fresh goat's milk.

"Mata." Ange ran to her and she hugged her.

"What is it Ange?"

"I saw a man near the river, he wasn't moving, his eyes didn't move, and he looked like this." Ange poked her tongue and rolled her eyes.

"Noai," called Elanai concerned. "Ange, tell him."

Ange went to him and swallowed hard. "I saw a dead man near the bend in the river. He is lying in the grass."

Noai looked at her. "Are you sure he was not just resting?"

She shook her head. "He had the marks on him like the goats that were dead in the water that day and blood came from his nose and mouth."

"I will ask Koi and Janun to come with me." Noai stubbed out his pipe and got up. He looked at Ange and saw the fear there. He went to say something, but he couldn't bring himself to say anything. Ange shrunk back towards her mother and cried a little. Elanai took her inside and gave her some milk sweetened with honey.

Elanai looked at her daughter and wanted to cry, the family had been celebrating Tessi's betrothal while this had happened to her little one. She should have been with them here.

"Were the flowers very blue this year, daughter?" she asked, picking a small corn flower out of her hair. A deep resentment welled up inside Elanai towards Noai at his treatment of Ange. The betrothal was assured now; she would not let Ange be sent away again.

Ange brightened a little. "Yes and I found some stones. I will polish them to give to Tata when he returns." She smiled up at Tessi and Elanai with a milk moustache.

Later that evening, the men came back with torches and the body tied to a litter made from branches. The body was burned.

Noai came back in, the girls were sound asleep, but Elanai had waited up.

"We will scout further up towards the next tribe. He had the spear marks like those of the Junta. His flesh was eaten like the jackals had had him."

"Ange is not to be sent away anymore; the betrothal has been agreed. I will prepare some food for you in the morning." Elanai looked at Noai darkly. He looked away.

On the second dawn after the scout party left, a windstorm blew across from the great desert. Elanai and the children sat in their huts deafened by the howling wind. It lasted from dawn to dusk, longer than any storm Elanai could remember. The wind sounded like a great booming voice screaming the coming of death. An eerie silence followed, with blackness. The dust was so thick it blocked the sun and choked anything caught in it. Ange, Tessi, and Elanai huddled with veils over their faces. Beneath the bellowing rage of the wind someone could be heard lost and hopeless. Their piercing cries magnified the ferocity of the storm.

Suddenly the roof came off, and they could feel the sand scratching their skin. On Ange's legs, it felt like claws not wanting to let go. Soon one of the walls gave way. They all screamed as the full force of the wind suddenly penetrated the hut. They pulled the mats and rugs over themselves to protect against the lacerating gale.

When it finally passed, a red dust cloud blocked the night

sky and crept over the entire village. Elanai stood in the hazy darkness. She felt the wetness of blood dripping on her legs and arms from the cuts of the eroding sand. Her eyes and mouth were full of grit and her throat felt like sharp needles pricking the flesh. A goat lay flung up against the wall; its flesh was flayed off to the bone. Ange and Tessi were coughing and spitting. They were both shivering and too afraid to move. Elanai walked out and saw most of the village had been razed to the ground. Only a few huts were standing and even then, it was only the walls. She saw their neighbour, Challo come out from under one of the walls of their hut. She held her son Kit in her arms. He was limp. She began to scream. Elanai ran to her and grabbed her. The boy's head rolled to the side. The white bones of his skull were exposed by a large gash.

"Tessi, you and Ange gather wood to start some fires."

The girls began to drag bunches of thatching that had come off, towards their hut. Others soon joined them. More cries of grief came as people found bodies under walls and debris. Ange and Tessi huddled as Elanai helped the old man, Denda, who had half his leg stripped of skin and muscle. She swaddled it as best she could, but the blood would not stop.

Dawn eventually came, dusky and pink, a small relief to the crushing slowness of the night. The relief was short-lived. The sun revealed the devastation. The whole village was surrounded by massive dunes of red. It was as if an ocean of sand had washed in but had been suspended just before crushing the village. Tessi looked over towards the people huddled around the dying embers of a fire. Denda had died. The old man's son covered him and wept silently over him.

Elanai stirred. "Come, we must fetch water and find food. The men will begin to gather the dead."

Elanai was distracted as she spoke. She was looking at the massive dunes that now lay around them. The desert had been creeping closer every year, but it had now finally arrived. They would have to walk over the dunes to find the well. They had managed to salvage some pails. Everyone carried two. A procession of fifteen began to climb the largest of the dunes towards the north. Ange stumbled a few times but eventually managed to scramble to the top. What met them filled them with despair. For as far as the eye could see there was dune after dune of desert. The well would be covered over. The river still flowed in the south but was now dammed by the desert as it passed beyond the village. Ange saw dark branches bob to the surface and then dip under it. She couldn't quite figure out what they were until some of them bobbed straight up revealing their flail arms and heads.

The group moved towards that side of the river to see who they were. Kamet went over and rolled the bodies over. "They are from the Junta; the storm must have come from that far south."

"I don't think it was the storm that killed them. They have the same pox on them like the animals and man found here," said Takob's father, Makab.

Soon over a dozen bodies had piled up.

"Where will we find water?" Elanai asked.

Heading back to the village, Elanai knew that they needed to leave. There was no water that they could drink, and no food; all the animals and crops had been swept away by the desert gods.

Ange screamed for something to drink and her belly would not stop growling. Not even the fear she felt could stop her wanting sustenance. She fingered the beads around her neck making sure they were still there.

Mensat called out. He was one of the village elders; the chieftain of the tribe for the last twenty summers.

"We must decide if we are to stay, the river is dying, and the wind has swept the desert to our huts."

"Where will we go?"

"We must go east towards the city. The pox is in the west and south and moves north. Burn your dead and bring any animals that are still alive."

"What about the others, Noai and Cheka and Koi?"

"We will leave a sign; if they have survived, they will follow."

Elanai found a sack of millet. For the most part, it was free of sand. A goat and her kid suddenly ran towards Ange. The mother limped and was bleeding from a cut on her rump.

"Quickly, milk her, Tessi, and then make some cakes with this flour. I will ask Mensat to kill the kid for meat."

Ange patted the goat and slipped a leash around the kid's neck as Tessi took as much milk as she could from the udder. They were both so thirsty they drained the bowls and then re-filled them. Ange began to make the batter for the cakes. A few of the other children waited for the cakes to be made. Ange handed them out to the children to share with their families.

"It will do until we find another place with food and water," spoke Elanai.

When all the milk and flour was used, Elanai took the goat to Mensat.

Tessi found some of her dowry. She gathered the cloth and polished beads that were given to her from Bensah. Ange gathered up any of their shawls and blankets she could find. She shook the sand out as much as possible.

"If we find Liet's family, then you can stay with them, Tessi. Use your dowry to pay your way." Elanai busily arranged the shawls and veils on her daughters for the journey ahead.

The night came silently with only the occasional noise from other huts. Everyone stayed near their own place, they would gather in the morning to begin looking for a new home. This village had been here for as long as Elanai and Noai had lived and as far back as their great grandparents. Their oral stories ran back many generations, but where they came from originally was lost. It had been told that Noai's ancestors were the members of the original tribes that settled here, considered to be born from ancient peoples that were the first peoples of the earth. Tessi and Ange's blood ran with these ancient memories.

Elanai sat down, feeling very tired and not very well. She felt something on her back, itching, she scratched it and felt it get wet. Looking at her hand, she saw it was wet with blood. She turned around and asked Tessi to look at it. Tessi's heart sank when she saw the oozing sore on her mother's flesh.

"Lay down, Mata, you are tired." Tessi gave her some more milk and placed a shawl over her. She looked away not wanting her mother to see the fear in her eyes.

Within hours, Elanai lay in a painful fever, with more sores forming on her legs and arms. Ange ran to find Mensat only to find the others had been struck as well by the sickness. Ange heard screams coming from behind a ruined hut. Further along, she found Chelli lying dead against a wall. Ange went faster to find Mensat. When she arrived at his hut, she found Mensat lying on the floor. He was shivering. His body covered with welts. His son lay next to him, blood oozed out of his mouth and nose. He was barely breathing. Ange ran out and looked for anyone who was walking, but there was no one. She went back to Elanai and Tessi.

"Everyone is sick, Tessi." Elanai opened her eyes they were blood shot and feverish. She breathed very rapidly. "Find Bensah, leave here, it is cursed." As she coughed blood began to run down her mouth.

Both the girls burst into tears, terrified at what was happening to their mother.

"No, Mata! We will not leave you," cried Tessi. Elanai lay back, and her eyes rolled back into her head. She had begun to shiver with the fever again. Tessi kept the fire going and put an extra wrap over Elanai, but soon the pox appeared on her face. She began to moan, and blood oozed from under her legs and between them. The girls cried watching their mother die before them. As the first rays of dawn crept over the dunes, Elanai lay dead in a pool of blood and excrement. Ange and Tessi covered her and went out into the middle of the ruins of the village. They wandered for a while to see if anyone was alive. They found Takob dead inside his hut along with his family.

"Ange, we have to leave."

"Where will we go?"

"I think we must go to the city. The storm came from the south so we cannot go to Tata Bensah." Tears welled up again in both of the girl's eyes.

"We will burn Mata and then leave a message for Pata to tell him where we are going." Ange nodded. She swallowed; she didn't want to look at her mother again.

The girls began to carry thatch and lay it over Elanai. Ange found the small feather mask she had worn at the marriage feast and placed it on her mother's chest. They lit the thatch. The flint caught the first time and began to burn quickly. Ange sobbed and Tessi had tears streaming down her face as the fire consumed their mother. The wisps of cleansing smoke curled up into the air along with the sickness. Both of their hearts became engulfed with fear and sorrow at the devastation that now surrounded them.

As they walked away, only a smouldering blaze remained of their home. Tessi wondered why she and Ange had not gotten sick. Maybe it was to come for them soon.

Walking over the first few dunes, they saw in the distance a hazy dark shape, giving them hope that there would be water and people who might help them. It was mid-afternoon when they reached the spot where Bensah's boabs grew. They were nearly covered to their tops. Sitting to rest, Ange and Tessi shared a cake between them, chewing with cracked lips. Ange leant on the branch of one of the trees and it broke. Water dripped out of it onto her back. She quickly captured it in her hands and gulped it down, instantly soothing her mouth and throat.

"Quick, Tessi, drink." They lapped it up. It tasted sweet and very much like a tree. Tessi tore some of her tunic and let it soak through and put it in her sack. They could suck on it until it dried.

The girls rested and drank as long as the water ran. The sun was dipping low again.

"We will rest here and start again tomorrow." Tessi looked at the imposing wave of sand ahead and guessed it would be un-climbable. "We will have to go around it, Ange."

Pulling the shawls over themselves, the girls curled up together. They felt safe here.

"Do you think Pata will find us?"

"I don't know."

Deep down Tessi knew Noai was not coming back. Her heart ached for themselves and their parents.

"Go to sleep, Ange, we have a long walk tomorrow."

Ange dreamt of raging storms and searing flames. Tessi saw darkness, pain, and sorrow in her dreams. Both girls fidgeted and whimpered in their slumber. Ange dozed with her body aching. It had been arduous for her to walk on the soft sand, her short leg would give out frequently, and her back would twist. They lay down, cradled by the broad trunk of the tree, and entwined in each other's arms.

"Some of em survived, look at this." The caravan of slavers stopped. Sek, the leader, kicked some pieces of thatch that had been arranged at the end of the destroyed huts. "It's Kensai for east. There is an oasis along the way, we can replenish there."

The slavers were from the far northern lands. At the back of them stood four young girls, tied at the waist and dressed in hessian tunics and veils. One had a fat lip and black eye. She had tried to run away.

The men had two pack camels. They had travelled from the south. The storm had swept to the west instead of heading towards the great southern plateau.

"Pity, this village had some good stock, better than this lot. We coulda made a decent profit."

"What about here the Choasa is just over…"

"Nay Michal, chunt bastard, the water teems with the pox, look at the dead that lie here!" The ruddy man had scars all over his face and was kicking the carcass of the dead goat. A pustule burst as he did so. "Fucken sickness everywhere. Sooner we get home the better."

One of the girls started to whimper with fear seeing the charred remains of the dead bodies. She clutched a charm to ward off omens, working it furiously between her fingers. One of the men, Nathan, yanked at her chain to shut her up.

"Over there, see that large rise directly ahead, fresh water lies below, untouched by the curses of this land. Its in the trees."

The wind brought the smell of the rotting flesh. They trod on the cindered remains of Ange and Tessi's home, and their mother's bones. One of the men tripped on Elanai's skull, kicking it in agitation. It splintered into moist pieces, some of it sticking to his boots.

"God forsaken, shithole," he said, swearing under his breath.

———

During the early hours of the morning, Tessi woke first. The sand had blown over them in the night; the shawls had blended with the desert they slept in. Tessi stood up gently, not wanting to wake Ange, her mouth was dry, and her lips cracked. Suddenly, she heard voices, men's voices, in tongue she didn't understand, but had heard before. They were men from the north. She slowly peered over the lip of the dune and saw two of them sitting up, while three others were sleeping. She heard the jingle of chains. Looking over further, she saw a sight that filled her heart with terror; girls like her chained like animals. She sat back down silently. Her heart thudded. There was nowhere to run or hide from them. For leagues there was nothing, they would see them trying to flee. Ange stirred. Tessi went to her quickly, pulled the shawl over her, and then tried to put sand over them again. She lay with her hand over Ange's mouth and whispered, "Shh, slavers." Ange's eyes bulged.

For a long time, they lay there, the sun rising in the sky, baking the sand and them with it. They could hear the men begin to stir. Someone shouted and then the chains all jangled. Suddenly there were footsteps nearby. Ange felt the pressure of the sand change as a foot trod close to her head.

"Nothing here. By the spirits, look at that, chunt bastard's too high, it would collapse if we tried to walk on it." As he moved, his foot landed straight on Tessi's foot. She bit her lip to stop herself crying out from the pain. He kicked it thinking it was a rock. The shawl flicked up and exposed her toes. He reached down and yanked her out. "What's this?" Tessi and Ange screamed.

"Eh, Nickov, look, I've got us a few more." He picked the girls up, one in each arm, and threw them up to where the others were sitting.

"Hmm, a gift from the sand gods." A man with hair that was as white as clouds chuckled. He picked Tessi up and placed his hand in between her legs. She screamed. "Unused, she'll fetch a good price."

He picked Ange up then, and looked at her, curling his lip

with disgust. Ange was paralysed with fear.

"Leave her for the desert."

Dragging Tessi over towards the other girls, they began to shackle her. She kicked and screamed. Ange began to cry. She had sunk down into the sand. Then there was a loud slapping sound and Tessi was suddenly quiet. Ange looked up through her tears. Tessi was stunned, and her lip and nose were bleeding. The man checked the chains were secured and walked away.

"What about her? Nah, leave it, she'll be a dead weight, and we won't get much for her anyway. Move, I want to make Ancrid City by dusk."

Ange began to sob. She ran towards Tessi and clung to her. The other girls just watched in a stupor. They had been through this in their own villages. Tessi began to rouse from the shock of being hit. She latched onto Ange. The fair headed one pulled Ange off and threw her towards one of the boabs. She struck the trunk hard sending a wave of pain radiating into her back and legs. She didn't stop looking at Tessi and Tessi kept watching Ange as she was hauled away. Each of their hearts tore in two with terror and sorrow. Ange's head slumped. Tessi screamed thinking that Ange had been killed from being thrown. The chains abraded her wrists as she bridled against them trying to get back to her sister. She reefed at them, pulling one of the other girls over and screaming, then all of a sudden everything went black.

"Put her up there until she settles." The slaver threw her over the saddle of the camel.

The sun rose to its zenith, baking the sand and earth below.

It felt no pity or remorse about its unrelenting gaze. The desert reflected the searing heat back, mocking it almost, not letting anything else exist along with it. Death thrived here and sorrow was its bride.

Ange lay near the boab, blinking through her tears, her body lying in a contorted pose unable to move from the pain. In the shimmery haze, she peered across the barrenness and could just make out the caravan disappearing into the horizon.

"Tessi." She sobbed until the heat and pain made her faint.

10

Blood Memories

Sa, Tuan and Kim had camped on an outcrop of rock high in the Mountains of Hosian that separated Ko's lands from the Hosiaan Province. The mountains were lifeless except for the buzzards who perched on their tips. No foliage grew to break the blandness of the slate grey rock.

Sa kept a look out as Tuan and Kim slept. The night had fallen quickly and while she had traversed these mountains many times before, the cliffs were littered with hideouts for criminals. She did not want to take any risks of being killed while they slept. The wind whistled around her but did not penetrate the steely single mindedness that had protected her throughout her life.

Sa's mind was sifting through each minute detail of the journey ahead. She would send Kim to the Iron Coast. He could scout ahead and bring back any news of the new ruler of the desert land. She and Tuan would continue to the citadel.

The chamber that contained the archives was beneath the main palace. It held the ledgers of the trade agreements for any weapon supply and the old surveyor's chronicles of the first explorations for the ore in the middling lands. She had planned how she would break into the archival chamber. A contact from long ago had been sent a message that she would be visiting. Sa trusted few, Marco was one of those few. He had grown up in the same interment camp as Sa and then Marco had been sent to serve in the kitchens of the Hojin dynasty. Her escape route would need to be finalised once she arrived at the citadel. Ko was right to be wary. The provinces lay disgruntled with the Emperor's brutality and seemingly inexhaustible wealth. It was no surprise that some of the feudal lords sought allegiance from any who were willing to challenge Ko's rule. She had seen the menace of Ranik and knew that he was amassing an army and seeking supplies to arm himself. The westerling was brutal even by Ko's standards. The Matavians, while considered enemies, were normally no threat to the Drax Empire, but something had changed. The tyrant grew in strength; his navy and army now almost equalled Ko's. The eagle masts were fitted with huge cannons and catapults. Ranik had full control of the main supplies of orichnite, and his bulwarks always returned loaded with the ore from the southern desert. Such quantities could only be explained to make weaponry. 'A war was coming,' Sa thought matter-of-factly.

Feeling confident that nothing pursued them, she let her mind drift into the mantras of discipline. Kim woke and went to her as she meditated.

"I will keep watch now, Elder Tuc." Sa gave an almost indiscernible nod as she continued to clear her mind and slowly drift into sleep. She remained sitting upright against a rock, her legs crossed beneath her.

Sa never usually dreamed, but this time her mind was full of red sky. She was walking with someone in her arms and blood washed around her feet. She couldn't see who it was that she carried as she continued towards the setting sun over rivers of blood.

On the dawn, they made their way to the peak of the southern ridge. They could see the hazy outline of the southern lands. Down below, lay the great windswept plains. The Hosiaan region was proud of its fine breeds of horse and horsemanship. Their soldiers were the finest archers under Ko's reign. The grasses on the plain blew like a straw-coloured ocean, with the currents matching the gusts of the wind as they rippled through the blades. The land was mostly empty this time of year as it was not the breeding season. The mountain lions and buzzards were often driven down looking for food and would prey on the farm animals in the fields. Sa and her protégés reached the bottom of the cliffs by nightfall.

"Kim, you are to go to the Tirolan crossing and make your way to the southern tip. There you will be able to sail to the Iron Coast. In one moon and five sunrises, you are to return and meet here at the base of the mountains. We will return to Drax City together. You will need to disguise yourself. The people are used to us as traders, but to linger for so long on your own will draw attention."

Kim studied the map carefully memorising the main landmarks, nodded, bowed to Sa, and left.

Walking through the tall grass, Sa gently let the seeded heads gently caress her fingers. The sensation was soothing, as was the sound of the rustling of the field that surrounded them. She and Tuan walked in tandem and meditated, the two assassins made minuscule lip movements as they recited their mantras; the serenity of the fields belied their lethal purpose to do their master's bidding.

The walk to Hosiaan Citadel was flat until two leagues away from the walled city the road made a long slow climb to the gates. They would not bother hiding their arrival as the large towers had a full view of all roads that led to the city. Interspersed throughout the grasslands were old nomadic camps from the summer before. There were pegs still in the ground where the great Yurts had been erected. The nomadic tribes were used to tame the horses before they were commandeered into Ko's army. The training circles of the horses were still evident where the grass had been trampled down to almost mud. Storm clouds began to gather with thunder urging them on. The yellow of the slender blades intensified as the grey and indigo clouds exploded their fury. The sweet smell of the lightening and wet grass reminded Sa of a time when she and her mother had run across the plain as indentured workers. The rain drove in between hers and Tuan's scarves stinging their eyes. Within minutes, they were soaked through. By night fall, they had reached a road that would join the main route to the city.

"Look." Tuan pointed. In the sky, streaked a flame. Sa saw it briefly as the clouds rolled together in readiness for another storm.

"What is it?"

"Perhaps the spirits are playing or are angry."

Up ahead was a grove of bushes. They took shelter and

made camp. The mud covered their black trousers. Taking off their layers, they strung them over the inner bushes and lit a fire. The rain had at least eased, but the thunder and lightning remained. Sa sat with only a grey cotton wrap around her chest and hips. Tuan had kept his loin cloth on. They had found a marmoset and were eating it. The flesh was acrid and barely edible.

"The Emperors cooks should be rewarded for making this rodent a delicacy, Elder Tuc."

"Indeed."

That night Sa dreamed again of a red sky filled with a fireball streaking over her head towards the sun. This time Kado's face appeared, but he was barely recognizable as if a disease had taken hold. The falling star hit the sun and the dream ended in a massive explosion of blood and fire.

They woke before dawn and by nightfall, they had reached Hosiaan City. Sa had placed her tunic over her pack and both of them had removed their head scarves. Tuan walked ahead to appear as spouses. Their plan had been to separate in the citadel and then rendezvous at the mountain pass. Once inside, Sa bid Tuan goodbye and headed towards the slum districts. Tuan made his way to the trading district to find any information on the buying and selling of the ore. The smugglers often needed to involve legitimate traders to fund their operations. The channels of information were lucrative with the nexus the smugglers weaved to maintain contacts and opportunities.

Sa arrived at a large boarding house with a laundry underneath. She looked up the façade of the piece meal architecture and saw a tiny window on the very top eave – an attic. She walked around the other side of the block and saw that the building abutted the central canal that ran through the citadel and directly toward the Palace. It could be scaled from the top roof without being seen from the busy street. There was a larger window at the rear. She returned to the entrance of the boarding house.

"Board until the next moon. Something small. It is only myself."

The landlord looked at her as he studied her scarred face.

"I have some rooms, seven ducks a night."

He led her up the stairs and showed her a large bedroom which overlooked the street.

Sa shook her head. "I want security. Do you have something that is away from the street and other lodgers? I am a nun from the Sadom temple and wish to meditate."

They trekked up five more flights of stairs. The landlord was wheezing and sweating. He took a key and opened the attic door. It was the only one on the floor. It was tiny and had a pitched ceiling and the windows she had seen from the street. There was a cot with a stained mattress, basin, and jug on a small table.

"There is fresh water in the laundry beneath. Madame Zosa will sell it to you for half a duck a bucket."

Sa nodded and placed ten ducks in his hand. He looked at her enquiring why there was not more to pay until the next moon.

"I will secure some work as a tutor. It is all I have."

The landlord left. Sa closed the door and unrolled her bedding. She checked the window; the panes were loose. She took her dagger, chiselled the wood away, and removed one whole panel of glass. It was long and just wide enough for Sa to climb through. Taking a leather scroll out of her sack, she perused the citadel's layout. The palace of Lord Hojinex was located in the southern corner of the main plaza. The map showed the sewer tunnels and culverts for bringing water into the buildings and centre of the palace. She would make her way into the chambers, unseen like the rats. She checked her purse. There were enough coins for Marco.

The night was veiled with clouds as Marco watched Sa descend into the old service tunnel beneath the palace. He breathed quickly, anxious to leave. He would be hung and quartered for this betrayal, but Sa-Tuc was even more lethal than his master. He closed the hatch as she disappeared into the ominous mouth of the tunnel.

Sa felt her way in the dark. In the distance was a spec of light that signalled the intersecting tunnel. She turned left and followed again until the hot air met her from above. Placing her hands on either side of the stone walls, she shimmied up to the grate in the floor of the library. She pulled on it and suddenly one of the sides dislodged from the stone. Marco had made sure it was loose for her.

Inside, the torches burned warmly. It was an inviting room Sa thought, as she made her way to the far end to a chamber sectioned off by bars. She heard a faint shuffle. Someone was in here. She froze and waited. The sound of parchment moving was magnified in the dim emptiness of the library. She moved in closer around the stone pillar. Inside, she saw Lord Hojinex and his General.

"There was more to be found in the central deserts further south. The coast here is calm and can be sailed."

"Ko is suspicious," spoke General Tranxo.

"Yes. I need to reinforce the stocks under Jun. He is still unaware of where it lies, but he is closing in. We still don't know where he keeps the treasure of the dragon," replied Lord Hojinex.

"Have you followed the slaves that deliver the wealth to the hidden Drax coffers?"

"We have tried. But at all times the messenger never returns to tell, nor does the slave."

Sa stood. They had the scrolls she needed, and she now knew where the cache was. War was coming if she didn't move. She spun without making a sound and flicked a knife directly into Tranxo's throat. Speeding past the collapsing soldier, she latched onto Lord Hojinex head and twisted fiercely. The crack of his neck echoed in the chamber.

Quickly she rolled up the map and placed it in her tunic. She went to the far wall and saw where they had been removed. She grabbed the other scrolls and stashed those as well.

She peered into the semi-gloom to check no-one had come in and climbed back into the tunnel.

Sa woke and looked through the window over the rooftops. The alarm would be sounded, and the city's gates closed as the palace guards began to search for the assassin of Lord Hojinex. She looked across at her satchel. The scrolls were safely stowed away inside. She watched the city's life below. Dusty whirlwinds floated up to her attic window from the street carriages.

Noises and smells rose to her in the little room she had rented. Below she heard sounds of pots and shouting. The steam evaporating off the canal water gave the roofscape a hazy appearance. Sa stood silhouetted in the window with hands behind her back, straight backed, angular and petite; a tight coil. Looking down to the narrow alley that led to her room, she noted guards knocking on doors. She stood a little back so as not to be seen. Sa quietly closed the window and sat back on her straw mat.

She waited. Nothing happened for a long time. Then there was soft tapping on the door. She rose and opened it. It was the landlady with a bucket of water. Sa handed her a duck and took the bucket. She took a drink and then splashed some of the water on her face and daubed the rest of her tiny frame. Wiping herself off, she dressed and packed her rucksack and left her room.

As she descended the stairs, muffled sounds of cleaning and cooking below rose toward her. Most of the doors were shut in the other rooms she glided past silently. On the third floor one door was open. Within the room, a group of young girls stood before a man sitting on a large bed. He rose and went to close the door. Sa noted his features and kept walking down. On the next floor, she heard the business of a family preparing their morning meal. A mother retorted to a child to hurry and sit. Another door banged and a young boy whipped past her and out into the street. Someone called to him in the corridor, but he did not stop, as he sped on his way. Steam wafted up through the central space of the stairwell from the washing room below. Sa came to the front entrance, blinked at the brightness of the sun, and stepped into the quagmire of the city. It pricked her senses after the pristine palace. The mud and filth clung to her shoes, as did the stench of the sewers to her nose. Children ran to her begging. Turning up her nose to their filthy faces, she batted them away. One little girl started to cry. Sa did not stop. The smell of the lily fern rooms penetrated; it neither delighted nor repelled. A man waited outside with a carriage behind him. It was ornately decorated and well maintained, suggesting a wealthy patron was visiting. She would need to be careful, as the search for Lord Hojinex's assassin would include places where criminals and the elite may gather; places such as the dens.

She continued along the streets towards the market alleys. As she neared the markets, the crowd became like a swarm, blending into one and pushing the mass in its own direction. Sa's face flinched at the proximity of others. Her life as an assassin had kept her isolated in a world of obedient precision. She headed towards a stand where rice and other staples were sold.

"Where do you purchase your teas?" she asked, as she inspected the goods on the stall.

"From the Indraan province."

"How fresh is it… and the rice, where is it from?"

"The same, the rains make for good harvests there, but it is three days journey from here, so the farmers bring their produce halfway and we bring it here."

"How often do you replenish it?"

"Every seven days."

Sa noted the man had begun to relax. "And these… how old? My master's family is visiting. The welcome feast must be worthy for my master's honour."

Sa attempted a smile but the scar on her face made her appear like she was grimacing instead.

"I will be leaving tomorrow for new stock. Perhaps if you come back the day after tomorrow, I will have better choice for you."

Sa looked behind the merchant and noted a cart. It was large enough for a person to lie down in.

"I will purchase some to sample for my lord and consider coming back if he is pleased."

The merchant bowed as the sacks of rice and tea were handed over.

Sa walked through the markets; the Indraan province lay to the north, which suited her. She bought some more leather scrolls to place the maps into and an undershirt made of goat's hair. She would wait until the dawn and return.

Turning down a side alley, she saw the man from the boarding house with a group of young girls around him. His hand rested on one of the girl's shoulder as he inspected her, his other hand forcing her mouth open. It looked like a vulture's claw clutching the tiny girl. Something sparked in Sa's mind; a memory long shut down. Over behind the group, skulking in a doorway stood a skinny emaciated man with jaundiced eyes, watching. The lodger turned to him and nodded at the girl he had been petting. The man in the doorway indicated three fingers and clapped his hands, instantly the other girls scattered into the street. The lodger from Sa's boarding house walked off holding hands with the girl. Sa saw the dulled eyes and knew that the girl was no longer innocent to what her life had become.

For Sa Tuc, emotion was foreign, her only consolation was order and precision in fulfilling her duties, but her disgust at one such as this, not willing to overcome a weakness but feed off the truly vulnerable, agitated her sense of discipline. She followed. If they were heading back to the boarding house, then they would need to pass through a quiet alley off the main laneways. She saw a walkway above them. She stashed her purchases under a stair and climbed up onto the overhanging planks. She crept ahead of them. The alley was almost like a tunnel and semi-dark all day. It had a bend in the middle so that each end was cut off from view. When she reached the darkest part of the alley, she elegantly climbed down. Wrapping her scarf around her face, she waited silently like a spider in its web.

They came to her. She let him pass. Then reaching her hand over the man's head, she deftly glided the knife over his neck and sliced cleanly. He dropped to the ground. Sa grabbed the girl, smothered her mouth before she could scream, and carried her to the end of the alley. She looked at a pox-scarred face and dead eyes. The girl coughed bringing with it a droplet of blood. Sa felt compelled to end the girl's life as well and stop the misery she would continue to endure. Her knife was poised but she did not act, instead, she grabbed a bag of rice and gave it to the girl.

"Run to Madame Song. She is in the western edge of the citadel. She will give you work in the kitchen along with food and shelter." The girl realised it was a woman's voice and suddenly looked directly into Sa's eyes almost like she was waking up for the first time. Sa watched the emerald slits widen slightly. 'You are not dead yet,' the assassin thought.

"Run, Go! Tell her the spider sends you and offers this gift as payment!"

Sa watched the girl disappear in the direction of the old concubine of Ko: one of the few to gain her freedom while she was alive. She rewrapped her scarf, took the rest of the tea and rice, and walked into the street. Back at the boarding house, as she ascended the stairs, she noted the room where the man had been, the door was shut. Sa tried it and found it was unlocked. On the floor near the bed was a wet stain, where someone had been mopping. The room was empty of anything personal except a half-sucked lolly on the table. A small dot of blood was on the wall behind the lantern.

Sa entered her own room, placed her pack on the ground and took off her head scarf. It had been a hot day and the filth of the street was encrusted in the parts of her face that had been exposed. She poured some water into the bowl and washed away the day's work.

Looking down into the canal and across the city, she could see the palace guards everywhere. A writ would have been sent by now to the Emperor with news of the assassination. It had been necessary.

Sa took out the scrolls and opened one of them. It was clever of Hojinex and Tsung to hide the caches of weapons deep in the Feet of Jun; directly under Ko's amassed supplies so that any deliveries looked to be part of the Emperor's own stock. The other two dragon dynasties were ready to go to battle against Ko. She remembered Chalac, and his prediction of the vice of Ranik of the west and the Lords of the south-eastern provinces. Ko didn't stand a chance.

She suddenly felt tired. Rolling the parchments into the leather binders, she lay down on the bed. As she drifted off to sleep, the face of the young girl came to her. She dreamed of her time in the orphanage. She had been working in the laundry, her hands raw from scrubbing. Her back ached from where she had been beaten the day before by one of the older girls and then by Madame Peregrin for the injuries she had inflicted in retaliation. She was walking up to the yards. As she entered, she saw Madame and one of the Palace soldiers standing at the end. She walked towards them.

"Kneel!" barked Madame.

Sa kneeled.

"This runt did that?" asked the soldier incredulously

"Yes, and I've seen it before, but worse, General," replied Madame.

"Where is this one from?"

"She was found in one of the old dens in the south quarter. Her mother was an indentured worker there. She came to us when she was five."

"What did the scar come from?"

"She came with it, her mother was being attacked, and the girl jumped the man to stop him. But the mother punished her with a cut, as she did not get paid. She was abandoned after that as she would be no use as a whore with a face like that."

"Here, girl!" ordered the soldier.

Sa came over to him and Madame Peregrin.

He inspected her teeth and felt her muscles and lean body.

"Bring her for the initiation trials. We shall see. Make sure she is washed and dressed. Feed her more. The Lord is not pleased with his current recruits and neither am I. They lack a strength and fury."

It was the day of the trials, Sa stood in line opposite a row of boys. Her body and mind remembered the adrenaline coursing through and how she felt like she was going to explode with impatience. Her eagerness to prove herself wound tightly like a coil in every sinew and muscle.

"Begin."

Sa's body jerked in her sleep as she remembered being winded by the first blow.

Getting up, she copped another kick in the face and salty blood filled her mouth. Instantly, Sa's mind saw the boy preparing to land a blow to her gut. She looked directly at his throat. In a flash, she had jumped up and landed a side kick directly into the boys adam's apple. He fell dead from the blow as his windpipe was crushed. Her mind cleared as she stood defensively waiting for the next. Blocking a jab to her flank, she ran at the next boy who was twice her size. She threw both feet at his chest in mid-air. He kicked her away, causing her to fall heavily. He laid into her, jabbing and thrusting. She tried to roll and duck, missing at least every second pummel. Exhausted after only a short time, she knew she would not survive. She rolled away, making the other boy follow. She felt a pole marking the boundary of the field hit her flank. Whipping up she grabbed it and snapped it out of the ground. In one swift move, she thrust it at the approaching attacker and rammed it into his stomach. Pulling it out, she went for the lethal blow.

As he fell forward, she staked him in the back. Twirling around in a pose of utter savagery, she stabbed and belted in blind fury at the others around her. Suddenly, she felt something knock her to the ground. She looked up and saw the General standing over her with a glint in his eye. He reefed her up. She stood and looked around the yard, only five out of the original dozen stood.

"Enough!" The General smiled. "Sa Tuc ; at last, the weapon I have searched for. The Emperor will be pleased."

The echo of his whisper as they stared into the coldness of each other's eyes remained in her memory.

———

Assumpta stared at Sa jerking on the mat. She had been drawn to Sa by a shadow which echoed with memories as ancient as her own. She drank Sa's essence only to be engulfed by a great vault. She gasped at the void within Sa. Never had the emptiness been so great. Nestled in a malignant silence, lay the seed of one never wanted and never belonged. Within the chasm, rose the screams of those who lay dead at the blade of this assassin. Assumpta attempted to fill the space, but could not, for as she entered more deeply into Sa's lost soul, she saw the eyes of an ancient creature that had first dwelt there, staring, piercing her elemental form. The god bowed to it and withdrew knowing this one belonged to another's dominion. Assumpta also knew that if Voloc would find a powerful ally and home in this one.

"You are to come to the grove by the moon's rise. If I am not there, then you are to wait for the northern warrior, Gildas.

There you will find guidance on where to go."

Assumpta plucked a memory of two children playing, it had almost faded into obscurity in Sa's mind. "I leave this for you, it was a token of a friend you once had but may have forgotten. Hang onto it, your darkness goes deeper than the warrior's. For you Sa Tuc, there may be no place to run."

Assumpta placed a pouch on the mat near Sa and left.

11

Ira's Covenant

Paulus came down off the lectern and turned to face the candelabra burning above the stone tabernacle. The other monks kneeled on cushions in meditation. As always, old Brother Frederick was to his left, and to the right was Vronius. Paulus closed his eyes; a slight sweat had broken out onto his forehead as he knelt beside his fellow monks. He breathed slowly, implementing the well-practiced meditative poses. He heard a snore drift from Frederick. He let his mind wander back through the details of the last few days. Then the image of the dark corridor came to him again. For a full cycle of the moon, this dream had not left him. It was as vivid as the first night it had occurred: the voices in the chamber had drawn him along the hallway. As he had neared the direction of the whispering, a door opened. At first, no one came out from the chamber, but then Paulus realised a shadow moved briefly before blending with the darkness. It turned and hissed. Just for a moment, red eyes peered directly at him. Even now, fully awake, the sting of those eyes made his heart leap with fear. What had happened after that had eluded Paulus. He forced his mind to listen to the great bell of Tarnoc as it faithfully tolled in long sonorous booms. Made from the iron of the great southern lands and forged in the fires of Mount Draag, it sang as if it was the heartbeat of the world; calling all the faithful. Eventually the beating in Paulus chest slowed and the beads of sweat worked their way off his forehead. At almost ninety summers, he felt his age and bone-deep weariness of being alive for so long. He had spent the last thirty summers as Abbot of the prime Irasian temple. He continued his prayers trying to calm the feeling of unease that had been with him since the dream. On the edges of sight, he felt something watching him.

Slowly, the Sanctuary of Reflection emptied as those who undertook chores left to complete them. Finally, Paulus left as well, leaving Frederick in peace, and made his way to his room. Located in the high tower, it overlooked the eastern side towards the ocean. The vista from his window was inspiring. Today he could almost see the shores of the Aeserean coast to the north. He noticed some parchment on his desk. Opening it, he read that an emissary from the territory of Matavia was waiting for him. Inside the scroll was a request to mine the lands surrounding the temple for the mineral Orichnite.

"Of course, I should ask how you came to be aware of the mineral's abundance under our temple, Ranik. And since when do you amuse yourself with the coloured fires that the mineral can be made into?" Paulus spoke to himself.

He called out to Flet who was in the ante chamber preparing tea. "Find Vronius and ask him to come."

As he waited, Paulus looked over the great expanse of the Sea of Ira. He remembered the time long ago when his ascetic mind had revealed visions in his dreams and brought the same hollowness that afflicted his heart now. He remembered the conversation with his predecessor, Ursula the 5th, when he told the old woman of these haunting visions.

"It is time. These visions are not unusual, for I too have had them."

"Is it a sign the ascetic ways of Ira have been inculcated fully?" Paulus asked.

Ursula had smiled at his naïve question. "For most brethren who report visions it is probably a lack of food and water when they have fasted for too long, eh." She winked at him. "But for a very few it is a sign that a new custodian of our faith and purpose is being sought."

"What do you mean?"

"For those endowed with the gift of sight beyond what the light reveals, the journey beyond the shadows toward enlightenment is arduous. Have you ever considered why the Brethren have never evangelised beyond the northern lands, Paulus?"

"Not really. Were we not kept busy enough here?"

"Seven millennia ago, when Ira first began his proselytizing across the world, he made his way to the south. The people were welcoming but had their own god and ways of paying homage to the world. No weaponry or alchemy, they abided by the lands and its providence as it deemed. Ira began to speak to them of learning, offering knowledge on how to till the land and our mantras of peace. However, the elders of the tribes showed him their customs and belief in the ancients. He was taken to their sacred sites. There he learnt of the old histories of how this world came to be and what our destiny could be if all was made clear to us. He fasted and prayed for many months to find enlightenment. He lived with the elders of those lands to learn their ways and understand this knowledge that the northern peoples had never known. Eventually, his self-denial and meditation bore fruit in the form of a visitation from a great custodian of the eternal. The god Norbu rose from his Keep and spoke with our founder. He asked one thing of him; that he would not bring the new religion here but teach the northern lands of Arglethium's mysteries and the wisdom of the ancients. He asked that he leave these children to honour and do homage to the ancient ones, for in the desert stood the way into the world of the spirits, unseen to our eyes. The Elders of the land have been given the duty to protect it. The god also spoke of the lost destiny of creation and said that a time will come when it could be restored. The god gave Ira a gift. He said it contained the eye into infinite light, a god called Caemeris and two beings would seek it. Our hope only lies with one while with the other holds our destruction. He showed Ira the gift and the power contained within it was indelibly printed onto his soul. The stone revealed the ancient light of the first dawn, but its power was too great for a child of Arglethium to bear. The potency of the stone destroyed his body. Thus, the few depictions we have of Ira were as he was after being touched by this gift – maimed and unable to walk. A blood covenant was made then between Ira and the elders of the tribes in the south and to this day that covenant has never been broken."

"What of the gift?"

"The whereabouts of the gift is passed only to the new Abbot when they take the chair of Ira. The gift chooses who is to succeed and continue its protection. It is the solemn duty passed down to each successor to protect the gift. If an Abbot divulges this to any other than the successor, then a calamity greater than any known on the world will befall us. I have meditated long and now know that you are worthy of the Chair of Ira. The gift has chosen and thus the dark things of this world are drawn to you, hence the dreams that haunt your sleep. Many things will be revealed to you if you assume the seat, Paulus. Not all of them will come from the light of our sun or the wisdom of Ira. Come, I will take you to where it is hidden."

The Abbot led Paulus towards her room. Ursula moved toward an old camphor tree box filled with blankets at the end of the cot.

"Help me."

Grabbing either end, they moved the chest over towards the bed. Ursula placed her hand on a brick in the wall. "Remember this." The only identifying feature that made it different to the other bricks was a small chip in the upper left-hand corner. As Ursula pushed on the brick, it depressed slightly. Beneath where the chest had sat a hatch opened, leading to a winding staircase.

"As we go down, pull the chest back over the centre and the hatch will close under it."

Paulus pulled the chest over the opening. As the hatch closed a sudden darkness enveloped them. Ursula lit a flint and then a torch bound to the wall. Looking down, Paulus saw a staircase descending so steeply that he began to feel giddy.

"Watch your step. There are rocks to hang onto in the wall."

Paulus instinctively grabbed the wall and felt a jagged edge there. Ursula's flame passed over it briefly as he steadied himself. The rock looked like the skull of a man. Ursula heard his gasp.

"It is a dark period in our history, Paulus, one which all Abbots must make amends for. That also forms part of the great pilgrimage that a new Abbot undertakes as atonement. All the labourers who built this place for the gift, died along with the knowledge of its location. Their remains are a testament to their sacrifice."

Paulus shuddered at this, astounded at the length taken to keep this part of the brethren's history secret.

They made their way slowly, taking what seemed at least a full turn by the hourglass. Eventually the staircase came to a vault. Paulus could hear the ocean beating against the walls. Walking into the room, the air was heavy with a musty dankness. A feeling of uncertainty pervaded Paulus' thoughts as though he and Ursula were no longer in the temple. He was beginning to understand that all that he had served existed for an entirely different reason than what he had been taught to believe. For the first time in his life, Paulus felt real fear. The muted wash of the ocean came to him, but instead of soothing him, it sounded like something was scratching at the walls trying to break in and take it all away, leaving no memory of the lives spent here in their search for wisdom and humility. Paulus felt like he did not matter.

Ursula lit another torch and brought the light across the cavern they had entered. On the far side, was a wall made from the cliff that formed the temple's foundations. It was heavily filigreed patterns were carved into the stonewalls. Ursula went to the opposite side to the entrance. She took out her scapula and removed a small key from the silver canister. She placed it in the centre of one of the panels. Instantly, the patterns moved like ivy tendrils and formed into a small lever.

"Do the patterns speak to you? Take the torch and look at them more closely."

Paulus moved in to inspect the wall. Nothing; he recognised neither a language, nor a repetition of the carvings beyond each panel. Then he stared for a while at one spot. Peering in the half-light, he realised he was reading the old text of Ira from the time he founded the order. It was not used anymore as all the scriptures and correspondence were in the common tongue.

"It's the old text in places: This panel has excerpts from the mantras of Ira "Wisdom's embrace … peace …""

"That's right the script is heavily disguised. See here, 'Wisdom's embrace shall lead a soul to peace and justice, and within will be found compassion for all things.' Each swirl extends over a letter or word, and the geometric patterns form the end of one mantra and the beginning of another. Remember these things, Paulus, for you will need to pass this knowledge on to your successor or, may the Great Ira forbid, take this gift to its rightful owner."

"What is the gift?"

"It was never fully explained by our founder, but not even the fiery pits of Mount Draag could destroy it. It is forbidden knowledge except for those chosen to be its steward. The god who gave it to Ira said it is not of this world. Even the god warned that it was not its to command. Come, we have dallied long enough. Do you understand that this must never be revealed until the next Abbot is chosen and is ready to receive and accept this knowledge? It is under pain of death if the covenant is breached."

Ursula pulled and turned the stone lever that stood out from the wall. A rumble resonated around them and Paulus could feel the vibrations beneath his feet. Suddenly the wall and floor disappeared, and the darkened cavern became a transparent glistening cathedral of crystal and glass. In the middle stood a massive pillar of what looked like diamond. A tiny beacon of colour sat in the middle; radiant like a star.

"Behold the temple of the custodians of creation. Here, upon the dirt and stone of the world formed late in their waking memory, sits the doom and saviour of all that is known to the children of the world. Come, for you are about to see the great gift of Norbu the mighty. The indelible dream and nightmare of what lies between nothing and something; being and non being; awareness and blindness; the questions never asked and their answers; the seed of creation and the uncreated; life to death and non-existence; chaos and order; a vision of glorious annihilation and no memory of destruction at all; the light before dawn's memory and the final death of the sun. Go now, Paulus, and be baptized by the gift of Norbu and become one with the memory of light."

Ursula had pushed him forward. He walked toward the pillar. He placed his trembling hand on the smooth cool surface. He pulled away as he felt the vibration begin to enter him. Ursula's hand suddenly lay on top of his and pushed it gently back onto the diamond pillar. Both hands penetrated the clear, water-like crystal. It was cool and felt alive. Their hands reached the aureole of colours suspended in the middle.

"Light beyond memory and dawn, accept this new steward of the gift of Ira. Swear your oath, Steward." Ursula's voice was low and fierce as she spoke into his ear.

"I swear to be steward of the first light."

"Do you swear to hold it in your heart until it is given freely to the next steward or a custodian from the dawn of time holds it once more? Swear it or you will burn."

"I swear."

Paulus stopped breathing as the watershed of creation entered him. His mind became black and then exploded over and over again. He felt himself be burned inside out. He watched his silhouette melt into dust and reform again in his shape, but something different. He heard distant cries of long sorrowful laments and rupturing agony as something was torn and wounded, pierced by a presence that disturbed the order of first chaos. All the threads of existence became visible before him and then shattered – again and again. An impenetrable darkness washed over him and he could feel himself suffocating, but still alive in its placental embrace. He began to weep as he watched himself become consumed by a oneness that every part of him could not comprehend. His body began to fight against the vision eating away at his mind. He fell backwards into the arms of Ursula. His body shook in violent convulsions as if it would split into a thousand pieces.

"Do you see? Live now and be ready to carry this within you. When the time comes, you will know what to do. Annihilation or memory of what can be, that is the path before us all."

Paulus woke. He was back in the darkened cavern of stone.

"Remember." Ursula was dripping some water from her cupped hand. She scooped some more from a small pool in the bedrock for him.

He nodded as tears welled at a lost memory that lay at the edges of his vision. He felt burning inside like a constant itch in his chest. He began to rub at the spot, but nothing would relieve the sensation.

"That feeling will remain. Once I have passed the scapulet of protection to you, you will be safe and the burning will lessen, but never fully leave you. It is considered the penance of Ira. It will bind you to this most sacred and unrevealed covenant. The pillar of the first dawn is what protects the temple from natural destruction of the oceans, and perhaps, also a time when the world is no longer safe from the unknown darkness. The wound of the custodians' light is what will chain you until death and beyond. If the gift is used by any other without the Steward's consent, then the Steward and the thief will be burned into ashes for a thousand cycles. If the jewel is taken unwillingly and not given to the hands of a custodian in five dawns, then it will incinerate any who hold it."

"I am not ready," Paulus wheezed.

"No, neither was I. But you will never be released now, not even in death. Use this time before the balm of the scapulet is given to lie in meditation in the room of quietude. Let yourself become strong from the sorrow and pain. Let the joy of the truth of our existence sustain you. Lament the passing of the brethren, Paulus, and be ready to be the next to follow in the footsteps of Ira; to be the next steward of this first light. My death will come quickly now that the inheritor of this gift has been found. Your suffering will soon be anointed."

Paulus nodded as he watched Ursula lock the panel stone again. The lever retreated without any trace. Hiding once more any existence of the great chamber of crystal.

"Come. We are now in the time of waiting."

The light in Ursula's room revived Paulus, lifting the heaviness he felt in his heart. Ursula sat down in front of the hearth. She gestured to Paulus to join her. He was panting from the climb up.

"Share a drink with me, Paulus, your initiation to follow in the seat of Ira the Great has begun. I see the fear in your eyes. Do not be alarmed. These truths are difficult at first, but take heart, for the Lord of the world entrusted Ira and his brethren to safeguard this gift. For many millennia, we have done so and continue to do so. Be assured that the wisdom of things beyond our knowledge will mark your way and the faith of Ira will be your staff."

A knock on the chamber door roused him from the memories. Ursula had taken ill two days after his initiation and died seven nights later. Paulus had assumed the chair of Ira. The visions, which had overwhelmed him in the crystal cathedral those many summers ago, had not returned until the last moon when he had seen the red eyes flash at him in the corridor.

"Come in." Vronius entered and bowed slightly.

"Brother, Emissary Dhat from the Kingdom of Lord Ranik is waiting outside. He is wanting to speak to you in regard to the mines."

"Yes, usher him in. Ask for some refreshments to be brought."

"Ah Emissary Dhat, please sit, you must be weary from the long journey to our temple."

"Thank you, Abbot Paulus. Your hospitality and cooperation on this matter is most humbly acknowledged by our Lord Ranik." The emissary spoke fluently in the common tongue but was heavily accented. The gaunt man had a grey pallor about him with small spider naevi criss-crossing his face. It was apparent the tyranny of working for Tias Ranik revealed itself with an addiction to the ghan root spirit.

Paulus nodded, wondering what the cooperation was, as this was the first time that he had any discussions regarding the minerals. Dhat handed some papers to Paulus, "These are from Lord Ranik."

Vronius placed a pitcher of cooled tea and herbs before Dhat and a platter of dried meats and cheese with bread. "Thank you. I believe you come from our lands, Brother."

"Yes, I do, Emissary, from the north. A village called Crina."

"Hmm, the winter was harsh in that region this year. Do you still have family there?"

"I do, My Lord, my mother and one sister. But it has been many months since I have heard from them. If they are snowbound, then that may explain why."

"I will make enquiries upon my return."

"I am grateful, My Lord." He bowed. Vronius moved further back towards the hearth.

Paulus looked up from the emissary scroll. "The largesse of Lord Ranik is notable; for every pound of orichnite mined, one quart is to be given to the temple. It is almost too generous, for one such as your Suzerain. There is also the question of who will mine this mineral. Our stonemasons tell me it is only found deep within the bedrock and is not easily pried out. Then there is shipping it back. Of course, the Brethren's mantra of peace would not abide the mineral being used for weaponry. Also, the village council and the temples' council of scholars will need to discuss this proposal to mine so near to our sacred house. My other concern is; will the mine be so deep that it may affect the foundations of the temple."

Dhat grimaced. Obviously, this man was not a fool, but worse, he did not seem to have a price. "My Lord Abbot."

"Brother is perfectly acceptable, Emissary."

Nodding slightly at the correction Dhat continued, "The labourers will be brought from our lands. They are hardened and well used to working in such mines. They are loyal to their Lord's will."

"How will the miners or their families be rewarded?"

"Ah, well, Lord Ranik offers sanctuary and food and shelter."

"Yes, but if they are labouring here, then how do they provide for their families."

"Abbot, be assured that our people are well seasoned for such conditions and expect no more than is their due. The women work as hard as the men – hardy folk you might say."

Paulus recoiled at the flippant expression. It was known only too well that Lord Ranik's wealth was built on slavery and cruel submission. He was also a warmonger. At least if he could negotiate a mutually beneficial arrangement for the brethren, the tyrant, and the labourers, then he may succeed in containing Ranik's ambitions and keep the brethren free of his leash. "Be that as it may, these lands are far from your kingdom and these mines you have said go deeper than any others. It would mean a long weary journey for the workers as well as danger. I would expect, as would the council, that some recompense be given to whomever must delve into the mine. Of course, there must also be an assurance in bond that the minerals purpose is not for weapons. There will be demarcation of how far the mine shall be dug. I will ask the master stonemasons to mark out the boundaries of where the mineral is believed to be. You may accompany them to ensure it is accurate. This temple has stood for a thousand generations and I do not wish a foreign sovereign not akin to the way of Ira be the cause of its destruction.

"Lastly, Emissary Dhat, I will need to take council from the scholars and garner their support before I can give Lord Ranik my permission. The village council will meet in three nights. However, the scholars will not adjourn again until the next full moon. I will send letters that all members must attend as some are on pilgrimage. So, Emissary, if you wish, we can prepare a room for you in the eastern wing. Please make known any requirements you have for your stay and I will ensure that you have them."

"I will need to let Lord Ranik know of the delay. I will need parchment and ink and your swiftest kite."

"Of course. Vronius, will you take the emissary to his room and arrange for everything he needs. Emissary, you are most welcome to join the brethren for the evening meal. It is simple fare but hearty, and of course we are always keen to hear of news in the lands beyond Irasia."

"Your offer is most kind, Abbot, but there is much to report back and after such a long journey, I will beg your leave." Dhat stood. His irritation was obvious as he gave a forced bow to the Abbot.

Paulus walked to the window and let out a breath. His face was flushed with anger. Ever since the decree from Ranik had arrived, he had been on edge. Even if a deal was struck with Ranik, if at any time it no longer suited the tyrant then he would simply renege on it and take what he wanted anyway. Paulus wondered why the despot was treading lightly and why the offer was so generous. Paulus stood at the window. He felt the furry brush of the temple cat on his right hand. He began to stroke it on the cheek. "Well puss, perhaps the end days are here at the hands of Ranik. What do you think, eh?"

The ocean looked spectacular beneath him. Blue as topaz with twinkling diamonds of sunlight across its surface. The waves were mild today, only nudging the rocks below. He saw an albatross in full flight, its wings on display. He secretly envied birds, the freedom to take flight and soar above all below, lofty in their judgment and vision. For the first time Paulus could feel his mortality and it had begun to weigh on his mind. The next Abbot had not presented himself. Vronius considered himself a strong candidate, but Paulus did not. He walked over to the desk, the cat following. It jumped up onto it and sat down expectantly waiting for a pat. Paulus pulled some parchment out and began to write the summons for the Council of Scholars to gather. There were twelve members altogether, seven of whom presently dwelt in the temple. Rictus and Joab were on pilgrimage in the east. Malachi and Tristian were visiting the western temple located in the Hunjavant Region to research some scrolls recently found to make reference to Ira. That left Benedicta who was on sabbatical to be with her dying father.

As he sealed each of the papers with the order's ring emblem of seven circles with a diamond in the middle, he called Flet.

"These two will need to be sent using a kite and the others delivered in person. It must be done today, and it is of utmost urgency that the brethren attend. I have stated this in the letter, but it may need to be stated again."

"Yes, my Lord Abbot." The young man nodded and raced out with the parchments secure in his arms.

The drone of the prayer bell for twilight devotions was calling from the temple. Paulus got up to make his way down. He noted the pilgrims were also more numerous now as it neared the twilight of summer and the beginning of the leaf fall festivals. It was also nearing the eve of the decicycle turn of the sun. Some of the villagers still clung to the old ways, blended with the mantras founded by Ira. The pilgrims would come to the temple to watch the red dawns of summer change to the indigoes of leaf fall as the brethren would bless the rise of the next decicycle. Paulus felt it made for a peaceful coexistence and helped maintain a harmony amongst all believers. Vronius came back in, startling Paulus.

"Emissary Dhat has been attended to, Paulus."

"Ah good, not too put out I trust."

"No, certainly not," he said, missing the old monk's wry smile.

"Good, tell me about your land, Vronius. The legends around Lord Ranik's cruelty and prowess on the battlefield are surely exaggerated."

"Lord Ranik is not to be underestimated, Paulus. His pursuit of domination knows no bounds. My people are hardy as Dhat mentioned, but that is borne out of a life of struggle and oppression. I'm afraid, to have the great Eagle's eye turned towards you makes you his prey rather than his ally."

"Yes, it is as I thought." Paulus considered this, and the generosity that Ranik had displayed so far. He decided that he would pay the master stonemason's father a visit after the evening meal. He would not be missed as he often went for a stroll to meditate in the long summer twilights.

The sun was low in the sky, creating a beautiful hazy dusk of reds and magentas, contrasted against the ocean, made the sunset even more spectacular. Paulus made his way along a well-worn path towards the village. Normally, he would detour to the right towards the cliff edges to meditate to the soothing sounds of the ocean. However, tonight he walked towards the old master builder, Krarne's hut at the end of the village. He was a similar age to Paulus and in a time long since passed, he and Krarne had gone to the river fishing together. The old man's hut was built amongst large cedar and fir trees.

Paulus knocked on the door. The hut had a visible lean to it as the aged cedar's trunk pushed its way higher and wider into the wall of the dwelling.

"Who is it?"

"It is Paulus, Abbot of the temple." Paulus heard a humph and some shuffling. The door swung open. Krarne had aged visibly. He had become so hunched over that he could not even look up, unless he turned his head to the side.

Paulus followed him inside. The old man went straight to his cot and lay semi-reclined on some pillows and cushions. He wheezed heavily.

"My apologies, Krarne, for disturbing you, but I feel you may be able to help me with some difficult business."

"Yes, priest, what is it?" he said half dozing.

"When the foundations of the temple were restored well on fifty winters ago now, you were the chief builder?"

"Eh yes I was, bugger of work it was, Monk; dirty and back-breaking, diggin' them tunnels to get to the stone pillars. There must have been some sorcery to build the dam things in the first place."

Paulus grinned slightly. "On those digs was there anything unusual to be found, like minerals or gold or something else."

"Eh, ah, priest, I am too old to remember if there was. Nothing sticks in my mind about it, nothing but the darkness and infernal damp. The ocean will eat that temple, Monk."

"I gather that scouts were sent to look for other riches or water wells at the time of the tunnelling."

"Guesso, but I was never made privy to it. Need to check the village records or your own. Probably with the maps of the tunnels, to know if beams were needed to keep the tunnels open. Yes, it would be with the local town ordinature. Why?"

"Oh, there may be some mineral wealth under the temple that appears to interest foreigners."

"Humph, if there is it would be taken by the sea. The salt gets inta everything, ruins it. Whatever may be there would be no good for anything anyway."

"What about orichnite?"

"Ha, especially that. It's full of salt! Salt loves it and the same back. We tried to use it for blasting the stone, but it was useless."

"Would you know that when you dug it up?"

Krarne nodded. "Should be like fine black sand, but the salt makes it into pebbles."

Krarne began to wheeze then cough, blood shot out onto the calico apron Paulus wore over his robes.

"Begs me," he said and lay back wheezing heavily.

"Not at all." Paulus rose to leave. "Thank you, Krarne, we may not meet again. I will offer alms for you that things are swift."

Krarne nodded slightly and then began to doze off.

Paulus closed the door and left the old man. He was more anxious than ever now. What was Ranik up to? The tyrant was no fool, he would know how low quality the minerals were here. The Abbot decided that he would request the maps of the foundations from the archival chamber.

The sun had set as he began to make his way back to the temple. The path was completely shrouded in intertwining branches and vines, giving the effect of a long tunnel. Soon it was completely dark. Up in the distance he could see the torch light that was the entrance to the kitchens. He felt a sudden gust of wind behind him. Walking along, he felt watched. He reached the door and knocked to be let in. It opened.

"Thank you, Igna..." Looking back down the lane, Paulus' heart froze. In the gloom amongst the trees two red eyes glared. They were surrounded by a dark shadow blocking the lane way. The shadow seemed as tall as a man. Then it disappeared. Paulus stumbled, grabbing his chest at the same time. He fell into Ignatius, the head cook.

"Abbot?"

Paulus righted himself. "I am okay." Breathing heavily, he looked again into the woods, but there was nothing there.

Ignatius came to the door. "Are there gypsies?"

"Eh, no, just an old man's mind playing tricks. Have you noticed anything strange, like animals in the woods?"

Walking over to the well in the middle of the kitchen, Ignatius lowered the bucket in to fetch some fresh water for the Abbot.

"Sit, no, nothing."

He brought the bucket back up and ladled some water into a bowl to drink. "Here, Abbot, it will refresh you."

Paulus nodded gratefully. "I thought I saw something staring at me just now."

"I will ask some of the brethren who go to meditate in the woods if they have seen anything."

"Yes, please do, but do not alarm anyone, as I said, it could be my mind playing tricks."

Paulus got up and made for his chambers. "Thank you, Ignatius."

"Of course."

Ignatius watched Paulus hobble towards the stairs. He motioned Micah, a novice who had just returned from evening prayer. "Follow the Abbot to his rooms. Make sure he reaches his door safely."

Micah nodded enthusiastically. He bounded up to Paulus and gently placed a hand under the old man's arm and walked with him.

Paulus looked up, hesitated slightly, but relented and nodded in agreement. He kept walking, assisted by the young man.

Ignatius went to the door and looked out once more. He could see nothing but decided it might be worth placing some extra torches in the main pathway.

Paulus and Micah reached the door of the Abbot's chamber. "Thank you, Micah, I will be fine now."

Paulus walked into his room and closed the door. The sound of the ocean came to him at once soothing his nerves and racing heart. He walked over to his cot. Undoing the rope around his waist and removing his outer robes, he lay down on the bed and closed his eyes. The red eyes burned there in his vision. The shadow had the shape of a man with long fingers, almost claw-like. He shivered again. Those eyes stared straight through him, as if searching his mind to find something lost. He grabbed the penitential scapula around his neck. He felt the constant burn in his chest slowly grow as the vision of the eyes began to overtake his mind. He tried to meditate but the searing eyes would not go away. He concentrated on the ocean, its tides washing the shore clean, taking away each day's memories and clearing the way for new ones to be made. He began to drift. Faces came to him – Vronius looking back over his shoulder, Dhat, Flet and then Krarne, then Ignatius. But behind all the images, something scraped at his mind; full with a desperate longing, wanting to get into the world. Its impatience was palpable, quickening with every passing summer, and now it knocked as the ocean knocked on the foundations below. A far roar pervaded the scratching. Suddenly Paulus mind was engulfed in the most appalling darkness. He saw a vision of a man swinging in the wind from a cross beam, his eyes gone, his mouth in a grimace of pain. Fluttering at the top of the main beam was a flag, shredded. It was black with a red eagle on it. The image faded, but the blackness remained, and the scratching became closer and more intense. Paulus writhed in fear and tried to wrench his mind back. But the scratching became so loud he could feel it ringing in his ears. He saw the flag burst into flames and the man's body decay into oblivion. A thousand screams seemed to come from the tongues of the fire as they consumed the man.

In the room, Paulus' body was soaked in sweat. He shivered and convulsed as he tried to take control of his mind. His knuckles were white, and blood dripped between his fingers where his nails had dug into the flesh as he gripped the relic of Ira. He felt the protecting power of the amulet stopping him being subsumed by the darkness. He woke briefly, the nightmare dissipated, but as he closed his eyes, again the scratching began, once more lapsing him into a fever.

Vronius and Flet tended to him. Paulus had never been this ill before. The brethren prayed and the villagers offered alms for his recovery. The old man shrivelled before their eyes. It was as if something was eating him from the inside. After two days of no change in the Abbot a meeting was called with the council to determine what to do if Paulus did not recover.

Godryn, the apothecary stood before the council.

"What is it that ails him, Sister?" asked Edram the lead scholar.

"I do not know. There are no pox or animal bites. Ignatius said the Abbot came home agitated after a walk, believing he had seen something in the woods, but no one else has seen anything. It could be a malady of his mind that makes him convulse so. I have seen these fevers before, in the Middle isles to the south, during their warm rainy seasons, but never here. The people believed that it is a bite of a demon. I know of their remedies for fevers and one in particular that may alleviate whatever afflicts the Abbot, but it requires a herb. Its called thorny janafille and is only found far to the west along the Aesearean coast. It will be at least two days walk there and back."

Brother Edram sighed heavily. "It seems there is no other choice, Godryn, you will need to remain here to tend to the Abbot, send one of the novices to fetch this herb. The council needs to decide what to do if Paulus passes into enlightenment of death. With no clear indication who will be suitable to continue in the Abbot chair, the law decrees that for two summers and winters there will be mourning for the Abbot who has passed, and none shall replace him. After this time, an invitation will be sent out to all the brethren for a great gathering. Those who wish to fulfil the legacy of our founder and become Abbot will be scrutinized by the council members. It will then be decided by voting who shall continue in Ira's steps."

The members agreed with Edram. Godryn rose and left to find Flet.

Paulus lay in his excrement and sweat. His hand firmly clenched on his relic in his rigour. His mind was blank. He heard no voices nor felt pain. He had been entombed in the darkness. Every now and then, he would hear the scratching come back, but his hand would tighten, and the hateful noise would lessen.

Vronius bathed the old man to keep him cool but showed

no emotion. Brother Ignatius, overwrought at the sight of the man he had helped and served, became frustrated with Vronius.

"What are you made of? The black obsidian that holds this temple up? The wooden beam that no one can bend? Waiting for him to pass from us to take his place? You are constantly hovering but do nothing to ease his suffering. Always at his side, quickly, too quickly. You are barely forty summers and yet here you are, tending him and placing yourself almost in the chair that this man is most worthy of holding. While you, no scholarly advice has been handed down yet, no sermons in the temple, no offerings and pilgrimages. What sort of Irasian are you?" It was as if Ignatius unleashed all his fear and grief onto Vronius.

Vronius had been listening to the tirade, but again did not display one bit of emotion or offence. As it was contrary to the brethren to be vain and ambitious particularly for the place of the Abbot, a reaction would be expected, but Vronius merely wrung the cloth out, refolded it, and placed it on Paulus' forehead. Turning to Ignatius, he said, "I only serve the brethren and Paulus. It is the Abbot's suffering that we must pray to end, not our own fear, Brother."

"Hmph! We shall see what Sister Godryn is able to do."

Ignatius left but thought he saw a flash of anger in the monk's eyes. He walked off to the kitchens to begin preparing the evening meal. He was annoyed at the lack of reaction again by Vronius and at himself; he knew he had disgraced himself as an Irasian; and to have done it in front of Paulus' obvious suffering only made his regret the greater. He would make a pilgrimage if Paulus recovered. The cook thought of

Vronius again. He had an aloof demeanour. Ignatius could not remember one sermon or great act of self-denial in the time he had been in the temple, but somehow, he had risen to become Sous-Abbot to Paulus. And now the hateful Ranik of Matavia, the same land of Vronius birth had his eye turned on the holy temple.

"None the less, Ignatius, you will do pilgrimage and alms once Paulus is restored," he muttered to himself as he began to chop some carrots.

Godryn prayed ardently beside Paulus's cot. Every turn of the hourglass, she would place two drops of lotion onto his lips. She rubbed it onto his hands and feet, hoping that Paulus' body would go limp and lose its rigidity.

Godryn was worried, she saw how the old man's hands had clenched onto the penitential relic, and nothing would budge it from his grip. None of the remedies worked, by the fifth day, any hope in the apothecary of being able to restore her Abbot was destroyed when she saw the emaciated body of Paulus.

Flet arrived back with pouches of the janafille. Godryn met him in her chamber, which was full of scrolls and bunches of herbs and ground powders. A heady pungent smell struck Flet – not unpleasant, but it made him feel light-headed.

"Fetch me some water and ask Ignatius if he has any goat nettles and dandelions. Bring them to me. I may need a lot, so ask for all his stores. I am not sure how affective this will be or how long it may take."

Flet shot off as Godryn began to prepare the janafille. It had a peppery scent. As she pulled the leaves off, her fingertips tingled from their sting. She pounded it into a paste. Flet entered with sacks full of nettles and dandelions and buckets of water. Two other kitchen hands walked in carrying more of the plants.

"Good. Place the water in the pot over the fire and put half of the nettles and flowers into it." Godryn scraped the paste into the pot. Then she went over to a crate on a table. Something moved inside. She had a grimace on her face. Stopping, she looked towards Flet and the other novices.

"You may leave now. Thank you for your help." The two girls scooted off while Flet stayed. "You also, Flet. I will call when you are needed." Flet nodded feeling a little miffed.

Godryn saw his look of disappointment. "It will take many hours to brew, Flet. I will fetch you when it is complete."

After he left, Godryn went to the crate. Inside was a guinea pig. Godryn disliked the old ways for this reason. She had not mentioned that the fresh blood of an animal and the flesh and blood of a newly dead babe were also the ingredients for the tonic. Neither of these would be allowed by the brethren. As she broke the pig's neck, it made a little squeak.

"Sorry, little one."

Slitting its throat, Godryn drained the blood directly into the concoction on the hearth. She threw the carcass into brew as well. An acrid smell rose into her nostrils.

Then cleaning the knife, she made a cut along her left arm and let her blood drip into the brew also.

"Hopefully the blood of a celibate will do just as well as a babe's." She sighed over the bubbling mixture.

She let it drip until the bleeding stopped from the wound. Stirring it once more, she noted from the old parchment that it must simmer overnight.

Godryn relaxed slightly. She placed liniment on her arm and wrapped muslin around it. She went to the window and looked out at the ocean. Memories of Paulus came back to her, in particular, her first meeting with him. They had travelled together a long time. Paulus had seen Godryn's aptitude for the nature of things, and how they worked. To her father's chagrin, the Irasian life called more than the earthy toil of a farmer's concubine. The smell from the hearth became more overpowering as the ingredients began to breakdown. She began to meditate concentrating on the dotted night sky. The moon stared at her, instilling its silent watchfulness in her mind.

Up above Godryn, the Abbot lay entombed in dreams of terror. In the paralysed body, the old monk's mind felt the scratching nearing. It was crushing all the walls Paulus put up to stop it reaching the locked knowledge the presence sought. The sound of something ripping violently entered the darkness so strongly that it jolted the lifeless body. Something wanted to penetrate it, scry something out of him. Then he felt the claw catch him. His body began to perspire as he tried to flee whatever it was peeling away the layers of his mind.

Vronius watched the old man writhe with the pain. He understood what the old man was seeing. He quietly meditated as well, waiting for the lesser one to break under the clutches of the shadow. Ignatius entered the sitting room. He quietly put a tray of soup and bread there for Vronius. He saw the candlelight flickering in the room where the Abbot lay. He briefly looked over towards the bed and saw Vronius leaning over Paulus with his lips moving. He turned towards Ignatius looking at him with a derisive smile. Vronius' eyes looked vacant and did not appear to recognize Ignatius. As he looked away, they were slightly tinged with red. Ignatius felt a cold dread come into his chest and left hastily. When he reached the kitchens, he took a bottle of cooking brandy and swigged out of it.

Morning came and Godryn woke up suddenly with a cat purring on her lap and a stiff neck from sleeping against the wall.

She went over to the pot. In it was a thick stew, dusky green colour with a smell of grass and of something sweet and rotten. She scooped out the pig's bones and threw them into the hearth. She ladled some of the soup into a bowl. Noting again, what the recipe called for, she made her way to Paulus' room. The first thing she saw was how much Paulus had deteriorated during the night. She sat next to him. She opened Paulus' mouth and began to ladle the soup into it. It would need to be done four times a day until the person was released from the fever. She also placed some bushels of the janafille around the Abbot, threw some into the hearth, and lit them. They sent aromatic fumes throughout the chamber.

Vronius reappeared after breakfast and walked into the room. Instantly, he could smell the tonic Godryn had prepared and recoiled from it.

"Sister, what is that?"

"It is our last hope otherwise ..."

"It smells like poison," he retorted.

"Yes, it is potent, no doubt. We will wait and see. Go see to your other chores, Vronius. I must wait with the Abbot and follow the recipe closely to ensure the best hope of curing him."

Vronius hesitated, but the smell made him ill forcing him to leave.

On the dawn of the fourth morning, Godryn was running out of the first batch of tonic. She had another batch brewing in her chamber. As she just finished ladling another dose into Paulus, Godryn saw the right hand unclench around the relic of Ira. A deep long sigh emitted from his mouth. Then stillness. Godryn thought he had died, but then the Abbot's eyes flew open and grabbed Godryn's arm. He took great gasps of air and stared wildly around the room.

"Paulus, it is Godryn."

Paulus looked at her stunned. "Godryn," he said weakly, "Godryn."

He relaxed slightly. "Water."

Godryn bought a bowl over to him and helped him sip.

Paulus closed his eyes. "Oh, Godryn, how long?"

"Fourteen sunrises and sunsets have passed you by, Abbot."

"I did not relinquish it. It wanted something, but I did not relent, by Ira's strength I remain, and the covenant is still unbroken."

"Rest, Paulus, you are very weak still. I will bathe you. Flet, bring warm water and salts," she called out to the assistant. Flet instantly flew in to see what was happening. A look of relief came over the boy's face to see Paulus awake.

Paulus closed his eyes, but the darkness startled him. He opened them again, sucking in the light.

"Don't leave, Godryn. Brighten the light, bring in flints and torches."

"It is good to hear your voice, Paulus."

Paulus nodded.

Vronius and Edram entered and saw that Paulus was awake.

"Perhaps it is best if we give the abbot time to recover a little more," Godryn said.

"I will look after him, Apothecary Godryn, you have served the abbot enough. Surely you are tired."

Godryn felt Paulus squeeze his arm as Vronius suggested she leave.

"I think I can manage a little more, Vronius, thank you."

Flet brought the water and some fresh linen. Godryn ushered all of them out. She gently propped Paulus up and began to feed him some more. He took a few sips and bought them up.

"What is that?"

"A tonic I have prepared to break the fevers you were having."

Paulus finished half the soup and lay down again.

Godryn gently removed the Abbot's robes. She saw how emaciated Paulus had become. On his skin were welts and sores from lying down for so long. There were other marks as well, like long thin scratches as if a claw had grazed him.

Placing some salts into the water, Godryn washed the wounds again. Then she redressed the Abbot in a fresh robe.

"You must rest now; the fevers may return."

"Please stay with me."

Godryn watched Paulus fight his exhaustion for almost an hour but eventually his eyes did close. She noticed the fear in Paulus' eyes. Once his chest was moving in a rhythmic fashion, she got up to stretch. She walked into the sitting room and looked out onto the ocean. There was a gentle knock.

"Come in." It was Flet and Edram.

"Paulus is asleep again. It is too early to tell if he has recovered from the fever."

"What do you think it was?" asked Edram, looking over Paulus and sniffing the bowl of tonic.

"I do not know. There were strange scratches on his back. Perhaps a wild animal unknown to these parts attacked him in the woods."

"The full council have arrived as requested by the Abbot before he was taken with fever. I will let them know that Paulus has awoken but needs to regain his strength."

"Thank you, Brother. I would also ask that visitors besides yourself and Flet, not be permitted to see him just yet. I think it would be wiser for Paulus' sake."

"As you say. I will announce it at the noonday meal. Thank you, Sister, Ira's peace be with you."

Godryn nodded in gratitude and sat down to eat some bread. The temple cat walked in and began to rub against her leg purring busily.

Paulus slept for almost a full day and night with nothing disturbing him, even when Godryn ladled the tonic into his mouth.

On the third day since the fever had broken, Godryn had been dozing near the hearth when she heard Paulus stirring. He had managed to sit himself up on the bed with his legs touching the floor.

"Water." He quickly glanced towards the window. "It will be daylight soon."

"Yes."

"Help me up."

"No, you are still too weak."

They both heard the gong for the morning gathering. Instinctively, they both went to rise.

"I will help you to the chair." Putting her shoulder under Paulus' arm, she walked him over to it. She noticed the abbot was as light as parchment.

"Take some more water."

"Oh Godryn, do you know what I dreamed of last night?"

"No, Paulus."

"The sound of the waves below."

For another seven sunrises, Godryn nursed Paulus until he was able to stand. Each day his strength and appetite returned. Still gaunt and drawn in the face, his eyes were more alert and seemed a little less fearful. Edram came to see him as Godryn walked him around the chamber one morning.

"Emissary Dhat has inspected the foundations and old tunnels with the stonemason. They will have the writ completed by the time the council meets."

Memories began to come back to Paulus of the meeting with Dhat and Krarne.

"Can you ask Flet to bring the maps of the tunnels from the first restoration. I wish to check something before the adjournment of the council."

"Of course. It's good to see you are more robust, Abbot."

Vronius began to spend more time with Paulus as his strength returned. Godryn saw no point in trying to stop him now.

"Your tonic was certainly very potent, Godryn. Who taught you the recipe?"

"The female chieftains in the middle isle called Tarus. They cling to the old ways, but they have the wisdom of ages as well. By the faith, Ira's favour certainly looked upon the Abbot also."

"What is in it?"

"Mostly the janafille from the Aesearean Sea, nettles, and dandelions."

"It seems such a simple concoction."

"I think Paulus resolve and hearty Aeserean constitution also had a part to play."

Godryn got up. "If you will excuse me, I have some errands to run, Paulus. I will need to find some more herbs that will be more restorative for you. I believe the council will meet tomorrow."

"Yes, of course, Sister, I may even attempt the temple today and I'm sure Vronius has much to discuss. Godryn, we have known each other many summers. Do you remember our first meeting, old friend?"

"Oh, I do indeed, Paulus, nearly fifty summers ago, now. I am glad that we may yet see the end of another one as well."

Godryn lingered a little bit, touched by Paulus attempt at a thank you. Ever the ascetic, emotion wasn't his strongest attribute. Leaving, she saw a strange look on Vronius face and noticed how dark his eyes were.

12

Fear and Courage

Ange woke. The sudden movement sent a bolt of pain through her. Her tongue was swollen and it was so parched it scraped the inside of her mouth. She slowly rubbed the sand from her eyes and tried to move again. The pain returned. She began to cry softly as she thought of Tessi.

"Oh Tessi, Mata." She kept crying. Her stomach cramped with dehydration and hunger. She moved, the pain bloomed, but she kept going, inching herself upright. Eventually, she got herself up against the tree. She felt a drop on her hand. The tap the slavers had made was still open. She raised her hand, whimpering as the pain seared into her ribs. She sucked the water off her knuckle. She reached for more. She made the almighty effort to twist up towards it, but the burst of agony made her blackout briefly. Panting with fatigue, she remembered Tessi tearing some of her tunic and soaking it in the water. She moved under the drip and let her shoulder get soaked. Once it was saturated, she sucked on the cloth greedily. The sun had almost set again. Tessi would be far away. She looked for her sack but could not see it. It had probable fallen down the edge of the dune. She settled back against the great boab. Its bark soothed her as the night breeze cooled her face. She sucked some more of the cloth. The nipple in the great tree was plentiful as the sap dripped continuously. She dozed again, but her dreams were bombarded with images of Tessi screaming, her mother dying, and dead bodies floating in the river.

A shadow with peering red eyes silently walked in the night. The wolf sniffed the air. It could smell something alive, not the stench of decay it was used to but old blood and memory. It wandered off. It was close, but its eyes were too veiled. It could taste the deepness of time in this place. There would be great strength here. The moonlight came out from behind the clouds suddenly revealing Voloc's form.

"Voloc what do you sense?" came the voice of the master far off in his cave.

"I smell the blood of an ancient, but it remains hidden to my sight."

Soon the Belmaris would move into its leaf fall slumber weakening its gaze, setting Voloc and the god free to roam beyond the protection of nightshade.

As Ange slept, oblivious to Voloc, her fingers moved minutely playing with the beads Bensah had given her. She didn't see their dim glow as the demon of the void neared and then moved away. The power within the stones and the elemental nature of Voloc were drawn to each other.

The shadow loped across the dunes catching Tessi's scent and blood on the sand. "One has walked on this earth who is drawn from the same ancients."

It turned away from Ange and began to follow the slaver's caravan.

Again, Ange woke, shivering from the cold air of the indigo dawn. A little pool had formed near her from the dripping wound in the tree. She soaked the cloth and drank again. She tried to stand, but her legs were numb. Weakly, she got to her feet. Steadying herself against the tree, she stood. Her breathing was raspy, and her ribs ached terribly, but her hunger made her walk. Stumbling over the dune she found the sacks they had brought. Inside them were the cakes they had made with their mother.

They were stale and gritty with sand, but she ate them greedily. Her stomach grumbled loudly breaking the silence around her. Looking through Tessi's things, she found her set of beads and put them on, and another shawl. There were some coins and the cloth of Tessi's dowry. She put them in her own sack and buried Tessi's. She cried again. Ange didn't know what to do. The man had said Ancrid City, perhaps she could follow and try to find her. Going back to the trees, Ange rested again. That night while she slept, instead of nightmares, she dreamt of the lady who had visited her at the well.

"Go north, to the grove. Leave while the moon is full and blinds the shadows of the night."

With the words, a dream washed over her of a moonlit grove with thin trees. It made her feel at peace, as if none of the nightmare she lived in now had happened. But the soft brush of a lizard crawling on her to drink at the little pool of water startled her; it skittered away at her movement. She gazed at the moon and realised how close it seemed all of a sudden. She tried hard to see faces inside its mottled surface, but nothing came. She willed herself to think of Tessi and Mata. She remembered sitting with them as they weaved a mat for the sitting area in the hut. Tata had brought the fine but sturdy calico yarn. Elanai had let Ange choose the weave pattern.

"One day, Ange, you will be able to sell your own mats and have a place at the end of the village. You will be called the weaver woman and you will be remembered for your nimble fingers," spoke her mother.

"But what if I want to be a sunbride, Mata?" she had asked innocently at the age of nine summers. No one answered her as they sat happily bringing the mat to life. Tessi had hugged her closely.

"It is because of my leg and my shape. I see how I am different, but I am the same as you all, Mata. I don't understand why Pata does not see it."

Her mother had remained silent for a long time. They had finished three rows before she answered.

"We only choose what we want to see. I often look into the night sky and think it is not Ancrid our god who lives there, but eyes which are snatched from us when we are born. One day they will fall to the ground again and we will put them back into our heads and we will finally understand how foolish we truly are. The elders and Pata wanted to kill you, Ange, when you were born. It was our tradition for it served us as a people. It was from the days of being wanderers and the desert was hard and had no mercy. You didn't walk until the seventh summer of your life and that is too long for nomads of the desert. But when you were born, I looked at those stars and felt a prick in my eye. Then I saw you in my arms. And I saw me and my mata and her mata before her, and all the way back to the beginning days. I asked, if I killed you, then do I forget the flesh and bones of a hundred generations of women with the same blood that has brought you here to me. So, I said, no, you must live, or my history dies along with you. The elders and your pata will never let you be a sunbride. I even think, deep down, I do not wish my life for you, Ange. It is difficult…" Mata had looked at Pata sitting outside. "But I do know that you made me look at the sky; and I could see for a thousand turns of the sun, like I had the memories of the great god Ancrid. I wept at the scorn I had thrust upon your shoulders by keeping you alive and almost broke with the weight of all those who came before you and Tessi. But the love, Ange, between us, and you and Tessi, and even when Tata Bensah comes, with his mongrel, Nekoda, then I know the grief is worth it. Please forgive me daughter, but I know the weaver woman who sits before me now at one time revealed to her mata what only the gods and stars can see."

A single tear slipped down her face at the memory. Mata was strict but she was strong. It was the first time Ange felt love and grief, for she knew how despised she truly was for her form and how, if not for her mother, she would not be at all. For Ange love and grief would always lived together within her heart.

She rolled over. Her back was less painful, and her breathing was less noisy over the last day and night. Deeply frightened, she knew she must leave for Ancrid City. On the dawn, she began to ready herself to walk as far as possible before the heat of the day reached its full strength. The man had said it took a day to Ancrid City. It lay to the east, where the sun rose. She still had some millet cakes and she soaked one shawl in water and wrapped it up tight so it would not dry out quickly. She also found a small leather cask on the sand. It had been dropped by one of the men. It smelt very strange like Pata's drink. Ange took it to the dripping water and let it fill. Her side still ached and occasionally a sudden pain would shoot through her, but she could bare it. The sand dunes looked like ripples of the Choasa river in the moonlight spreading out forever before her. She stepped out, daydreaming that she would find Tessi and they would walk to the grove together. The boabs remained steadfast in their constant vigil over the desert as she departed across the great sandy ocean. Ange was too young to be afraid of death or understand it fully, but her fear of not having anyone filled her heart with such sorrow that it almost ached more than her broken body. It would be a long hard walk as her little feet climbed up and down the sand. Loneliness engulfed Ange. She pined so much for Tessi and Mata that a dry sob escaped her.

She watched the sun rise in the east. The rays that spread their way along the dunes did not warm her or make her feel comforted. Ange could see in the hazy distance the city outskirts. It frightened her more to see it. She knew she must go there, but what would happen. Covering herself over with her shawls as she walked, she munched on a cake. She could buy some more food with the stones and coins she had. She was thinking of Nekoda for some reason. His warmth at night would have been welcome. By the end of the day, Ange had reached a few outlying huts which had been hastily erected by other refugees like her. Not many people were about so she made her way around as far as possible from the dwellings. She would be in danger if someone saw her on her own. She made camp in a clump of bushes. A red wren squeaked its indignation at her intrusion and hopped crankily around the twigs at her. She smiled a little. She was so tired, her lips were cracked, and her face was peeling from sun burn. A dull throb remained in her ribs. She swigged a little more water and biscuit and went to sleep. Murmurs from people walking by occasionally woke her, but she remained hidden from them inside her sanctuary she shared with the little wren.

Bensah and Nekoda walked into Kensai. He stopped to look at the destruction. Bensah had not held great hope of finding anyone alive. His own village had been decimated as well. He had barely arrived back when the plagues and storm struck. Sara was dead by the time he had reached his home, as was most of his livestock. A few like him had survived. They were making their way west towards the highlands, not realising that the same fate had struck there as well. Bensah had decided to head back towards his trading route, he would check on Noai and then head toward Ancrid City. If need be, he would re-establish there if it had not been affected.

Bensah felt little emotion at the loss of everything; he believed the earth took back what it gave. Inspecting the place that was once Noai's, he found the remains of a body. The charred garment looked like a woman's shawl. There wasn't any trace of the girls. He saw the trails of camels leading out of the village, typical of a slavers' caravan. He hoped deep inside that the plague had taken the girls before the slavers had arrived.

"Time to go, Nekoda."

Nekoda had been foraging in the cinders of the burnt relics of Kensai.

"We will go to the boabs and then towards Ancrid City." Nekoda gave a bored yawn and trotted off.

The wind blew again. Bensah braced himself for another storm to come, but it didn't. He eventually reached the boabs: still and constant in the land, like eternal keepers of the desert on watch for the weary and thirsty. Bensah sighed. "It gives and it takes."

The large dune was still there and even more menacing than when Bensah first sighted it so many moons ago now. He noticed the well of water, which had grown to be quite large since Ange's departure. Nekoda helped himself to it and gulped it all up.

Bensah smiled at the simple brashness of the dog. He inspected the tap. It was done very cleanly, but it was unusual to be left open. Whoever did it either wasn't a seasoned traveller to the desert or was not intending to return.

He refilled his casks and let Nekoda lap up more and then blocked it again. He would sit out the noon-day sun and leave again in the early dusk. He had traversed this part so often that even at night he could navigate the desert. He began to spread out his scarf over some of the branches to make shelter. He noticed a sack lying at the other side of the Boab. He went over to it and looked inside. It held some braids and at the bottom was a bead. It was like the ones he had given Tessi and Ange. They had come here. He searched around and noted another camp had been made. He pulled a flask out of the sand and sniffed it, the brew the northerners drink, usually slavers. His heart sank with the thought that the girls had survived only to be taken by the slavers. Perhaps he may find them again in Ancrid City. He lay down under his tent and dozed. Nekoda came over after a little while and settled in as well.

Ange walked around towards the main entrance of Ancrid City. It was bustling with markets and traders selling all sorts of wares. A rivulet of sewer and refuse flowed down toward the western side of the city. She had wrapped her shawls around her body and head to disguise herself. There were so many drifters coming in from the plague that ravaged the land she blended in. Ange could smell food. Patiently waiting, she mingled in amongst the crowd. She had often seen Mata barter at the markets. She would not give in straight away and would try to be firm on her starting offer. She took a deep breath and pointed to some flat millet cakes. Holding her hand up she made a signal for ten and for some flour and flint as well as some cinnamon sticks and taro. She could make food on the way to the grove and it would not be too heavy to carry. Her stomach roared at the smells that hit her. She saw people buying fresh goat's milk and honey.

The merchant gestured five kapos for each. Ange shook her head as she picked out three beads she had taken from her necklace. He nodded. She took the goods and went to the man selling the milk.

"Milk and one pot of honey."

The clay pots were as high as her knee, too heavy to carry for long distances and had no lid, but she could make herself some sweetened cakes to carry. She stacked the pots on each other and and placed the flour and cinnamon in her satchel. Reaching her camp she sat straight down and drew the milk to her mouth. She dipped her finger into the honey and stirred her finger through the milk and sipped again. She drank it down quickly. She felt sick as the richness of the milk and honey bombarded her stomach but was satisfied as well. Getting up, she decided to risk walking into the city. She had felt a little braver since the market. Too many people had been uprooted by the plague for anyone to care who she was. The goat milk man had called her El samata, meaning old mother. Her limp and cracked skin made them think she was an old woman. Entering the main gates, the city was a series of high red mud brick buildings, laid out in a circular fashion around the temple dedicated to the city namesake Ancrid, god of the desert. The buildings were very imposing as they only contained narrow slit like windows, making the facades unwelcoming and impenetrable. The desert winds that sometimes tore through the city often destroyed whole areas, therefore there was a full-time quarry of bricks, and labourers, just to keep the buildings erect.

It was quieter within the walls as it was the mid-afternoon when people normally took a meal and a rest from the heat. The houses had muslin shrouds hanging out of the windows and entrances. They gently swayed in the breeze almost like sailing boats in mudbrick walls. Women had gathered around a well to wash their clothes. Some smaller children played around them. One of them pointed at Ange walking past. His mother told him to run home. Ange continued into the next square. Men were gathered in groups tossing pebbles, Ange's heart twinged when a memory came of Noai and Bensah and the other men in the village playing the same game. She began to cry a little as Tessi came to her mind. Waddling past, she went further in towards the temple. Eventually, she reached the inner plaza and immediately saw a running fountain of water. Women were filling clay jars and then hoisting them on their shoulders. They walked in an elegant procession back to their homes. Ange noticed some of the women left alms while others did not. A high priest from the temple walked past her into the temple itself. Its imposing facade had only one door that opened like a black mouth. Ange could see nothing inside. Someone touched her on the shoulder, and she froze with fear. Turning around, a guard of the temple was looking down at her.

"You cannot loiter here, El samata, take water or leave." The guard looked at her hesitantly, realising that she was younger than he thought.

Ange bowed subserviently as she tried to conceal her face and quickly left. The guard was staring too long and she suddenly lost her courage. She would come back tomorrow to fetch some water before she left. She darted back down the alley the way she had come but took a wrong turn. She began to panic as she became more lost. Tears streamed down her face. Looking behind her fearfully, she expected to see the guard following her, but there was no one there. She sunk down against the wall and started to cry again. She silently whispered Mata and Tessi's name. Slowly her fear subsided, allowing her to get up again. The shadows were becoming long, and she didn't want to be lost in the dark. Walking back the way she came, she scooted back down the alley leading toward the temple. The guard was not there. As she approached the main square again, her heart froze. Lined up outside along the road were women in chains. Just briefly, a glimmer of hope came to her that she would see Tessi. But as she scanned the unfamiliar faces her heart sank just as quickly as the hope had sprouted inside her. Two men came along with a pail of water for the girls to drink, they were not like the northerners but tribesmen from the plateaus. They had bones pierced through their noses and shaved heads. She quickly walked past, fully covering her face. Ange recognised the lane she had entered by when she saw a small cart with tangerines laid out for sale. The smell of them had struck her and their colour. She had never seen such food before. She sped down the lane past the vibrant piles of fruit relieved she had remained unseen and still free.

When she got back to her little shelter, she sat down. Suddenly a wave of grief engulfed her. She just wanted Tessi to be here so much. Through her tears, she struck the flint to make a fire. Pulling out the clay bowl, she put it on the fire to warm. Then she began to make her millet cakes. She only needed a little water with each as she mixed the honey and crushed the cinnamon into the mixture. She wished she had some more milk to drink with it. A vision of a dark night that never ended loomed in front of her, as she realised that many more days would come which she would need to face alone. This thought made her eyes well up with tears again as she scooped the cakes off the hot bowl and ate them. She licked the dregs of the honey from her fingers. It was completely dark now. The stars twinkled in the sky. She noticed the little wren asleep on her eggs in her nest. Rolling over, Ange eventually slept. Her legs and body jolted as her dreams were bombarded with the ugly faces of the slavers and dead people floating in the Choasa.

Waking just before dawn she quickly packed her things. She slung her satchel across her chest and winced with pain as it touched her ribs. She would go to the well, fill the casks she had bought, and leave. She remembered there was a road leading away from Ancrid City towards the mountains. The gates to road to the north were on the other side of the great temple.

On reaching the entrance to the city, the main gates were still shut but she saw a small hatch open for a merchant arriving at the same time as herself. She walked through unnoticed, as it was usual for women to go to the temple early for worship before the men arrived. Quickly, Ange made her way to the fountains. She was the only one there. A priest opened the doors to the temple. It looked like Nekoda with massive jaw's yawning. Ange filled her flasks and left two beads. She walked as quickly as she could, lopsided as the water made her sack heavy. A group of men walked in from the main alley way. Ange bumped into one of them.

"Eh, el samata," he said and nudged her aside. Ange hesitated at the voice, as it sounded familiar. Not wanting to draw any more attention, she kept walking. The man had stopped and turned, looking at what he thought was an old woman. He stood thoughtfully looking at the creature waddling away.

He went to the fountain to drink before entering the temple. He drank generously. As he scooped more water up, he looked into the bowl where the alms were held. He stopped suddenly when he saw the two beads. Standing up quickly, he searched the square for the old woman, but he could not see her.

"Eh, Bensah, where are you going?" called a man at the entrance to the temple.

"I will be back." He went down the alley hoping to see the woman. Nothing. He turned down another alley.

Bensah began to run over the other side of the temple plaza. As he got to the other entrance, he saw in the distance the hooded figure walking with a limp amidst the crowd. He couldn't get closer as people began to flock in for the morning markets. He watched the figure push further through the crowd in the opposite direction and then turn onto the road that led away towards the north. A gust of wind blew causing the shawl that covered Ange's head to fly off. She glanced around her briefly to make sure no one was watching. She pulled it back over. It was enough though for Bensah to see her.

"Praise be, Ancrid! But where is she going?"

"Bensah El Bunani, we're waiting" called Antsa. Bensah had arranged a meeting with some slavers.

"I'm coming." Torn between searching for Tessi and following Ange, Bensah decided that at least he knew which direction to look for Ange. Tessi was still unknown and in danger. He turned and headed toward his friend.

Once Ange had broken free of the crowds leading into the city, she made a better pace. She felt more relief when she was away from the city. Its slit-like windows looked like black eyes watching her. There were still a lot of people about, so she made sure her face was fully covered with a tiny gap for her eyes.

By mid-afternoon her legs and back were beginning to cramp. The number of travellers on the road had dwindled so that now she was walking alone for long periods. The path had slowly become steeper as it neared the smaller ranges that hid the ocean from view of the city. With the climb, the desert slowly gave way to scrub and grasses. Seeing a cluster of trees, she decided to go towards them. Ange made her camp, ate a millet cake, and drank some water. Lying down she waited for night and the stars to appear. "I can see your eyes watching, Mata. I hope they show me how to find the grove the lady spoke about."

She drifted off with Tessi and Mata on her mind. Waking with a start, she heard voices. A family had camped near her. She gathered all her things around her.

A man got up when he heard her move. Bowing slightly, he greeted Ange. "Sister." The group were laying their bedding out for the night. It was still dark; the only light was coming from their fire. She lay down again waiting for them to go to sleep. Eventually, the fire died, and everything was quiet. She got up slowly, put her things in a sack, and crept back onto the road. Walking until dawn, she slowed down realizing that there was only one road and she would see the same people travelling in her direction anyway. As the sun rose it lit up an imposing wall of grey rock, extending along the full line of the horizon. It was the northern ranges. Her heart sank as the forbidding wall of rock seemed to glare at her, telling her not to come. She shivered as she continued. She saw the same family that had she left behind during the night. They would walk with a quicker pace than her, so she decided to hide behind a bush until they were ahead. As she crouched behind, a scorpion ran onto her hand. Startled she jumped and shook her hand to flick it off but tripped over a rock. Landing heavily, she blacked out and rolled down a small embankment. Her water and flour spilled out of the sack. She got up, desperately trying to save her water. She managed to salvage one flask, but the flour was ruined. She burst into tears again. Just then, she felt a sharp sting on her leg. The scorpion came running from under her tunic. She kicked it away. Her leg began to swell rapidly and throb. She pulled herself up towards the bush again. The bite was on her strong leg. She began to sweat and then everything went blurry. Ange blacked out as the poison coursed through her body. She lay slumped on the edge of the road like a little doll. People walked by, thinking it was an old woman who had died while on a pilgrimage to the temple, or that the plague had found her. The sun watched all these things below as its indifferent rays shone on a heart full of sorrow and loneliness inside a broken body. The ragged form that lay now in the baking heat held within it the knowledge of love and cruelty by the same world.

Ange woke with fur in her face. She tried opening her eyes as the pain shot through her head from the glare of the noon day sun. Then squinting again, she put up her hand to push away whatever it was against her. There was a whiny yawn and big lick on her face. She realised in her fog it was Nekoda, but thought it was a dream. She lay back down and stroked him.

"I wish you were here, Nekoda."

"What do you mean sister, he is here." A throaty chuckle came to her. "It must be the fever."

She looked up and saw Bensah stoking a fire. A bush fowl was roasting on a stick above the flames.

She sat up and inspected her leg. It had ulcerated where the bite was, and the skin was taut all the way up to her knee.

"It will clear quickly. I had some tea to bathe it with."

Ange started to sob, she wanted to hug him, but he didn't move to reciprocate.

"Tata, they took Tessi. The slavers. Did you see them in the city?"

Alarmed at her crying, Nekoda began to put his paw on her and lick her tears. She hugged him tightly around the neck, making sure he was real, and that he didn't leave. She lay back down. Nekoda settled as well, panting as Ange stroked his neck.

"No, but when we return to Ancrid, we will search for her. You are fast for a cripple. It took me a full day to find you after leaving the city. Where were you going?"

Ange's tongue was slightly swollen from the sting. "The mountains, Tata, a lady told me to go there. It would be safe."

Ange vomited all of a sudden but felt better after.

"Good, the poison is beginning to leave your body. Sit up and have some tea. It will help."

Ange propped herself onto her elbow. Bensah gave her the tea and bread to eat as well.

"Why the mountains, Sister, that is too dangerous for you; thieves and jaguars live there. One or the other would see the end of you."

"I don't know. A lady was in the village before the sickness and she said I should come to her grove. She said it was over the mountains. She said someone was looking for me and I would not be safe until I reached her place."

"We will go back to Ancrid. I have family there. They will give you shelter in return for working for them. They are fair people, and I will probably stay now as my own place has been taken as well. I know some of the northerners that sell our girls. They may even have Tessi."

Bensah clicked his tongue. He stopped, seeing the look on Ange's face, a mixture of hope and fear at her sister's fate.

"Ancrid is the place we will go, both of us will remain there and start again. The earth has taken but she will give again in her own time. We will leave on the morning. You should be able to use your leg by then."

Ange lay back down, tired and sad, but happy also that Nekoda and Bensah had found her. Deep inside, a small hope flickered that Tessi lay not far from her.

The wind came again to Ancrid City and pestilence found her home. The city was emptied in the two days it took for Ange's leg to heal. They watched the wind roar over the landscape. Bensah thought that this would be the end of it, but the storm swept towards the south and away from them. The dregs of Ancrid City began to file past them. Ange scanned them desperately searching for Tessi. Her heart thudded, but as the survivors finally dwindled to only a few, the small hope that had been enflamed with her reunion with Bensah diminished just as quickly.

"We must go north, Tata."

Bensah looked at the passers-by also trying to see if there was anyone he knew.

"Yes, sister. It seems the sickness and spirits of the wind will not go north."

Ange nodded and patted Nekoda. "Tata, did you hear the voices on the winds during the night? They were sad and angry."

"Nay." Bensah looked at the winding path that led north. His dreams had been haunted with visions of waves of blood washing against the feet of the mighty northern ranges driven by a demon on the wind. He had not heard Ange's sad voices.

"Stand and let me see how you are."

Ange got up and looked almost comical, limping from one side to another, but her good leg could carry her weight.

"We will take a longer route around to the east of the mountains. There is a well-trodden path, which I think will be safer. Doanda village lies there and we can search for Tessi as well. It has a large slavers' market. Our land is finished child; this land is old; ancient. Did you know you are a descendant of the first tribes that came here?"

"Yes, the lady told me so," replied Ange as she patted Nekoda.

13

Godryn's Flight

Paulus rested against the windowsill and looked out at the first leaf fall dawn. This decicycle would be the fifth in the one hundred season Irastian calender meaning it would be coldest of the five leaf falls. The gold and red leaf harvests would be short and the barc-branch seasons longer. There was already a deep indigo shadow in the dawn, normally not seen until ten seasons had passed. It was a reflection of the heaviness which lay around Paulus' mind and heart since the fever had taken hold. He heard Vronius enter and place some papers on the table.

"What things have I neglected in my absence?" Paulus looked at Vronius and a slight chill went through him.

"Oh, nothing of import, Abbot, it is indeed a miracle of Ira that you have come to back us." Vronius began to place scrolls in front of the abbot.

"Sister Godryn is renowned for her apothecary skills, even the Feudal Lords of the middling territories have called upon her knowledge and insight for curing maladies."

Vronius nodded, "Perhaps she is too attuned to the old ways. They are, aftcr all, considered barbaric, even sorcery."

"That is where her skill lies, Vronius, to know where the real healing is found without offense to our ways of Ira."

Paulus began to feel agitated at the tone of the questions.

"I remember when her parents brought her for worship on the festivals. She was precocious and curious then for a daughter of a peasant farmer. Often, she would be looking up at the sky seeing how the birds soar. One time, I think her mother found her rummaging through the old cook Gabriel's herb stores inspecting the fine patterns on the leaves. I remember hearing Gabriel cursing loudly when he found the herbs neatly arranged in size and colour of their leaves all over the kitchen floor. No, Vronius, Godryn is no sorceress. Her mind is made to draw the tapestries of this earth that are hidden from us. She is a healer and a sister of rare insight. She and I have known each other for a long time. We must prepare for the council's sitting. Have you met with Emissary Dhat?"

"Yes, he has been inspecting the tunnels beneath, along with the master stonemason. We are coming to agreement on where the mining can take place. Emissary Dhat has also informed us that Ranik himself has decided to come and complete the negotiations."

Paulus looked at Vronius intensely. The monk's dark eyes made him shiver. He sensed that Vronius was old, ancient almost. He wondered if it was his fevered mind playing tricks.

"This is grave news. Does it mean war?"

"Possibly," replied Vronius.

The abbot sighed. "And I am still weak."

Vronius simply stared at the old man with no reply.

"You don't seem concerned, Vronius?" Paulus probed, half

wanting to shrink into the bed again and half wanting the shadows to reveal themselves for what they were.

"I am Matavian. We are babes born and baptised with fear and subjugation. It is simply what life can bring for some. I noted that some of the old maps have been sent to you?"

"Yes, I will look at them later."

Vronius curiosity grew more with no explanation offered from Paulus.

"Is there anything I can help you with, Brother, you are still not back to yourself."

"Have all the members of the Scholars' council arrived?" asked Paulus, deflecting Vronius question.

"Yes, all of the members are here."

"I will need more parchment, Vronius. After that, I will not require you. I may attend temple this evening but Flet will assist me with the stairs." Paulus did not look at Vronius when he said this.

"Of course, Abbot."

Paulus breathed a sigh of relief when Vronius left. He was still tired, and all the fussing was beginning to wear on his patience. Unrolling the first map, he placed the ink well and the blotter on each end and began to check the notations made at the side. Mostly the inscriptions were about the water and salt levels, and some mineral deposits found, including the orichnite. Krarne was right, the salt pervaded everything. Going to the next map, he saw how much exploration had occurred, almost to the central bed of rock that was the main support for the temple. Its central spire rested directly upon it. He also noticed how the orichnite levels petered out well before the inner walls of the temple. He would be sure to point this out to Ranik.

He unrolled the last map and noticed a tunnel that had begun to be dug under where he now sat with the notation of "XOAI". It was the lettering after it that caught his attention OAI. It was an abbreviation used when an Abbot had given an express decree. He noted that three blockades had been placed in the tunnel. He guessed why the order had been given based on its location. He would need to meet with the master craftsman to ensure the blockades were maintained.

Placing all the scrolls in their satchel except the last one, Paulus went towards the fireplace. He put the map in the flames and watched it burn. He sat again to rest before evening prayer. Why was Ranik here?

Paulus dozed off in front of the hearth as a cool breeze passed over him. A memory came back to him; the first night he had seen the figure in the corridor. The mumbled words he had forgotten came to him, 'Find it, Dhat, and bring it to me, destroy all who stand in your way'. The voice was low and menacing and not familiar to Paulus, as the figure turned and looked, it faded, but Vronius came a moment later, walking towards him.

"Abbot?"

Paulus jumped. It was Vronius. Paulus looked up at him and froze; the monk's eyes were black, pitch black; he had seen that darkness before. The lingering remnants of the dream, and what had been shifting on the edges of his memory, became clear. The fear it instilled in Paulus' heart chilled the wizened old man to his bones.

"Abbot, are you okay?"

"Yes, Vronius." Averting his gaze elsewhere, he stood. "The gong tolls for evening incantation. I slept longer than I thought."

"You are too tired, Paulus. I will ask them to bring you supper in your room."

"Nay, I am rested. Ask Flet to come to assist me with my robe."

"I can help you," Vronius said, heading off into his room. "Did you find what you wanted in the maps, Brother?"

"Yes, there is wealth of this mineral below us, but I fear that the sea has claimed much of it already. I will explain this to Ranik when he arrives."

He noticed Vronius examining the empty vial of tonic. As the young man sniffed it, Paulus saw the look of revulsion on his face. It was as Paulus had thought – the old ways have a deep wisdom that had been lost.

Paulus noted how agitated Vronius was. "What do you detect in it?"

"This is unusual, Abbot, I am not sure. I have taken the liberty of looking at this elixir. I went to visit Sister Godryn, but she was not there. The door was ajar, so I went in. I found the recipe, and these were in the hearth."

Vronius unwrapped some small bones that were charred from the fire. Paulus looked at them carefully. They were small like those of an infant's hand or animal.

Paulus inspected the scroll. Indeed, the tonic called for human and animal sacrifice. The language was strong, but so were all the remedies of the old religion, but it was understood these practices were no longer followed. It was especially heinous for one of the Irasian order to partake in these rituals.

"I think Godryn will provide an explanation for these, Vronius. I'm sure she has not reverted to sorcery." Paulus noted a flash of anger in the young monk's eyes again.

"Indeed, Abbot you have not fully recovered from your affliction and it is still unknown what it was that assailed you. I think it is better for the council to determine what action needs to be taken."

Paulus did not respond immediately. The tonic was protecting him from whatever it was that had come into this world.

"I will consider it, Vronius, but it cannot be done lightly. Sister Godryn is a council member and her skills as a healer and steadfastness to the ways of Ira are unquestioned."

The Abbot placed his robes on. His heart thudded with fear and agitation. 'Where was Vronius going with this enquiry?' A sick feeling welled in his stomach.

Vronius followed Paulus down to the temple. The stairways were not steep but long and wound in a circular pattern to the lower levels. He watched from behind, wanting to rip the old man's heart out. He knew the old man knew where the gift lay, but his mind was impenetrable. He needed to find a way. 'The apothecary's tonic will wear off,' he thought.

Paulus could feel the eyes burning into his head. He wheezed slightly at the effort to make it to the temple. His heart pounded slightly. It was here for it. He wondered, how long it would take before it knew where to look. He could feel a slight pressure like a band wrapping itself around his head. Just then, a procession of brethren came into view below them. Paulus could see Godryn, Benedicta, Malachi, and Rictus. Instantly,

Paulus felt the cold grip on him release.

"Abbot, good to see you and Brother Vronius"

"Thank you, Benedicta, and you; Godryn, Malachi, and Rictus," replied Paulus.

"You still look pale, Paulus, I have some of the tonic left. I will give some to Flet to leave for you in your room."

Paulus grimaced as the taste came back to him. "As you say, Godryn."

The brethren entered the temple together. Paulus' spirits lifted and his mind felt clear. As he was going towards the main sanctuary of the temple, he knew now what had to be done. The time had arrived when those created before our world had come to destroy it. "Forgive me, Godryn." He sighed to himself.

On the morning of the council, Flet assisted Paulus into his robes. He took another sip of the tonic. Paulus, Flet and Vronius made their way to the great hall, which served as a dining chamber as well. Entering, the council members were seated in a semi-circular fashion with the Abbot's chair in the centre.

All of them stood. Flet assisted Paulus up onto his chair and then left, acknowledging the council. Vronius placed the Book of Lore on the lectern and also left. Closing the doors, Paulus stood and began to recite the Litany of Ira.

The council members responded in perfect harmony and tone. Once they had finished, all the monks sat.

Paulus began. "My Brethren, I have called a meeting of the scholars to request your permission for Lord Ranik of Matavia to use our land near the temple for mining of the mineral orichnite. It has been found to be in abundance along the coast as far as the very foundations on which we stand. His offer is a generous one, allowing the brethren one fifth of the gold danats made from the mines. As you are aware, the upkeep of the temple and the alms for the villagers is always with us. These added donations would help immensely in our missionary work and maintenance of this holy place. I ask then for you to consider this request. May the light of Ira's faith guide us in a wise and fair decision."

Joab spoke first. "Lord Ranik's reputation for brutality and war mongering are well known. Not only does an association with this tyrant go against our teachings, but it may jeopardise the allies we have forged in our missionary work in the northern and eastern territories."

"Yes, Joab," continued Benedicta, "What of the labourers – are we to watch these people be brutalized, while we take the profits they pay for with their lives."

"I have asked that the people be paid in silver and their families be recompensed."

"I think the brethren should say no to this alliance. He cannot be trusted. Any terms we agree upon he will renege on them."

Paulus nodded, "I agree Malachi, which makes me wonder how much of a choice we have."

Joab sat back and wiped some sweat from his brow. "My time in Lord Ranik's feudal territory makes me only too aware that the brethren are now in a precarious position. If we do not agree to his demands, he will simply invade our lands and enslave the people. If we ask for nothing, then we will receive nothing from him."

"I agree, Joab. I have requested that boundaries be placed on where the mining shall occur. If the brethren can at least ask for recompense to the miners or their families then surely, we have not breached our creeds. I see no way forward if we do not accept. Yet, if we do not ask for protection for the poor souls who will deliver this wealth, then I fear the brethren shall have abandoned the goodwill of Ira and of people across the lands our temples occupy. I will now ask for a vote to resolve this matter."

Each of the council members placed their vote either a stone or a coin for yes or no in the basket. Paulus drew them out and counted the yay and nay. It was resolved that the alliance with Ranik was to proceed.

"My reply to Ranik is a conditional agreement — our acceptance of the one fifth of all gold danats, and that the labourers be paid in swine and goats for their families to subsist on and be rotated regularly. With the profits we receive, one third will be placed toward feeding and sheltering the labourers who are sent here, and the rest shall be placed towards the village and temples across the lands. I have already stated that there shall be boundaries where the tunnels are permitted to go."

"What if he breaches these terms, Abbot?"

"We will consider that if it happens. Lord Ranik's strength is formidable as you know. It is the eagle and the field mouse at play."

"Abbot, if I may," interrupted Joab, "I have fostered good relations with the City of Esteron. Princess Nene has developed an affinity with Irasian thought and has given permission for us to evangelise in her lands. It is interesting that she would seek a religion for her people based on peace and harmonious tolerance when her army is larger than any other kingdom, save Ranik's. It is also worth noting that these two suzerains are bitter enemies. I'm sure if some of the profits we will garner from this unholy alliance could see their way to the great Citadel then a valuable ally would be attained, and the peace of Ira will spread to new believers."

"Ahh, Joab, I remember fondly when your father first bought you to the temple. I think if the brethren could learn to live more austerely, then some of these funds will indeed be put into your sagacious hands to foster a friendship with Princess Nene. Once the council has adjourned and agreement is reached with Lord Ranik, then I think you will be free to continue your missionary work in the City of Esteron."

Joab sat back quite pleased with himself, his hands on his generous stomach – made the more so because of the Princess's fascination with Ira and many diplomatic feasts.

"Thank you. Brethren, I fear that we are now in the race with the eagle for our lives, so be vigilant and offer many alms that he will turn his gaze once he has his fill." Sighing audibly and his shoulders slumping, Paulus continued, "Now for something else which pains me greatly. As you know, I have been unwell, with a deep fever that still chases me even now. It was by the good grace of your alms and skill of our Apothecary, Godryn, that I have recovered to this state now. However, it has come to light that a grave breach of our sacred oaths may have occurred in order to cure me."

Paulus rang a little bell. Vronius entered with a small bag and vial on a tray with the a scroll of parchment.

Godryn stiffened. 'What is going on?' she thought, recognising the tonic vial and scroll from her room.

"Thank you, Vronius. Sister Godryn, please stand. Long have I known you, and our association has been one of trust and good faith. I call upon this goodwill to help understand the veracity to this charge laid upon you by the nature of these things found in your chamber. Is the tonic that you gave me from the recipe written on this parchment?"

Vronius took it to Godryn.

"Yes, it is, Paulus."

"And these bones?"

Vronius opened the bag and spilled the contents onto a mat. Every councillor looked curiously at them.

"Yes, Paulus."

"Have you spilt human blood to make this tonic?"

Godryn hesitated. "Yes, Paulus, I have." There was a slight gasp around the room.

"Are these then the bones of a babe?"

"Indeed, they are not, Abbot!" Godryn was astounded. "I used a guinea pig and my own blood made from a small cut. These bones are too large for a guinea pig. If I may, Paulus?"

"Of course."

The Abbot felt a wave of revulsion well up in him at the thought of drinking more of the tonic.

Godryn inspected the bones. They were too large for the pigs she had used. Besides, she was sure that only ashes remained in the hearth.

"Brother Edram, could you look at these bones?" Paulus gestured for him to inspect them.

Edram was an apothecary and performed the burial rituals for the villagers.

He picked them up and looked at them closely.

"Are these the bones of a child, Brother?" asked Paulus.

"Yes, indeed they are, only of the foot though."

"Paulus, this is not of my doing. Where were these bones found?" pleaded Godryn.

"In the apothecary's chambers," replied Vronius.

"Sister Godryn, do you not know how it pains me to think that you may have used such dark sorcery as this, albeit to save my life. You know that this nulls any justification for what you have done."

"Paulus, how can you think that I would do such a thing? I used the rodents given to me by the village midwives and I cut my own wrist to fulfil the recipes requirements. See here is the wound." Lifting her sleeve and unrolling the muslin, she showed the wound on her arm. "When in all of my time in servitude, have I ever stepped beyond the vows we are beholden to."

"Edram, can it be a mistake?"

Edram looked again. "Nay, My Lord. When the plague came four winters ago, the babes were the first to succumb. It was then that I saw the bones of the innocent pile around me. Indeed, this is the foot of a child." Edram looked at Godryn. "While I am dismayed and wish that there is another explanation, you have always explored unorthodox ways, Godryn. The brew was potent to bring the Abbot back to us. Such fevers I have never witnessed even in the southern isles where the pox is deadly."

"But, Edram you have seen my work. I know that I have sometimes looked at the old ways, but never outside what is acceptable and a child – please by the faith of Ira."

Benedicta stood up. "I will not accept that Godryn has done this heinous thing. She may be guilty of using the old ways, but this is dark sorcery, and I will not accept that an Irasian of such renowned skill would stoop to mere devilry."

"Nor I," came the response from Joab.

"Malachi and Rictus, what is your opinion?"

Malachi spoke, "It is impossible for me to say as I was away at the time of your illness, Paulus. Indeed, by the stories told to me it was as if you were raised from the arms of Ira himself. However, Sister Godryn, while prickly and unorthodox, has many times displayed an exceptional skill in healing, so if anyone were to pull a soul from the very infinite's grasp, then I believe it would be Godryn."

Edram spoke. "I have seen the great bond between you and Godryn, Paulus, indeed I came as a novice on the same day as Godryn. She has grown in her skill as an apothecary, as you have as our chief ascetic. Your questions are not asked lightly, Paulus, and without good reason. I will defer to your judgment." Edram lowered his eyes without looking at Godryn.

"Rictus."

"I am new to the council and coming from the northern temple, I am unaware of the prowess or methods of Godryn as an apothecary. I understand the fervour the faith of Ira can stir and the desire to heal and restore. Indeed, if this thing were done by one of the brethren then surely it was only out of good intentions to end suffering."

"This is entirely objectionable to me. I have not desecrated the life of an innocent. Ask the old woman, Ladra, she will say she gave me the rodents." Godryn's face began to go red at her indignation at the accusation she had slain a child.

"I have done this, Abbot, in the hope that we would clear Sister Godryn, but the old woman passed away not three days ago," Vronius interjected.

Godryn looked at Vronius instantly suspicious as to what had killed the old woman. Paulus stomach churned at what was happening. He also wondered what had happened to the midwife.

"Please, Paulus, you cannot believe I have done such an abhorrent deed."

Paulus looked down to the stone floor. He felt the fever returning. A deep pit of grief bloomed and overflowed in his heart as the words formed on his tongue.

"Nay, Godryn, I will make my judgment. For disobedience to the oaths of Ira and taking the life of an innocent you are to wander penitent and in exile. It is however understood that the deed was done to restore life and end suffering then the exile shall not be to the end of your life but when shadows thicken on the skies and sun no longer brightens. You will live as a hermit far from the temple for the next decicycle of the winter face of the sun. At the completion of the twenty leaf falls, you will return penitent, not as the apothecary, but only to do penance fasting and labouring in the temple gardens. Your exile shall begin on the third dawn, where I will place on you the scapulet of the penitent. On that day you shall learn your litany of penance contained with the scapulet; which you shall recite daily until the end of your exile. Only you shall deem if there has been true penance and regret at the actions you have taken."

Godryn stood, completely stupefied at what had happened.

"Paulus, is it the fever speaking? I have done no such act. I breached a minor law in regard to taking the life of an animal other than for sustenance and I used my own blood to fulfil the tonics ingredients."

"Nay, my judgment is made. I adjourn the council."

Paulus got up. Vronius stooped to gather the damning articles and followed the Abbot. As Paulus walked past, he saw the hollow look in Godryn's eyes and her utter confusion. Normally fiery in her persona, all he saw was a dejected shadow. Paulus wondered how the accused monk could not hear the blood rushing in his head or his heart pounding in his chest at the pain he felt of what he had just done to an innocent brethren and his friend.

Back in his chamber, Paulus sat down in his chair facing the window.

"Please leave, Vronius."

"Abbot..."

"I will be fine, it is never an easy decision to make, and even more so with someone I have known for so long. It is a grave breach of our codes and laws and could not be left unaddressed."

"I understand, Abbot. Do you want some fresh water, or tea perhaps? It has been a difficult morning."

"Yes, some tea, but just send Flet. You will need to begin the counter response to Ranik to be ready when we meet with the tyrant."

"Of course."

Paulus got up and went to his desk. He felt weak, washed out from the inside. Taking out some parchment, he dipped the quill in and began to write to an old friend. Paulus was not a sentimental man. A life devoted to ascetics and searching the interior labyrinths of the mind and soul, required no attachments to the heart and the body. The lessons were hard to endure at first, but age was kind to this way of life; as the mind and body fatigue so the ties to old desires break also.

After finishing the letter, he rolled the three pages into a tight scroll. He took off the pure silver scapulet of protection and placed the scrolls inside, around the small key. He sealed it with the cap and then held it briefly over the embers in the hearth, soldering the tube shut.

"May the faith of Ira be your strength and his peace your staff to guide you to the infinite's wisdom and love," he whispered over the silver pendant.

Flet arrived with the tea.

"I have completed the litany of penance for Godryn. I will take it to her on the third day before the solstice of the fifth cycle of the leaf fall. Is she comfortable?"

Flet saw the silver pendant lying on the table near the ink well. He placed the cup and pot down next to it. Being a novice, he was required to learn the discipline of not letting his personal thoughts spill out but considering everything through the teachings of Ira. But even Flet felt a well of anger toward his Abbot at the injustice toward Godryn. She had saved his life. Surely that was greatest teaching of Ira, the value we place on our existence to preserve it as much as possible, to reduce suffering as much as possible within our understanding.

Suddenly Flet felt Paulus hand grip his arm.

"Abbot, are you not well again?" Flet asked, concerned.

"If anything should happen, this pendant must be given to Godryn. She is the only brethren I have encountered with her intuition and vision which is worthy of this gift. Her penance must be given, Flet. Do you understand?'

"I will, Abbot. But rest. You are still weary from the illness." Flet could see a deep fear and desperation in Paulus. His own heart raced. 'What was happening in the great holy temple of Ira. Bring us your peace and wisdom Holy Ira. Guide us and let our minds be at peace once more,' he prayed silently.

On the third day, after Godryn had been exiled, Paulus stood looking out over the ocean. His eyes squinted slightly from the brightness. 'Brother Sun, you are very generous with your cheer and light today on the last of the summer before you turn to us with winter,' he thought. The fever had returned during the night and vaguely he thought he heard the scratching again.

Vronius walked into the room silently. Paulus turned from the window and saw the early rays catch the monk's eyes. They were red flames dancing in pools of blackness. A low growl came from Vronius. Paulus stood back against the window his hand on his chest. He felt the burning of the precious stone flare within his chest as the shadow's claws descended into his mind. Paulus pushed himself back against the window and tumbled out. The blackness in his mind let go just as his body crashed onto the rocks below and the waves engulfed him.

Godryn sat in the chamber of quietude. There were no comforts only a small window, hessian cloth and small jug and bowl. The privy was a hole in the corner where she could squat to piss. A sudden chill washed over as the dawn came on quickly. Inside, her heart churned with anger, confusion, and remorse at both feelings. She sat up and gingerly rose to her knees to pray at first light. Such an automatic ritual physically, but internally she still found resistance to the discipline.

Whispering the litany, concentrating on the words, her mind didn't falter. Slowly, she felt the obeisance consume her as she thanked Ira for a restful sleep. When she finished, instead of getting up to eat, she stayed there a little longer, thinking. For the first time since her noviciate had ended and she had not been on mission. Godryn had missed partaking in the first meal of the day with the brethren. The thought of being in exile for twenty winters overwhelmed her. Tears began to stream down the old woman's face. She would miss the communion of her brethren — the prayers and fasting; each person an integral part of harmony and quest for peace.

She thought of a conversation with Paulus before the fever had taken him.

"What is the greater, love or faith?"

Godryn sat silently pondering the question. It was difficult to answer. After much thought she answered, "I do not know. I only hope I may know both in my life."

"What is the opposite of love, Godryn?"

"Fear."

"You have answered well, Sister. Why is fear the opposite of love and not hate?"

"If a person lives in fear, they will seek dominion over that which they do not understand, or they will be destroyed by it.

Either path leads to destruction."

'I still don't understand, Paulus,' she thought looking at the purple light of first dawn of the leaf fall cycle. Paulus would come soon with the penitential litany on the solstice. Then her exile would begin in earnest.

Flet entered Paulus' chambers with his morning meal. He saw the room was empty and the bed not slept in. He grew worried. The call to prayer had not been rung yet. He looked out from the open window and horror struck his heart. He could see the grey and black tunic of the Abbot being thrashed in the waves against the jagged rocks. Flet raced out and down the stairs.

"Help. Abbot Paulus has fallen into the ocean. Please ring the call for help. Get the fisherman to come with their poles."

Ignatius came up from the kitchen. Flet almost knocked him over as they collided on the stairs.

"Ignatius. Hurry. Fetch the fishermen, Tollo and Janus. The Abbot has fallen from his window and lies in the ocean."

Flet ran past him and out to the path which led down to the ocean. He scrambled over stones and eventually came to the cliff's edge. The body was still there, being heaved up and then battered down onto the rock. It was too far for Flet to safely pull Paulus out. The body flipped and Flet almost vomited when he saw the pulverised face of Paulus. He tried to reach forward and latch onto Paulus robes, but a wave came up and snatched the body out of reach. Flet fell back trying to stop falling into the violent surges of the ocean. Something glinted out of the corner of his eye. Flet looked toward it. Squinting in the spray of ocean he saw it was the penitential scapulet. It had become snagged on a branch of bush which grew just above the waterline. Flet remembered the desperation in Paulus' eyes two days before. The Abbot knew something was going to happen. He scrambled up to the path. He lay flat and stretched out to where the bush jutted out of the sandstone. He just managed to grab the silver pendant. Suddenly he heard voices. Getting up, he saw Vronius coming slowly, and behind him, was Ignatius and three fishermen.

Flet placed the pendant inside his tunic. He felt the piercing gaze of Vronius.

"The Abbot has fallen to his death, Brother."

Vronius stared over the edge. He didn't react. Ignatius flew up behind him. Tollo and Janus peered over. They began to scramble over the edge with their great fishing poles. Paulus had sunk below the rocks and only a tiny fragment of his habit showed where his body lay.

"By the faith, what other evil befalls us now," Ignatius exclaimed.

Everyone looked up. On the horizon, the black ships of Matavia were entering the bay of Irastia. Leading them was a massive bulwark with the mast head displaying an eagle. The beak was chiselled to a razor-sharp point.

"Our guest has arrived. I will ready to greet them." Vronius left without saying anything about Paulus.

Flet and Ignatius looked at him in confusion.

"It is no use. We cannot reach the body, brethren," spoke Tollo as he climbed back up to the path.

"Can you post a boy here for the next few days to see if the ocean will give his body up?" asked Flet.

"Yes, of course."

"What is happening, Ignatius?"

"I have sensed a shadow for the whole of this cycle. The red dawns have had a darkness behind them, which I have never seen before in my sixty summers as a brethren, Flet. I fear that shadow has awoken."

They stared once more into the water but there was no trace of the Abbot. Flet's heart pounded with grief and frustration at not being able to save Paulus.

"Did you see what happened, Flet?"

"No, I left Paulus last evening and I came this morning with his meal and the chamber was empty."

The gong for prayer began to boom across the wind and out across the ocean. It sounded like a death knell to Flet and Ignatius.

"Come, we will tell the brethren as they gather for prayer. By the faith of Ira, my mind and heart have never felt such turmoil."

"Nor mine, Brother," replied Flet.

— — —

Lord Ranik sat looking at the monks gathered before him. Mostly he just wanted them dead. The Scholaria had often come to his lands to study their ancient texts and healing methods. While it had agitated him at the time, Faad, his main advisor, had suggested that the information they could gather from the gormless monks could prove to be of value. Faad was right. It was how Ranik had become aware of the vast amounts of mineral that lay under the temple.

Vronius stood before the assembly. "Brethren, I have gathered you here today in the presence of Lord Tias Ranik. After much negotiations and discussions with our guest, it has been agreed that the Great Temple of the Irastian order be relocated so the mining of the orichnite can continue. The foundations have been reached and our master craftsmen have stated the weight of the great stones above will not be borne if the tunnelling continues any further."

There was a quiet murmur that moved around the refectory.

"Abbot Vronius, this cannot be allowed to happen, this temple was built on sacred ground when Ira came to enlightenment. The mining must be discontinued. Lord Ranik, have you not gleaned enough for your needs?"

It was Micah. Ranik looked at him and nodded subtly to one of the guards. Moving off the dais the soldier went to the old monk. Raising his sword, he ran him through. Micah collapsed with a heave.

"You are a demon. Ira save us," he wheezed as his blood spilled out.

Vronius didn't flinch. The other brethren, including Flet, stood stunned.

"You are a cursed man, Ranik." Edram knelt over Micah trying to staunch the bleeding.

"Enough! Your choice is this, monks; leave or be killed. My mercy is shallow and brief, so decide quickly."

"Vronius, this cannot be allowed. We must defend the sacred place of Ira. To the death if need be," pleaded Benedicta.

"That, I will leave you to decide. For those who wish to leave with me and begin anew, then we will make pilgrimage, otherwise you have heard Lord Ranik."

The brethren did not move or speak. Flet looked at Vronius and saw a flash of shadow in his eyes and a tiny smirk on his face.

"So be it." Ranik stood. "We begin blasting at dawn. Take me to the eastern shoreline. I wish to inspect the ore that was found there." Vronius nodded and moved to leave with him.

Brother Edram grabbed the Abbot's arm. "Lord Abbot, we must stand our ground with this tyrant. Ask the city council, they will send their army to defend us. Send for Princess Nene of Esteron," implored Edram.

Then suddenly a sword flashed. Its blade decapitated Edram.

"Hear me; leave or be killed." Ranik left with the sound of his voice thundering in the monk's ears after he had he wiped his blade on Edram's tunic.

Flet saw the bloody mess in the great council hall. His heart was beating like the waves on the cliff in a thunderstorm. He raced up toward his room to begin packing. The temple was in chaos as the guards and slaves of Ranik had inundated the temple and its grounds. The villagers were being terrorised and driven from their homes so that the slaves could be accommodated. They were made to work the fields for food. There had not been any homage paid to Paulus and his body had still not been recovered from the ocean since yesterday.

He began to fold his clothes. He took the leather pouch which held his quills and scrolls of precious parchment. He pulled his bedding up. As he did so the scapulet fell from his tunic. He looked at it. In all the melee caused by the tyrant's arrival he had forgotten about Godryn. She was locked in the chambers of quietude. He packed his satchel. Then going to the hallway, he checked if anyone was about.

"We are all exiles now Godryn," he whispered.

It was drawing toward night again. He found the winding stairs to the chamber. The rest of the brethren were beginning to pack their few belongings and arrange satchels of food for the pilgrims. As he made his way through the kitchens, he saw poor Brother Frederick lying on a litter in the kitchens. Ignatius was giving him water. He had refused to leave and had been forced out by one of the soldiers, preferring to die in the place it had been his home since he was fifteen summers old. Flet's heart thudded with anger and fear seeing the old monk. The memory of seeing Edram and Micah dead remained fresh. He continued down toward the chamber of quietude. Reaching the door, he opened the chamber. Godryn lay on a hessian sack. She sat up.

"Flet what has happened? Why has Paulus not come? And what is all the commotion?"

"Paulus is dead, Godryn. He fell from his chamber window and was taken by the ocean. Ranik has arrived and has invaded the temple. He has told the brethren to leave or be executed. I have come to set you free. I also wanted to give you this. Paulus, on the last night I saw him, told me that it was important that I give the scapulet to you. He knew something was going to happen to him."

Flet gave the pendant to Godryn. She rolled it hesitating out of shock at everything which was happening. Prying off the metal lid a scroll of parchment fell out of the cylinder along with a key. She put the key on the table and unrolled the paper.

*From Paulus X, Abbot of the Brethren of Ira
to Godryn, penitent monk,*

If you are reading this then all hope is not lost. What I write here cannot be fully explained but know that what I tell you has never been divulged to any other than the Abbot-Sous in seven ages since Ira. The demon remains. Its claws still pierce my mind bringing the cursed fever with them. The talons burn my flesh and the scratching never ceases. It seeks a precious gift. This gift has resided here in the temple and is the reason our temple was built; to protect and guard this gift until its true keeper reclaims it. If the demon finds the gift then my soul will know no peace, only the chaos of the dark, and the truth of light will never be known by those of us who dwell here. Godryn, I tell you this as the demon commands Vronius and it is he who seeks the gift.

It is found in a chamber beneath my bedroom. The way down is under the cot itself. Look for the brick with a corner missing. It will open a passage. Search for the lock. I have drawn it for you. Use the key to open the door to where the gift rests. You will know it when you see it. When in the presence of the radiant stone of colour, place your hand on it and read the incantation.

"By Ira's grace and with fidelity to the ways of peace, I ask to take this gift to the custodian to whom it was made from and the rightful ruler of its ancient power. By five dawns, as the sacred covenant commands, I will relinquish this mighty watershed, gifted to the safe keeping of my faith, Father Ira. Bless me and give me safe passage until the rightful steward is bestowed."

If the gift allows you to possess it, you are to hasten to the sacred grove found on the great table to the north of our lands. It lies between the twin falls Oda and Uda. You must relinquish it by the dawn of the fifth day otherwise you and all those near to it, will burn to ash, but never die.

The demon Vronius must never seize it. The gift has the power of the ancients and may only be commanded by them.

I wish it were not in our time, sister, that the fate of the world is to rest on our shoulders. But the darkness has breached the light and consumes all that lay within its realm. The last protection to stop the utter annihilation of the infinite's vision was entrusted to Ira and his brethren, and so it falls now to you to keep it from the claws of the most unclean beast of darkness that walks amongst us.

Forgive me for your exile, friend, for I saw no other way to hide any trace of the gift's existence from the relentless pursuit of this shadow. Even now it claws at my mind so it may discover the location of the sacred jewel and consume its power. I am growing weak. I fear it will not be long before it has the knowledge it seeks and with it our death.

Hasten to the sacred grove Godryn, and Ira's protection with the speed of a kite upon you my friend.

Paulus X

Godryn saw a swirl of old text similar to that in which the scholars wrote the sacred writs. She read the note again. Paulus was not himself when they last spoke.

"Flet. We must go to Paulus chambers."

The stair well was deserted and unlit. Normally the novices would be given the chore to light the passageways. The climb was not steep, as the turret was located on an outcrop of cliff, but the walk still pricked her knees. They entered the chamber. The door had been sealed after Paulus death and was difficult to budge open. It was dark and silent. Godryn's mind flicked back to the last days she had been here.

"Paulus wrote that the entrance is under his cot."

Inside the bedroom, they found that all of the furniture and the texts of Paulus had been pillaged. Scrolls lay in chaos on the floor and the bed and desk had been upturned. Inspecting the wall carefully, Godryn found a brick with a corner chipped. She pressed the corner and underneath the cot, a trap door opened.

"Quickly," spoke Godryn.

Godryn went first, thrusting the lantern down and finding the winding staircase. They descended slowly, having to stop, as the blasting seemed to draw closer with their every step. The tunnel shook and some of the wall collapsed from the force of the explosions. Eventually, the pair reached the bottom and entered the stone chamber. Godryn took the scroll from the metal scapulet and unrolled it.

"Look for this, Flet."

They searched each of the carved stone slabs meticulously. Almost at the point of giving up, Godryn saw the inscription. Taking out the key, she inserted it in the minuscule slot. Suddenly, a lever popped out.

She turned it and just as another blast pounded around them, the stone transformed to the crystal cavern. Flet and Godryn froze with awe and thudding fear. They looked at the great diamond pillar with its corona of colour bleeding out into the chamber.

"Come, this must be what Paulus wrote about." Godryn gulped, not wanting to walk toward it in case the glass floor was an illusion and would crumble to dust beneath her. An almighty shudder went through the room.

Godryn neared the column cautiously. Remembering the instructions, she pushed her hand into the pillar. It resisted, but then gave in. Her fingers began to tingle as the coloured light washed over them. With her other hand, she held the scroll open.

"By Ira's grace and with fidelity to the ways of peace, I ask to take this gift to the custodian to whom it was made from and the rightful ruler of its ancient power. By five dawns, as the sacred covenant commands, I will relinquish this mighty watershed, gifted to the safe keeping of my faith, Father Ira. Bless me and give me safe passage until the rightful steward is bestowed."

At first, there was nothing, then suddenly the colours seemed to draw into themselves and Godryn could feel a small stone in her fingers. Pulling her hand out, she saw a diamond in the shape of a tear drop.

"What is it?" asked Flet.

"It is what Ranik seeks, Flet. Come now, the race begins, or all shall be for nought. I must take this to a place between the falls of Oda and Uda in five days or it will kill me and anything near me. It was what Paulus told me in the letter."

Ascending the stairs was a slow business for Godryn, but eventually she made it. She collapsed on the floor wheezing. As she lay, recovering, the tunnel caved in on itself causing the flag stones of the floor to loosen under her body. Dust plumed up into the room, choking them both.

Flet grabbed Godryn by the arm and hoisted her up.

"Hurry, I know a passage that will take us out to the coastal path towards the woods."

Godryn placed the prism in her silver scapulet and followed the young monk. They entered complete darkness for five hundred paces. Stepping out onto an unused path, they both nearly tipped over the cliff edge and into the ocean below. Over in the distance, the protrusion of ragged stones that supported the abbot's chambers exploded in sparks and rocks. Godryn and Flet stood and watched the six thousand decicycle old temple disintegrate before them. The large turret where abbots had sat and pondered the mysteries of life, stars and gods, crashed into the ocean: its hungry waves finally sated.

Sighing heavily, Godryn spoke, "Come, Flet, we must head east towards the river. I must be at the falls of Oda and Uda by the fifth dawn."

Flet nodded, too stunned to speak. The path they were on led around the very edges of the coast was only ten spans above the waves. It was extremely narrow in places. A roar came across the breeze. Godryn shuddered thinking that was no earthly creature making that noise. They reached the woods and rested for a bit. Wheezing heavily, Godryn slumped against a tree stump. In the distance, they heard shouts and a malicious bark seemed to come with them. Flet climbed a tree and saw guards and a massive black shadow suddenly disappear under the canopy. He almost didn't believe he saw the shape it had been so fleeting.

"We are discovered, Flet," Godryn cried with panic and

defeat in her voice.

"Hurry!" whispered Flet pulling the old woman up.

"Nay, Flet, I am too old I will not make the journey in five dawns. It is hopeless."

"You must, Godryn. It is only you that can do this now. It is not far to the river. Keep on the path ahead for another five hundred paces and you will find a fork. Take the one that has the mulberry bush blocking it. It is well hidden. It will take you around the base of the western ranges until you can cross the Hunjasat River. Let the current carry you until the mighty bends of Hun. Then, when you see the great oak tree which weeps over the flowing water, grab the branch which reaches out over the current. It is sturdy enough for you to climb out on the banks in the lands of Aeserea. Then follow the fields keeping the mountains to your right until the eastern tip of the Northern peaks comes into view. Follow them until the foot of the upper fall is heard. I have taken this route many times as a boy returning to my homelands. It will take the five dawns. Ira's blessing on you, Godryn and remember me in your odes to the faithful. I will lead these dark tormentors far from your path."

Godryn left as she saw Flet run back the way they had come. "Ira's protection for all of us."

Godryn ran at an old woman's pace as the agony in her knees bloomed. She found the fork and entered the path signalled by the mulberry tree. She found a path well covered by the understory of the forest. She prayed for Flet and thanked the great spirits for the monk's valour and fidelity.

Flet had sprinted most of the night. His legs felt like jelly and his chest burned. The guards were still chasing, and they were closing in. Then he heard the growl not far behind. His time was drawing near. Deep within, he prayed to Ira for a quick death and for Godryn's safekeeping to deliver the gift.

The dawn of the next cycle of leaf fall and indigo nights was breaking over the ocean as Voloc lunged at Flet. Standing on his chest, red eyes blazing, the beast stared into Flet's mind. Flet began the mantras of peace to block the image of Godryn.

"Search his bag!" commanded the demon.

The guards threw everything on the ground and the wolf tore at Flet's clothes. Nothing; Voloc ripped Flet's throat out and then his torso. The guards stood back when they saw the savagery of the beast at work.

Godryn stood at the edge of the great River Hunjasat. It was flowing slowly, and its surface twinkled with the setting sun. Flet had been dead two days and Godryn was being hunted. Stepping into the water, she waded across, letting the current carry her at a swift yet gentle pace. The water was cold but soothing to her screaming joints. The current was strong beneath the calm surface allowing her to cover a league quickly. Soon she saw the bends of Hun and sure enough the huge limb of the oak reached out almost like it called to her to come. She readied as it neared and then grabbing onto it, she heaved herself up onto the limb. When she walked out of the bushes towards the east, she came out onto an open plain of wheat and barley crops. It was too exposed to rest here, so she made her way towards a shadowy area about a league straight ahead. Her habit was heavy from the water and the satchel she carried dripped down her legs as she trundled towards the woods. Her wheezing breaths echoed into the silent fields as she rested against a tree. She saw the massive peak of Tarantess and knew she was following the right path. The night was ushered in by the full gibbous moon. Anyone on her trail would still be able to see her even at night. Getting up, she continued on into the empty darkness until dawn broke. Her feet were numb and her muscles spasmed with each stride. The forested wall of the great plateau loomed before her just on twilight. She still had not heard or sighted her hunters. Reaching the vertical staircase cut into the rockface of the cliff she began to climb up the roughly hewn steps. After only a few paces, her foot slipped, and she plummeted down to the ground. She heard the snap of her bones as her chest hit a rock sticking out of the surface. In the distance, faintly, she could hear a waterfall.

"Get up, Godryn!" she wheezed to herself as the fourth night slowly began to descend around her. She began the climb again. The pain of the movement dulled her mind to the noise of the barking dog and thundering hooves of the horses coming across the plain towards her.

The moon illuminated the forest as she crawled to the top of the plateau. She did not know how much further there was to go or how long to the dawn. Standing upright again, she began to head towards the sound of the huge waterfall of Oda. She prayed to herself that Ira's guardianship would remain a little more. The moonlight and dappled shadows danced around her but slowly faded as the forest became denser. Suddenly she realised how quiet it had become; even the leaves did not rustle. She could no longer hear the sound of water. Fear filled her mind as she thought she had become lost. Stumbling on, the trees changed from hoary old oks to slender birches. With a few paces the forest ended and she found herself standing on the edge of a circle of grass with a pool in the middle. A pale sliver of the dawn's light mingled with the light of the full moon, gently caressed the grass and silvery flecks of the branches of the trees. She went to the pool and collapsed on the edge. She dipped into the water and gulped in its sweet nourishment. A pain lanced through her chest as she lay down to rest. Her breathing was ragged and shallow. She pulled off the scapula around her neck and held it in her hand.

Godryn saw herself sitting with Paulus in the sanctuary beneath the great bell of Tarnoc.

"Tell me of all these, knowledge, beauty, strength, obedience, reason, faith, good deeds, which is the greater?" asked Paulus.

Godryn replied, "Reason and knowledge."

"What of good deeds, apothecary?"

Godryn's hand let go of the silver canister as she slipped deeper into the dream.

Lido stood above her. She could feel the presence of the prism. A low growl emanated from the far side of the grove.

"Tormented one, be gone from my place. You have no power here."

"Not yet spirit, but the time will come when all shall be under my dominion."

"You had your chance, why didn't you take it?" No answer came.

Voloc snarled as Assumpta appeared. "Ahh, old one, you have delivered the gift. Rest now, for when the war between light and dark is over, your courage shall be remembered." Placing her hand on Godryn's chest she took the monk's last breath, the god felt the essence of the monk enter her.

Assumpta picked up the silver scapulet and opened it. She held the tear drop in her hand. She saw all the memories held inside. The ancient memories of the Fourth realm of light were held tightly inside the crystal, made by Norbu from her tears at the time of the sundering and imprisonment of Baachelaus.

Voloc's eyes blazed when it saw it. Its mighty form strained against the power of Lido.

Assumpta stepped towards the black shadow, and with her gaze, thrust it towards the sun. A yelp came across the skies as the rays of the great Belmaris touched the black hide.

"It is not complete, Sister." spoke Assumpta.

"Our brother has hidden the other half for a reason, Ascendant" replied Lido.

"Yes, he has foreseen something. I will need to find him to join the two pieces, sister. But those of the ancient blood come. They still remain ignorant."

"I will wait for them. And, of this one, and the jewel?" asked Lido.

The gods looked at the lifeless body of Godryn. Already her cheeks had hollowed.

"Let her body return to the earth. I have her in my heart now and there she shall remain to be free from anymore suffering. Norbu's gift, my tears, will be safe in your blessed spring, Sister."

Assumpta walked to the edge of the pool and dropped the prism into the silent water. It only sank an arm's length beneath the surface where it came to rest on top of a giant waterlily. The petals slowly closed around it concealing it once again from the world.

"Sister, hasten your quest, for your tears have drawn the destroyer to my realm," said Lido as she carried Godryn's body into the sacred water.

Ascendant left once more to seek out Norbu.

14

Chains of Freedom

As the moon reached its full face the slender birches glistened under its spell. Gildas slept soundly underneath their glow, letting the night zephyrs caress his skin. The grass was soft and downy making an excellent bed. His body was still ravaged from the days in Banrock but some of the deeper wounds appeared less menacing. His escape had been easy in the end. After seven days of not accepting food, they had found him unconscious on the floor, barely breathing. They removed him from the vest and had placed him back inside his old cell and forced food into his mouth. Then, when he was strong enough, they had thrust him out into the yard for another of the death battles. He made the decision he would escape or die. He had pinned his opponent to the wall and using the body like a stepping-stone, managed to heave himself over the wall. The thorny brambles bit into his emaciated body as he landed on them, releasing the scent of his blood into the air. Instantly, howling echoed across the plain as the hounds of Banrock began their hunt. The dogs chased for many leagues, but, even after the fifteen summers of imprisonment and torture, the exiled

Graan warrior outran them.

The grove was easy to find, as any of the paths through the forests on the table above the Hunjsavat River seemed to lead to it. He had decided to stay, if only to heal his wounds. The witch may have led him to a trap, but it would do until he was stronger. While he slept, his mind was raging with battles he had fought and won. Memories of Jarrod fighting beside him and their father. Gildas had eventually made his enemies kneel to his suzerainty, the revenge swift for the loss of his father from the blade of an Unstaadt savage. Men's faces flew into his vision, screams and agonising pleads for mercy bombarded him. He twitched on the grass. He was back in the darkness again. It was silent. Then he became aware of something else. Suddenly, a wolf flashed into view; never this real, this close. He ran, a hot breath whipped past his cheek, he didn't stop as he heard the growl behind and then the abrading bark. Gildas focused; run to where it cannot follow echoed in the dream. He raced. The stench and lust for blood drew closer as the great wolf and the hounds of Banrock hunted their prey. Suddenly, his pursuers stopped. Gildas dared to look back. In the distance tiny green specs shone out. Gildas could feel their coldness before they saw him. A wraith wolf came into full view as it turned and sped towards the green eyes on the horizon. Its head was larger than Gildas full stature and within its huge jagged teeth were remnants of chewed flesh.

Now the victory of the Easterlings appeared and Gildas found himself standing on a rocky outcrop overlooking a vast plain. To his back was the azure of the majestic eastern ocean, magnificent and lethal as the mighty waves roared up the face of the cliffs. Before him, spread out on the plateau was the aftermath of a bloody battle. Soldiers lay dead or dying while others stood looking up at Gildas and Jarrod – always his brother was standing beside him. Gildas spoke, all the men before him kneeled, and those who did not were slashed down by those loyal to the Graan warrior.

"I am Gildas Gol of the Graanar; born in the reaches of the vast northern wastes, suckled on the tit of the Great Ice Bear. You are now beholden to my rule and at my use as I deem. Be loyal to me and I shall reward you with my protection. Choose treachery and know my wrath."

Cheers went up from the clansmen, while the vanquished sat in fear at the enslavement of their lands and lives. Gildas eye was drawn to a child crying so loudly he ordered it be smothered. Jarrod asked him to stay his hand, but he was disgusted by the noise of it. The face of the child remained in his dream; its expression changed to sneering then its eyes changed to those piercing green specs. "You have done so much already," it mouthed. "A loyal servant you have been and will become."

Gildas woke with a start. He was shivering in-spite of the warm earth he rested upon. The pool rippled slightly. Gildas sat up and noticed how dry his throat was. The nightmare lingered leaving him feeling washed out. He went to the pool. Scooping the pristine water into his hands he gulped it down. It was soothing and refreshing and cleared his mind instantly.

Sitting down again, his body still sore from his escape, he thought of what to do. Jarrod was on his mind a lot since the witch visited him. Had she cursed him? Those bonds were broken long ago. His brother would not have survived the hatred Gildas had chained to the Gol clan. 'By now, I should be searching for some mercenary work to earn some money, but instead here I am lying like an old woman, nursing wounds and a fevered mind,' he thought. He began to whittle down a few small branches to set a trap. He had noticed some droppings of shit near the pond, a marmoset or possum. It would return for water. His mind went back again to the steppes. He, Jesse and Jarrod skinning the fur off the marmosets his father had bought home. Gildas was gauging the quality of the fur. It was nearing his time to choose a companion, not to be joined yet, but betrothed. He knew it would be Jesse, just like everyone else, but it had not been approved by her father. Clot of the Clan Clotte was not opposed to it, but he was wary of Gildas. The chieftain was torn, as he knew for the Graan, the union was a good one. But even at that young age, Gildas had begun to show his belligerence to all that opposed him. However, the clans of Gol and Clotte had common enemies amongst the seven, and the in-fighting was beginning to weaken the tribes-men, making them vulnerable to invaders. This union would provide a formidable faction.

Inside the hut of Clotte sat Gildas, his father, Jesse and the talisman. Gildas eyed Clot and could see something weighed on the chieftain's mind.

"Nadas, could you ask Gildas to leave, I wish to talk between ourselves."

"I will not leave. It is against traditions. All must be present at a betrothal." Gildas protested at Clot's request.

"He has the right, Gildas, as the betrothed's father and clan chieftain. Show respect." Nadas gestured for his son to leave.

Gildas walked out, angry at being asked to leave, knowing that with or without permission, his clan wife would be Jesse. They had already lain together. It did not matter what the chieftain's decision was. He went around the rear of the hut and lay in the snow to listen.

"Speak your mind, Clot."

"I have asked the talisman to look into the future to see what the spirits see, and he sees shadow all around Gildas. My thoughts often dwell on this, Nadas. My daughter is a good match, and her betrothal to your son will make a strong bond for our clans, and all of the seven will see our strength and unite. But Gildas is wilful and I fear for my daughter and the Graanar tribes. His strength and temper will make him a strong warrior, but as for my daughter, will she fall under these and be lost to his domination so that even her own kin will not know her? Jesse is strong and the spirits have given her much heart and lust for life. The mother of the ice flows strongly in her blood. Would a father wish to see that trampled under the weight of a strong, but I fear hateful, betrothed who when challenged seeks revenge and not counsel."

"Have you not seen the two together? I see Jesse look at Gildas straight and without fear. I have seen Gildas step aside for her. Naught else, I have seen this with, including myself. Yes, Gildas will be strong and mighty and too quick to temper I agree, but never with your daughter have I seen this, Clot. I cannot foretell what shall come, but I think this union is fate with or without our agreement." Nadas looked directly at Jesse. She looked away quickly. She knew Nadas spoke the truth but did not wish to agitate her father.

"Is this true daughter, speak freely here."

"I have known Gildas since we were babes in furs. I have bested him in our childish games for he let me do so. We sit beside one another and he does not rage. He stills with me for I see when the anger comes and consumes his thoughts. It is not for me that I fear, but for him, for I fear it will be his death or the clans. I fear if I were not with him, no peace would he ever know. I also see his bravery and Gildas' love and pride for the clans and might of the icy wastes. I know that he will do all he can to make the clans strong and unafraid. Carry all his people on his shoulders and leave a legacy for our younglings so our lives here will endure. My life, for whatever reason, is with Gildas. I will walk with him, I will bed with him, I will fall with him, and I will die with him."

"But daughter, I fear that with time he will become blind to you and all will fall or die with him, for it is the way of the mighty that nil else is clear to them but their own vision."

"Gildas was put here to be something. His strength and tenacity are only bettered by the ice mother herself. I know within my heart that I must be part of his story, or I fear all will not only fall but shall die, and the clans of the north will perish into time without memory or name. Gildas sees my heart when his gaze lingers on me and knows no hurt or deceit lies there. His rage comes from his pride. When wounded, a mighty bear is released. I know the terror which can dwell there, but I have stayed his hand. And when this happens, I can see it is the ice mother herself which rages, and it is her who listens to my counsel. But fear also lives next to love and duty. I too have asked the talisman what may lie before me. Tell them."

The old man spoke. "I see a land ravaged at the hand of Gildas and in the distance stands a demon eating the great ice mother that roams our lands and protects us. As the demon comes to strike our mighty chieftain down, Jesse, with her knife, wounds him so that as he falls, the demon's gaze passes over him. The spirit of the ice mother dwells inside Gildas and she is saved by the blade of Jesse."

"What does this mean, talisman?" Nadas asked feeling concerned for the first time.

"I know this came from the spirits who have willed this union. Dark days and much blood shall wash our lands at the hands of your son, Nadas of Gol, but a greater peril lies beyond that and your son's destiny is bound to it also. He will be our destroyer, but also the ice warrior that may just stop the end days of the Graanar. The ice mother blesses and curses, as is her way."

Jesse spoke, "I will fulfil this fate and duty if only to protect the Ice Mother from complete destruction."

Their union was agreed upon. The memories had been long buried, there was much he had forgotten. Even Jesse's loyalty had not stirred any feelings. The nightmares that haunted his sleep pricked the fallen Graanar's stony heart more closely. He had seen the presence of another shadow in them: a presence that was stronger in its will to conquer and destroy than his own. At fifty summers, Gildas guessed he was getting old and along with it came deep exhaustion and fear.

He wondered about the talisman's vision regarding the demon and shivered again at the nightmare of the green eyes in the distance. The witch had won in the end. He had no choice but to go where she had told him was safe.

He heard the trap go off and went towards it. Inside lay a possum. Gildas killed it and took it back to the fire. Nothing seemed to make a sound except the spitting flames. Jesse's face formed in front of him as he tested the roasting carcass. He had killed her in the end, just as her father said he would. 'The mighty always become blind to all except their own vision.' He thought on the truth of those words. His heart had not even broken when he saw Jesse lying dead before him; but her eyes remained ever looking into his deepest thoughts, never letting him go. They had made him see his own weakness. He drove the stick into the ground in anger. What purpose would he serve now? He was a prisoner and exile, useless except to run with common thieves or a bandit in the forest. The black wolf of his dreams chased him. After so many winters of being caged, the world had forgotten Gildas Gol, the great Graan Lord of the North.

"The ice mother curses and blesses as is her way," he whispered as he sat watching Jesse's face dance in the flames.

15

Forsworn

The dawn was magnificent as the sun ascended over the horizon leaving the death and venom of the world at the grove behind her. The old monk lay within her. She felt the weariness of Godryn's soul being torn between intimate desires and the unreachable quest of enlightenment. Assumpta wondered about the chains the clay born used to bind their weaknesses and strengths. Their blindness led them to these dark places with no way of reprieve. Why had she not been let forth into the world instead of being held in the realm of light? It was as if each thing existed independently of everything else. The realm of light was breached anyway, would it not have been better to let her and Baachelaus rule here amongst the creatures made from clay.

"Oh, great Belmaris, brightest of all the stars and light of the darkness that surrounds this place, can you not reach forth and pluck the sorrow and malice and destroy it in your cleansing flames? Save these ones from the torment of seeing their own death."

The clothes she wore glistened with its rays and reminded

her of its makers. She smiled thinking of the little worms, under-standing now how lethal they were to the people here as well. Did all that dwelt here seek to maim them?

As she made her way over the first of the peaks, she saw a structure built into the side of the mountain. It seemed an impossible feat to build it on the very edge of such a sheer cliff face. There was a man standing looking out over the valley below, arms outstretched as the sun grew to its fullness. He then lay down prostate on the stone ledge not moving. Assumpta quested into his mind and found quiet solitude. She went forward curious about this one. As she rose higher in the sky the man did not move and his mind remained silent and still with one thought; the rising sun. She then directed her mind to others in the building. One was meditating but annoyed at the same time about the young novice who had forgotten to fetch the milk. Another was trying to remember the litany of the dawn, but he couldn't remember the main verse. Then she felt an implacable darkness pierce her thoughts. A palpable fear washed over her and she began to shiver. She felt the blood of old fire and memories. This was one of the descendants of the first to walk the earth. An ancestor to those who made cove-nant with Norbu. His face returned to her from the image in Lido's pool. She walked through the entrance with her hood pulled over giving her the appearance of a pale shadow. Since her time here, she could no longer fully disguise herself as she became more connected to this world, but the magic of the worms had its wisdom as their silk threads hid her form in the shadows. Inside the temple was dark and heavily timbered, with huge beams of oak interlaced with granite colonnades carved from the mountain. A large metal disc hung in the far end of the chamber and dotted on the floor were several monks. She had not sensed them earlier as they were deep in meditation and had entered into a trance state. All she could feel was silence.

She continued until she found the one with the darkness inside him. It grew stronger as she neared him and a niggly pain began to burn and prickle her skin. On the mat lay Kado, emaciated and feverish. He had bruises all over his back and sores on his arms and face. He had inflicted deep gouges from the itch made by poison of the lily worked its way out of his body. He twitched and rolled over moaning. His eyes opened as she neared him. Placing a hand on him, the searing pain that met her was as the prick of the scorpion bite. It washed through her making her collapse with pain. She fell away from him, as did her hood, revealing her face. He looked confused thinking she was a monk.

"Water, wretch!"

Assumpta rose and seeing a bucket of water with a ladle went to get some.

He drank it thirstily.

"The scorpion chases you."

He looked at her for the first time realising it was a woman.

"Who are you?"

"You are one of the descendants of the ancient blood that walks the earth; Kado last son of the Dragon Dynasty."

He stiffened slightly as he heard his name. "Who are you? Tell me your name."

"You do not know me. I know your friend. Sa Tuc is her name."

He relaxed a little and she felt a small dot of light enter at the name. He still held affection for her. "Did my father send you? Am I forgiven?"

"Your father is dead."

Kado sat up and propped himself upon the wall. The room was dark with only light from the doorway. He was dressed in a loose hessian robe and sandals.

"More," he said, giving the ladle back to Assumpta. She refilled it and handed it back to him. His mind was racing, as was his heart. He had an illness inside him. He coughed heavily bringing with it spots of blood.

"What do you mean Ko the Emperor and war monger is dead? By whose hand?" Assumpta was confused at his feelings. She had felt the grief in Ange when she thought of her mother and sister, and even in Bensah. But this one was different; there was alarm at the news, but no regret or sadness. She sensed a twinge of relief.

"Your father's kingdom has fallen. What festers inside you, for I see a worm there that will not leave, but slowly eats you away?"

Kado looked with jaundiced eyes at the woman for the first time. She was unlike any he had seen before. Her skin was like a moon and her eyes shone brilliantly, green with yellow speckles, which caught what little light there was in his chamber. Her dress was unknown to him – pants and a long tunic with boots. He noted the unusual weave on her belt.

"Who are you, woman?"

"Your world changes around you, Kado Kodrax. The demon and the destroyer now walk this place. He has come for all that exists here, to draw it into himself. I seek the descendants of the first generations of the clay born; one such as you."

"I do not understand you. Are you a spirit come to me in my dreams about my father's passing?"

"You are awake, not dreaming. When the sickness inside you has healed, you are to come with the one called Sa Tuc. Your purpose is not revealed, but the blood of the dragon must not be consumed by the shadow or its power will not be defeated. Remain here until you are healed. The scorpion is close, Kado, but it has not devoured you yet."

Kado looked at her suddenly. How would she know? She must be of the spirit realm to see into his mind. Assumpta felt the fear rise in him as the memory of being hunted came back to him.

"It gets closer all the time. But they are only nightmares as my body purges the lily from itself. It cannot harm me here. I fear the sickness in my chest will eat me first."

"Do not fool yourself. Once it would only have been a shadow on the edges of your dream, but the destroyer has breached the void and now these things that hunt you are real. I could not be here if this were not so."

Kado was beginning to feel tired again as the next wave of cramps began.

"What of my mother, where is she now?"

"She is dead as well. Your father's kingdom has been trampled to the ground, Kado. Voloc, the shadow, seeks the power of your ancient heritage, and has driven the one known as Ranik through your lands. The bejewelled city adorned with my brethren's work is all but destroyed."

"Was their death brutal, particularly his?"

Assumpta probed carefully for she did not wish to feel the malice wash over her as before. "I do not know. I was not a witness to their deaths. Voloc's mind is full of hatred of all things born of Caemeris. The shadow's vision does not lie with that of the brethren. Believe me Kado, you are now the prey of the scorpion and its master."

"So, what am I to do then, this pathetic son of a dead emperor, loathed and feared by all under his gaze. No kingdom to rule and a body weak and diseased from all my insatiable appetites."

"I will have need of you. Dragon sired, you are one of the ancients, the Ko-Dragon birthed of the loins of the great lizard who first walked into the middling lands. Your father's dynasty has dwelt in feudal suzerainty for almost seven millennia. Face the scorpion that seeks you. This illness has not made you completely rotten. You have an unfound strength with which to fight it."

"I am of no use. If I jumped from the cliff now no one would care and the Drax Magisterium's demise would have a fitting end."

"Nay, for your death will only leave your blood to spill into the earth for the shadow to consume it at time's end. Your ally, Sa Tuc, is useful also and I sense that more is to come where she will be needed."

She hesitated, looking at the creature that lay before her. "Kado Diamond Fang, I have found you now and I take all your malice and putrid mess inside for it will serve me well in the battle to come. Strong or weak, you are entwined with the great custodians of your world. If it is not the scorpion that devours you, then it shall be me. Come with your assassin and friend when you are strong. So much more lies ahead in these the last days of the Custodians of Caemeris."

Kado tried to stand but collapsed again as fatigue and pain began to take over. A deep visceral cough racked his body causing blood to dribble down his lip. The solemnity of Assumpta's words seemed lost on him, as his mind became clouded by the demands of his body. Rousing briefly, he stared at the spirit in front of him. "Where is mistress Sa? It would be nice to see her again."

Wiping his chin with his robe, he inspected the red spittle. "Spirit, I will stay here, but I fear the Drax Magisterium demise is closer than you think. I think that the lily candy has truly addled my mind and rotted my innards until they cannot be cured. If I wake, my father shall still haunt my steps and my fretful mother will scold herself in obeisance to her inferiority to the mighty Ko. If you see Elder Tuc, let her know the monks have finally beaten me into a compliant puppet. Something she could never do."

He chuckled to himself causing him to go into another violent cough. The spasm exhausted him as he lay back down and let his eyes close. Then the fevers began. Assumpta felt fear creep in and it made her shiver. Kado stood on a massive chasm of darkness. He had his arms spread out ready to fall. She left just as the claws of the scorpion could be heard in the distance.

"Face it, Kado and you shall prevail. Run and you shall die, but the pain will never end."

Leaving the temple, the silence of the occupants' minds and hearts quelled the turmoil that she had taken from Kado. If he chose to, he could become strong again. Stepping down off the entrance to Sa Dom temple, she walked into the heart of the forest, which was so dense in places that the sun never broke through. She did not notice the shadow behind her fade into the trunk of a massive fir tree. Assumpta suddenly heard the low growl. She froze. Turning around she saw standing behind her one of the ancient guardians of Baachelaus. It was tall and towered at least three heads above her. Its massive talons scraped the ground. She steadied herself waiting for it to attack her.

"You have the stealth of your prisoner in you, gaoler. What do you want?"

It stood swaying not speaking in the dappled shade. It approached and stretching its long talon out it touched her forehead. She felt power drain from her and pervade her as well. The knife-like claw left a mark on her skin of a small diamond without the bottom point.

"Who are you gaoler? Why not do the shadow's bidding and destroy me? You know who I am and why I am here."

Just then, a breeze blew and caused the branches to sway and separate for a moment, letting in the morning sun. A ray glanced onto the guardian's upper limb and burnt it. It jumped onto the shaded side of a great conifer. Assumpta could barely see it. A chill whisper floated down from where the creature sat.

"We are bonded to the shadow until our queen commands us. You shall bring her to us. It has been promised by the prophecy of Caemeris and our progenitor Stonthrax."

And then it left. Assumpta let out an audible breath. The surge of the power that had emanated from the creature left her and made her faint. So strong were these creatures; but they were unknown to the brethren. They were potent with an ancient strength, made even before the realm of light. She rubbed the mark on her skin. It still tingled slightly. The creature had looked inside her and had seen who she was in her elemental state. It would know why she was here. Yet it did not seem to care. Perhaps they were an unknown ally. Their queen? Perhaps Norbu would know. She had never seen the guardians bind Baachelaus in chains. These creatures and their destinies were unknown to her. Her grief and confusion had blinded her to these last moments when the realm of light had been ripped open. This is the legacy that the children of Arglethium endure. Their ignorance like her ignorance, their sorrow like her sorrow. Perpetually doomed to exist in the memories of light and yet never touch it or understand it.

Ascendant journeyed on, reaching the greats hills of Jun. Belmaris was strong and at its zenith.

"Rise, brother sun and smote this poison that has cursed the realm of light and this cage of clay which has existed since the first colours of the dawn of time."

But nothing came from the great star, and in her mind's eye, she heard the screams of Kado as the scorpion hunted his blood.

16

Fire and Water

The heat of the day was cooled slightly by a breeze from the sea to the east. Bensah and Ange walked on the steep pathway stretching along the coast. They had turned towards the north separating from the last survivors of the Ancrid City. He had tried to warn some of their fellow refugees not to go south even near the coast. Bensah looked behind him and saw Ange limping along with Nekoda beside her. She was staring out towards the ocean. She was overwhelmed with its beauty and grandeur the higher they climbed.

"It will take until the next full moon to reach the mountains, Ange. It is eight dawns until we reach Doanda."

As they walked, occasionally Ange would ask a question, but mostly it was in silence. Bensah thought of what they would need and who could provide them with the safest way to cross the mountains. Ange would sometimes think of playing with Tessi until it hurt too much and made her cry. Nekoda would give her an affectionate nuzzle and trot off looking for something to eat. Soon the road evened out onto a plateau that ended abruptly at the feet of the Doanda Ranges. The mountains divided the south desert lands from the northern trade route which connected the western territories. The cliffs were high enough that they trapped the clouds from moving south so that the northern lands were green and fertile, while Ange and Bensah's lands were hot and dominated by desert. The road wound closer towards the edges of the cliffs so that their sheer and unwelcoming faces imposed themselves on travellers beneath as well as the ocean. Ange was glad that she had Bensah and Nekoda with her as she peered over the edge down toward the crashing waves.

They eventually reached Yena. It was about the same size as Kensai, but stretched along a small stream with no central market. Ange saw the dwellings were in the shape of mounds. Bensah placed a leash on Nekoda before he entered. He knew of a trader who would sell him supplies and information. Ange followed along behind.

Coming to a humpy, Bensah called out. "Woop Woop, Tchata."

A man about the same height and age as Bensah came outside. His head was almost fully covered, as was the fashion in the coastal villages.

"Eh, El Bunani. Many moons and a new wife, eh."

"The plagues have come, Brother, and we seek new lands. Have many come this way?"

"Only a few. We had heard rumours."

"Yes, a demon drives the wind, Brother. All is lost in my homelands and as far as Ancrid City. I am going to the other side of the hills."

"Hmm, you will need supplies, a camel."

"Nay, just food mostly, and the safest route."

"Come we will eat. Jekta!" he called, clapping his hands. A woman and two girls had been preparing the midday meal and ushered Bensah into the small dwelling.

Ange and Nekoda waited outside. One of the girls bought Ange some yogurt and cakes.

"Thankyou." Ange's mouth watered at the food. Nekoda lapped some milk from a bowl.

Bensah emerged several hours later. Ange had fallen asleep on Nekoda.

"Come, we will camp here the night and leave early."

On the morning, the bartered supplies were given to Bensah. They consisted of two flour sacks, five water bags made from the hides of goats, honey, and cinnamon with yoghurt for the morning meal.

"Remember, the path closest to the ocean is the most trodden but be beware thieves are easily hidden in the bush. I do not know of this lake you speak, but I rarely travel over the mountains now."

Bensah grasped arms with his friend.

"Farewell and safe travelling, Bensah." Tchata patted Ange on the head and Nekoda.

"You must be strong to survive the plagues, little one." He spoke looking at Ange's bent shape and tiny body.

Ange looked Tchata in the eye. "Yes I am strong." she replied.

The village disappeared behind them, and soon they reached the steep path that led down to the beach where the main route through the mountains could be found. Ange stood on the pebbly sand and looked at the ocean before her. The blue of the water matched the stones Tata had given to her. She touched some of the water as the waves lapped on the sand and pulled back, instinct telling her that they might drag her in. Nekoda frolicked joyfully and splashed both Bensah and Ange. Its huge expanses made her feel small and lonely for some reason. The waves movements made her chest ache each time they crashed into the shore. A sense of doom came with it and she wanted to yell out, to stop whatever it was destroying her world. Tears came but she wiped them away quickly, "You can't have anymore, you have enough," she whispered to the ocean.

Eventually, they came to the point where the mountains met the coast and turned towards the north. A small staircase of chiselled steps worked its way up along the face of the cliffs, disappearing under the foliage of the forest that grew at the top. The waves crashed onto the outcrops of rocks, forming a natural barrier to crossing the base of the mountains. It was getting towards night and the trio made camp. As soon as the sun set and darkness engulfed them, a roar of wind and waves soon swept onto the lands. The tide was massive, and the blue became obsidian black as the might and terror of the ocean rose up. Far off in the horizon, Ange could see the twinkling lanterns of a ship climbing the huge swell, its hull almost disappearing as it dipped down the slip-face of the waves. She went to sleep hugging Nekoda, thinking the dangers in this world never ended. She dreamt of being swallowed by one of the waves. It was like claws larger than the vultures of the dunes were tearing at the earth, wanting to devour everything.

The dawn rose and soon the threesome were climbing the

ladder of steps. Half-way up the almost vertical climb Ange stopped and rested against a ledge. Her good leg still ached from the scorpion bite. "Tata, I can't walk anymore."

Bensah came up from below breathing heavily. "We will rest when we get to the top. We can't stay here, Sister, the tide can reach this far, see the white line along the rocks there."

Ange saw it and nodded. Getting up, she looked back down to the sea. Stumbling back against the rock, she steadied herself as her head spun from the height. As she went to step up the next ledge, her weak leg scraped along a jagged shard of slate. The blood dripped down.

"Keep going, Sister, I will patch it when we reach the top." Bensah pushed her to keep moving. He stayed behind her to steady her if needed.

Nekoda went ahead, easily climbing the rocky face. He soon disappeared into the canopy. A flurry of birds with brightly covered feathers suddenly appeared out of the trees, followed by a bark. Nekoda poked out onto a ledge with a bird in his mouth and tail wagging with pride.

"Whoop, good dog. We have a meal, Ange." His fingers fell into a small pool of blood that had dripped from Ange's leg. He hoped it didn't fester before they reached Doanda.

They camped under a large fern. Ange had scratches on her face from the spikey fronds of the elegant plant which covered their path. There had been no light at all as the forest grew denser towards the summit. As they set up camp, the rain began. The drops were so thick and heavy Ange thought it was like stones hitting her. All night it continued soaking them through.

"Nekoda you smell." Ange pushed him away as the dog rested next to her. His fur was soaked. He sneezed but did not move enjoying the warmth of Ange.

In the middle of the night, Ange heard voices. She woke to find Bensah sitting up with his machete in one hand and holding Nekoda's snout with the other. He had Nekoda's leash wrapped around his arm. The dog was straining so hard that the leather strap was cutting into his flesh. The voices carried up through the leaves. It was accented but Ange could understand it.

"I saw em come this way. Go higher."

Bensah looked at Ange. He put three fingers up to tell her how many. As they came close, she saw they had large knives on their belts. Suddenly Bensah let Nekoda go. The dog instantly dragged one of the men to the ground. Ange watched in the moonlight. Nekoda's large jaws ripped out the man's throat. The one behind, after recovering from shock, went for the dog with his knife, but Bensah's machete flew into his chest. The third one, realising he was outnumbered, started to run, but Nekoda got his scent and chased after him. Bensah pulled his machete out and cleaned it on some fern leaves. He came back under the fern and sat down.

"We will continue on at first light. We will need to be more careful." Nekoda came back covered in blood. He sat down snorting and panting and began to lick himself. Ange pulled away, shaken at the ferocity of the fight.

"Never mind Ange, this is the way of the world." Bensah spoke.

Shivering she lay down again.

They reached the highest peak of the path three days later. Ange was completely exhausted. Her leg that had been bitten had not healed fully and was still throbbing. The wound on the other leg had begun to look ugly. Bensah dabbed some ointment made from tea onto the sore.

"There is a healer in Doanda, Sister. It should be okay until then."

"Tata, why do you stay with me?" Ange watched Bensah rewrap the wound carefully.

"I do not know, Sister." He genuinely did not know. He knew he could go ahead and begin again, but why he chose to take Ange; he wasn't sure. Perhaps it was his affection for Noai; loyalty and friendship were strong bonds to Bensah. Ange was also the last remaining link to his life before the plague had come. Deep down, he wondered as well if Ange was the daughter he still grieved for even after so many seasons had passed. It was that grief and mutual bond he had shared with Sara his wife. They had been ostracised by their village when the twins died and remained with her. His trading was also considered to be unfair. He understood the isolation which can build walls more sturdy than fortress when you were judged to be different from others.

Breaking free of the profuse canopy they saw the walk down would be difficult as well. The view stretched in front of them for leagues; green open fields interspersed with forests and valleys. It was magnificent. The mountains continued to their left along the ocean, blocking any noise from the waves.

"The lady said we should walk for nine days until we find a lake after we crossed over the mountains." spoke Ange.

"Who is this lady?"

"I don't know, she was there at the well the day Takob broke my beads. Her eyes were like looking into a rainbow. I think she was a spirit. She said a man was looking for something I have."

"We shall see." Bensah wondered if it was Ange's mind playing tricks on her from the sorrow and hardship she now endured. If it was real then it was no comfort either that spirits had been awoken. Did they bring this destruction with them? He shivered at this thought. "Praise be Ancrid, protect us." He muttered.

They began to make their descent towards the valley. A small glimmer of hope formed in Bensah's heart that they could settle here. He could farm again. The area had been settled long ago by the north and south and was one of the few territories where the two peoples mixed.

"Perhaps life could begin again." He sighed.

Ange slipped on a rock. She slid halfway down a slope until she caught a branch. Nekoda came loping after her. Giggling, she hoisted herself up. Just as she was about to continue, her face was met by a massive green snake that hung from a branch; its long, forked tongue fluttered on her cheek. Ange froze as the head glided past followed by a massive body. Its belly was wider than Ange. The scales scintillated in the dappled sunlight, brilliant yellow's and greens. It hitched on a branch momentarily, as something bulging inside its skin got caught. Slowly the great leviathan slid off into the jungle and disappeared from sight. Ange let out a breath of relief. Nekoda started sniffing some scales that had been fallen on the ground.

"It didn't think you were tasty enough today, sister." Bensah patted her on the shoulder laughing.

They made camp again halfway down the mountain path under a massive fir tree. Bensah walked to an out crop of rock. He saw buildings in the distance to the northwest. Plumes of smoke drifted up from some of the buildings. 'Doanda would be good place to start again,' he thought. He scanned the vista and looked directly to the west, Bensah could see a red band extending across the horizon. 'The sun does not want to sleep tonight,' he wondered at the ferocity of the sunset. The red was like a blood of freshly killed goat.

It had been almost two full moons since he had left his home. As he made his way back to their camp, he knew they would not go any further. He had enough to buy his way into a new life here and the weariness of living crept ever more into his flesh.

Ange had started to make a fire and pluck a turkey Nekoda had found. 'The girl has strength,' he thought, and a swell of pride bloomed in his chest as he thought of his tribeswomen. He did not say anything about staying in Doanda.

Reaching the village, they found it deserted. The huts had been almost destroyed by fire and there were no remains of animals or people to be seen. It was built on the edge of a river called the Funasa. The river continued on its path oblivious to the destruction that lay on its banks. Its silent flow was swift and hid its lethal strength which could drag a grown man down to its unknown depths. Across the other side, the rest of Doanda was in ruins, some of the humpies were still smouldering in places.

Bensah's heart sank as his hope of a life here drifted away with the smoke. He stared disbelieving at their misfortune. Ange saw the disappointment in Bensah's face.

"I think we need to go to the lady's place, Tata," she said taking his hand.

He looked at her and thought how pathetic they must seem to the world, homeless, no food and only the things they carried to call their own. But he saw Ange's broken body and how she climbed the mountains, survived slavers and a plague and stood here before him. It was weak of him to feel sorry for himself.

"Yes, Ange it seems we are not welcome here either," he finally managed to say to her. She squeezed his hand slightly.

Smoke began to drift across again from the west. They left the little village and continued walking. Nekoda had been drinking from the river. "Well dog, if you don't get sick then at least we will know the winds have not poisoned the water."

As they continued throughout the day, the smoke began to get thicker. Ange found it difficult to breathe. Her leg had begun to ooze pus again.

"Tata, my leg."

"Come, we will go up higher away from the river. I will go back tomorrow and see if I can find the herbs to clean it. The smoke may have cleared by then."

That night they camped up on the side of a hill inside an empty hut. Nothing had been disturbed and there was plenty to eat. Towards the west, epileptic fits of a massive wildfire were devouring the vast forests.

Ange sat up. "Look, Tata."

In the distance a figure walked amongst the fire. It looked like a man but made of flames. It flung its arms and hands, igniting everything it touched. It jumped onto a hill and burnt the crops. Then it flew onto the canopy of trees and incinerated them. It went towards the Doanda mountains and lit the jungle so that the green that normally crowned the granite cliffs soon turned to orange and black as the fire spread.

"The spirits of the earth have awakened, and they are angry, sister. Come, I think we must make haste, for while the wind did not capture us, the fire will."

They hastily packed their satchels and made their way toward the crest of the hill. The moon was full but had a red glow around it from the flames. It gave enough light to allow them to make their way down the other side of the hill and continue due north. Ange was limping badly. She sat down, exhausted.

"We will rest near the river. The flames did not cross before. The water may protect us."

Suddenly the roar of the flames could be heard behind them, as the fire demon spat its fury onto the earth. Ange looked back and screamed, the spirit was just on the other side of the river behind them. Bensah grabbed her and began to run.

"Quickly, it pursues us."

The smoke was choking and they both coughed. Nekoda was sneezing. Rabbits, and lemurs and monkeys were scurrying with them in the same direction. 'Good,' thought Bensah, 'we are going away from danger.' Eventually it became too thick and choking and Bensah could feel heat.

"Into the water."

They splashed into the river. It was deep and the water washed over them both. Ange panicked as she didn't know how to swim. Nekoda dogpaddled towards her letting her clutch his fur. The flames roared at the side of the river. Ange could feel the water heat up around them. She could barely breathe from the smoke. Bensah found her and Nekoda. Swimming back to the bank they had come from, they found the muddy bed underfoot and trod water. Then through the flames, the fire spirit appeared. It went to leap over the river, but suddenly a figure rose out of the water and grabbed the spirit of flames. They wrestled, they spoke and roared at one another in an ancient tongue. Flames and water hissed, and steam rose into black vapours. The fire god's face changed shape as its mouth broke into a ragged maw issuing a different voice. The water spirit did not relent. Suddenly the river around Ange and Bensah began to recede leaving them standing in mud. A massive wave was forming. It came towards the fire spirit and pummelled it into the riverbank. The flames broke apart. Suddenly, the fire reformed stronger than ever as it became a massive behemoth. The water rose again, and the two figures were lost in a haze of vapours and ashes. The water spirit turned briefly. It saw Ange, Bensah and Nekoda, standing watching; Nekoda whimpered while Ange shrunk in fear. Turning back, it reefed the flames into itself to douse the raging fire. Everything exploded as the massive wall of water flooded the lands and suffocated the flames of the fire spirit. Suddenly, the stream of the river began to flow back towards Ange and Bensah.

"Hurry, we will drown."

They hopped out and began to run towards the trees. Bensah hoisted her up onto a branch as he followed. In the distance, the two figures could still be seen fighting, but the fire spirit had been weakened.

"Something has angered the gods, but something protects us, sister, we should be dead."

Ange cried softly, "The grove, Tata. We need to go there, or we will die."

"Yes, sister." They watched the water overtake the village and rise almost as high as the branch they sat on. As it flowed back into the riverbed, it washed away with it the remains of Doanda. The land was scoured clean.

"What are those spirits, Tata?

"My grandfather used to talk of the spirits of the earth. They help to keep life in balance; Fire, Water, Earth and Wind. But they remained hidden in their real form. Something has awoken them for them to show themselves to us."

The night was barely different to the day as the smoke lingered in the air choking everything. They made a camp. Bensah had managed to salvage some stores to take with them the rest of the way. A deep fear rose in Bensah's heart. If the spirits were at war, then no one would survive. He also thought of the water spirit seeing them there, witnessing its battle, and knew that something still fought to protect the land.

Ange lay sleeping as he smoked his pipe and thought of what they would do. He lay down patting Nekoda and fell asleep.

Lido walked towards the three lying on the ground sleeping. She touched Ange's leg and healed the wound. "Run, children of Norbu. I cannot protect you forever. Seraf sees only darkness and malice. He will destroy all in his path. I cannot go against Baachelaus. He is the higher brethren. I cannot stop his will, which drives Seraf to such rage. Go to my pool as my sister has commanded."

17

Assassin

Sa woke. She saw the pouch on the mat. Someone had been here. Standing up she looked around her small room and then went to the door. She listened for any sound that someone was waiting to attack. It was dark, with only a waning crescent of the moonlight filtering into the window. Deciding it was safe, Sa opened the pouch. A small jack carved out of ivory fell out. It was ornate but worn down, showing its age. It stirred something in her, but she couldn't place where she had seen it before. She sniffed it. 'It isn't a tracking token,' she thought, not detecting any odour. The Feudal Lords and Ko trained dogs to follow scents. Tokens could be rubbed on a belonging or person of someone they wanted tracked. Sa put the jack back into the pouch and slipped it insider her tunic. Swiftly she gathered her satchel with the stowed maps. Peering into the empty corridor she stealthily left the boarding house, unheard or seen. The streets were quiet apart from a few brothel workers and their masters and beggars asleep on the pavements. Sa quickly made her way to the sugar trader's stall. Her black eyes were constantly scanning and checking if anyone was following her.

The cart had been moved in readiness for the morning's trip. The tarpaulin was taut over the top. Pulling up the tarp she decided she could fit long ways. There were empty hessian sacks three layers deep lining the cart; waiting to be refilled with sugar, flour, rice and tea.

Hearing voices she ducked down and waited.

"Yes, I will leave in the morning before dawn. The guards are inspecting everything. It will delay the journey. Jhan said he took nearly half the day to just leave the city."

Someone came over to the cart. Sa could hear them checking the tarpaulin again and testing the ropes. Waiting a little to make sure they didn't return, she slipped under the sacks. Noting her feet jutted out she exhaled and twisted her feet outwards to the corners, flattening out the sacks. The cart looked undisturbed.

The cramping in her body began just before the dawn as the voices returned. She tensed; this would be the test. The tarpaulin flipped open and something landed on her torso. She felt the cart start to move.

"Where are you headed?"

"Pohl town, and then to the crossroads."

"Go!"

The cart began to move again, jolting heavily as it crossed the ditch that marked the boundary of the city. Sa relaxed slightly until the next cramps began in her legs. She started to recite the mantras of control to herself. It would take most of the day to reach the crossroads. From there, she could make her way to the mountain paths and aim directly north. She would be back in Drax province by the next moon. She breathed deeply trying to control the pain.

Sa lost track of time but knew that it was not yet night, as small shafts of light still broke through the cracks between the planks. She had felt the air grow cold, which meant they were moving higher into the mountains.

The cart had not moved for some time and the chatter of the men seemed further away. She stole a glance through the sacks. She could not see anyone sitting on the bench seat. She heard the ass swish its tail. Sa took the chance and lifted herself out of the cart and hopped quickly underneath. Her legs cramped instantly. Placing herself fully under the axle in the hope that no one would see her, she rubbed her feet and calves to get them moving. She felt the blood coming back and tested that her legs would support her. Looking around, she saw a rock and some trees on the opposite of the road. The trader and his companion had made a fire a little way off and were talking behind her. Sa couldn't make out what they were saying. She bolted and cinched herself up against the rock face away from the cart. She waited, breathing slowly to lessen the adrenaline. Sa slid into the bushland and disappeared from the sugar trader and Hosianne Citadel. She kept running until the half crescent of the moon was almost perpendicular to the earth. She had managed to cross two leagues to the north. Sa made camp and began to plan the next part of the journey. The sandstone cliffs were too sheer to climb where she was, further west the ranges flattened allowing travellers to cross them.

She heard voices and quickly slipped into a crouch behind an outcrop of rocks. A group of men walked past, massive in stature. They laughed and spoke in a tongue of the northern clansmen. Their voices faded as the group moved on. Sa waited until she could not hear them. Deciding it was safe she continued her flight back to Drax City. The caves in the mountains were full of criminals not only from the provinces of Ko but also from the men of the east and the far northern lands. Men Sa could best one to one, but they tended to form raiding parties on the local villages. If she happened to meet with one of these parties, she considered that she would not survive. The northern clansmen had fierce reputations for their fighting prowess, even Ko had tried to enlist them, but they were unwieldy, lacking a subtle discipline and only making up for it with brute strength.

Sa came to a large expanse of grassy plain dotted with rocks. It stretched almost a whole league, with no shelter or cover of trees, leaving her vulnerable to attack. Thick bracken and thorny bushes, covering uneven rocky ground, made the trek harder work than Sa expected. After half a day, Sa rested. She took out a small sack of nuts and grains. As she ate, she pulled out the jack that had been left in her room. Looking at it frustrated her. She had seen this before, but where. She flipped it between her fingers. It was a child's game she used to see the other children play in the courtyards. The counting chants came to mind. She put it back. Swigging some water, she got up and began a slow jog. She was hoping to make it at least three quarters of the way around the plain today. Suddenly she heard men's voices again. She crouched flat under the bracken. It pricked her face and hands, making them bleed. They were speaking the same tongue as before. Sa heard the word 'west'.

"It's a woman or boy. They were too small to be a man. They

have to be heading to the Xian path over the mountains. There is no other way to climb the ranges," spoke the largest of the group.

"Yeah I reckin' Inat. Theys has to be here somewhere. Nowhere to hide on the plains," agreed Knut.

They had guessed that was the direction she would be headed. Standing directly beside her, she saw a leg dressed in heavy leather strapping around the trouser of the clansmen. It protected their legs from the thorns. It was like a timber pylon towering over her. Suddenly, Sa felt something grab her back and hoist her up.

The men laughed when they saw her. They threw her down. Sa sprung up in her defensive stance and looked at each man, quickly sizing them up. There were four. They were massive. Each would have been twice, almost three times her stature easily. Their arms were as thick as tree trunks. They had the tribal tattoos of the Graanar clansmen. One of them feinted at her to get her to jump, but Sa's reaction was far more lethal. In a flash, she had whipped herself up onto his back and slit his throat, darting back to face the other three as they watched their clansman fall to the ground with blood gushing.

"Bitch!" one of them muttered and pulled out his machete and swung at her. She ducked easily and landed a blow to his diaphragm. It was like a rock and jarred her leg. He went at her again, then, the others came behind forming a circle around her.

Picking up a stone, she speared it up into one of the men's head. He fell, stunned. Sa landed a blow to his neck and crushed it. She whipped over to another menacing with an axe. She stumbled as one from behind slashed at her back. It glanced off her swag. Sa rammed her dagger into the knee of the axeman, he fell as the ligaments gave way. Sa grabbed his head and reefed it back; the whites of his eyes glistened as she dragged her blade along his throat. The blade caught briefly on the bone in the clansman's neck. She watched his eyes dull as the warm blood oozed onto her hand. The last man standing made a run at her, grunting heavily. With lightning speed, she leapt up onto him and taking his head twisted it with a ferocious force and broke his neck. Sa put her knife away and stood looking at the bodies.

"That was too close, Sa Tuc. You were clever trackers to find me like that. Too close," she whispered to herself.

By night fall, she had crossed the exposed plain and was making her way along a gentle slope of the mountains. It was three nights past the full moon, Tuan and Kim will not have waited for her, so she did not expect them to rendezvous. In two more days, she would be able to cross the cliffs and be within the Ko territory.

She looked towards the mountains as they began to loom over the landscape. Running at a fast sprint, she did not notice the body lying in the grass. She tripped over it sending her into a somersault. Looking back, she saw Tuan lying in a pool of blood. She crouched down. More than likely, it was the men she had encountered earlier who had done this, but she didn't want to risk being caught. She lay still for a long time. Not hearing anything, she crept over to Tuan. She reached inside his coat. His bedding and roll had been ransacked and his tunics torn, but Sa knew where anything important would be hidden. She found what she was looking for, a metal tube lodged in the side seam of his undershirt. As she took it, she bowed to Tuan. "You have died honourably."

Getting up she put the tube in her tunic and sped towards the mountains. She looked like a black panther streaking in the night. Sa made it over the first rise of the lower mountains. Just as the exhaustion from the climb up began to bite, she found the ledge where they had camped on their way to the Hosiaan province. As she slept, Kado came to her again in her dreams. She and he were playing jacks in the courtyard. He was teaching her this time. Three days later, as she made her way back to the forests surrounding Drax City, she found Kim. He was lying against a tree, sheltering from the wind, pale and taking shallow breaths.

"What happened to you, Kim?"

"Elder," he gasped, "a demon rises in the south. He brings desolation to the lands. He breathes fire like the dragon legends of old and drives the winds until all is scoured from the land. He seeks the mines of the Emperor."

"Kim, Lord Ranik rises in the west also seeking the mines of our Lord."

Kim gripped her arm, nodding strenuously. "It is rumoured that Lord Ranik sought a parlance with the demon and now Ranik's armies are under the rule of him. They march towards the Palace."

Kim relaxed his grip.

"I cannot wait, Kim. I must warn the Emperor."

Kim nodded. "The demon brings its own kind. They were made of legs and arms like spiders. They cursed the water and poisoned the villages. One of them scratched me with its talons."

Sa lifted him up to inspect his back. The back of his coat was shredded and underneath, festering, was a deep cut, to the bone. The flesh was already black, and pus oozed. It smelt of decay.

They looked at each other and nodded slightly. "Know that you died loyal to the end Kim."

Sa took her knife and ended his life. Sa left Kim against the tree facing toward the Emerald Citadel of the Drax empire that he had served to his death.

————

As she stood in the watch tower at the very top of Mount Gian, she saw the armies marching. Normally, there were two guards there, but it had been abandoned when Ranik's armies had been sighted. She watched the kite fly towards the palace with the news that Ranik's legions were positioned along the western ridges of the river. It would have been a surprise annexing as the ridges were considered to be impenetrable, except for secret tunnels that had been forged many generations ago. Sa wondered how Ranik would have known of the siege tunnels.

She made her way down to reach the palace by the early afternoon. She saw the smoke rising in the distance and the clash of swords. Ranik's soldiers outweighed Ko's, both in number and size. Each force was equally as lethal as the other. Angsung Warriors were subtle compared to the brute strength of Ranik's. Sa sprinted. She saw soldiers streaming out of the hidden tunnel that entered the first section of the Palace city. Screams floated to her across the wind. She looked up at the directions they had come from and noticed two figures scaling the walls in great strides. One of them turned its head and seemed to stare straight at her. She dropped to the ground. The creature did not appear to have seen her for it continued on its way, climbing to the palace walls at an un-natural speed.

Sa saw a group of soldiers rushing around towards the culvert that emptied the sewers on the eastern wall of the main quarter. She deviated towards them. This tunnel led directly towards Ko's quarters. She sprinted like a raven crossing the sky. The men didn't even hear her. She leapt up onto one of them, slit his throat, then launched herself at another as he turned. The three at the front were too far ahead to hear their mates fall. She flung a dagger at the one in the rear and then, facing the other two, flew into the air, knocked one out with a kick to the face, fracturing his nose into his head. He staggered back, swiping with his axe, half dazed and bloody. Sa drove her other dagger up into the leader's sternum, twisting it into the heart. The last one was crawling away. She could hear him gurgling as the blood and fluid oozed out of his face.

Grabbing him she asked, "Who commands you?"

He looked at her and tried to speak, but there was too much muck in his mouth. "The destroyer," he gurgled. Sa twisted his neck.

Near the grate covering the sewer, was a sack of explosives; they were trying to block it to prevent an escape route. She removed the grate covering the culvert and ran into the stinking tunnel.

She climbed up the shit laden walls and eventually reached the top. She went into the drain that sat beneath Ko's private kitchen. It was pitch black except for the embers of the hearth. The acrid smell of burning rice in a pot met her. She stole toward a doorway, concealed mostly by a large cabinet full of spices. She moved the latch and walked into a tiny hallway between the walls towards Ko's chambers. As she neared it, she heard voices. She looked through an air shaft grate. The Empress lay dead on the floor, and Ko had been bound by the hands and was kneeling with blood streaming down his face. A figure blocked her sight, but she heard it all.

"Where is the stone of Norbu? I can smell its power."

"I don't know what you are talking about," replied Ko.

Ko screamed when the creature dug his eyes out. Sa wondered at the question. While the general of Ranik's army spoke in a broken native tongue, what he asked made no sense. Suddenly, the creature crushed Ko's skull. Sa waited. The figure moved away, a hand came up, a large talon pointed at something. Sa stood back, realising it was one of the creatures she had seen scaling the wall. The soldiers and creature left the room. Sa waited a long time before stepping through the door. The room was washed with blood. Ko was barely recognizable, and the empress' face was frozen with fear.

Sa thought of Kado. Checking the hall was clear, she ran towards his chambers. Nothing. The room looked abandoned. His bed unmade, his washroom cleared. Smoke began to fill the room. With it came the stench of burning bodies. Then she heard something moving in the corridor. She dove under the bed. Kado's servant Ming was under there also. He was stunned to see Sa. A soldier came in and began to ransack the room. Ming and Sa squashed up against the wall and slid behind the curtain that formed the bedhead. The soldier looked underneath then left. They crawled out from under the bed. The city was being burned to the ground.

"Where is Kado Kodrax?"

"He was sent to the Sa Dom temple after the harvest festival by the Emperor." Sa relaxed a little.

"Who are the invaders, Elder Sa?"

"Lord Ranik, but he is no longer their suzerain, another over-lord commands his army."

"What do they want?"

"I do not know. I did not understand what they were asking the Emperor. Come, Ming, all will be dead by nightfall. We must find Kado and raise Ko's allies against these usurpers. We will leave for Sa Dom while it is dark."

"But none have come to his aid, Mistress."

"Not yet, but the attack was without warning." However, Sa saw the truth in the comment as well.

They returned to the kitchen to find supplies. They left through the tunnel in the sewer. The fighting had begun to die down. Ming looked back over towards the main route. He saw people being herded together. A large dog was barking. It attacked a woman who had fallen. In the distance a great bonfire raged. They were being burned alive. Ming vomited, being only royal staff, he was not used to such violence.

"Come," Sa whispered.

Ming stumbled, and a soldier standing with a large hound heard the noise. He began to walk towards them. He then saw the bodies of his comrades. He called and others came. Sa began to run. An arrow sped into Ming's back. She did not look back for the servant. She saw red eyes piercing the darkness amongst the death and chaos. She bolted into the woods and began to climb the hill that led to the eastern ranges. She heard the footfalls behind her and the low growl. She climbed a massive maple tree to its very top. It was gently swaying in the wind. Just in time, she realised as she saw the soldiers run underneath her. One of the dogs paused briefly, sniffing the air and ground. She held her breath waiting to see if it saw her. It continued on to follow the others. Sa climbed down when no other soldiers came running beneath. It was approaching the dawn. Sa Dom temple lay to the northwest from here, which meant that she must circle around the rear of the army and then head towards the temple. Climbing up the steep hills which surrounded the citadel she made her way towards a cave. It had a good vantage point across the embattled palace. Her mission now was to find Kado. The Drax Magisterium had given her refuge and purpose. Perhaps she could restore the House of the Dragon so that the tyranny of the Matavian did not bed in her homelands. Finding the cave entrance, she stepped inside with daggers ready. It appeared empty save for some scattered remains of animals. The darkness clung to her thickly as she walked further into the cave. She tripped over something; it moved.

"Who is there?"

Sa went rigid.

"Please help, I have hurt my leg."

"Who are you?"

"I am a priest from the temple Sa Dom. I have come to ask for Emperor's Paidrax's help."

"Why?"

"An army led by demons has ransacked our city. I was sent to bring help back, but I was attacked by a soldier and now my leg withers and I with it. Please go for help. Ko is loyal."

"The temple is destroyed also?" asked Sa as she lit some flint to see better.

"Almost, it sits too high for the enemy's catapults of fire to reach it easily. But I do not know how long it will last. The scourge of the invaders grows stronger."

"Ko is gone, and the palace is overrun. I seek Kado Kodrax, heir to the Drax Magisterium. His servant said he had been sent to the temple."

"Kado, yes he was there. I do not know if he still lives. I am left to die then?"

Sa nodded. Her mind raced thinking of what to do.

"Water, do you have water?"

She fetched some from a small stream that trickled down the cliff face. She could smell the rotten flesh of the priest's leg. He would be gone by morning.

The priest fell to sleep. Sa sat at the mouth of the cave. She could go to Ko's ally Lord Jiang and ask for refuge and offer her services. Eventually, she fell asleep. In her dreams, a voice echoed 'Go to the grove, assassin. Wait there until you are called.' Then she saw the red eyes of the demon and a woman standing looking in the distance. They turned to Kado as he marched his way across a large desert. He had fear in his eyes. He kept looking behind him, as if he was running from something. Then they were children. Sa remembered Kado asking her to play jacks. She saw the jack in his hand. She kept missing the jack as she flipped it between her hands; they were both giggling. A smile curled on her lips as the memory came to her. Kado had bruises on his legs and arms where his father had beaten him for being bested in the sparring.

"If no one else will love us, Sa Tuc, then perhaps we can love each other." Sa remembered looking into the lonely eyes of Kado as they sat together playing and knew she saw a kindred spirit there.

The priest took his last breath as the sun rose. Sa stood looking at the smoke rising from the ruins of Ko Palace. The shining jewel of the ancient dynasty lay smothered in blood, and smoke and ash. None of the feudal Lords had come to Ko's aid, such was the vitriol for their suzerain. 'Perhaps they would regret the day they did not defend the mighty Emperor,' she thought. She gathered her things to leave. She would go to the place that had come to her in her dreams. Perhaps she would find some answers there and then seek allegiance with Lord Jiang. If Kado lived she would be able to seek parlance for him with knowledge of who remained loyal to the Drax empire.

PART THREE

The Bonds of Stone and Water

18

The Grove

Ange stared at the trees, fascinated by their elegance. It was like they were alive, and their bark had been made by the full moon reflecting on water. She wondered if they were made of silver. The boabs from her home were plain compared to these beauties. They were tall and thin and as numerous as the reeds that grew in the great River Choasa. She swayed with them, dancing lightly as if she were a dandelion seed caught in the wind. As she walked into the opening of the grove she saw a man asleep on the grass. The sight of him made her instinctively move closer to Bensah. She took his hand as he drew her around to the far side of the pool. Bensah saw the tattoos on the man and the wounds. He guessed he was at least twelve spans in height and had the marks of Graanar clansman.

"Sit, sister, we will wait as you were told. At least it is sheltered and the air fresh."

They both swigged some water from their pouches and Ange nibbled on some berries she had found along the way. The silence of the birch forest had made her heart ache as the image of Tessi and Mata played on her mind; more so as she knew that there was no hope that Tessi would know how to find this place. A tear trickled down her cheek as she came to the realisation that any hope of seeing Tessi was vanishing with each passing day. Bensah was her only link to her home. Tata was tolerant, but he did not love her like her Mata and Tessi had. She wished the lady would come soon and explain it all. Nekoda came over and licked her face, sensing her distress. She smiled and then giggled as the dog took it as a sign of encouragement and placed his paws on her to play.

Gildas rolled over with a groan and sat up. He jumped up swiftly pulling his dagger out in alarm when he saw Bensah and Ange sitting on the far side of the pool.

"Who are you?" He eyed Nekoda, sizing up his jaws. Bensah held him tightly as Nekoda's hackles rose on his back.

"We were asked to come by another," Bensah replied, "I am Bensah El Bunani and this is Ange Tsaed. We are from the lands of Akras in the southeast. Who are you?"

"This other, is it a witch, dressed in black robes?"

Bensah looked at Ange and asked her if that was the same woman. Ange nodded, too shy to speak up.

"She has asked us to stay here until she comes but has not told the girl why or who she is."

Gildas relaxed a little. "A witch," he retorted.

The sun arrived suddenly, breaking through the leaves in dappled spots on the grass. The spots moved across everyone's faces. Nekoda snapped at them as they danced around his feet. Everyone was quiet as the dawn brought with it the hectic sounds of awakening in the forest. The cacophony of birdsong was overbearing compared to the serenity of the grove.

"How many days journey has it taken you?"

"Two new moons," Bensah replied. "Our village was wiped out by a plague leaving only a few of us. The woman came to the girl and told her to leave and meet her here."

"What pox cursed you?"

"I do not know. I have never seen anything like it. Death came swiftly to people and animals alike. The water soured overnight, and desolation swept the land. A spirit or demon walks the land setting everything ablaze with its gaze. We have seen the Spirit of the Water rise up to meet the God of Fire smothering its flames turning it to smoke and ash."

"Where were these demons?"

"In the lands of Doanda. I believe they are what drives the wind that brings the curse of sickness to our people."

Gildas looked at Ange intensely. He saw her deformed body and wondered how such a weakling would survive the devastation of a plague and fire of the demon from the underworld. He curled his lip in disgust as she tried to hide her weak leg under her tunic.

"Tell me of the demon?" Gildas demanded.

"It was in the shape of a man on fire, but larger than the tallest trees and swifter than the wind that fed its flames."

"Was there a wolf that walked beside it?"

Ange pushed into Nekoda; she could see the anger behind the man's eyes and knew it meant danger.

"Nay, only the spirits of fire and water."

Gildas thought, 'Is, the dream he had real or has the witch put a curse on us all and this place is a trap. Either way he would be ready for her.' He seethed inside preferring a curse to the possibility of his nightmares being real. He stood and kicked a clod of grass out in frustration.

"Where are you, witch, enough trickery, and veiled talk. Show yourself!"

Ange was scared. She could see the fear in his eyes, deep like the trapped calf 's cries for mercy as the lions and hyenas seize them. Ange saw the scars on his arms and legs and wondered why he would scowl at her when he was so maimed himself. Bensah should be careful. Gildas reminded her of the slavers who took Tessi.

Gildas spat on the ground and walked to the pool to take some water.

"We must eat," Bensah announced, feeling Ange shivering in fright next to him. He had trapped some pheasants in the forest.

"Here, Sister, prepare these and we will gather firewood." He gave the birds to Ange to begin plucking them.

The trio sat warily while they ate their breakfast. It was still cool so Bensah wrapped the remaining food in a pouch made from the hide of the hippopotamus, making it waterproof. He placed it into the pool. It rested on a large lily.

It was midmorning. Bensah was tired after the long journey and made himself a camp to lie down. Gildas got up and started to take smaller branches off the lower limbs of the birches to make a bow and some arrows. Ange was lying on Nekoda's back in a sunny part of the glade. She watched Gildas whittle the arrows into shape. After a short time, he had made nearly two dozen. Seeing that the bark split in the ends of some, Ange remembered the twine she had salvaged to use for mending.

Taking it out, she walked over to Gildas and left the spindle near him. He eyed her but did not stop shaping the branch in his hand.

"What are you doing?" he growled at her.

She pulled away quickly and gestured at the twine and arrow and indicated how to bind the ends to make them stronger. She could see how icy his eyes were. They were almost white like the silver bark of the trees. Her heart thudded with regret thinking he would grow angry again.

He picked up the twine. He tested it between his thumb and finger and then his teeth. It didn't break or fray. He began to twirl it around the shaved arrow end, but it kept coming loose. In frustration, he flung the arrow and thread at Ange. He began to whittle the next twig.

Ange deftly threaded the twine around the blunt end of the arrow, stopping halfway. She inserted a feather symmetrically on each side and neatly tied off the twine. She handed it back to him. He took it and placed it in his bow and shot it off. It flew in a perfect arc into the trunk of one of the trees. Gildas grunted his satisfaction and continued to whittle as Ange began working on the next one. This went on until Ange had finished most of her twine and all of the feathers. She wanted to keep some of her string in case she needed it.

Gildas had made over two hundred arrows, he put them in his large pouch along with the bow. The bow extended the full length of Gildas' back. He stoked the fire. It was not good to be idle for so long. He was nervous again.

Should he leave and make for the eastern shores. Merchant ships were always looking for crewmen. His wounds were healing quickly, another day or two he would be back to full strength.

Bensah rolled over, refreshed after his nap and hungry. It was mid-afternoon by the sun and Ange had fallen asleep alongside Nekoda. It was good; the girl must be weary. Bensah took the pouch of food out of the pool. He removed one of the birds and placed it on the hot embers to roast.

"Why do you think we are here, southerner?"

Bensah saw the wounds on Gildas, and how he winced when he twisted. He saw the shackle scars on his ankles and wrists. They were purple and gnarled like an old tree caught in a crevice of rock. Bensah guessed that the northerner had been imprisoned until recently. The only gaol within walking distance of here was the Banrock Prison on the Dranak Coast. The stories of the terrors were legendary. Bensah wondered what crime Gildas could have committed to be sent there. He looked at the tattoos and the legends of the fierce Graanar came back to him. They had once tried to invade the upper regions of Akras, but the desert is a different beast to that of the ice lands, and they inevitably retreated, to the relief of Bensah's people.

"We have no reason to fear the woman. Why are you suspicious of her? We would be dead, Brother, if not for her."

"I have my reasons." Gildas was curt. "I will decide soon." His voice trailed off in thought.

Bensah wondered as well what the woman would want with such as Gildas and indeed himself and the girl. The clansman was something. He'd been someone. The arrogance in his gaze said that one time he was a strong man who had either ruled or tried to seize power.

The sun was waning. It would be dark soon. The trio finished off the rest of the kill. Quite sated, they all sat back to enjoy the fire, each deep in thought. Gildas had decided to leave the day after tomorrow. He would catch more food to take and head east for the trader ships. He'd seen the desert dweller watching him at times. He knew he had guessed where Gildas had come from.

Ange had woken to eat but she was still so weary that her body felt like it was weighted down by a great sand dune. The trees were magical to her and the grass so soft. Slowly drifting off to sleep, she was remembering her mother walking through the door of their hut. She always had something in her arms, wood, pails of milk, yams. How many times had she seen her – so familiar. Realising it would be no more, she felt a pain in her chest as it swelled once again with the sorrow that had dogged her every step since the plague. She rolled over and saw the large man on the other side of the fire. He had strength and knew how to place fear in a person's heart. She wanted to be like that, gruesome and strong. Mighty enough to fight any demon or spirit that may rise out of the earth. Closing her eyes, she dreamt of running like the other children. She felt so free and fast. Nekoda bounded along beside her. She was giggling watching the dog trying to snap at a butterfly. They were running through the forest to this place, amongst beautiful lush ferns draped with the sweet smell of blossoms. A hand grasped her. Long fingers pinched into her flesh, hissing, and a foul breath met her. She looked up and saw a terrifying face with no eyes, only blue-green specs. She screamed and struggled, but the face just chuckled as black ooze dribbled through its torn lips onto its chin. "Come to me," it hissed at her.

Ange wailed in utter panic and horror. She woke with Bensah shaking her. She grabbed him around the neck.

"Another, Sister?" the concern in Bensah's voice alerted Nekoda. Ange was trembling and almost strangling him, so tight was her hold around his neck. She was rubbing her arm. Bensah saw burn marks on the skin. Gildas was looking at them, alert after waking so suddenly.

"What is it she dreams of? The wolf?" he asked.

"Well, is it the wolf, Sister?"

"No, Tata," replied Ange, "It was a spirit with green and blue spots where its eyes should be. He was a monster. He..." She sobbed as the fear rose in her chest. "It was worse than the fire god."

"You have seen this as well, Northerner?"

"I have seen the dots of light staring, but it is the wolf that haunts my dreams. Where is the witch? This bitch has cursed us all with faeries and imps of the underworld to torment us more. She leads us to our death."

Ange snuggled into Bensah and she motioned Nekoda over to her so that she was wedged between them. Bensah could feel her shivering against his leg.

"T'is only the spirits of sleep. We are safe here." He spoke trying to reassure Ange and himself.

"Everything is bewitched here. I will take my chances with the seas and merchants. I have had enough of this madness that hunts me at every turn. Do you hear that witch? Whore of the underworld, show yourself!" he roared.

Turning, he saw the eyes on the far side of the grove. Gildas rose slowly and unsheathed his sword. Slowly he crept to the where the red eyes burned, not daunted by the growl. Gildas sprang at the wolf and flung the sword directly at it. Its enormous head, large and black, lurched out in a lathered snarl. Its fangs were illuminated by the full moon. The wolf caught Gildas' arm, gripping the flesh and tearing it to shreds. Gildas flinched momentarily but continued. With adrenaline and blood oozing, he thrust forward with his free arm, but the sword did not connect. The demon disappeared. Gildas went to give chase.

"No! Northerner." Bensah grabbed his arms. "It wants you to follow it."

Nekoda bounced into the ferns and shrubs after the shadowed wolf.

Gildas stopped. Heaving with pain and anger, he flew around at Bensah, blade ready for cleaving the trader in two.

Ange screamed. Gildas hesitated just enough.

"Cursed witch! Where are you? You have brought me to a cage full of demons and phantoms to haunt me, not real enough to be cloven. Giving no quarter to be defeated or even to be killed by them, only torment."

Bensah backed away sensing the rage within the clansman. He did not doubt for one minute that if the warrior snapped, he would kill Ange and himself. Ange cringed with as much fear of Gildas as the wolf.

"Where are you?" Gildas raised the sword again, his gaze falling on Ange again, causing pure disgust to rise in him at the sight of her. His own dead son's body rose to mind; the injustice of it, and that the fault that lay with him.

"How does a chunt-bastid spirit do that? Curse me more whore and demon, naught else is there to strip from the hide of this son of the Ice Bear."

Rivulets of blood ran down his arm and onto the sword. He threw it with a mighty heave, and it lodged into the largest of the birches. He sat and began to strap the wounds to stop the blood.

Ange watched Gildas heaving with exhaustion and pain. She saw him awkwardly trying to staunch the blood with leather straps, but they only tore the flesh even more. She removed one of her shawls. It was one of Tessi's. She edged towards Gildas and quickly left it near his leg.

"Ange, leave be," uttered Bensah.

Bensah shooed her behind him. They had both seen the look Gildas had given her. Bensah decided they had to leave. Maybe the woman was a witch after all, leading them here to their death. They were caught in a trap with a wild beast, who knew how to wield a sword.

Nekoda came bounding back and barking in excitement wanting Bensah to come join the hunt. The dog nudged him in the arm urging him to get up and then stood barking at he and Ange.

"Shoo, mutt!" Bensah strapped the muzzle on him to settle him down.

The moon came out and shone on the pool. The water shimmered in muted tones and the birches dispersed the lunar glow around them. Silence settled over the group. They waited until the sun rose to make their decisions regarding their journey.

Nekoda sat on watch, half hoping the wolf would come back. Ange was lightly stroking his tail trying to think of a way to convince Bensah to stay. She knew that it would be better to wait for the lady, for the other path always led to darkness, at least that is what her dreams showed. Nekoda sat up suddenly and started to whine. He shot off towards the pool. Gildas and Bensah both stood up, watching the dog.

Gildas saw the woman on the far side patting Nekoda.

"Witch," he hissed under his breath.

Ange ran to her. "Hello, daughter. You look rested."

Assumpta's gaze spanned the grove. Her eye caught Gildas and noted his wounds.

"This ugliness intrigues me, Gildas Gol. The pool here replenishes and heals all that come near it. Come here and bathe the wounds. Always at war, come!"

"Leave it, witch. The wounds will settle."

"Nay, they are from the fangs of Voloc, a creature of the void that has ever hunted me. The venom will remain with you all your days if it is not cleansed by my sister's blessed waters."

Gildas ignored her.

"Ahh... you!"

She walked to Bensah and touched his forehead. "Sorrow lies within you, but not deep. You have profited from your kin, to make trades with those whose currency is flesh. You have placed chains on your own blood kin in-order to fill your pocket with their wealth. Still, you are kind to her and watch her. Not all in you serves your own need first."

Bensah stood looking at the lady Ange had told him about. He had not really believed she existed. He pulled away as he realised she had seen into his memories.

Suddenly a blade appeared at Assumpta's throat. It was Gildas. The god did not flinch.

"Tell us your purpose or let us go," he hissed.

She pushed the blade away from her and swiftly took Gildas sword arm and thrust him to the ground.

"A day will come that your blade will destroy me, warrior, but while I remain full of the light of Caemeris, it cannot harm me. Please sit and I will tell you of my purpose."

Gildas kept straining to get up and attack her, but he was held fast by the power of Assumpta. He gave up as the blood oozed from his arm and the poison began to work its way into his body.

"Eons I have walked since the sundering at the dawn of creation, looking for him who was lost to the eternals' sight. Ever the dark's vault steps ahead of me, a chasm of despair before me. In fading light as the moon rose and the brightness of the sun waned, my brother came. Gently wiping the tears from my face, he smiled as Seraf, Lido and Aerean gathered, 'Get up, Sister, the favoured ones of Caemeris in the realm of light awaits your hand to pull him from the great emptiness that chains him'."

"Riddles, woman, you are a demon like that wolf, leading us to our death."

"Yes, Gildas, I will probably lead you to death."

Gildas became defensive and snarled at her. "I knew it."

"Look."

Opening before them appeared a vision of all that had passed in the mind of the god. A tear came to Ange's eyes, for she too understood that longing for those cherished and now gone. Realisation dawned on Bensah. He dropped onto his knees knowing that truly, the gods of creation had woken and come to their lands. In the vision sat a pulsing star, arrayed in a corona of colours, ebbing and changing. Just faintly, a shadow appeared, but so fleeting the witnesses doubted their own vision. In it they saw the light coalesce into six figures. One of them had reached forth gathered the vision and transformed it into a tiny spec of power which Ange, Bensah, Gildas and Nekoda could feel inside themselves. Its light speared across eons of time. Then a great shadow descended and only four figures remained surrounded by an ocean of dark. A cry echoed across the emptiness as the realm of light shattered into a thousand pieces, piercing the void and sun. A miasma of colours pooled beneath the sun and then a world formed. Suddenly the vision disappeared.

Ange fainted as she felt the power drain from her while Bensah sat down. Nekoda barked at Assumpta to bring it back.

Gildas was stony-faced. He showed no emotion to indicate he understood at all, but inside his heart thundered. He had seen that emptiness before and also what lay beyond the darkness. He had never dared go beyond his desire to conquer, to test the limits of his ambition and be something other than a warrior and collector of victories. Anger rose inside him.

Assumpta knew he would be the one to fight. He would know Baachelaus when they found him. Gildas had stood on the chasm of that eternal emptiness most of his life, and he would know the wretchedness when he neared it.

"Nay, witch, I will have none of your trickery." He drew his axe and thrust it at her. Bensah shot forward to stop him but he was too late. Gildas' blade sliced into her chest. The god drank in the hatred, felt the searing pain in the body she had assumed, but did not fall. She put her hand on the axe and pushed it out of her. Gildas watched, and made to do it again with his dagger, but Assumpta thrust his weapons away and flung it onto the trunk of a tree behind his head.

"Stay your hand, Gildas. You cannot harm me. I was birthed by the spark between light and dark and sculpted into being by the first colours of time's dawn. The ones of this place were formed here and so their flesh shall remain. Your deepest desires and emptiness belong to the Cameris, not your flesh. It is your choice to stay, but the darkness in your mind will condemn your wife and child to the chaos for eternity. They are the one place of refuge for the mighty warrior of the Ice Bear."

Gildas' face became apoplectic with rage as Assumpta's barb sank in. She saw all their hollow weaknesses, Gildas rage, Ange's fear and Bensah's opportunism.

Gildas groaned in frustration "Who are you, witch? Why do you want me? I have paid my dues for my pride. I owe you nothing," he bellowed.

Ange cringed in fright. Nekoda growled with his hackles rigid, pointing straight up.

"You know what I showed you. If he is not found, then Voloc will place Baachelaus on its throne to rule here. The ancient gaoler and shadow will become the usurper of the rule of Caemeris and the first remembered realm of light. And in breaching the laws of first light so destruction shall come. Arglethium will be doomed to groan under the tether of Voloc.

But I fear worse than that; all the first light has wrought will be undone. I cannot harm you any more than what you have already been through, Gildas. Your blood calls me and the demon, for it flows with the power of the first colours of this world's dawn. My spouse is weak and only the ancient forces will restore him and allow him to remain here. If Voloc still cages him when he is fully restored, then the void's dominion will never be vanquished not even by me or my brethren. I need your help, warrior – your strength, your malice, your resolve, your blood, for if I do not have it then Voloc will."

"Nay, witch, I will not do your sorcery. I will leave here and be rid of your curses and tricks."

"With that demon at your heels? It has tasted your flesh now. It will hunt you down and throw you into the abyss, chained to its command for eternity."

"I will take my chances, bitch."

Lido had risen to the surface and silently made her way across the grass. She strolled near Gildas and stroked his arm. He flinched at her touch. He watched the flesh fold over and bind together healing the festering gouges Voloc had inflicted. The spirit sneered at the venom she washed away from the torn flesh. He grunted at her, stepping away, suspicious of Lido.

"Addled is your mind and spirit, corrupted that you should shun the purity of my blessing and yet be ready to face the shadow of the void." She pushed Gildas to the ground. He fell asleep on the grass without trying to attack the water spirit.

Ange watched Lido. She couldn't believe what she was seeing. She didn't feel frightened but wanted to be strong like that. To be able to fell a dangerous man like that was unthinkable to her. She could defeat the slavers who had taken Tessi. Ange's heart became filled with a deep desire she had never felt before. She wanted to be powerful like the gods who stood before her. She turned and saw Assumpta staring at her with a knowing look.

"Ah, foul thing that treads my brother's keep, beware beast of the dead stars, tread near my waters and know my wrath. Sister, long has been your quest, tired grows this world and all in it. Faster and faster it spins, pulling the darkness to it. Your spouse still lies weak in the south and the demon roams," cried Lido.

"What of our brethren, Seraf and Aerean?" asked Assumpta.

"Great destruction they have wrought. Seraf, with Aerean at his back, has ravaged the most blessed of lands of Norbu, killing all that dwelt within it."

"Why is this? Why this malice? The custodians are in awe of the eternal. Their gaze should not be clouded." replied Assumpta.

"Norbu must be found for none have the strength to go against Voloc. I have called for my brother many times and he does not answer. Long have I yearned for his growl, deep and rolling throughout the lands. Take the jewel to my Keep and the girl. It will be safe there until Norbu can be found. You must seek for Norbu on his throne. I cannot see him there for it is in the highest peak in the middling lands. His home is found where the eagles sit on judgment on the earth, for they are Norbu's eyes and ears. The mountains of Norbu have a crown of clouds so that they are shielded from all below it. Only you will be able to scale its heights."

"I will go there. When another called Sa-Tuc arrives, send her and the warrior to Norbu's keep. I shall meet them there. They are hardy as the stone of the mountains and will endure the journey. There I will either find our elder brethren or build my army to bring Baachelaus back to me and seal the breach so the light of Caemeris to reign once more."

Lido watched Ascendant but did not speak aloud 'You know it will bring destruction to this place if Caemeris realm is restored.'

'I know sister, but once Caemeris created all this, but if its memory is usurped by Voloc then, nothing will ever exist again. At least in one death then hope may remain for more creation to come. Annihilation or hope, these are our fates.' Ascendant responded.

Ange had gone to sit near the pool and watch the fish. They seemed to be waiting there to be caught. She tickled one on its nose. She saw the massive lily in the water below. It was large enough to hold her, Nekoda and Bensah.

"Look Tata, it is so big." Bensah had been listening to the gods. He felt fear rising in his chest. 'What had he and Ange been drawn into?' he thought.

Droplets began to form on Lido. "I must go. I have lingered long enough. Go to my Keep with the gift, Sister. These ones and the jewel will be kept safe. Seek Norbu. I will continue to search, but I fear Voloc's mischief will keep me busy. I will send the others on your quest to Tarentess."

Lido gave Assumpta the prism that had been in the lily. Assumpta watched Lido, disappear into her pool. She turned toward Ange and Bensah.

"Enough for now, our journey may be long, and I sense your weariness. Take rest."

Bensah and Ange sat, suddenly feeling a strange calmness come over them and wanting to lie down and sleep. Ange vaguely remembered watching the god holding something bright on the other side of the fire, the flames dancing in its facets. She thought how beautiful it looked as her eyes closed. She sensed the power in the jewel, the same power that she felt from the gods in the vision.

On the dawn, Ange woke for the first time since the plague with a peaceful mind. Her dreams, while tinged with sorrow, were of happy memories with Mata and Tessi, walking along the river Choasa collecting caper flowers to dry. She noticed the grass where the northern man had lain was still flattened. He was nowhere to be seen.

Bensah beckoned. "Come eat, Ange, then pack your things."

Nekoda was busy foraging at the edge of the grove. Seeing Ange, he whined with excitement at the thought of moving on again.

A large bumble bee making a loud drone sped past Bensah, directly towards the god. It stopped in front of her face and hovered. Ange looked at it and wanted to touch it. It was bigger and fluffier than the ones she saw at home. Its buzz was lower too. Nekoda went to snap at it but it simply glided out of the way and resumed its rendezvous with Assumpta.

Assumpta nodded slightly and then asked, "Have you seen your father?"

The bee buzzed and then turned away. As it left it almost hit Bensah in the face.

They gathered all their things and walked into the forest of Lido. The sun was weak on the horizon, tingeing everything with a dull pink.

"What of the northerner?" asked Bensah as he looked at the impression in the grass where Gildas had lain.

"In time, he will decide where his allegiance lies but for now, he has been blessed by Lido's most sacred of waters. Let him heal. The abyss inside him is not completely bereft of memories of the great ice mother who my sister suckles. He will remember this in time and much more," replied Assumpta.

The spirit must have bewitched them all as Bensah had not heard the Graan man leave. He looked back at the grove, fascinated by its beauty and solemnity.

"What is this place?"

"Each of my brethren has a place where they first stood when the eternal thoughts came to this world to protect the lands from the wars of creation. I am only privy to them when my brethren allow me to come."

"So where is your place, Lady?" asked Ange.

Assumpta looked down at Ange and bending over, she placed her hand on her heart and head "In here, Ange. I lie in the place where our inner most desires and thoughts exist. I am the hope of things asked for and my spouse is the throne where they may remain until they are fulfilled."

"Even the hatred and hurt we can desire?"

"Even the shadows which lie deep inside. We are not as you call good and evil, but we affirm each other and bring things to their fullness. It is then that the light of Caemeris is weaved and made real in this place called Arglethium. This place of

dense light is bent and shaped until it makes you and Nekoda."
She smiled.

19

Hunted

Sa walked into the grove and immediately scanned the verdant space. She saw a pit with cold ashes. On the edges moss had just begun to grow. She kicked the ashes with her toe wondering how long it had been since anyone had been here. Sa went to the pool to drink. She knelt down and as she scooped the water with her hand she noticed fish swimming close to the surface of the water. She let her hand rest in the water. The fish gathered around her fingers, she gently grabbed one but decided not to take it for food. Not yet anyway. Washing her hands and face, she gulped large mouthfuls of water and felt instantly refreshed. Sitting back on the grass, Sa looked about her. She had felt compelled to walk in this part of the great forest which in the Drax Kingdom was called the veil of Jun and in the Aeserean and Matavian tongue the forest of Vran. Her mind was calm, sensing that no harm lay close. Sa took out her blades and began to polish them. They were clean except for the hilt. It contained the remnants of some hairs and blood of two Unstaadt soldiers that she had stumbled upon. She dipped them into the pool to clean them properly.

Lido rose out of the water silently, disgusted at the blood that had washed off Sa's dagger. Sa stopped washing the blades and slowly shimmied back from the pool as the spirit came to form in front of her.

"You are the one my sister asked me to send to her."

Sa slowly manipulated one of the daggers into a strike position.

"Put it away. You cannot harm me."

"What god are you?"

"I am no god, for only the Caemeris claims suzerainty over creation. I am Lido, guardian of the water. You are stained. I taste blood on your hands and feel the chill in your heart. Why would my sister wish to use one such as you? Voloc would have better use for you."

Sa relaxed slightly. "I do not know of whom you speak."

"Ascendant has asked a favour of you. You are to go to the great mountains you call Tarentess and find my brother Norbu. Eons have passed and none have heard his voice. My sister said you are one who shall be able to scale the walls of his Keep. Your journey will be long and hard, stained one. Cleanse yourself of the foulness that lives in you before you leave. Your heart would freeze my great oceans, so mired is it in the shadow. If the warrior returns, then you are to take him to the great throne of my brother also. Take nourishment, for many days lie before you when your body shall crave food and the blessings this great realm of the mighty Norbu sustains."

Sa saw some fish flopping onto the grass in front of her as the god slowly descended into the pool. She hesitated briefly, watching in the silence around her, waiting to see if anything else may appear. Eventually, she took the fish, cleaned and gutted them. The raw flesh tasted of the water and sweetness of water lily roots. Lying on the grass, she thought of the great ranges of which the spirit had spoken. It made no sense to her. She had not heard of any god called Norbu or of these demons but remembered the creatures at Ko's palace. The eyes of the wolf had watched her in her dreams ever since.

She had traversed the base of the northern ranges, near the behemoth rock called Tarentess many years ago, on mission from the Emperor. Its height were unseen from below. The peaks, supported by feet of craggy rocks, disappeared into sheer cliffs rising directly up without ledges to allow travellers to scale them. It was mostly slate rock, which could crack at the slightest tremor. On one of the western edges, an outcrop of cliff contained a large black lake, formed from a waterfall from above. That had been as high as she had managed to reach. She remembered the icy blackness reflecting back at her, and how its purity and solitude had reminded her of her own existence. Sa had felt a presence there that was not completely strange to her. Re-focusing her thoughts, she remembered the path of steps leading up from the other side of the lake. At the time, she had been curious about where they went, but had not had the time to find out. She closed her eyes and finished her incantations.

Fear is the doorway to defeat
Defeat is the path to weakness
Weakness is the step to destruction
Destruction is the door to death
Fear is death

To defeat death then kill fear
Strength must endure over weakness
Strength of the mind will defeat fear
Strength of the body will destroy weakness
Fear is defeated by the destruction of weakness
Sa slept.

Gildas crashed through the glades, pale and barely breathing as the torn flesh on his legs and arms spouted blood. In his stupor, he saw the woman asleep, but did not stop. He crawled into the pool and immersed himself into the anointing water. The red eyes stayed at the edge of the shrubs glowing brightly, the guttural growl that came from the direction of the eyes did not wake Sa.

Gildas was sinking into the depths of the pool, his blood flowing out freely with blooms of red staining the crystal purity. He was in the darkness again, but there was no way out. He couldn't find Jesse. He drifted away, his heart slowing as the black emptiness engulfed him. No memory of himself seemed to come back, only the face of the wolf snarling and the voice of something calling out its name. Gildas sunk ever deeper until his body lay at the bottom of the sacred pool. Within days of leaving the others, it had found him. The wolf had hunted him to exhaustion and almost to his death. But Gildas lay there and knew that death would not be his salvation either. He had seen his fate and knew the witch had been right. His doom had come to face him from the nether world, to follow from his dreams to waking. The torment that would never end had bitten his flesh and would not let him go. Something grabbed Gildas and began to heave him up. Suddenly, he could feel air on his face. Lido carried him to the grass and laid him down.

"Stained as well; my pool is full of the blood of murderers and assassins. Ahh, Sister, you have bought much profanity to my sacred wells. Begin your battle quickly so that all may be restored."

Lido poured water over his wounds helping to slow the blood spouting from them. Even she was not sure he would survive the poison that now pervaded his body. Voloc had done its work. She saw the demon's eyes watching from the edge of the glade. She sent a jet stream of water directly at it. As it contacted, the wolf yelped in pain, but it did not flee. It was getting stronger. Gildas began to rouse, but the guardian touched him again and the peace of the grove filled his mind. Lido went back to her pool to leave Gildas and Sa sleeping.

Dawn broke, the sun revealed in its ruby shades two figures, each warriors in their own right, formed to bring subjugation or death to others. Sa slept with her dagger in her hand, ready at all times. Gildas wounds lay angry and raw. The bleeding had stopped, and the flesh was beginning to heal over.

Sa rolled over and saw Gildas. She jumped ready to attack. Gildas stirred but was too weak to move. His eyes fluttered open for a moment and then closed again. Sa noticed the fang marks on his arms and legs and the brute size of the man – three times her height and width. He had the tattoos of the northern clans. 'What had done that to him?'

She backed away and sat legs crossed in readiness for any attack. For him to find this place must mean he was invited. For several hours, Sa sat there not moving. Gildas eventually stirred. He groaned as he tried to stand, but a large gash on his stomach threatened to reopen, so he lay back and tried to relax. He passed his tongue on his lips and noticed how dry he was.

Lido rose again, walked over to him, and let water drop on his mouth.

The spirit turned her head to Sa. "If he survives Voloc's bite then he is to go with you to the Mountain and beyond. He is needed by my sister. My pool runs with the blood of the innocents slain at the hands of both of you. You are both stained and unworthy of the eternals spark. I grant him this sustenance as granted to me by the eternal, but Voloc grows strong and the warrior may yet die. The darkness comes to my pool, dank and lifeless. Children of the world, forsaken you are by the descendant. May my sister's quest to find him to bring be fulfilled soon; whether it be annihilation or restoration. For I see now the sorrow anchored to my sister and the malicious veil that blinds you all."

"Why does the demon not kill me?" croaked Gildas.

"I fear your blood is valuable to the one it cages. Voloc needs its prisoner's strength restored to restore itself."

"What is this quest and who is Voloc?" asked Sa.

"My sister will enlighten you, vicious one, as for Voloc, he takes the form of a wolf here. In the void, the fell creatures came to be. Voloc was the first spawned, but he is also the destroyer of the light, hater of the Caemexa. It is weak here amongst the favoured of Caemeris, but the emptiness in all things feeds him, most of all in the Descendant. You, vicious one, he has not seen, but if he does, a feast awaits him, so vast is the chasm of no light that grips your soul."

Sa could feel the spirit's gaze penetrate her.

"I shall leave you now, for my brethren still wreak their mischief on the lands. Leave by the wane of the next moon. If the warrior is still not healed, then go without him, for I can do nothing more for him."

Sa remained watching the huge Graan that lay panting on the moss.

Sa took some fish from the pool and filleted them. She tilted Gildas head forward to give him some water. He opened his eyes, briefly sipped, then coughing slightly, he took more. He lay back and remained unconscious for the rest of the day.

Sa practiced her daily routine and meditated. She sharpened her blade. She kept a pouch of salt in her belt and let the fish cure in the sun.. Sa had been mentally visualising the route she would take to get to the mountains. It would be difficult, but the best way would be to head west towards the Aesearean border and follow the road of Yullaan. The route steadily climbed the peaks of the north for at least fifty leagues. She estimated that if the man was strong, it would take them less than two cycles of the full moon. 'That path would have a more plentiful food supply at least,' she thought, remembering the spirits warning. It would also be sparsely populated for most of it. She sized Gildas up again. His food intake would be twice hers if not more. The night fell again, and Sa slipped into her incantations and examinations of the mind.

Gildas groaned again and croaked, "Water."

Sa gave him some. He opened his eyes; he was more alert this time. Sa noted that the wounds were slowly knitting.

"Who are you?"

"I am Sa-Tuc. I am here because the spirit of flesh and mind called me."

"Spirit of flesh and mind? You mean the witch." Gildas let his head drop back again and closed his eyes.

Sa did not continue with the conversation. 'He may not survive,' she thought. Had she been elsewhere, she would have ended his misery long ago, but he was wanted for something as well by the spirit.

Seven more days and nights passed. Sa saw the gashes closing over. Each time Gildas awakened for longer. The darkness he moved in and out of was fading slowly. Occasionally, the red eyes would appear, circling, menacing Sa and Gildas, but the water in the pool would ripple and the wolf would retreat.

On the dawn of the eighth morning, Gildas sat up on his own. He still felt weak, but the wounds were thickening into purple knotted scar tissue. Sa came over to him. Surprisingly, he let her firmly clasp his head to help him drink water from the pouch.

"Food," he croaked as his stomach roared suddenly.

She broke strips of fish into smaller pieces for him. He chewed vigorously and ate more. Suddenly he vomited on himself and groaned at the pain the heaving caused in his ribs. The flare of pain bought back the memory of hearing the snap of his ribcage when the wolf had thrown him against a tree.

He drank some more.

"Slower," said Sa.

He nodded and took some more. He gestured towards the trees. "Let me rest against it."

Sa helped him to his feet. Every single one of Gildas' bones and muscle screamed with pain. Sa noticed tears in his eyes. He kept walking until he reached the large silver birch and slid carefully down to rest. Sa placed her pouch behind his head so he could rest. She walked away as Gildas closed his eyes to sleep. 'He would be a worthy adversary,' she thought.

Each day, Gildas walked a little further and the pain lessened. He ate and drank more. There seemed to be a never-ending supply of fish. Sa had gone hunting once and bought back a hare and some wild fowl. They were roasted and eaten lasciviously by Gildas.

"You are from the Drax Kingdom?"

Sa nodded.

"You are no monk or priest by the look of the daggers you hide in your sleeves."

Sa looked directly at Gildas. "That is right Graanar, I am no monk."

By another seven dawns, Gildas was walking on his own. The scars were well-formed and beginning to harden. The ones on his chest pulled as he breathed, but it no longer hurt nor did his chest crackle. Gildas began to pull little branches off one of the willows and asked for Sa's paring knife. He began to make his arrows. By another dawn over one hundred arrows sat neatly piled. He began to work on the bow. A memory of the girl came to him; the twine would be useful.

"It will be time to leave soon. The journey will be long, but you should be able to strengthen as we walk. The most diffi-cult part will not be for another hundred leagues. Food will be plentiful at least for that part of the trek. Do you have a sword?"

"No, the wolf chewed it from my grasp." He rubbed a mottled scar near his wrist.

"We will purchase one as we travel."

"Where are we going?"

"To the Mountain of Tarentess to find one of the spirit's brethren."

"That is near my homeland, but you can only cross the northern peaks near the western shores."

"I know of another path. Rest! Tomorrow you will hunt for food."

Gildas flinched slightly. Sa knew fear, she had seen it often in men's eyes just before her dagger would slit their throat.

"You will hunt tomorrow, for you must be able to while we travel."

He nodded. Deep inside a fear had been planted. Gildas had tasted the reality of pain and torment at the fangs of Voloc.

The pale dawn broke through and Gildas rose with it. He slung his bow and quiver and went into the forest. He hesitated at the edge knowing what awaited him. He noted Sa sitting with legs crossed, very still with her eyes shut. He begrudgingly gave her the respect due to her for her discipline.

He stepped into the trees and ferns and made his way towards a path that was lit by the sun. He followed for a half a league. He found a sheltered hollow beneath large ferns and sat down to wait for a deer to come. It wasn't long before a doe and her calf appeared. He would take the calf, it was smaller, and the meat would be sweeter. He aimed his arrow and let it go. It made a clean hit and the calf dropped to the ground. He stood watching as the mother fled in fright and confusion, wondering where her calf was. Gildas winced a little as he stood to go and collect the carcass. He stood looking down at the fawn and the blood oozing. An image flashed into his mind. He and Jarrod had been hunting. They were dragging the body of a small ice bear home to skin and eat. Gildas remembered feeling proud of his little brother and his prowess as a hunter. They were laughing and joking about how they would use the animals hide to play a trick on their mother. Jarrod had stood by Gildas as much as Jesse. Every victory, even ones Jarrod had counselled him against, he had followed dutifully – out of fear or fraternal allegiance, Gildas wondered for the first time. Another memory flashed into his mind. The day he had claimed a rival clan's land. In his relish to avenge for disloyalty, he had ordered all the elders to be scalped and their heads staked outside each of their huts, as reminders to their families not to seek retribution against the Gol Lord. Jarrod had objected vehemently, but Gildas had ignored him. But this act had sown the seed for the other Graan's rebellion against him. It was one thing to denigrate the enemy, but another thing to do it to blood tribesman. Jarrod had understood the effect it would have on the tribesman and how it would fester and rise.

Gildas hefted the fawn onto his shoulders and felt a sharp pain shoot through him; the wounds were deep and still healing. He steadied himself and began to make his way back to the grove.

When he arrived at the pool, he threw the fawn onto the ground. Sa set about skinning the carcass and smoking the flesh. Gildas sat in contemplation as the sun began to wane that day. The witch had known he would barely survive an attack by the demon. Next time he knew he would be captured by it.

"We will leave in three nights. If we make good time, then we will reach the northern steppes by the solstice. From there we can head west to the steps of Yullaan where the Mountains begin. We follow them until we reach the base of the cliffs, unseen to men, as the clouds veil their faces. It will take many days and nights, and even then, the climb to the mountain's summit is not known. Another three nights, northerner, and then I leave with or without you."

Gildas didn't respond. He had no choice. The night arrived and Gildas slept. Sa watched him twitching. Whatever haunted this man was persistent. Sa rubbed the pouch around her neck unconsciously and lay down. Her mind now full of the journey to the north, she had pushed her desire to seek Kado and allies of Ko aside. It was her way. Ever seeking a purpose or a master, Sa Tuc, the assassin, never waned in her duty, but also never understood why she had become a weapon for the malice of those who wielded power. She had never contemplated being anything other than an assassin either.

The following days, Gildas' strength increased, and his courage began to return. It had been a full cycle of the moon since the others had left. Gildas and Sa sparred. Gildas was impressed at her nimble stealth. He became more confident, letting the lingering doubts subside as he attempted to outstep her subtle manoeuvres with his powerful strokes.

The night before they had decided to leave, Gildas lay down to sleep. His eyes watched the fire blaze back and forth. He was drifting off when he noticed the eyes in the flames.

He blinked and looked again. They were there watching him.

Gildas stared at them directly. "What do you want? Kill me now! Why do you wait?" The redness flared slightly more brightly and then disappeared. Gildas closed his eyes and waited for the chase to begin again. He would run to where it couldn't follow. Voloc caught him once and whipped him through the air, his body twitched. Sa watched it all. What she didn't see was Gildas getting up and running from the demented shadow that pursued him, to the faces of Jesse and Jarrod, their blades glinting as they wounded the foul beast, momentarily stopping its relentless pursuit.

20

Lido's Keep

Nekoda bounded ahead of the others as they walked through the dense forest. Sometimes, Ange and Bensah would lose sight of him and Bensah would whistle to bring him back. They had left the grove without any sightings of Voloc. The forest was quiet and aloof compared to the warmth of the grove. No birds sang, nor did they hear any small animals foraging in the undergrowth.

Assumpta had been deep in thought for most of the journey. She held half the prism but wondered where the rest lay. Only Norbu would have the strength to sunder it and would have only done so to hide it from Voloc. As it swung around her neck, the awakening memories came back to her again, but always the grief would return, magnified now by her time here in the presence of the clay born. She felt the fear and sense of loss in Ange and Bensah but could do nothing to relieve it. Worse was yet to come.

Bensah had lost his bearings after the third day. They had gone on a steep decline after leaving the birch grove and walked into thick unyielding forest. He also questioned what use he and the girl would be to the powers that now walked amongst them. He did not entirely trust this spirit with them, she was always unsure of any answers. For all he knew they could be going to their death. Perhaps the visions she had shown them was just sorcery. Ascendant looked at him when she sensed Bensah's misgivings. In his head, he heard her voice.

'Yes, Bensah El-Bunani, you could well be walking to your death, but where now can you walk and that will not be your fate. I take you to where you will be safe for a while and all will be made clear in time. I can only show you what you have already seen and know that deceit lies not with the brethren, but the shadow who seeks their death. Ange would not have made it this far if not for your protection. The time will come when she will no longer need you, but until then you are her keeper.'

Bensah looked at her and mumbled his dissatisfaction at her reading his mind. 'Perhaps she was a witch as the northerner called her,' he thought, and then realised that she would have heard that.

He looked and of course, a wry smile was on her face. 'Nay, I am no witch or demon. My essence remains that of the first and the great star Caemeris, the wanderer and maker of the realm of light. But be warned, the shadow and light are entwined in an eternal struggle, so with one comes the other.

'Then what are you?'

'All that is unfulfilled.'

This cryptic comment did not make sense to Bensah and he strode ahead to Ange. He felt the firmness of earth under his feet and the touch of fern leaves as he walked. These familiar sensations helped calm his mind to know some things were still real. Nekoda came bounding out of a very dense meadow of ferns. He held a large possum in his mouth. Bensah rubbed him on the head and put it in his rucksack for food. Nekoda whined a bit and pawed at the bag, disappointed at not being allowed to eat his catch.

"Nekoda you always have been and will always be my friend. You don't know how much that means to me right now," spoke Bensah.

Assumpta felt the affection in Bensah's heart for the dog. Such harmony between them. 'Light and dark are entwined together. Here, in Norbu's world, where the bonds of stone and water ran deep, it is also awash with the consummation of light and dark. Their binding together is unbreakable. Has the rendering of the prism, my tears which hold the last image of Baachelaus, made this world, the world of Arglethium happen? Would it have been this way if the Ascendant and Baachelaus Descendant had remained in their realms? Aloof rulers constantly in each other's gaze blind to all else.' Assumpta wondered how Voloc was able to breach the realm of light. This question had never occurred to her, lost in her sorrowful quest to find Baachelaus. But seeing the world of clay and dense light, was there some other purpose to it all?

'Norbu, brother, Baachelaus and I are bound here in this world. Where are you mighty one? The sundering, which destroyed the realms of the custodians will come here as well if my tears, our memories are not re-made. For we were the shadow and light until we were unmade. Reveal yourself and remake this thing so we may learn of our fates.' She watched Ange and Bensah from behind as she prayed to herself and her missing brethren.

Ange stumbled. "I am tired, Tata."

"Is this place much further, Spirit?" asked Bensah.

"Yes, another day. We will rest a while."

They made camp and Bensah prepared the possum. Ange found some roots; she scraped them clean and put them in the fire to roast. Peering down on them was a dim shaft of light. The forest was so dense that it seemed impossible that the sun would ever penetrate here. Ange nibbled on a root that had roasted in the coals.

"Tata, the root is delicious." She handed some to Bensah wrapped in a leaf.

After eating she lay back and began to think of Tessi. The ache inside her welled up again each time she thought of Tessi and Mata. Ange had been alone many times in her life, shunned by most of the villagers. It wasn't being alone that made her sad it was the loss of the happiness she and Tessi always shared.

'Perhaps not all is lost, little one.'

'Can you see if she still lives, Lady?'

'I cannot be sure, but I sense there are more of you whose flesh flows with the blood of the ancients. Whose memories are the same as yours.'

Ange was a little heartened but rolled over and quietly began to cry again.

'It will make sense in time, Ange; not all has been in vain. Nevertheless, you are hardy, are you not, you have endured a life that would test the mightiest. Most would fall under the weight of the scorn you have had thrust at you. Is this so much more to bear?'

"Yes, it is. I had Mata and Tessi to help me. I loved them very much. You would not understand this. You are not from this place."

Assumpta pulled away from Ange's mind and let her sleep. 'I am what you feel, Ange. But yes, even I do not understand it.'

Bensah stirred, hearing Ange call out suddenly, realising that Ange and the Spirit had been talking to each other. His mistrust of Assumpta made him wonder if she was teasing the girl or trying to comfort her. "Where are you taking us, spirit?"

"To Lido's Keep. It is impenetrable. Voloc runs freely now and will become stronger with each passing moon. I must find Norbu and the other half of the stone. I cannot guard you and Ange as well. My sister's keep will protect you until Norbu can be found."

"Why do you need us? It seems to me this is a war from the heavens. Why bother with us at all? We do not have strength to fight a battle between gods."

"You have seen the place from where I came but it has been destroyed. Norbu has forged your world and he has done it with the memories which lie deep with me and Baachelaus. Ange and the others are needed, for they were descendants of the first peoples and are in covenant with Norbu. She is needed to heal the breach and stop the sundering of light and shadow. All of Caemeris memory even that contained the first covenant maker's blood is needed. It is the end days of the custodians of Caemeris but not for the shadow, which existed before light. In time it will make sense Bensah El Bunani. You are both needed," Assumpta looked at Nekoda as well as Bensah, "and

Ange will need to be strong. She has lost much already, and more sorrow will come."

Bensah patted Nekoda on the head. "Ugly mutt, you are wanted. You are right I still don't understand of what you speak. But all other roads seem to lead to death or the curse of this demon which hunts us. What choice do we have?" he mused not expecting an answer.

"There are difficult times to come, Bensah El Bunani, but nothing can be stopped now, the war must begin, and destiny fulfilled one way or another."

"Such dark words, Spirit, and yet we men seem ignorant to whatever this fate is supposed to be."

"Yes, you are, and if the void has its way, not only ignorant will you remain, but you will not even count as a spec in the vastness of times light. Whether you understand or not, and whether you wish to continue with me, darkness has come to you, and my brethren and Ange and the others are what stand between you and your annihilation."

'Hmm.' Bensah yawned, not one for melodrama normally, he still did not quite get the gravity of the situation, but he was concerned for Ange. This spirit had other use for her, which she would not reveal. He would be watchful. He rolled over while Nekoda went over to Ange and nuzzled into her back.

Assumpta looked at them all. She sensed his wariness. 'Of no good will it be to him if he chooses to take the girl.' Gazing into Ange, she saw her dream of a time when she and her sister were playing in a field near a large river. There was a tremendous sense of calm and happiness inside her heart. Ange was special. The pure love she looked at the world with shone like Norbu's beautiful stones that he fashioned from the earth. Bensah was cool, removed, and wily. He was not cunning nor deceitful, but loyal and hardened to survive. Nekoda was just plain happy. She giggled a bit as the dog looked at her.

Assumpta began to walk in the forest. She lived between waking and dreaming. Her form was adapting quickly as her essence and the physicality of the body were blending. She thought of Ange's dream of her sister and began to search for Tessi. A tiny thread of life found its way to the spirit's essence. The girl was still alive, but awash with sorrow and pain. The girl's longing to be let free even to die overwhelmed the custodian. She wanted to take Tessi away from the shadow she now existed within, but Assumpta withdrew her questing for Ange's sister. She decided not to tell Ange that her sister was alive. It would distract Ange away from her destiny if she clung to the hope of finding Tessi. The grief of her sister's death would serve to harden such a pure heart. A hardness which would be needed in the days which lay ahead.

The forest was dark and indiscernible in any detail. She could feel the fronds of the plants against her skin. She thought of what may come. She could sense Descendant now. He grew stronger all the time. He was trapped by Lido's oceans, but he would grow strong enough to defeat the custodian of water as well. Then it would be him and her. She thought back to the beginning, and how they were both on the horizon of their fullness. They looked at the first stars forged by them, brighter than now, as the emptiness of the void dimmed their glory when it took him.

They drew near to Caemeris and let its flares touch their

essence, baptising them and bonding their energy together so that for all eternity they would be spousal to one another. She remembered the sheer heat and force that the star thrust at them and realised that was the beginning of light where no darkness could penetrate the heart of the entire universe. They pulled away, depleted from the rawness of the light but also stronger, emboldened by the knowledge of its power. They stood still for an eternity, each bonded to the other's glory, not wanting to leave. However, he became too strong, his gaze was averted away from her, and she could not draw him back. He pulled her with him as he went to the core of the majestic star. They both saw the eye of Caemeris, they both felt the power and strength and ancient memories. They saw what made the custodians and the fourth realm of light. But then came the spear of shadow splitting them apart. The memory of Caemeris remained with her while he was draped in shadow. Light and dark no longer bound but sundered. Norbu bowed in grief and in his hands, he captured her tears as she wept. The colours of light and the heart and memories of the Caemexa born swirling into them.

She woke up from her thoughts to find sun breaking through the large trees towering above her. It struck her face and lit up the foliage around her. Nekoda barked as he saw her glory. She got up and went to the others to begin the day's journey.

She led them down even steeper valleys until they eventually reached the bottom of the ravine. A small rivulet ran swiftly at the base of the valley. It was not deep, and thc pcbbly bottom could be seen clearly. Bensah tried the water. It was sweet and refreshing.

"Nothing like home," he said to himself. Ange stooped as well and noticed brightly coloured fish swimming in the water. Their scales were like the colourful rain spirit which came out after a storm. Nekoda grabbed one and ate it. Ange splashed water at the dog, but he ran away into the bushes to enjoy it. They continued along this stream until midday of the next day. They had to follow the sound of the water. It had become dark from the canopy; the forest blocking the sunlight. Ange had some flint and hessian cloth and made a small torch to help see better. Assumpta guided for the most part and Lido had come to join them briefly in between battles with Seraf and Aerean and searching for Norbu.

"No news, Sister. He slumbers deeply, our brother. He was old and huge though." She chuckled.

Assumpta smiled. "He had reason to sunder my tears, Sister. He has foreseen something."

Eventually the forest began to form a corridor along the stream as the fronds and branches touched on either side of the stream forming a canopy. A light began to penetrate, not from the sun but from something glowing in the distance. Slowly, an opening came into view. Nekoda bounded ahead and disappeared into the light. They came to a cave whose stonewalls were completely covered in vines and ferns. The light shone forth at the mouth of the cave. They entered and immediately spilled down a waterfall formed from the stream. Assumpta laughed and Ange screamed while Bensah swore. They came to a gliding halt on the floor of a wondrous pool, surrounded by waterfalls in all directions. Ange spluttered. Not being a swimmer, she floundered in the water. Nekoda, who had been swimming and dunking for fish, swam to her, so she had something to grab onto. Then one of the waterfalls opened into a doorway, and a voice called them.

"Come," beckoned Lido.

They swam into a swirling shroud of water. Ange held her breath, but the swim was taking too long and she needed to gulp air. Panicking, she grabbed Bensah's hand. Suddenly Lido appeared.

"Breath the flesh and blood of Lido, custodian of the blood of Arglethium, betrothed of Belmaris, bringer of life to dirt and stone, leaf and bone." Suddenly Ange opened her mouth, her heart thudding, thinking she would drown, but instead she found she could breathe.

They continued to swim. All around them the light pierced the torrent and diffracted into rainbows. Ange felt like she was swimming inside the beads Bensah had given her. A mound of water solidified before them for them to sit upon. Lido rose before them in her real form. Here she was strong and beautiful. She wore a gown of mother of pearl, bejewelled with white and pink scales. Her eyes swam with the colours of the waters upon the earth. Her hair flowed around her like delicate reeds woven with small lilies.

"Welcome to my home. Rest and be safe, for no darkness may penetrate here. Feed yourselves with my pets, they are sweet and juicy."

A little crab crawled up her arm into her sleeve. She pulled it out and gave it to Nekoda, who gulped it down with one snap of his massive jaws. She laughed.

"It is many eons since others have been here."

"Beautiful you have become, Dearest, since your infancy in the custodial realm. The wisdom of the Caemeris is fully wrought in your beauty and majesty. I bow most humbly that I come here to your sanctuary with my bonds of sorrow and death. To see the bride of Belmaris and the life blood of the realm of heavy light, flesh and stone, clay and leaf."

"Nay, Sister, all this is for the clay born, so that they will one day grow enough and see all this in its fullness for themselves, and I shall no longer be. Then they shall be the custodians of this realm and not I." A ripple rose through the watery world of colours and eventually surrounded Assumpta in a column of water.

"I bless you, Ascendant, in your journey that your beloved is found and returned. May your questing heart find its peace and its home. May your unknown destiny be made known. May the questing light of Caemeris find its way and remember Arglethium in its quake. Remember what lies here and seeks mercy to remain if the rule of Caemeris is restored."

The column of water disintegrated splashing into the lake that surrounded them.

"I will remember Brethren of water." Assumpta bowed to Lido and then turned to Ange.

"I must leave now and make my journey to Tarentess."

Ange started a little. "No, we will come with you. I do not wish to be here." She pleaded with Bensah. "I want to go home." She began to cry. "You will not come back for us. We will die here, and no one will know we are here. Tata, I want to leave."

Bensah held her. "Where would we go, we are in the hands

of the gods of the world now, sister and our fate is not ours anymore. I see now that more is hidden to us than is revealed and we are full of arrogance at what we think we know. The demons we have seen will kill us as they have already our families. So, I ask you, where would we go and not be swallowed by the destruction we have seen?"

"No, I want to be with Tessi. I know she is alive. You could find her if you wanted to," she said, looking directly at Assumpta.

Assumpta hesitated. "Yes, perhaps but I will not, for it is not required that we find your sister yet."

"So, she is alive."

Now for the first time, Assumpta began to feel the chaos that could exist within a heart as the lie formed on her mouth.

"I do not know."

Taking out the prism, Assumpta turned to Lido. "I leave this with you, Lido. I shall return, I hope, with the other half. Ange, I know you are sad for I see it in your heart, but you must understand, your fate is now not your own. It is not safe for you yet. Voloc the demon will find you. Stay here until I return. Tessi is no longer your concern."

At these words, Ange felt a hatred swell in her heart for the first time ever. She looked directly at Assumpta, who knew what lay in Ange's mind.

"You will understand in time. You must trust me."

'I will not!' came the defiant thought.

Assumpta placed the prism inside a shell and walking to the huge sandstone wall that surrounded the lake they sat upon, put it inside a crevice. Lido shaped a small waterfall, which cascaded over the crevice to conceal the jewel.

"I go now to find Norbu. We will gather when I have found him." Assumpta left, she felt Ange's anger and Bensah's fear. Her resolve became stronger to bring the quest to an end and relinquish her sorrow. Lido took her hand and guided her up to the entrance. She walked into the dark forest and felt a heaviness come over her again. Lido left her. Assumpta walked back along the stream they had followed. She felt loneliness engulf her. The warmth of the bonds between Bensah, Ange and Nekoda had been comforting and now all she felt was the weight of her fate and unending chasm of sorrow again in their absence.

In the Keep, Bensah had caught some little crabs, and feeling not a little bit squeamish, ate them.

"Try one Ange, they are tasty." He caught another one. The little creatures seemed to be posturing to be eaten as he plucked another from the edge of the water.

Ange had gone over to the far side of their watery dome and was lethargically patting Nekoda. Sensing Ange's low mood, he was trying to comfort her with a paw and nuzzle. She shook her head.

"It will be alright, sister she will come back and will know what to do. How can we be out there, imagine the people..."

He stopped himself short realising what he was about to say, 'the people who would be hunted down by the wolf and creatures it now held power over.'

"We are lucky, Ange. The gods have been good to us for whatever reason. We have no choice now but to listen to them. We don't have to trust them, but there is no other way that I can see that would protect us, at least for a little while longer."

"I miss Tessi, that is all, Tata, and I believe the lady could help find her if she wanted to."

"Perhaps, but it is not what she chooses to do. Come, eat."

Ange came over begrudgingly and ate a crab. Lying down again, she wondered how long she had to wait here. Sleep began to wash over her. She dreamt she was walking along the road to her village and she was wearing a long flowing gown. Mata and Tessi came running to her and danced with her. She was so happy. Then her mind was blank as they both disappeared from her, but she did not feel sad, only a longing to see them again.

'One day, Tessi, we will meet again, and dance together along the river.' Assumpta heard the sigh in Ange's heart. She turned her gaze to it and snuffed out the longing that lay there.

"Your quest will be long one, Ange. You need to become Ange, not just the sister of Tessi and daughter of Noai and Elanai."

Ange lay there and rested for the first time in the four moons since the plague had stolen her life and family. Her body ached from all the walking and her heart ached from losing Mata and Tessi. By the time she woke, outside, the world had turned a full cycle of the moon, but inside here, it only felt like a few hours had passed. She got up and drank some water. Bensah was still asleep and Nekoda was playing with a crab, which deliberately outstepped and outwitted him each time he snapped at it with his large jaws.

Ange became curious and began to explore the cavern. The dome of water they sat upon sloped down towards the large lake. She went away from it towards the caverns of the walls.

The waterfalls were gentle but constant and sparkled with blue and aquamarine. Ange put her hand in and realised that there was nothing behind the watershed. She stepped through tentatively and after a few steps she entered another cavern containing a transparent columns filled with creatures. Strange multi-coloured tentacle creatures that looked like the lizards from her home, walked up the sides of the columns. Huge fish with sharp teeth and massive fins swam past as Ange walked around each of them trying to figure out how they fitted in there. On the floor were oysters open with massive pearls on display. Ange took one and felt it. She remembered long ago when a trader had passed through with one ear pierced and a pearl hanging from it. Ange had asked what it was; she didn't believe him at the time but now understood. A snout poked out of a tower on the far side of the chamber, massive jaws extended revealing large white teeth. A huge lizard crawled out and into a pool and swam away. Unbelievably, she saw a blue mass gently break the surface of the pool as well. It blew a spout of water and then ducked under the surface again. Its body was so large that Ange sat on the edge and simply watched it pass, until its tail came up and swept a wave over the floor and her. She giggled as the water drenched her. Walking further in, the columns continued mesmerising her at the wonders of the earth, showing its anthem of creation. Eventually, the cathedral ended, and she turned back.

Slipping, she fell through the stream and came across the wall where Assumpta had hidden the prism. She plucked the shell out of its watery receptacle. She opened it and took out the prism. It felt warm, like it was alive. She inspected each of the sides and then held it up. It swirled with all the colours of the rainbow, only brighter and more alive, like they were oceans of colour ebbing like a heart beating. She felt the prism become hot as a shaft of the light from the cavern caught its bevelled edge, suddenly a spear of white heat struck Ange directly in the chest and flung her into the pool. The prism remained in her hand. She could not let go. She saw in her mind whiteness, so pure that her mind rebelled at it. Her heart beat so fast that she was gasping. A vision began to open in her mind not meant for clay born. Ange saw a raging gold pit of fire spewing forth and opening to reveal the heart of the sun and the world's lost destiny. Her mind broke as the fullness of the images pervaded every part of her being. Just then, something thrust her out of the water. She took a huge gasp of air as she landed on the floor again. Lido stood before her

"Get up girl and take the prism back to its receptacle. Up now!"

Ange blinked in disbelief. The prism was still burning in her hand, but the vision had disappeared. She quickly placed it into the shell and slotted it into the cavity. Lido sculpted a thick column around it.

"Are you hurt?"

"I don't think so." Ange's mind cleared instantly.

Lido lingered. "Sister, you have chosen well. I will set the great serpent to guard here while I search. None should survive what you have seen, Ange. Is your mind clear?"

"I think so, what is that?"

"From now I shall call you Keeper of Sorrow and Guardian of the Tears."

Ange looked at her not understanding what Lido meant.

"Go back to your companions and rest, for you will need your strength."

"What are these?" Ange asked pointing at the columns.

"They are creatures that are given to my care. They are what I have wrought as the Norbu has seen. Some were here at the dawn of time and no longer linger on it while others are yet to come."

She watched Ange go back to Bensah and Nekoda; neither had seen what had happened, indeed Bensah was still asleep. He dreamed of times with Sara and as a child with his brother and father fishing. He felt content for the first time in many moons.

Lido left, with a new hope, the girl was strong with the ancient blood of the earth. The spirit of water drifted back to the beginning times when the wars between the light and dark had stopped and the lesser children had come to be. The first ones did not know of each other, for all had grown in their lands that Norbu had prepared for them. They lived in isolation for many generations, until Norbu called the leaders of the children of the earth together to form a covenant. A time that has been seen in the mind of the infinite would come, when the earth would be for the children to keep as their own. Their fate would not be guided by the dark or light, but by their own hand. And not until the earth took their bodies back would their true destiny be known. Blood was spilled by all the tribes in the sacred caves, known as the Gate of Belmaris. It was here their brother had entered. The oldest of the tribes came from the girl's land. The first parents of each tribe spilled their blood into the soil of Arglethium. Norbu took the prism of the realm of the custodians and formed a rock. Lido blessed it with her waters. That rock became the throne of Norbu.

"Why do you slumber, brother? The covenant of water and stone sits on the precipice of destruction. The Keeper is found; the Keeper of the Tears and the last memories of the realm of light. Wake yourself now and show the world who you are and master the earth so that the malice that abides here may be smote by your mighty fist."

21

The Orynth

Assumpta placed her hood on her head to protect against a heavy shower of rain which broke through the forest roof. The smell of damp earth and sweetness of the lush greenery revived her spirit. She noticed the droplets of water running down her tunic sparkled with the colours of dawn, keeping her dry. The path suddenly turned into a steep rise, forcing her to climb up vines and roots of the trees. As she emerged out of the dense canopy she found herself standing on outcrop of rock. She could just see in the distance a solid black horizon of the northern mountains that formed the border of the middling lands and the ice plateaus. The vista before her took her breath away. The northern ranges looked like great fangs ready to devour the earth, as if a leviathan of the old wars lay buried deep beneath the land. Below, mist rose in small wispy bands like fingers, reluctant to let go of the warmth of the earth. The storm clouds moved away swiftly, revealing a crystal cerulean sky. 'The world waits for you, Belmaris, to reach your strength,' Assumpta thought, as she sensed life waiting to draw the light in and grow. She breathed in the air and felt how her body became invigorated and renewed, so immanent was this place for the flesh to survive and her heightened senses to all the clay born, she felt her whole body breathing in harmony with the sun and earth. Each minute pulse of life and death over and over again was flowing through her.

She fell, stunned. A sudden bolt of white heat pierced her, as the surge of the tear's power passed through her. Lido's voice came to her, "The Keeper has awoken."

"Ange, your suffering shall be your strength and now my death is near. Mighty Norbu hasten to me. For the memory of light has chosen another to wield its strength and with it has been born the new Caemexa. Hasten brother so the custodians of light maybe reunited once more to restore the realm of their birth."

She made her way towards the escarpment below. An eagle flew above her looking for prey. It swooped on a field mouse. Assumpta heard the little squeak of the tiny rodent as the eagle's claws crushed its chest. The descent to the ground was hard going. It was mostly rock, and she had to scrabble along outcrops of slippery stones. She noticed she began to tire quickly. The eagle still flew in circles above her as if it was waiting for her to fall so it could swoop on her as well. It landed on a cliff ledge, and sat perched looking into the distance, and then occasionally back at her. Eventually tiring too much, Assumpta came to a large flat expanse of rock, where a pool of water had formed from the rain. She dipped her hand in and drank it. The eagle sat just above her.

"Who are you?" Assumpta asked the bird, gulping the water.

It squawked and flapped its large wings.

"I am seeking Norbu, the god of the earth, have you seen him with your keen eye, bird?"

It bobbed its head. Assumpta stared at the large creature not knowing if that was an answer.

"Show yourself, for I think you play with me."

The bird transformed into a man with a beaked face and claw-like hands.

"I am EY, loyal servant and brother to the mighty Norbu."

"I am blessed indeed to be visited by a friend of my brother. Have you seen him?"

"Nay, my kin and I have not seen our brother for many sunrises now. I sense a force has come that is malevolent to all things here. Are you here to destroy us?"

"For a hundred of Arglethium's millennia have I wept and now the end is near. For whether the victory be to light or dark, my toil and sorrow shall end."

EY began to form back into an eagle again but stopped itself.

"I am mostly bird now and find it difficult to remember my old form. Our brother and Lord's counsel is sorely missed. He slumbered many uncountable dawns but it is not unusual for the mighty Norbu to take such lengthy repose."

"My sister and I seek the protector of this world and stayer of the hand of the great star. My other brethren have been lost to us now. I have found the last of the ancient blood lines that formed the covenant and the new Caemexa have been chosen but do not know it yet. I journey to Norbu's Keep, in hope that he dwells there still or has left a clue as to where he may lie. The gift he forged of my last vision before the destruction of the realm of light needs to be remade."

"I will follow you there and help guide the path. What is your name?"

"Ascendant."

EY knelt. "You are the Keeper of souls and wielder of the spark espoused to the vaults of Caemeris. You are born of the kernel of creation."

"Up, EY, you are not less than me, for my custody lies in the hearts of the clay born, whom this world sustains. You are unknown to me, but you are brother to my brethren, and we shall journey together as kin."

EY rose and walked towards her. He jerked his head forward in the fashion of a bird. He looked at the god quizzically. "I thought you would be different."

"This body has been chosen, as in my true form I would exist on the edges of the world and would not have been able to come into it. Come, EY, guide me to my mighty brother's throne and tell me of your kind, for I have no memory of you. I know of the beginning and the end but am blind to all else between."

"Spirit, who is it that seeks to destroy all he sees and spews forth his malice into this realm of the mighty Norbu?"

"The Descendant has come to this land, but it is truly the great shadow, Voloc, who seeks dominion here and whose poison seeps ever more into the heart of Arglethium."

EY squawked at hearing the name of the Voloc and changed back to an eagle. It stretched its wings out fully to alight into the air. They were three times the length of the body the god now existed in. It took off hovering just ahead of her as she began to walk.

"This way, spirit, the path is more defined. There are only

six of us left now in the world. We choose to live in the highest eyries, away from the children of Arglethium and as close to the great star as possible. Our memories are haunted by the slaughter of our brethren in the wars of creation. My father, YU, was the first to come with Norbu to help build and shape the world. YU and the mighty custodian made large beasts that stood as tall as small hills and grazed on the highest trees. This form the Orynth now live in was much larger than now. We ruled the skies and hunted the smaller beasts below. Norbu shaped the mountains and valleys and let us nest high, so that we could survey all around us. Great serpents and lizards roamed freely and tamed the oceans and mountains. With each age that passed the bonds of light and dark grew stronger and the world thrived. But destruction of your realm brought the darkness and bled into world. It found its way to Arglethium. Belmaris was blinded by the belching fires of the demons of the void. The sky became black with cloud and ash and choked the rays of light so that nothing reached the life below. All life died and the giant beasts succumbed to hunger and illness. But Norbu was not satisfied that life be quelled so easily and called his servants to his side.

"Fight with me to destroy this darkness and you shall be granted your freedom to dwell here in any form you choose."

So, our legions gathered, a thousand-fold, the Orynth, servants of the mighty Norbu. We stood at his side. Norbu called the demons forth to declare the first war of creation. His mountain was destroyed as the dragon of fire broke into the world – large and ugly, a behemoth with opaque eyes from never needing to see. It belched its hatred at us and incinerated most of the world. We gathered half our legion in the choking ash in the sky and the other half remained below on earth. The ancient snake, Vipax birthed her young and bid them join together, and a great leash was made. We called the bastard dragon back to us. Its fires took almost a hundred-fold of us that day. We wept for the loss of our brethren, but still the battle continued. We drew it forth. It chased, belched, and burnt all in its wake. So full of fury it did not see the mighty god with his lasso waiting. Norbu drew himself up and thrusting the leash over the dragon's head, he reined the putrid beast in and bought it to its knees. He took its blind, dumb eyes and squashed them into its skull. It screamed with the agony of it. It reared back whipping some of us into the air, sniffing our essence it ate more; my sister IU was one of them. Norbu pulled the beast back and wrapped the serpents around its body. Striding towards the great maw, he ripped its jaw off and crushed its head in his hands.

Ascendant had been so enthralled by EY's recall of the beginning days the night had fallen without her noticing. She suddenly realised how hungry the body had become.

"I will fetch food." EY sped off, seeing a marmoset foraging in a bush.

Assumpta had learnt from Ange how to make fire. She was grateful for the warmth it gave, as well as cooking the flesh of animals. A twinge of sorrow passed through her heart thinking of Seraf's capture. A dead marmoset landed near her. She looked at EY perched on a branch of a tree above her.

"There are no lesser one's here, EY?" She began to skin the rodent.

"No, there is a tribe of children that pass this way occasionally. The ruler of this land is brutal and frequently they are enslaved. I have seen some of the ways of the children and I wonder why Norbu brought them to fruition."

"Yes, EY, I see it all and more, and I also cannot guess the wisdom of the Caemeris for I am all of their love and hate in one mind. Why I do not know. It seems cruel to make it this way."

The darkness was soothing around the gods as they sat on the borders of Unstaadt. EY tucked his head under his wing and dreamt of his glory days; when he and his kin fought side by side and forged the land and the creatures that dwelt upon it.

Assumpta ate the rodent and lay back to sleep. She was glad for EY and felt a bond with him. They shared the same sorrow, for they mourned the loss of the majesty and beauty first wrought. She shed a tear for her brethren as she fell asleep.

They started their journey the following morning. EY resumed his story of the first wars. The land around them changed from the verdant escarpment at the foot of the western lands of the forest of Vran to a vast white desert stretching for leagues to the north. Shimmering in the distance were the northern peaks. To the south, the desert was surrounded by the green plateau whose edge formed a meniscus of cliff around it, but it was so large that the edges were not visible from side to side. Soon Assumpta heard the crunch of salty sand under her feet as they continued into the heart of the massive salt plain. EY let out a few cries that reverberated across the emptiness to call out the Orynth's who dwelt in this land.

"I have told the Orynth, Ascendant custodian of Caemeris

walks beneath their perches."

Assumpta nodded looking up into the sky for any more eagles.

By noon, Belmaris' blazed, bringing thirst and exhaustion to the god.

"EY, this body will not tolerate such heat or dryness. It barely stays upright."

"I see a tree ahead. We will rest there until Belmaris sleeps again."

They reached a burnt stump with one branch of leaves producing shade. The god slumped down and took a slug out of her canvass of water. She panted slightly. "Tell me more of the wars."

EY perched on a branch, hesitating as he thought he saw something moving in the distance. It turned out to be a tumble weed.

"For an age there was peace, particularly after the defeat of the blind dragon, for it was sent to snuff out the light. And many creatures perished from its vileness. Soon its smoke began to thin and Belmaris returned. We began to restore the dead lands and let new things grow. But one dawn, a great roar was heard and suddenly Belmaris was hidden from us. Norbu called us all to his Keep.

"Be strong, my lieges. Hold steady, for your birth right to this clay and rock shall not be usurped."

Out of the darkness, a shape moved like a mountain but instead of fire its breath was frigid like death. Anything it touched would become brittle and shatter. Its red eyes shone in the blankness and pierced all they saw. Norbu watched and waited, for he knew this creature was the oldest of all time and creation. It had come from the depths of Magmeris' tomb, the sister star to our own, and it was this fell beast that had consumed its blazing heart, causing its demise. Where the new life had sprung from the fiery bellows of the blind dragon, the demon's venomous chill singed the new shoots. Norbu called upon Belmaris to revenge its sister's death and smote this eidolon. Norbu wrestled it, but its strength was great, and he could not defeat it. Norbu called for his brethren to help, but none could thwart the wretched power of the creature. My father, YU, came to the mighty guardian.

"Hold true and go to the Belmaris' light and call upon its fiery might, while we distract this phantom of terror from your flight."

Norbu considered at length, for he knew the earth could be lost if he left it unprotected. Without him it would let this demon run free, untethered. But, at last, when once more he could not defeat the fell beast he spoke. "My servants, nay brethren, for this you shall have your freedom to roam as you will in my protection, for your valour and steadfastness has no equal. I will seek the great star's mercy if you will but hold my fortress until I return."

With that, he left Arglethium as we gathered near to the demon. We surrounded the cursed thing. It looked at us and laughed at our pathetic stance. It blew ever so gently, and I saw half my brethren gone, shattered crystals frozen on the ground. We called Vipax again but the ice sheets that covered the oceans were so thick she could not break through to us.

"My father, YU." Assumpta saw EY's chest plump with pride

as he said his father's name "devised a plan. We ran towards the centre of the great icesheet that covered the southern end of Arglethium. It followed us. We ran faster and made it run. It tried to blast us, but we were quick. It then tried to stomp us in jest and cracked the ice it stood on. As soon as Vipax heard the high pitch of the frozen ocean shattering, she swam to the opening, and rising, she opened her mighty jaw and dragged the shadow under the water. We looked into the opening and great tidal waves erupted through the icesheets. The demon struggled to rise again, but Vipax pulled it under. We flew to the sky and awaited Norbu. The struggle continued until the ice was broken into tiny snowflakes. Finally, the tumult stopped. To our despair, the shadow rose silently and slowly over us. It chased us to the end of the earth until we could fly no more. It blew its lethal zephyr until only the six of us remained. In our last throes, a ray of light lit our hiding place. We blinked in confusion as the dark that had held sway for millennia, with the torment of the void and its creatures, suddenly shattered, blinding us. Then we saw Norbu stood upon the ray of light. Taking a spear from the belly of the great star, he thrust it at the demon and struck it in its dead heart. The light seared it into annihilation. The shrieking howl that emitted from it still haunts me. Then the skies opened and the great Belmaris shone forth and warmed the earth. Breaking its crust and piercing to the very heart of this world, it left a memory of its quickening flame so the dark would know its heat and the unsleeping eye of Belmaris. Vipax roared to the surface and standing in the golden rays, it too was blessed for its fearlessness against the dark. So it was, when the final battle had finished, Norbu knelt in honour and homage to our fallen kindred. And, keeping true to his words, he set us free from our servitude to him so that we may live under his protection, but not at his whim. Then, one of my brothers, VE, stood before the mighty lord and looking directly into the eyes of Norbu spoke, "We shall rebuild and create together, mighty father, as kin conceived through battle, to give glory to the great star, for the caemexa are bonded now in the destruction of war and in the work of creation. And so the last of the Orynth; VA, XI, YU, our father, AX, EY and PO soar in the skies as eagles to watch over all that was fought for and remade, out of love for the creatures who reflect the beauty of the myths of Caemeris."

"And Vipax, the serpent?"

"Slumbers beneath her oceans until called again, which I fear may have happened. Not so long ago, I felt the rumbling deep below the oceans and wondered if the great silver fang had need to waken."

The sun was fading, and the god felt replenished as she finished her water.

"How far until there is water, EY?"

"It is not far. By my wings it is only until the daystar reaches the high point."

"That will be most of tomorrow. Can you take my water bag and fill it? I will not be able to walk that far without more."

EY flew down and clutched it in his claws. Darting up into the sky, he screeched into the silent dusk. Night soon came and the chill of the desert reached her. She began to shiver uncontrollably. Lying down, she directed her mind to Ange and Bensah. She saw the mark in Ange now from the prism. It would never be removed. They were looking through her sister's palace, and inside each of them, lay fear and amazement at the wonders that were kept there. Ange's heart and mind churned with equal sorrow and anger. She pined greatly for her sister even though the hope had gone that she would ever see her again. Assumpta thought to look for this Tessi again and reaching out across the vast emptiness, she found the girl quickly. The god felt fear in her heart again and something else, yes, the girl was with child.

A fish landed next to her, and the water bag, followed by EY swooping down to land. She ate the flesh and only took a sip of water to save it for tomorrow. EY stood on the branch gently swaying in the wind.

"Sleep! For the next few days will be difficult for that body, and I will not be able to stay close once we reach the foot of the great ranges."

She walked with the eagle for most of the day across the salt pan. The hood protected her skin from Belmaris' heat, but her lips had begun to crack and bleed as the salt slowly drew out the moisture from them.

"What is this place, EY?"

"It is where Vipax pulled the great demon below the ocean. So tainted was the bed below that when the earth was finally rebuilt, nothing would grow, and the salt remained."

"How much further? This body truly imparts its fatigue across the mind and soul."

"Why create the lesser children and then not give them a means to live their life," asked EY.

"Caemeris never explained its ways. When the light first met the dark, it neither asked for permission, nor made offerings of shared suzerainty. It simply arrived and tore the void with its illumination."

The desert stretched before her like a timeline of grief and sorrow. It seemed never to end.

Assumpta grew wearier with every passing hour. Her voice cracked and her tongue began to thicken. Even the water didn't make a difference.

"Do you know why Norbu may have split the prism of tears, EY?"

"I do not know why Lord Norbu split the prism or where he lays. Those days came after the first wars and we were not privy to all in our father's mind, for our freedom had been gained."

She nodded and continued.

"It is not much longer. I will scout ahead for more water. Have you finished your store?"

She nodded without answering. Swooping down to her, EY collected the pouch and flew away. She collapsed about an hour later. Her tongue was swollen, and her mind was a sea of confusion from the dehydration. Then she felt feathers on her face as EY was trying to force the water into her mouth. She woke startled and batted the bird away. She picked up the bag and gulped down water. She got up.

"Come god, what use are you to all of us if you cannot even walk the dead lake." EY attempted to clutch her in his great talons but it could not hold her. It was like clasping mist.

"This body needs to harden, EY. It will not allow aid. It is how my essence strengthens itself."

After another three days of walking, they reached the edge of the northern ranges. She looked up at the height of the cliff face before her. It rose so high above, that sky and rock merged beneath the clouds. She felt as if she were falling. She latched onto a small ledge to steady herself. Her face had blisters on it and stung as the salt got into the raw flesh beneath. Above, EY was hovering in the air. Another two eagles had arrived. She sat near a bush that abutted the granite cliff. The cliffs were pale grey and white granite – mostly barren except for a few courageous shrubs that grew between the cracks. The dusk was just starting with Belmaris setting in the east, casting a pink hue over the salt pan and cliffs. EY flew down and transformed into his other form. The other two joined him. One had plumage that was a mottled grey and the other was jet black, while EY was brown.

"Ascendant, these are my brethren, VA and XI. They have come to see the final days of the custodians."

"See her as she is, worn and fatigued from the ways of this world. The flesh bound are to be honoured for their perseverance. You are most gratefully acknowledged, lieges and allies to my mighty brother, Norbu." Assumpta bowed wearily.

XI came forward. "How do we speak to that which is unknown to us and never shown to us?"

VA came forward also taller and with downier plumage, she squawked at her.

"Do you come to destroy us, Ascendant?"

"I do not know yet. My spouse and I are yet to meet. It is so long an age since our sundering that we will not know each other. But I can no longer bear my grief and an end must come.

With my end so might this place be destroyed. May I ask two things?"

"You may," responded XI.

"Do you know where the mighty Norbu slumbers?"

"We do not. We have not spoken with him since the last war. But we have felt the presence of another. Its stench is the same as the dragon and demon defeated long ago."

"I ask then," as the god bowed before the Orynth, "Will you honour the old bonds and seek my brother Norbu, for without him, the destroyer shall surely succeed and enslave all again in the darkness that began it all. I go to his Keep to seek him out of find answers so this quest shall end. A new Caemexa, warriors and defenders of this world are to be born. I have asked Lido to send two of them to the Keep of Norbu. There they will be pledged to be protectors of the Keeper of the gift forged by Norbu. This gift holds the last memories of Caemeris."

XI, EY and VA stood together, and bowed their heads. "We will search for our mighty Norbu. We shall call a council with our kin to ask if they wish to renew the covenant again between custodian and Orynth."

The god stood, "Show me to where I need to go, EY, and then go with your brethren once more."

"Who are the warriors you have chosen to fight, god?" asked EY.

"Gildas Gol of the north, and Kado Kodrax of the middle lands. The Keeper of the gift, Ange Tsaed, a desert dweller has been given ownership of the light of Caemeris. These will become the new caemexa, the custodians of light. There is another, Sa-Tuc. I do not know what awaits her, but her soul is ancient and draws me to her."

"We know of the great Gol lord, fierce and cruel. Why choose such as he, the darkness is more his domain."

"His blood runs with the covenant long ago when the clay born became of aware of the passing of time. He is a descendant of those parents and it is this bond, forged by Norbu and the great Ice Bear, that I draw upon."

"So be it, god. We will seek our brother and master Norbu for you but will seek council of our brethren before we pledge our lives to your warriors."

Ascendant nodded as XI and VA turned into eagles and flew swiftly into the sky. EY lingered.

"You must climb until you reach the very tip of the peaks, then walk directly north. The sun will always rise to the east. You shall know Tarantess, for its height even shades Belmaris. Be warned, until you are halfway up the side, Belmaris will be your enemy, but the cliff is treacherous without its light. So, you must climb after dawn and after the zenith of the day."

EY transformed into an eagle again and flew away after the others.

Assumpta sat down. Suddenly, the silence began to gather around her. The sun had fully set, and the moon was on its last gibbous wane, only dimly illuminating the desert before her. She curled up into the bush for warmth with the hood well over her head and went to sleep.

The next morning, she began the arduous trek to her brother's Keep. The rock beneath her feet was slippery from the dew, and a few times, she skidded grazing her knees and shins. By midday, EY's warning was beginning to bear out its truth. She stopped under an outcrop of rock for shade and sipped some water. Her climb was almost vertical. Her fingers were bleeding from gripping the jagged slate.

After three days with only water and her silken clothes to protect her, she reached the top of the mountain ranges. For the first time, she saw the sun setting over the vast ice sheets that stretched all the way to the north. The desert that stretched behind her turned black suddenly as the ranges blocked the rays of light with precision. Her wormsilk clothes warmed her against the frigid air that blasted her during the night. It felt like razors on her skin. The cloth, especially the belt, had stored the rays of the sun during the day and the nearer she came to Tarentess the warmer it made her feel.

"You call to your creator, little ones."

At the dawn, she saw the spine of ranges running directly west and traced her path as far as she could see. She tied the hood more closely around her face to protect the raw flesh that now lay exposed on her nose and cheeks. Her fingers were blue and bloodied where the nails had been ripped off by the climb up. Just vaguely in the distance, the tall shadow of Tarentess revealed itself.

"Mighty Norbu, welcome your kin and hasten her steps to your mighty throne."

22

Norbu's Keep

"So, this is a mighty god's lair?"

Gildas and Sa had arrived the day after Assumpta. Sa was cooking a pheasant as Gildas and the god inspected the cave. All of them were weary from the arduous trek to the throne room of Norbu. The cavern had been carved into the very tip of the Tarentess. A throne towered towards the roof at the rear of the cavern. It was carved from the same granite as the mountain, with one adornment: a diamond carved into the back rest. A vast emptiness greeted them inside the implacable stone, but a palpable energy of deep awareness and unshakeable constancy, as old as Arglethium itself, could be felt.

Assumpta ran her hand over the walls to try and feel her brother.

"There is nothing here. Your brother hides himself or is dead," provoked Gildas.

"Nay, warrior, for Arglethium would end if the mighty Norbu were to leave before all has been wrought."

"Is there nothing here to show where he lies?"

"I will seek further on the morn. The loyal Orynth hunt in

the day and roost in the night. They may know."

Assumpta sat with Sa who was stripping the flesh off a bird. The god was still impatient with the needs of the body she now inhabited. Her mouth salivated as Sa put the flesh onto the flames to roast.

Gildas stood at the entrance of the Keep smoking a pipe he had carved on the journey. The demon had left him alone since the grove. 'The witch, she attracted it,' he thought. He was more wary since he was back in her company.

He looked across the northern entrance towards the great expanse of his homelands. It had been twenty summers since he fled them. Would anyone remember Gildas Gol now? He wondered if Jarrod still lived. More than likely dead. The Gol name would be cursed amongst the clansmen for generations. It was their way to hold grudges and cling to superstition. The wind became cooler as the clouds descended obscuring everything above and below the entrance to the cavern. Gildas shivered and went back to the fire. He unrolled his blanket and lay back against his pack.

"Why now, witch? What has bought the spirits of the underworld to us here when we have dwelt for generations without knowledge of you or your brethren?" He eyed her carefully, waiting for the answer.

Assumpta roused from being deep in thought. She looked at Gildas as he puffed on his pipe. His gaze remained fixed on her.

"I am weary of the sorrow and the path that was laid down and I seek an end to this fate. It is unfathomable how long I have searched for Baachelaus. Voloc is drawn to me, Gildas." She smiled wryly. "The demon knows I am an agent of its destruction and seeks the same power that I do. I draw my strength from you and the others. Why now, I do not know, but I am grateful that soon it will end. You and Ange have been chosen to fulfil the covenant first wrought. I seek you and the destroyer. Baachelaus, the creature you see in your nightmares, seeks you, for your life force is tied to this place and has a potency which we can draw upon. We are both weakened. He from his shackles of darkness and myself, from the breaking of the realm which made me."

"What spirits of fortune are you if your only desire is to sate your heart at the cost of us here?"

"You are right Gildas, the brethren will remain as long as we can until it is determined who shall remain, the first born or the last born. The custodians are your progenitors so without us you the clay born, the last to come would not be. Together we must answer the call of Caemeris and then our destinies will be decided. The prism forged by Norbu must be remade to ensure these destinies are fulfilled."

"Bah, still speaking in riddles. What about her?"

Sa had been meditating with her legs crossed and eyes shut. She had heard Gildas' question.

"She is for something else not yet awakened. Her life is bound to this place in another way."

Sa nodded, not really understanding anything, but being pragmatic in nature, she understood that at this moment her life had no purpose with the Drax empire destroyed. She would remain until the path forward became clear.

"Rest now, we may have more news when the Orynth arrive. Make your choice, warriors. Your lives are no longer your own, for the gaze of the immortals is upon you and the ancient strength that lies within your blood."

Sa unfolded herself to lie down. Assumpta closed her eyes and sent her mind out into the night: Ange and Bensah were safe. Kado battled his way back to existence. Assumpta could feel the resentment rising within the Graan warrior. For Gildas Gol to feel trapped made him dangerous not frightened. 'Voloc's attacks had cowered him but would that be enough to make him loyal to the oaths sworn by his forebears so long ago. Would the fear of Voloc break his iron will and heart enough to see he must protect Ange and fight for her until the custodians are finished?' the god thought, as she sent her essence out into each of them.

On the next dawn, the three visitors stood on a precipice on the opposite side of the Keep. The view was still covered by the clouds, and the air was frigid. The eagles had not returned. Assumpta thought of EY and his family; perhaps they were still in counsel.

"We will wait until the eagles return."

Sa and Gildas began to spa again. They were well-suited to each other. Gildas' brute strength and size became more refined with Sa's precision and subtlety. Assumpta was running her hands over the walls trying to find any clue as to what had happened to make Norbu leave his throne. She could not sense any of his essence, which meant millennia had passed since he resided in this place. Moving along the rough wall, she found a small passage, barely wide enough to fit through. It opened out after one hundred paces into a small chamber. An unnatural silvery sheen covered the walls, as there was no break in the rock to let light in. Inside stood a basin raised up in a pedestal. It was full of water. Assumpta touched the surface and it rippled and danced in shapes. It formed into a face: Norbu. She realised this was the image in her head. It felt like liquid metal. Sa and Gildas came into the chamber as well. Gildas had scraped his shoulder as he squeezed his way in through the doorway.

"What is this place?" asked Sa.

"It is the well spring of Norbu. It is where the first elements were drawn to make Arglethium. Here lies the flesh and bone of your world. Norbu would kill you if he knew you were here, for a clay born with this knowledge could wrought the wealth of the world to keep as their own."

"But how?" asked Gildas, his interest peaked.

"Come here and place your hand in the basin."

Gildas came over and warily put it in. The liquid moved like it was alive. Assumpta watched closely to see what happened.

"Think of something."

"Like what?"

"Anything that can be wrought from earth and water."

"But everything can."

Gildas thought of a sword, and touching the liquid again, a sword formed on the surface. Perfect in its detail, Gildas grabbed it not expecting it to be real. He thrust it against the solid rock wall. He removed it and saw that the blade gouged a groove deep enough to fit his hand into.

Sa went over and put her hand in the basin, but the liquid retreated from her. She pulled away quickly.

Assumpta walked over. "I think I see now."

"Know this, Gildas, if you choose to run with the demon then I will kill you or my brethren will. This knowledge is sacred and I in my infancy have let it be known to a lesser one. It cannot be desecrated by one such as Voloc."

"Bitch, do you threaten me? What is this place and its sorcery? You speak of a god who cannot be found. Then you tell us of the sanctity of this thing but let it be known to us. You are truly addled in your mind or is it your own mischief that now plagues this world and our lives?" Losing his temper, he thrust the sword at her.

She flicked it away. It landed in the basin and dissolved into it. Suddenly, she thrust him against the wall and lifted him off the ground. Her eyes became black with venom and her skin rippled like the granite of the mountainside.

"Who do you choose, Gildas, the custodians of light or Voloc?"

"What is the difference? I knew you were a witch."

"Take the sword again and arm yourself, for when Voloc comes and I am not here, you will need to defend yourself. You ruled half the land that my brother wrought and now you are nothing; but the land remains. One day you may need to rule again. Will you do it with the favour of my brethren or not?"

"Gildas Gol rules by his own axe or not at all, witch," he spat back at her.

Assumpta penetrated his mind, heart, and soul and pulled at the thread of fear that still lingered. She saw the face of Jess and behind that the great Ice Mother and just as she went to pluck it out of his mind, she spoke. "Who do you choose the shadow or my brethren?"

She saw a tear well in the mighty warrior's eye as she lingered over the image of Jesse. "Who do you choose?"

She held him waiting for an answer. She probed deeper at the face of Jesse. The fear rose into his eyes.

"You, witch. I choose you, witch," he whispered.

Assumpta relented and let him go. The hope and sanctity of Jesse's image remained in the warrior's heart.

He walked out into the main cavern and stood at the northern entrance. Assumpta followed him.

"When the clouds break, I will leave you, witch. I want no part of sorcery or trickery. The Graan have ever lived by the axe and ice and I am no different. If the unending cold takes me then I will return to my ancestors and take my rightful place among them. I have paid for my hatred and anger."

Assumpta felt the rage and the pain within him, more so now that she had managed to prick the one place where no one else had gone; a rage that was directed at no enemy, but only at himself. It had been with the warrior all his life and in the end, it would destroy him.

"Remember who you have chosen, Gildas, when the time comes you must fight once more." Assumpta's voice pierced his thoughts.

Sa came to the entrance and looked out into the mist.

"And you, assassin, will you stay with her for this blind chase; the white fox chasing the white rodent in the snowstorm."

"I have always been hunted or been the hunter and ruler of nothing, including my own destiny. My mother saw me as the enemy and treated me the same. After scarring my face because a customer told her to do it, she sold me for fermented lily, as she knew I would not be wanted with a disfigurement. Then Ko Paidrax Blackflame found me. He saw a weapon that needed sharpening until the blade pricked to the bone with such precision, the cuts it inflicted closed over without a trace. I must follow and obey for I know no other way to exist. I will chase with the white fox as you say until I die, or another path is laid clear."

"Why do you not desire more, assassin? You have the skill and cunning to lead an army."

"You desire power and domination while I seek bondage for that is all I know. Warrior, before you leave, think of what you have now seen, and the demon that treads on your heels: this place, her and her brethren. Were you not blind to these things before? To spurn your brother and clan is one thing, but the spirits are not so easily distracted from their desires. That sword did not form for me."

Getting up she gestured for Gildas to rise also. "Come, let us practice or I will become an old washer woman before my time."

Gildas looked at the eastern female begrudgingly. He knew she spoke the truth as he rubbed the marks on his neck where the witch had held him. The witch had gone where even the demon couldn't. Looking at her, his temper flared again. She had the power to end this and yet she doesn't. The god was sitting with her eyes closed on the throne. Sa tapped him on the leg to get him to begin their sparring. He got up and took out his sword.

Assumpta smiled a little at the conversation that had taken

place. The assassin's soul was full of old wisdom.

EY, VA, PO, XI, YU and AX were perched on a ledge of rock at the roof of the cavern watching the trio sleep. The Orynth had arrived during the night after making council. The dawn had risen, but it was difficult from the height to know what time of day it was, as the cloud cover remained as thick as ever. Assumpta stirred first and saw EY above her.

"Ah, most faithful, you have returned."

Sa and Gildas woke quickly when they heard the god speaking. They immediately saw the six majestic eagles watching them carefully. EY transformed as it flew down to Assumpta. The rest of the Orynth followed. They stood a foot taller than Gildas and regally stood surrounding the throne of Norbu.

One of them stepped forward towards Assumpta and bowed. It was grey with silver flecks in the plumage.

"Brethren of the mighty one, you are welcome here. I am YU father of EY. I am the oldest and was first chosen by Norbu to set about his work here. You are unknown to us for we came to be in the wars of creation and beyond the realm of the mighty Norbu. But I sense the myth of Caemeris walks closely. Ever this legend is steeped in mystery for all creatures born after the dark."

"I bow before you mighty and valiant servant and brother to Norbu. This is Sa Tuc of the Drax Kingdom and Gildas Gol of the Graan from the north."

Sa bowed, but Gildas did not react, instead choosing to remain on guard. 'These bird spirits could rip them all to shreds if they wished to,' he thought.

"Have you taken counsel?"

"We have and it is decided that we are in covenant with the great custodian for he gave us our freedom and looks upon us as his equal. We will provide help where we can. We searched for him, but his slumber is deep. Seven millennia of men have passed since he and I spoke. Not all the world has been searched though. It is not unusual for him to rest and slumber for many generations of the children. We will begin again at the next dawn to search again."

"Yes, his scent is long passed from here. One boon I ask, YU, before you depart?"

"Ask, Ascendant."

"Food, we have none and this body is ever in need of it."

"XI, PO, and AX, hunt for food and bring kindling for a fire." The three became eagles again and flew away. "The malice that has come grows stronger. What is it that it seeks here? Its stench revives my heart for the glory of the beginning days," spoke YU.

"Voloc seeks Norbu's gift. It contains the last vision of Caemeris before the great sundering occurred. I need to have the custodians restored in unity again, for if Voloc wields its power, the light itself will be destroyed. I have found the one half but not the other. Only Norbu has the strength to break it for he wrought it. Only he can restore it."

"And these ones? Why do they accompany one of the guardians of Arglethium?" YU's eagle gaze peered directly at Gildas as he spoke. "You are known to the Orynth, Gol lord, for we witnessed the red stain in the ice lands by the blood spilt by your sword. Why would one such as you be worthy to serve the great custodians of this world?"

"It is not by choice, eagle, but the demon is stronger, for I have not found his bare spot to thrust my sword into and drain the sorcery and conniving from his body," Gildas replied in a low growl.

"Nor will you ever, you fight amongst the eternal. It is not by a clay born's hand it will be destroyed," replied YU.

Gildas grimaced slightly at the bird's warning.

Assumpta noticed Gildas' reaction to YU's words. "They are hunted by Voloc and me, for they are the ancestors of the first children. They are part of the blood covenant that your lord made as the first peoples walked the earth."

XI, PO and AX returned in a flurry of wings with several marmosets and pheasants. AX dropped a bundle of twigs and branches on the floor of the cavern. Sa went over and gathered the carcasses to cook the meat. Gildas began to make the fire, wary and inspecting the eagles above who had not transformed back into their other form. They eyed the pair as they began to prepare a meal.

"We have not searched the southern or eastern lands so far. We will leave again with the dawn, but you will have to wait, for a storm rages below. I fear that something drives the wind more than it should. As the first rays of light break through the rock above known as the Key of Norbu, leave here and return to the water spirit, for your lives are in danger while Norbu is unfound."

YU turned to transform back, to roost for the evening, when he saw the rock that stood at the entrance to the chamber to the well.

"Who entered the sacred heart of the Keep?"

"It was I, old one," Assumpta said.

The rest of the Orynth readied themselves to attack, their feathers bristling in a pose of fierceness.

"It is not to be entered other than by Norbu. Have these ones seen what it keeps hidden from the eyes of the world."

"Yes, and the warrior has been tested in it."

AX flew towards Assumpta in an instinctive move of threat.

Gildas became edgy; these predators were not to be trifled with. He unsheathed his sword slowly.

PO grabbed his arm and XI placed its wing around his neck. Gildas fought against the restraints, but only got a mouth full of feathers. EY stalked over to him and thrust his beak into his face. Cocking to the side like it was looking at a mouse in a field, it pecked Gildas on the cheek several times, drawing blood. The Graanar roared but XI's wing drew in tighter, almost choking him.

"That is to remind you of the price on your head, warrior, for the desecration that has occurred."

Released, Gildas took a defensive pose with his sword. "How dare you, demons. I asked for none of this. I did not seek this place of my own will but out of flight from one of your kind. Your god, this witch, has led us here. If your great master leaves his keep unguarded, then he must live by his own lapse of judgement. I will not be made the purveyor of misdeed here. Your gods and demons are as foolish and lacking cunning as a newborn babe. What of her, the assassin, she is privy to this sacred gift. Is her life now not forfeit as well?"

He heaved and as he finished, taking a deep breath. Spittle came out of his mouth.

"She cannot use it, Gildas, that is why, for it chooses who may take its gift and recreate the world. The knowledge of this is dangerous to all, and if it were wielded by a demon then death would come to all, including the great Belmaris, the one you call the Sun. With that and this jewel, the world that the Orynth and the mighty Norbu spilled their blood for lies on the perilous edge of annihilation. Therefore, while it is not by your design to be in this place, nevertheless you are, and you now have a knowledge and power to use as no other. You are so marked. Should destruction come from the well-spring of the earth then it will be known whose carcass shall be flayed and consumed by the mighty Orynth."

Assumpta stood before EY. "Enough, Orynth, the Graan knows his fate is now bound to this battle."

Gildas roared at the frustration of it, wrenching himself free of XI he stormed to the edge of the keep. White cloud met him. He wanted to jump but knew it would kill him. Assumpta tensed, as she knew what thoughts raced through the clansman's mind.

"Ascendant, surely your purpose was to bring questing thirst to the hearts and minds of the clay born, not their destruction. The mighty Norbu's wisdom has not failed to bring such potency here in your jewel and to reveal the life blood of the earth without reason, to restore what has been sundered."

Assumpta looked as all the Orynth as well as Gildas and Sa stood waiting for her answer.

"I do not know the purpose of my brother nor of my own destiny, for this vision was lost to me when our realm was destroyed."

A low chuckle echoed throughout the chamber. Assumpta looked and saw that it was Gildas.

"Our fate and our lands lie in the hands of the lost and worn whims of spirits that were made to watch us and keep us safe. Only, in their fevered state they bring the very thing that will ensure our destruction." Gilda spat on the floor and turned his back in disdain. He took out his pipe and lit it.

"The Orynth will honour our covenant with your brethren Norbu. We will depart at the dawn to continue our search."

YU looked carefully at Gildas as if memorising him. He turned and the six of the Orynth stood in a circle and closed the opening to the well. There was a faint trace of an outline of the doorway. Transforming back into eagles, they all flew to the ceiling and roosted on a rocky ledge. Huddled closely for warmth, they tucked their beaks under their wings.

Assumpta slumped onto the throne and fell into deep thought. She mused about YU's words. Had this been a trap all along for the great potency given by Caemeris to come together in one place, so that the Destroyer would devour it all and snuff out all memory of existence, including the dark?

Sa took some of the meat over to Gildas.

"Eat, either way you will need your strength."

"Would you not use the basin, even make a trade for the knowledge of its whereabouts, if it bought you freedom or wealth." Asked Gildas.

"Yes, I would, but it is to be allowed to wield its magic that is dangerous, not the knowledge of it. Place your hand on the rock. I cannot budge it, but I think you will be able."

He walked over to the passage doorway and the rock trembled

under his hand. Assumpta pulled his hand off the wall.

"The Orynth would kill you now if not for me being their master's brethren."

Gildas looked up and saw two of the birds had awoken and were watching him.

AX and PO saw all of it and remembered Gildas face and form.

The next dawn the cloud broke and sunlight streamed into the cavern. The small shaft of light directly above the throne beamed the star's rays directly onto it, giving the stone chair a silvery glow. Sa placed her hand in the light to feel the warmth of it. Gildas inspected the western wall, gauging the best route to descend the sheer cliff. Assumpta came over to the throne and sat herself directly below the light and let it stream through her. Tears rolled down the god's cheeks and spilled onto the floor beneath, forming a pool that seeped into the black rock. She had delved into her memory to find the answer to the Orynth's question but had found none. Now a deep despair had entombed her mind.

Sa noticed that the light extended down under the throne and into the dais it stood on, only it changed into different colours, reds and blues and golds. As the sun struck the god fully, the cave became illuminated with her essence. Sa and Gildas had to close their eyes at the brightness for fear it would blind them.

"Mighty brother, hear my plea, awaken now and harken to my aid." Her tears washed the throne of Norbu and the floor beneath sending tiny rivulets across the polished stones.

The god stood and faced Sa and Gildas. "We will begin our

journey back to Lido and wait for news from the Orynth. Gildas, it will be your choice to follow or make your own way in this world. I will not ask you again, but take this as a gift from the brethren, and as a protection, for the custodians are not without mercy."

The god held out a sword similar to the one the he had formed in the basin.

"Nay, witch, I want no part of this place. Keep it."

"You will need it, Gildas Gol."

Gildas took it reluctantly. He felt its lightness but remembered the gouge it had made into solid rock.

Stepping over the ledge first, Sa began the long climb to the bottom followed by Gildas and Assumpta.

Light mingled with sorrow and seeped into the deepness of the earth. As it moved further through the soil and rock, a tremor began to build, gathering speed and coursing all the way to the fiery heart of the world. The spark of the great star that dwelt in the bosom of the world dimmed a little as the tears of the Ascendant washed over them. As the unquenchable flames drew the sorrowful flows into themselves, a great shudder resounded throughout the earth and into the skies above.

As AX, EY, XI, PO, VA and YU flew a great heave rippled the cerulean sky around them, pushing them higher.

"Ah, mighty brother Norbu, you have awoken at last," exclaimed YU as it steadied its wings.

"EY, find the custodian and her warriors. Bring them to our brother and Lord."

23

Reunion

Something pricked and then began to burn in the place where his ancient heart lay. He took the scalding pebble and looked at it. It was such a tiny thing in his hands that he wondered why he had thought it so precious to place it next to his heart. Norbu, the great custodian of Arglethium woke up after seven ages of slumber. The rock and stone of his dominion had been his bed as he let his essence drip into the world while he rested. He stretched a little and saw around him a cradle of rubies, diamonds, emeralds and sapphires. The sacred power that bled from his beating heart issued the precious gems, in tenfold abundance. Standing up, a massive quake erupted and rippled through the primordial layers of the world. Upon the surface, a mountain side disintegrated into rubble and massive boulders crashed into the ocean below. A wave formed in the ocean and flowed over the middling isles pushing the islands together towards the southern lands. Even the great thick ice sheets of the north ruptured as the creator-god rose to greet Belmaris and his kingdom once more.

Deep in his cave, Baachelaus was roused by the force of the

avalanche of rock that slammed into the edge of the Iron Coast. Shudders cracked his red throne and caused the cavern walls to rupture and let light in. He screamed from the pain, but soon his agony was distracted by what lay behind the quake.

"Ancient power has awoken and reveals itself to me."

The guardians came to life once more. They and their prisoner began their march towards the ocean that had blockaded Baachelaus since his awakening. The fallen god roared across the desert as he saw the bridge of rock and rubble that now joined with the middling lands to the north.

Breaking into the light of the world, Norbu sighed and took a deep satisfying breath.

"Ahh Belmaris, you still warm my children." His voice rumbled across the sky and earth.

The prism pulsed in his hand. "Yes, now I remember. She has come and the other half must have been found. So, there will be a reunion."

The god chuckled, emitting such a deep visceral laugh the crust of the world rippled again. Norbu was not large, only two spans taller than a man, but he was strong, and this was his kingdom. His potency was palpable to all that lay around. The rock clung to him, not wanting to let go of its father. He sat on the edge of the mountain that was Sa Dom and looked below him. He saw the destruction around him, the mining tunnels, and bloodied remains of the clay born as they had battled one another. The devastation of the Drax city. The jewels that had been reefed from the dirt and then placed as adornments now lay mingled with mud and black soil. He raged when he saw the cart horses neighing in distress as their flesh was whipped.

He snuffed a group of soldiers out to quell the malice in their hearts and minds. He looked at the dying slaves at their feet and took their lives as well.

"Back to the earth and stone you go, give back what has been cruelly taken from you."

He put the prism in his heart and waited for his sister Ascendant, and brother Descendant. It was only she that could awaken him. She had been his favourite of all the brethren, and it was her essence he had wrapped into the prism; the last memories of Caemeris and the realm of the custodians. Norbu sensed Voloc watching in the shadows. He saw over the horizon more children marching towards the pit that used to be the Citadel. Voloc had been busy to cause such destruction so quickly.

He would wait until dark, and if all had not gathered, then he would return to his throne and await them. Picking up a handful of diamonds and rubies, he pegged them at the miners and villagers. Some of the soldiers began to gather into militant rows with sticks and rocks to throw at the mighty Norbu. Others just stood frozen in awe mixed with fear. The ones with spears and knives had begun to fight back throwing their weapons at him, but they fell away from his skin, not piercing it. They persisted and he began to enjoy the game. He chuckled to himself and watched the advancing group of swordsmen fall over from the ripples in the ground his laugh made.

"Brother, Norbu."

Turning, he saw PO and YU.

"My feathery brethren, long since we last met. The malice of long ago greets my awakening and the sorrow of she who has been set to destroy it lingers here as well. Have you seen them?"

"We have. She comes to you. The deceiver has returned. He is strong and he seeks the same thing."

"Hmm, perhaps our time is over, friends."

"We will see, Brother Norbu."

Assumpta stood on the cliffs near the Drax City and saw Norbu talking to YU and PO. EY had come to them with the news of Norbu's wakening just before they had reached Lido's Keep. She had collected Ange, Bensah and the dog and together they had swiftly marched to find her brother. Mostly what drew her now was the prism around Norbu's neck. Ange held the other half. Already she felt the crushing weight of the two halves as they neared one another.

Sa and Gildas had returned from scouting out a way to get to Norbu, but they had been cut off by the armies. The destruction of the Drax Palace had left massive ravines around where it once stood. The army of Ranik was gathering into formations after the chaos of the god's quake. Gildas stood to the rear surveying the scene below. He looked at the one called Norbu and felt the power in him. He wished he could face him in battle as the Chief Graan of the Northern reaches. The sword given to him by Assumpta was secured in his belt. Sa noticed that he kept his hand on it at all times.

"Ange, come to me. All are almost gathered," Assumpta called. "Give me the prism."

Ange removed the pouch from under her top. Assumpta took the prism out.

"When the time comes, after my tears have been rejoined,

you must take it and run to Lido's Keep. Nekoda, Bensah, Gildas, and Sa you must protect her from the demon. Flee quickly and do not let any other touch or look at it. Let the others die for you and fight for you but keep this safe. You are its keeper until the final battle is won. It has chosen you Keeper. Beware of Voloc, for he is known to us as the deceiver and his lust to extinguish the light of the Caemeris knows no bounds. The dark made him for one purpose only, to destroy the light. Do not betray it to anyone, for anyone or anything, for to lose it will mean the end of your life and all of those you love. Not for anyone, Keeper."

Assumpta looked deeply into Ange's eyes and heart and knew how much she missed Tessi. It was a wound that may fester and risk all. Assumpta dived into the secret grief of Ange and rose with the same venom as with Gildas at the well of Arglethium blood. Gildas flinched slightly at the memory of the same barb he had felt.

"Not for anyone. You are the Keeper of Sorrow and Guardian of the Tears. No longer is your fate your own to make, for your life is forfeited to the memory of Caemeris, the maker of light. It has chosen the new Caemexa and now the custodians go to meet their destiny, either we will remain or the light and shadow will destroy us."

Ange nodded, frightened. Assumpta placed a memory of Tessi dying into Ange's mind. It would ensure that the hope of seeing her sister again would not distract Ange away from her duty. 'You will understand in time, Ange. Do not hate me when you discover my lie. I am the custodian of the children of Arglethium, the creatures formed from the chaining of light and shadow. Baachelaus is the spirit of their breaking and I am the spirit of their bonding. The tears, the prism you hold carry us both and the last memories of our realm of light. Keeper, answer the questions of Caemeris mystery and you shall defeat Voloc.' She let her thought lay dormant in Ange's mind to be remembered when the battle here had been fought.

"My brethren are the prism, Keeper, and you are our protector but also our enemy." She spoke out loud.

"I don't understand how can I protect you and I am not your enemy." asked Ange timidly.

"Either one of us shall remain or nothing else will. I must go now. Remember all I have told you. Be true to each other and hold to your oaths your ancestors made with mighty Norbu."

Ange stumbled as the god let her go. She trembled at the fierceness of the god, the immense weight of what she had been given to bear.

Ascendant turned to EY. "Let the Lord of Arglethium know we wait for him and Baachelaus."

The sun set as the garrison of Ranik's soldiers made their way across the western plains of Drax province. The numbers were close to one thousand. Faad had ridden ahead to check the lie of the land and still wondered what the point of his mission was when there appeared to be no enemy to combat. Mounting his black stallion, with many misgivings, he re-joined the front line of the riders. He felt a doom weighing over his head and wondered if he would ever see the Bay of Tears again. He thought of the last meeting with his suzerain.

"Exquisite! Absolutely exquisite! Have the jeweller make a pendant for the queen from the diamonds and one for the concubine with the emeralds."

"My Lord do you…"

"Yes, won't it be fun to watch the queen be jealous of the young servant and see what she does with her. You know she is with child."

"The queen, my lord?"

"Nay, the concubine."

"There have been reports of a disturbance far beneath the tunnels. It began three nights ago."

"Keep digging until the guts of the stones spew forth, Faad, there is more to be found yet."

Suddenly pulling him back from his thoughts was the sight of a great wolf running alongside him. His horse shied away to the right, frightened by the beast. He drew his sword thinking it may attack him, but it transformed into a shadow in the figure of a man. Faad swallowed hard, as red eyes glared at him.

"Meet at the city ruins. I want you to seek out a youngling, from the desert country. Kill the assassin and the warrior that guard her."

Then it disappeared. Faad galloped with the soldiers behind him towards the ruined Drax Kingdom. Ranik's insanity and irrational orders still did not make sense to the Matavian captain. This spirit had possessed Ranik perhaps and now all of Matavia spewed war across the lands. Faad could see his death closing in on him with every stride his stallion made.

Voloc reached the city and slowed when he saw his mortal enemy. Norbu did not see the demon coming towards him as he was looking at Assumpta approaching in the distance. Voloc propelled himself at his enemy, snarling as it landed on

Norbu's chest trying to snatch the jewel. Norbu grabbed the beast by its hide and threw him against a rocky ledge. Voloc got up and started to circle around his feet.

"Deceiver, why do you come here? I have always defeated you in my kingdom."

Voloc rushed at Norbu again and just as he was about to thrust him into the earth a fiery hand grabbed Norbu and pushed him into the cliff. The heat was consuming and bit at the fleshly form he had taken. Then he felt the wind pin him down.

Norbu reacted with an almighty roar, which lifted the cliff and rocks into a cacophony of rubble.

He clapped his hands together and the wind and fire fell back.

"Nay, demon, be gone from here." He picked up the massive wolf and flung it far up into the clouds. The Orynth grabbed it by their talons, held the thrashing beast, and pinned the shadow to the cliff.

Fire and smoke surrounded Norbu clouding his vision. He felt the flames of Seraf burning him as the fire spirit went into a frenzy of destruction. Aerean formed briefly and looked into her mighty brother's face. Norbu saw her and grabbed her, quelling the fire and wind alike.

"Younglings, the mischief the deceiver has wrought has stained your pure hearts. Enough now. Quell your rage and lie at the feet of the mighty Norbu, who is still Lord of his dominion and brother to you both."

As the flame dimmed, he saw before him Baachelaus. The emaciated figure stood silently looking at the great god of creation. The sun had burnt his flesh. It now lay ragged and flaked as it was frittered away by the zephyrs of Aerean. Deep inside the hollow chest lay the remnants of the chain which had been thrust around him at his imprisonment eons ago.

"Descendant, you have cast down your bonds and walk in the light."

Baachelaus looked at him. "Who are you, god, that the earth trembles at your voice?"

"I am Norbu, first made of the custodians that came before you and your spouse. But you have forgotten us, and the dark has ravaged you so much that your form is not familiar to me anymore."

"I have no memory of you, but I shall have dominion over you and this place."

Baachelaus took Norbu in his grip, but nothing happened. Norbu simply threw him away. The guardians stood swaying behind but stilled when Norbu gazed at them.

"You have no strength over me, Descendent, for I was the first of the custodians. You are still weak, for your strength lies in the shadow. Your image has been stolen and sealed in the jewel. Seraf and Aerean come to me."

Fire and an aching moan echoed around them as the spirits tried to pull themselves free of Baachelaus. Baachelaus began to laugh. "Nay, they are now bound to me, as you shall be. Voloc has no dominion over me for we are one and the same now. The dark binds us together in essence."

Baachelaus opened his mouth and roared at Norbu. The ground shuddered and pushed Norbu back. The Orynth were shaken, losing their grip on Voloc. Drinking in the fury of the warring gods, Voloc sped towards the melee of the spirits.

"Enough." Assumpta stood behind them. She gasped when Baachelaus turned towards her.

"Oh, my beloved." She fell to her knees as the despair of his imprisonment consumed her. She held her hands out to him, but he only looked at her, confused. He could not sense her essence, but her voice sent an echo of pain through him.

"Who are you?" he growled.

"Where is the gift, Ascendant?"

She threw the prism towards Norbu.

Voloc leapt for it as Norbu's hand closed around the jewel. The demon latched on the arm of Norbu. It transformed into the shadow and completely shrouded Norbu. The custodian of creation melded the two halves together. Voloc's shadow magnified so that complete darkness fell across the world.

Baachelaus grabbed Assumpta by the throat. "Who are you?" The blue green specs of his skull shone brightly. The god gouged his memory searching for the voice and profound longing that it had stirred in him as he lay in the cage of darkness, but nothing came. The ragged mouth roared, and the long white fingers squeezed tighter around Assumpta's flesh, real and easily torn now from her time in this realm.

"I am your destiny. You must come with me now. Hasten, Lord of Arglethium."

Above, Gildas and Sa and Ange stood watching the struggle. Gildas wanted to go and fight until he saw the white god that now stood before them. A chill had gone down his spine at the sight of him. Gildas had sensed his own destiny lay along the same path as the god.

Nekoda was reefing at his leash. Bensah held tightly but knew he would not be able to hold on much longer. He saw the ravaged god snatch Assumpta.

EY stood behind them.

"We must go and help her," called Bensah.

"Nay, lesser one, this is beyond your strength and ours as well. It is the god's war and they must fight it," replied EY.

Nekoda let loose a visceral groan and broke the rope that had held him. He raced towards the shadow that covered Norbu. The animus within knew the father of all creatures was in danger and he went to protect him.

"Nekoda come back here," yelled Bensah.

Ange gripped Bensah's hand out of fear for the dog and herself.

The dog leapt up into the shadow and was blinded and suffocated by the poisonous veil of the demon. Ange heard the pet mongrel yelp. Fire sparked all around them and the wind shaped the flame into a tornado. All that could be seen was the dark shadow of Voloc and the wind of Aerean and the flame of Seraf lighting the lands in a corona of golds and reds.

Suddenly, a white light shot out up into the sky. Its force went through the ground. The cliffs above the city began to avalanche and the last ruins of Drax city sunk beneath the earth. Assumpta and Baachelaus were pulled into it. Baachelaus roared as one of the guardians tried to pull the god out of it. Assumpta's hand flew out and pulled the god back towards her. A shower of rain seemed to materialise as Lido was gathered into the miasma of light and heat. Then time stopped. The ground and sky heaved together. The white light stayed but the flame and wind stilled. The people below were flattened into the earth. A shadow was spun far into the sky and away. Nekoda flew out towards the ground rolling down the embankment towards a sink hole.

"Bensah, save him," screamed Ange.

Then the flame and wind were sucked back into the white light and everything disappeared. The world suddenly became silent. All that stood before them was the burnt earth where the explosion of white light had emanated. The sunlight was restored allowing them to see again. The air seemed to lighten as Gildas and Sa and Bensah raced to where Nekoda lay.

EY grabbed Ange and flew above them. "When I fly down, grab the crystal before the demon returns." Ange was too stunned by being picked up that she didn't realise what the Orynth had said. She was also trying to see Nekoda. Bensah was sliding down the rubble ledge reaching out as the dog scrambled up the loose gravel. Gildas and Sa were running along the edge of the sinkhole. Sa had some rope ready to lasso over the Nekoda's head.

"Now, youngling." EY swooped down to the burnt patch where the custodians had fought. "Now," screeched EY. Ange saw a diamond sparkling in the middle of all the ash and dirt. She latched onto it but feeling its heat she nearly let go.

"It will not burn you, youngling," EY spoke as it shot up to the sky.

Gildas and Sa had stopped and watched EY fly up and away with Ange. Then they heard Nekoda yelp.

Gildas quickly turned and slid part way towards the dog, grabbed its hide and threw it up towards Sa. Nekoda grunted as it hit the ground at the assassin's feet. His hide was burnt and raw flesh was exposed. Bensah arrived and bent down to check him.

"Dog, I could not believe that you could be any uglier but…"

Nekoda whimpered a little trying to lick his master but lay his head back down.

PO flew down. "Hurry, for Voloc still lives and comes this way. Flee now to the water spirits protection."

Sa saw EY with Ange above them on a rocky outcrop. "Come warrior and trader, we must go. The demon will be after the stone."

Faad watched everything from a distance. He did not understand any of it, as his mind reeled with the images of the spirits fighting. He saw the girl the beast had told him about.

"Quickly after them, the girl has something precious Lord Ranik wants."

Bensah had hoisted Nekoda onto his back. He and Gildas reached Ange quickly. He swept Ange up into his arms.

"This way." They followed PO and XI in the air up over the ridge towards the forest that they had come through. Suddenly, an arrow flew past and stuck in a tree. Then one struck Gildas in the back. It was deflected by his leather vest. He turned and saw a Matavian captain and a dozen men behind him gaining on them quickly.

Sa looked at Gildas. "They will catch us."

Gildas nodded. "Birds, take the girl." PO and XI flew down and lifted Ange high into one of the spruces. "Trader, do you have a weapon?"

"My axe, that is all."

Gently placing Nekoda under one of the trees, he joined Sa and Gildas.

"Are you with me, assassin and trader."

"We are with you, clansman." They responded together.

The soldiers advanced. Faad moved to the rear trying to see the girl. Sa flew into a frenzy and killed three of the front guards, breaking one's neck and slitting the throat of the other two.

Gildas' sword sliced easily into three more. Bensah rushed at one of the soldiers and received a glancing blow to the chest, but his axe managed to land in the soldier's head. Feeding the blood lust, he barged his way in towards the soldiers in the line. Finally, only three soldiers stood with Faad.

Sa didn't have a scratch on her, but Gildas and Bensah had blood oozing from their wounds.

Gildas rushed at one guard and then another slicing their heads off. Bensah's axe flew into the remaining one's chest. Faad stood back sword ready but knew he was defeated.

"Lord Ranik will not relent, you know his tyranny and resolve, and the fangs of the demon wolf now lie at his throat."

Gildas brought the sword to his throat. As he went to run the commander through, one of the guardians came from behind. Just as it went to sweep Gildas and Faad into the air, VA swooped down and attacked it. Faad fled into the forest to get away from Gildas, but also the creatures that now surrounded him.

"Flee now warrior, there is no time," EY screeched as he flew down. "The deceiver brings the god's gaolers; you will not defeat them."

The rest of the Orynth landed on the path in an imposing wall of defiance.

"You must leave now. We will hold off the guardians and deceiver. But go now. PO guide them to the place of the water spirit. Guard the Keeper."

Nekoda lay near a tree barely breathing. Ange had climbed down to sit near him. She was petting his head and crying as she looked at his mangled body.

"No, I will not leave him." She began to sob. "The water god will heal him. Please, Tata."

Bensah picked up Nekoda. He knew that the water god would not be there but hoped Nekoda would survive.

Gildas picked up Ange as he and Sa began to follow PO's shadow from the sky.

The Orynth gathered with YU at the front as the Guardians came up over the ridge. Voloc had become a wolf again. He leapt at YU. The eagle's talons grasped the smoky blackness of the demon. It burned his flesh, but he held fast. The ancient Orynth took flight and drove Voloc high towards Belmaris. As the face of the star neared, YU called to it, "Oh great star, sear the demon to its death and rid us of its curse."

YU began to disintegrate as Voloc shrivelled from the light and heat. They both plummeted to the earth. They struck the ground where Norbu and his brethren had stood, shattering the crystallised earth. The Orynth and the Guardians were catapulted half a league from the force of the explosion.

Gildas and Sa stopped to see what the noise was and watched as the red creatures that came gathered around the plume of smoke. PO screeched above them to keep going.

The Guardians gathered around Voloc and began to chant. The Orynth picked up the body of YU and flew towards Lido's Keep.

The flight to Lido's pool was unhindered. The foursome found the top end of Drax Bay had been partially filled with rubble from the massive quake of Norbu's awakening. They crossed the waters easily bringing them directly to the edges of the forest of Vran.

Bensah lead the way once they were in the forest remembering the path the god had taken. Ange never stopped looking at Nekoda in Bensah's arms. Bensah's chest heaved with the weight of Nekoda. The dog was barely alive. He splashed into the stream of water that led to the opening of Lido's Keep.

Ange was sobbing as Gildas let her go. She collapsed near Nekoda and placed her trembling hand on his burnt body. Sa, Bensah, and Gildas lay down with exhaustion, nursing their own wounds.

The Orynth flew into the cavern. XI and VA were carrying YU's body. They reverently placed him on the cavern floor.

The feathered brethren turned into their upright forms. PO knelt and cradled YU's head.

"Tata, Nekoda is dying," cried Ange.

Bensah sat down looking at Nekoda, amazed the dog was still alive.

"Ahh mutt, you were always ready to take on more than you could chew when it came to a fight." Bensah lightly stroked an un-singed bit of ear.

PO and EY looked across at the weeping girl and the mangled mess of Nekoda.

"Should this one, our brethren and mighty defender of Norbu be allowed to die at the fangs of the destroyer. Was Norbu ever a generous master and protector to all those made under the custodian's gaze?" asked VA.

"Father YU, we weep as our spirit breaks at the sorrow and sacrifice you have made to protect the custodians of water and stone. This one made from the desert and river water, who is now given the duty to discover the mystery of the realms of light. Send your spirit to her so she may continue with protection of the mighty father of the Orynth and the loving heart of YU," implored PO.

"Keeper of the Tears of Ascendant, come closer, bring our four-legged brethren, your defender and confider. A brave and worthy companion who flung himself into the claws of annihilation to protect our brother and creator Norbu." EY gestured for Ange to come over toward the grieving circle of Orynth.

"What do you mean? The water spirit can heal him. Lido, where are you?" she pleaded.

"The custodians fight their own battle now," replied EY.

She looked at Bensah through tears of fear and exhaustion. He nodded at her, not knowing what else to do. She put her hands firmly under Nekoda. She could feel his faint breaths pulsating against her arms. She crawled over to the body of YU.

EY took her hand and Nekoda's paw and placed it on YU's chest.

The Orynth stood in a circle and gazed down at their father and Ange and Nekoda.

"Bless us mighty one, once more, bless the Keeper of Sorrow

and let your strength be hers. Reward the brave anima caged in flesh and bone. Break the clay bonds of their forms and heal the scourge of battle. We lay the grief of the Orynth in the heart of the Keeper alongside the spirit of YU."

Ange felt the faintest zephyr touch her flesh. A tiny shiver went through her. She didn't feel any different. Most of all what she felt was the breathing of Nekoda become stronger. Suddenly, he lifted his head and gently licked Ange's cheek.

She hugged him fiercely, sobbing with relief.

"Thank you," she whispered to the dead body of YU.

"Ange of the sand and river, you are now steward of the Orynth. Your war has begun, for the deceiver is not destroyed, only maimed. The custodians have left this world and you are the one who must battle with Voloc. We leave now to honour the life of our father, YU."

"But what are we to do? The demon will rise again and hunt us down," growled Gildas.

"You must find a way to protect the Keeper of this gift forged from the tears of the Ascendant. Until the mystery behind its power is understood, you are beholden to this oath. Voloc's reign is about to begin. Look for allies in all places, the sky, the deep oceans, and the ice. We are all brethren made from the bonds of water and earth within the sight of Belmaris. By this light we are in communion and by this light we shall perish or prevail."

EY looked at Ange and Sa.

"The Orynth must mourn first and score the legends of YU so he shall be remembered. After this homage we shall return."

XI and VA wove a feathery shroud around their father.

Gathering the body of the ancient servant of Norbu, they flew from the Keep of Lido toward the highest peaks of Tarentess.

"What do we do now, Northerner?" Sa had come up to Gildas as he peered into the large cathedral of watery columns. Inside them lay lifeless creatures.

She looked down at Ange as she sat with Nekoda. Bensah was letting the dog lap water from his cupped palms.

"I do not know, assassin," replied Gildas.

The Story Continues in Book Two

VOLOC'S REIGN

Appendix

THE CLAY BORN OF ARGLETHIUM

Ange Tsaed: from the village of Kensai located in the eastern deserts

Gildas Gol of the Graan: former warlord and Chieftain of the Graan Clans of the Northern Icelands

Sa-Tuc: Assassin to Emperor Ko

Kado Kodrax: Heir to the Drax Magisterium

Bensah El Bunani: Trader and family friend of Ange and Tessi

Nekoda: Wild dog /hyena cross breed, companion to Bensah

Emperor Ko Paidrax: Ruler of the Drax Magisterium and father to Kado

Empress Shosunna: Wife of Emperor Ko and mother to Kado

Lord Tias Ranik: Suzerain of the Lands of Matavia

Captain Faad: Knight Captain of the Matavia Garrison

Sister Godryn: Monk of the Order of Ira

Abbot Paulus X: Abbot of the Temple of Ira

Brother Vronius: Monk of the Order of Ira

Brother Flet: Monk of the Order of Ira
Noai: Father of Ange and Tessi
Elanai: Mother of Ange and Tessi
Tessi Tsaed: Sister to Ange
Widjera: Tribal Elder of the Desert People of the Iron Coast
Tamatjera: Son of Widjera

CAEMEXA BORN OF CAEMERIS

The Custodians

Baachelaus (Descendant): Diarch of Caemeris, spirit of the unknown, binder of yearning & fulfilment
Assumpta (Ascendant): Diarch of Caemeris, spirit of the clay born, binder of light & shadow
Norbu: Elder of Creation, Custodian of Arglethium
Lido: Water Custodian
Seraf: Fire Custodian
Aerean: Wind Custodian
Voloc: Dark Custodian, Born of Oblyquixiton
Belmaris: Sun
Magmeris: Dead sun, sister to Belmaris

The Servants

The Guardians, Aracnine: eight in number, jailers of Baachelaus
The Orynth: YU, EY, PO, XI, AX, VA. Servants to Norbu
Uchala: Sentinel, Spider in form
Vipax: Sentinel, Serpent in form

About the Author

Clare Rolfe is an Australian self-published author. Her first novel was the dystopian fantasy *Ten Letters to Delacroix's Tomb*, released in 2016. Her inspirations for writing include philosophy, the natural world and science. She dabbles in poetry and flash fiction and is a routine blogger on-line of her work. In between writing and working in her day job she loves to travel. *Ascendant's Tear* is the first book of the Legend of Caemeris series.

Stay in Touch
Facebook: Clare Rolfe / CL Rolfe
Twitter: @rolfe_cl

9 780648 699408